D0122076

THE
OTHER
SIDE
OF THE
SKY

THE
OTHER
SIDE
OF THE
SKY

AMIE KAUFMAN
& MEAGAN SPOONER

An Imprint of HarperCollinsPublishers

HarperTeen is an imprint of HarperCollins Publishers.

Library of Congress Control Number: 2020936258
ISBN 978-0-06-289333-8

Typography by Jenna Stempel-Lobell
20 21 22 23 24   PC/LSCH   10 9 8 7 6 5 4 3 2 1

First Edition

To Kristen,
Who believed in magic with us.

ONE
NIMH

The floating market takes shape amid a flutter of torches and spellfire, each pinprick of light tailed by its glittering reflection in the river beneath. The sun is still below the horizon, though hints of peach and copper streak the underside of the cloudlands, hanging far above the clutter of our market. Monstrous shadows slip from the predawn gloom, gliding with the current toward the growing city upon the water, only to reveal themselves as houses and workshops, food stalls and vendors' platforms.

I used to watch the floating market arrive every month. Riverfolk from leagues away converge upon the floodplains below the temple, steering their homes by sail and oar and pole across the broad, slow river as it spills over its banks into the forest-sea. In mere hours, the gentle curve of the river becomes a bustling city, each solitary barge of reeds joining together in a single teeming, intricate whole. It has always thrilled me, watching the transformation of my world—but every time, the thrill pales a little more against the torture of not being able to enjoy the market with the rest of my people.

This is the first time I've been on the river during the mooring in years. The view from the temple sanctum is quiet and remote—from there I cannot smell the charcoal and peat as the cooks and bakers heat their ovens, cannot hear the laughter of the children still too young to help their parents with the ropes, cannot feel the pulsing syncopation of feet and currents shifting the floating market streets underfoot.

My memories before the temple are dim at best, but once I was one of those children. The smell of grilling meat and spice bread meant I would get a treat if I was well behaved; the laughter was the sound of my friends calling me to join them at play; and the footsteps that pounded up and down the thick reed streets were mine. Some years back, I tried sneaking into the market in a handmaiden's borrowed clothing. But whatever ease and safety I'd felt as a child in this place had long since bled away—I barely made it down one street before the crowds pressed in so close that I had to flee, straight into the panicked protection of the guards searching for me.

Now, I'm alone.

I'm not so foolish these days as to try to disguise myself, for it would be far too easy for someone to brush against me or take my arm in an attempt to sell me a bauble. Even the tiniest children know what the deep red of my robe and the kohl rimming my eyes signify—they know it before they can walk.

But even after all the time I've spent watching the riverfolk bustling to and fro, the crowds draw out a deep, quiet unease that throbs like the ache of an old injury. Despite the fact that I wear my red robes and gold circlet, the traditional garments of divinity that warn against coming too close, someone could still accidentally touch me. Being here is so risky it borders on reckless—but the politicians and priests who govern my life have left me no choice.

My eyes flick upward, as they often do, to rest upon the mass of darkened cloud overhead. The gods have not been heard of since they fled there a thousand years ago, leaving only one— the first of my divine line—to guide the people they left behind. Do they live there still? Do they care that their representative in this land has been pushed to such desperate measures to help her people?

Eluding my guards wasn't difficult, for the simple reason that I never try, not anymore. I am no prisoner, and they are all but ceremonial despite having been trained from birth to die fighting for me. But to come to the market flanked by a dozen men and women in the grim black and gold of divine guardians would be to announce my activities to the entire temple, and the city as well. Word will undoubtedly float back to High Priest Daoman's ears, but it will take time. By then, I will have secured safe passage for my journey, and can claim I only wanted to see the mooring.

The house I'm looking for is distinctive, with a roof that sprouts patchwork scaffolding like spindly arms reaching toward the sky. Quenti's house is one of the fastest on all the rivers and forest-seas, but when he's moored, he replaces his sails with skins and vines and reeds to dry in the sun, above the humidity of the river. Clutching my spearstaff, I scan the market for the trader's base.

Spellfire flickers to life above a one-room livestock hut, and in its steady blue-green glow I spot what I'm looking for. My heart sinks as I realize there's no quick route to reach Quenti—I'll have to join the thronging masses of people.

A sturdy warmth butts up against my calf, that single touch enough to give me courage. I don't need to look to know it's the bindle cat—his familiar burbling, insistent trill floats up to my ears, and I chirp back. His wide, furry face turns up to me and then, purring like an angry stormcloud, he butts against my leg again as I set out.

Though I keep to the edges of the market, avoiding the thickest crowds, riverfolk are still busy lashing their homes to others. I pause only long enough to reach for my chatelaine and draw out a pinch of fireseed.

I cup it in my palm, whispering the invocation against the powder. My breath sends a puff of it floating from my hand, each little grain beginning to glow like a nascent star as it showers to the ground. I raise my cupped hand and anoint the blade of my spearstaff so that it casts its gentle light in a watery pool around my ankles.

Now that I'm illuminated, my people scatter and fall back from me.

All I see are bowed heads and the backs of their colorful market garb as they kneel and touch their heads to the reeds until I've passed.

Lady, they whisper respectfully. *Beautiful Goddess. Divine One. Blessed Divinity.*

I murmur a blessing whenever I see a face lift, wishing just once that I could walk through a crowd without its many eyes following me, hungry for some sign that I am the salvation it desperately needs. Sometimes I think I see doubt there, behind the worship—sometimes I *know* I do.

All the living gods throughout history, my predecessors, embodied a particular aspect of the divine in answer to the needs of the land. There have been gods of poetry, gods of war, gods of the celestial heavens, and gods of green growing things. Before me, the temple was home to a goddess of healing.

These aspects have always manifested themselves within the living god a year or two after their calling. They say that Satheon, who led our people during my grandparents' time, was called to the temple as a boy of sixteen and manifested his aspect of farming just a week later.

I have been a goddess for nearly ten years—and still, my people are waiting to see what solace I will bring them.

If I ever do.

Sensing my emotion, the bindle cat gently and carefully dips his head, opens his mouth, and bites me on the ankle. Focusing on that sharp pain, I take a breath, grateful for my one companion.

I found him as a kitten in a sodden bindle sack, wet and half-drowned on the bank of the river, one afternoon a few months after I was first brought to the temple. Scrawny and pathetic as a kitten, he's a massive, muscled, fire-orange beast as a grown cat.

The bindle cat gives his own blessings in echo of mine— though they sound more like curses—as he trots along beside me, tail upright and round eyes alert. While everyone in my life knows I ought to have manifested my aspect years ago, and has hopes and expectations for me, he has none beyond his next snack. The bindle cat is just a cat. And unlike my servants and guards, he's allowed to touch me—and I him. Having a solid warmth to stroke and curl up with when I'm lonely makes the rest of it bearable.

I stop to avoid disrupting a procession of food sellers making their way down the reed street in front of me, mobbed by children hoping for a clumsy moment, for a hurried trader to drop some sticky rolls or a pouch of sweets. Another trader trails along in their wake, bearing trays full of charms to ward off pestilence and ill fortune. Such trinkets are often sold and resold without ever receiving a touch of real magic, but I can feel the faint tingle about them that tells me these are genuine, crafted by some local hedge-witch. Perhaps the trader himself, for he also carries a little spellfire lantern with a trail of curious, light-seeking insects buzzing after it.

The bindle cat sits at my feet, regarding the chaos with vigilant disapproval.

As I wait for the vendors to pass, I cast my eyes back toward the buildings crowding the narrow, winding streets that cling to the perimeter of the temple, above the flood line of the river. More than one roof flutters with pennants, those of red and gold gleaming even in the twilight. But as the morning grows lighter, I see the outline of the other banners, and my blood chills.

These flags are gray, as if camouflaged against the dim sky, and there are many of them. Many more than I knew were there.

From my rooms back in the temple, my audience chamber, the terrace where I address my people, only two of these gray flags are visible to me. The rest are hidden by draped textiles and trailing vines, by the architecture of the temple itself. So many are hidden from my usual view that I can't believe it's a coincidence. Was it someone among my priests, the high priest himself, perhaps, who ordered the placement of those decorations, wishing to shield me from the increasing threat against me?

Or was it the Graycloaks, deciding in their leaderless, faceless way to conceal from me as long as possible the momentum their movement has gained?

Either way, the decision was made, and no one consulted me.

"Out of the way!" a voice snaps just behind me, making me whirl around, my heart in my throat.

An older man stands there, a scowl creasing his leathery brown face where there ought to be shocked recognition at the sight of my crown and crimson robe. He wears the tattered, undyed wool of a villager from the western mountains, although a necklace of beads and bird's bones claims him for one of the riverstrider clans.

The bindle cat, back arched and body rigid against my calf, hisses a warning at the man. I raise my staff between us, stepping back. I open my mouth, but I've never had to identify myself to anyone, and the words *Do you know who I am?* stick in my throat.

Then the man's eyebrows rise, his eyes lighting. "You!" But where I would expect sudden shame and a scramble to repair his gruff manner, instead the man begins to croon, "Little fish, little fish, where have you gone . . . ?"

A shiver trembles through my shoulders, understanding dawning as I peer harder at the man's quivering features, into eyes wreathed by puffy skin. They don't focus, those eyes, not the way a normal person's do—their clouded depths look past me. Through me.

Mist-touched.

He must be harmless, or he wouldn't be permitted to roam the market, but a flicker of fear follows that shiver down my spine. He might not intend harm, but if he were to stumble forward, or leap for me . . .

The ravages of the mist-storms are unpredictable at best, decimating crops, transforming solid stone, ripping away by the roots trees old enough to have known a time when I was not the only god to walk upon the ground. But far worse is what a mist-storm does to an unprotected mind.

The man is still chuckling to himself, gazing through me and continuing to sing in his cracked voice. "Tell me truly, little fish, are you the only one?"

"Let me help you, Grandfather." The endearment, even from a stranger, seems to soften him, ground him a little. I swallow my fear, one hand already dipping into a few different pouches, gathering up spell reagents. "Let me bless you and see you back to your clan."

The riverstriders are known for taking in the mist-touched, even those exiled from their own villages for being too hard to care for. Life on the water, they claim, is a balm for the wounds left by the mist.

"The lastest and loneliest littlest fish left . . ." He blinks, breaking off mid-song to look at me. But when I lift my hand and open my mouth to begin the spell I hope will help soothe his inflamed mind, he interrupts with a loud guffaw.

"And so used to swimming with the hungry river-snakes, she doesn't even know she's alone." He wipes at his eyes, chortling, and then fixes me with a grave look. "It is an honor to meet the last of anything, Lady."

A tingle of warning makes the fear at his proximity flare. The mist is not malicious—it is a force of nature, the magic left behind by the world's creation. It only becomes dangerous when it gathers into storms, and even then, its effects are never twice the same. But sometimes, very, very rarely, its touch brings along with madness a thread of future-sight . . .

If the Graycloaks have their way and remove me from power, then I may well be the last.

The last living goddess to walk the land.

I bend down to stroke the bindle cat, whose muscles are bunching in preparation to pounce. When I look up, the mist-touched man is gone. The market is busy now, and I can see very little past the denser ring of people trying to avoid me. As I turn to search for the old man, the ring undulates away as if pushed by some invisible force.

There is no way with the mist-touched to tell addled ramblings from prophecy until the thing they speak of comes to pass. Even if I could find him again, he likely wouldn't remember what he said.

I straighten, trying not to let the nearby onlookers see me rattled. The riverstriders make up most of the floating market, and they're among the most devout and devoted—but I see flashes of gray nonetheless. What began as a series of whispers years ago, deep underground, is now an open movement.

The Graycloaks.

I will not let them see my fear.

I stride forward, the ring of onlookers stretching and then snapping away, children and adults alike scattering before me.

Quenti's houseboat has a cluttered, ramshackle look to it, as though it began as a one-room shack on a barge and other floors and chambers were added here and there as needed. Knowing Quenti, that might actually be the case.

I ease the door open a fraction and clear my throat. "Blessings upon this house," I call tentatively—like most riverstriders, Quenti's never been terribly formal, but he also houses half a dozen river children at any given time, and I err on the side of caution when it comes to announcing my presence.

A flurry of feet precedes a series of hushed exclamations. I look up to see a trio of round faces peering down at me from the second-floor landing. When they see the woven crown upon my head, two of the faces jolt and vanish again. The third—a girl, I think, although it's difficult to tell in the gloom—watches me with open curiosity.

"World's end, it's true." The voice is not Quenti's cracked

and kindly one. I squint in the low lighting at the young woman who arrives on the heels of one of the little riverstriders. She bends to whisper something in the child's ear, sending him off again before descending the stairs. "Welcome, Divine One. Our thanks for the light you bring this day."

Her voice is taut and cautious where Quenti's would have been warm. In the tension of her voice is an unspoken question, one she dares not ask.

"I come to see Quenti," I tell her in answer, once she's reached the bottom of the rickety stairs. "I must speak with him privately."

She hesitates, giving me the time to examine her more closely. She looks a few years older than I am, and wears the braids of a married riverstrider, black hair woven through with the iridescent blue-and-copper plumage of the crested flame-tail. Those feathers, and the bright bangles at wrist and ankle, identify her as a member of the same clan as Quenti. Olive skin at the neckline of her tunic darkens at her shoulders, telling of hours spent on the water under the sun, and muscle along the arm against the railing tells me she is more accustomed to river work than market politics.

The silence stretches, and I see that strong arm twitch. Realization hits me: she doesn't know how to be around me. She is frozen between a desire to avoid offense and a fear of disappointing me.

I draw a breath, trying to ignore the abrupt sting of self-consciousness that needles at the back of my mind, whispering:

Did you expect her to snap to attention? You've been too long in the shelter of guards and priests. . . .

"What is your name?" I ask her, letting go of the air of command that took me years to cultivate.

"Hiret, Lady." She swallows. "I am Quenti's niece. That is my sister, Didyet." She tilts her head without looking—the girl who'd remained at the top of the stairs to watch is still there, but now that I look more closely, she is not as young as I'd first thought. Younger than me, but not by much.

"Really?" I don't have to feign friendly delight. "I knew your mother when I lived among the riverfolk. I remember when 'Auntie' traveled with Quenti for a season. She made pirrackas." My memory of the woman is hazy—most of them are, before the temple—but the smell of fried dough and the dangerous lavalike ooze of hot honey, I remember with crystal clarity.

Hiret's eyes widen. Her right cheek bears a cluster of beauty marks just under the eye, and her quick smile makes them dance. "That would have been years ago—the last season she was here, I was still learning to walk the river. It would have been before . . ." She halts, the smile vanishing, her uncertainty returning.

"Before I was called to divinity," I finish for her, more used to speaking of those dark years between my time and that of the previous vessel of the divine. "Your uncle was kind to me then, when I was no one—as he has always been since. I am sorry if I frightened you, Hiret—but I really must speak to him. I must ask him about the use of a boat, and the loan of a few of your people. I must go on a pilgrimage, and soon."

Hiret glances past me, picking up on my urgency at the

same time as she realizes I am not accompanied by the half-dozen guards that usually follow me. A flicker of recognition passes between us then, a hint of the girl in her recognizing the one in me, who I keep hidden beneath the crown and the robes.

"My uncle is ill," she whispers.

"Ill?" My chest tightens, for her lowered voice tells me it is not a passing cough. "What—"

"Mist." Hiret looks away, up at the stairs and past her silent sister, as if she might stretch and bend her gaze along the cramped corridor and into the room her uncle occupies. The movement very nearly conceals the grief in her sharp, expressive features. "His ankles swell these days, and he was soothing them in the river mud when a storm rose quickly from the forest-sea."

"Is he . . . ?" In my mind's eye, I'm staring at the mist-touched man singing songs of fishes, and trying to imagine my old friend in his place.

"His mind is quick as ever. But . . . come."

Hiret turns and leads the way up the rickety stairs, shooing irritably at Didyet as she reaches the top. I would know her even if Hiret had not made the introduction, for Didyet's face is a softer, rounder copy of her sister's, though she has no constellation of beauty marks on her cheek and her unbraided hair stands thick and defiant in a half halo about her head.

The girl returns my gaze with a stare of her own, showing me another way she is not like her sister—the set of her mouth is sullen and tight. Angry.

"What can *she* do about it?" Didyet mutters, as if in

confidence to Hiret, though plenty loud enough for me to hear. She does not move from her spot, barring my way, since I can't brush past her. "She can't stop the mist-storms. She can't heal the mist-touched. She isn't even really the—"

"Didyet!" her older sister snaps, cutting her off with such vehemence and horror that the younger girl stops mid-word, a flicker of fear showing through her bravado.

Hiret stands in stricken silence, so appalled by the blasphemy her sister nearly spoke that she has to catch her breath before speaking. "You will not show yourself again while the Divine One is here, do you understand?" Her voice is low and quiet, but carrying such ominous promise and authority that I almost take a step toward the far bunks myself. "Go and tell the other children they must sit quiet in their rooms or there will be no time to visit the market this afternoon."

Didyet stiffens, hearing the tiny emphasis on *other children* in a way only someone chafing against the delay between childhood and independence could. But her sister's voice, it seems, is more intimidating than the robe and staff of a goddess—she only flickers a glance from Hiret, to me, and back again, then turns to flee toward a wobbly ladder staircase leading up. Only when she begins to climb do I notice that her ankles aren't decorated with the bright beads and bangles of her clan. Instead, she wears only a single strip of cloth, tied neatly into a gray anklet.

My head is spinning—*She is so young; how could she be a Gray-cloak already?*

Hiret lets her breath out in a rush and turns to face me, an

14

angry—or embarrassed—flush visible despite her sun-browned cheeks. "Divine One, I—"

"It's all right," I murmur, forgetting my lessons in diction, too focused on not letting myself think about that gray anklet. "Hiret, when did your mother pass beneath the river?"

"She . . ." Surprise overtakes her dismay. "It will be ten years, come the Feast of the Dying."

"May she walk lightly," I murmur, invoking the brief beginning of my blessing. *Grief*, I think distantly. *Didyet lost her mother, and that is why she turns to the Graycloaks—why she looks for someone to blame.*

"How did you . . . ?" Hiret's eyes have gone from me to my staff, brow furrowed, as if she half believes my magic might allow me to read her mind—though such a thing is impossible.

"You have been looking after your sister for some time," I tell her, a smile in my voice if not on my face. "Only mothers know that particular voice."

And high priests, I think uneasily, imagining Daoman's reaction to finding me missing and my guards unaware.

Hiret's lips flicker in an answering smile, then fade. "Come. He is just here."

She draws aside a curtain on one of the doorways and then steps away, bowing her head, leaving me room to slip inside with no risk of touching her. I nod—and then my breath stops when I see the man lying in the cot before me.

Sores travel up from the edge of the blanket to the crown of his head, the already-thinning hair there reduced to patches. His expression is drawn in pain even while he sleeps, and his breathing is shallow and irregular. A flash of him as I last saw him—round face wreathed by wrinkles and laughter lines—cuts across my eyes, and I have to swallow the bile rising in my throat before my vision clears.

The sores are like nothing I've seen before, though I've made many pilgrimages and done what I can for the mist-touched as far west as the mountains themselves. The welts don't come from within, rising with infection and disease from his own body; instead, it is as though some twisted sculptor melted his flesh, reshaped it from the outside, and let it set again around Quenti's skull.

He cannot help me.

The thought brings with it a wash of guilt, that I could think of my mission while looking upon the ruin of my old friend, someone who cared for me the way family might have done, had I been allowed one after my calling.

But I have no choice other than to think of it—I must put purpose before feeling, or else the mist will be all that's left of my people. Our gods abandoned us centuries ago to live unburdened in their cloudlands—now, there is only me.

I must have made some sound, for Hiret's voice comes from behind me, gentle with sympathy and shared grief. "I think sometimes he wishes it *were* his mind that the mist remade."

When I look back at her, Quenti's ruined visage is so burned into my gaze that for a moment I see his wounds superimposed over Hiret's face, eclipsing that constellation on her cheek. I shiver, and reality returns.

"I will do all I can," I manage, the words escaping in a hoarse croak.

Hiret nods, gratitude in the curve of her lips. But her eyes carry something else altogether, and I can't help but think of what her sister said as I climbed those stairs.

It is true that I cannot heal the mist-touched. The divine before me could. Healing was the aspect she manifested soon after she was called. She spent much of her time away from the temple, traveling to the remotest villages, tending the guardian stones that keep the mist at bay, and caring for those unlucky enough to be caught in a storm without protection.

But I . . . I can only ease their pain for a time, little more than what any decent hedge-witch with a healing spell could do.

I lean my staff against the wall, tell the bindle cat twined about my ankles that I need space now, and lay out the reagents for the magic I can offer. I would have been a powerful magician if the divine had not chosen me for its vessel—now my skill at magic seems paltry to those who need miracles.

Hiret is quiet while I work—at one point I glance over to find her slowly, rhythmically stroking the cat's back with one hand while gazing into nothing. The cat blinks back at me, ears flattening to signal his displeasure at this development, even as he draws in a deep sigh and lets it out in a grudging, rumbling purr.

Hiret knows what her sister said was true. I cannot heal the mist-touched. I cannot stop the storms, and while I don't know whether other deities before me could, none of them needed the ability so urgently. The storms come so violently and so quickly now, their frequency growing with each passing year. And yet I remember, as young as I am, a time when magicians could sense a storm long before it gathered; a time when it was safe to travel beyond the riverbanks, beyond the guardian stones.

"You said you came here seeking a boat." Hiret's voice is as vague and rhythmic as the way she pets the cat.

"That was before I knew he was—" I keep my eyes on my work, my throat so tight I can barely speak. "That was before."

"Quenti would have granted you as many barges as you needed, and as many of my clansmen too. I don't have his authority, but—I can do this thing for you instead, Lady. I can't leave my uncle, but my husband is as clever a strider as I am, and his brother too."

Hope, all the brighter for the darkness around it, flickers. "They can be spared? They are not needed here?"

Hiret pauses, then says quietly, "You came with no guard." Each word is hefty with significance.

The spell I'd been casting flickers and falls apart at my fingertips, dusting the blanket with powdered bone and elderweed. When I look up, Hiret's gaze is no longer distant—she's looking at me now, the hazel of her eyes thoughtful and keen.

"You come alone," she says, "and you ask for a thing that could be granted to you by your priests and your Congress of Elders a dozen times over, and each boat laden with gifts to boot. Instead of asking them, you come here, to your old friend, in the hope he can spare a single vessel."

"Hiret, I—I would tell you why I . . ."

But she's shaking her head, gaze clear. "I don't need an explanation. Half of your Elders have gray hearts, even if their cloaks still pretend otherwise. If they who are foolish and fearful enough to smother our only hope wish to stop you completing this secret task of yours—then I wish to see it done."

The conviction in her voice leaves me so moved I can't speak. I end up staring at her, my eyes and mouth wide, like a hungry child standing in front of a stall selling pirrackas.

"They *are* fools," Hiret says, a hint of that recognition returning—as if, somewhere beneath the goddess, she sees the girl who was pulled from her mother's side and dressed in divine crimson by the high priest all those years ago. "You are the only light we have against this darkening world, Divine One. They have forgotten what it is to live without guardian stones, but we have long memories. We remember why our ancestors took to the river, trusting the protection of the waters that flow from your temple to the sea." She kneels, touching her palms to her eyes in the ancient and uncommon gesture of piety and devotion. "The riverfolk are with you, Nimhara. Always."

"Thank you," I whisper, still half-dazed.

And then she's gone, to look for her husband and his brother, after promising to send another of her clansmen to escort me home through the growing market crowds when I'm ready.

I'm left in silence, but for the labored breathing of the man in the bed at my side. Carefully, I scoop the healing spell's reagents off the blanket and into my palm so I can begin again, though now I scarcely notice the incantation or the power it channels.

The riverfolk are with you. . . . Always.

And yet, I can't forget the anger I saw in the face of Hiret's sister, the face so like hers but for its fear and defiance. I saw the way she questioned Hiret's faith. And I know what Didyet would have said, if her sister had not stopped her.

She isn't even really the Divine One.

TWO
NORTH

The council meeting's pushing into its second hour, and I've got this overwhelming urge to clear my throat, like I need to check that my voice is still working. I grab for my water bottle instead, taking a long swallow. I close my eyes for a moment to try to relax. And then I wonder if now I'm going to need to pee in the middle of my speech.

Not for the first time, I consider postponing my pitch another month. But the timing is perfect now—Alciel's aeronautics show is in just a few hours. I can show them what I know—what I can do—if only they'd give me their support.

Skyfall, this *has* to work. They have to see what I see.

The world outside flies past in a silvery blur as we hurtle toward home, the train snaking its way around the edge of the island. We've got about an hour left on our journey, broken by a stop at Port Camo. By the time we reach the palace, my fate will be decided.

My bloodmother, Beatrin, my grandfather, and the eight councilors are seated around a smooth conference table, studying the 3D graphics projected above it, listening intently as

Councilor Poprin drones on about water reclamation. I'm standing off to the side, waiting for my turn to speak. Across the carriage is my heartmother, Anasta, who I'm pretty sure is here for moral support. If she knew what I was about to say, she probably wouldn't be shooting me such an encouraging smile, but unlike my bloodmother, Anasta always thinks the best of me. I think she's quite pleased I've actually asked to address the council, rather than being assigned a topic by Beatrin to limp through in the name of my education.

I drop my gaze, subtly twisting the band of my chrono around so the face rests over my pulse and I can take a sneaky look at the messages that have it buzzing against my skin.

MIRI: how's the meeting going princeboy?

MIRI: nearly time for your big moment!

MIRI: are you nervous?

MIRI: that would be terrible if you were nervous

MIRI: will you get nervous if I keep saying nervous?

MIRI: (i'm kidding, don't be nervous, you'll soar)

SAELIS: You can do this, North. Your presentation is *great*.

SAELIS: All you have to do is get them to listen, and they'll have to agree.

MIRI: . . . get them to listen

MIRI: I take it all back, you're screwed

MIRI: I mean, goooooo North! \o/

SAELIS: What is that?

MIRI: it's me, I am cheering

SAELIS: Is that circle your head?

MIRI: of course

SAELIS: Then shouldn't it be \O/? Your head is much bigger than that.

MIRI: hmmm, fair. I do have magnificent hair

I smother a smile, but Miri isn't wrong about my problem—getting the council to listen to me's never been easy, and getting this idea off the ground is going to be a particular challenge. Still, I've practiced this thing half to death. I've stood up in front of the council a dozen times—twice a year since I was twelve—but I've never cared like I do now.

I don't think I've ever wanted something this badly, or been so sure I was right.

"Thank you, Poprin, for that comprehensive report." My bloodmother's voice is smooth, slipping into the conversation like a blackwing into a flock of sparras. By which I mean she's perfectly graceful, while everybody else freaks out and flaps around in an effort to show they're paying attention to her. Beatrin never speaks loudly, but every word sounds as though she's selected it with care, crafted it just the way she intends. Her words are as precise as the gold paint that lines her cheeks and marks her as royalty, as carefully sculpted as her sleek, black hair.

My own paint would normally have been smudged hours ago, when I propped my cheek up on my fist in what my heart-mother, Anasta, would call an "unprincely posture." Today, though, I'm carefully put together. Whatever it takes to convince them to climb aboard.

23

"Your Highness," says my grandfather gravely, expression solemn, eyes smiling.

"Your Majesty," I say, pushing away from my spot by the wall and moving to the open space at the head of the table. I already feel the need to clear my throat again.

Augh.

Here I go. Time to somehow convince them I'm not just chasing rainbows.

"Your Majesty, Your Highnesses, esteemed council members," I begin.

My mothers, my grandfather, and about half the council are looking at me, while the other half are checking their files to see what's next. But Talamar's dark eyes, so like my own, are fixed on me, and he gives me a tiny nod of encouragement. So I take a breath and begin the words I've rehearsed.

"The great chambers at the palace have seen countless hours of debate on the altitude problem. I know this council has never reached agreement on the question of whether the islands are sinking or not. Perhaps that agreement—for or against—is years away. But there's a reason for that, and it's that we just don't know enough about the problem.

"One thing we *can* agree on is that in the centuries since the Ascension, we've lost the knowledge of our engines that we once had. We don't know how they keep the archipelago aloft, only that they do. We don't know how they repair themselves, only that they do. Most important of all, we don't know whether they can continue doing that forever. They might be failing as we speak, allowing the islands to sink, or that day might lie far in the future. Either way, I think there's one more thing we should agree on: we can't afford to wait until the problem is dire before we begin to solve it. We need to reclaim our understanding of the sky-engines, or one day they'll fail beyond our repair, and it will be too late to do anything about it."

I have everyone's attention now. The argument about whether the cities are sinking has caused more shouting matches around the council table than any other topic, and if I'm declaring my position on it, then they all want to know where I stand.

Talamar breaks the silence when he lifts his inhaler to take a quick, hissing drag from it, and my bloodmother fixes me with a *better make this good* kind of stare. She'd have preferred me to talk to her before I said anything in public, but if I had, she'd have had the chance to stop me.

I push on, taking advantage of the silence because in a minute, I'm not going to be able to shut anyone up.

"Two years ago, just after he was elected, Councilor Talamar proposed an expedition Below." Brows go up around the table. A couple of the councilors sit forward in interest, and my heartmother closes her eyes, because Talamar's wild ideas are the last thing she wants me involved with.

"He said that the only way to recover what we lost is to go back to the place it came from," I continue. "Our ancestors built Alciel down there. They launched Alciel into the sky from Below. And somewhere in the ruins, maybe the Royal Academy could find evidence that tells us how they did it."

Even now, in the middle of this moment, my heart thumps harder just thinking about it. To go Below, to see the place where our history began, to walk in the same places our ancestors came from . . .

To visit a land of ghosts, empty of people, but full of forgotten stories.

"That would be fascinating." It's my bloodmother who cuts into my speech, smooth as a sharpened knife. "Unfortunately, the academy members would be dead—everything Below, from the insects on up, is a threat to life. And in the extremely unlikely scenario that they managed to defend themselves, they would have no way to return to us. Their no doubt valuable insights would be lost, North."

Here I go.

"That's true, Your Highness," I say, as respectful as I know how to sound. "And I know it's dangerous down there. But as for our chances of discovering what they learned? That, I can do something about. I have found a way to return to the sky from Below."

The room explodes.

Everyone starts talking over everyone else, and the only ones silent in the room are my heartmother, my grandfather, Talamar, and me. It isn't Anasta's place to speak at a council meeting, so she's biting her lip, but I can tell there's going to be a Conversation about this later. His Majesty's simply leaning back in his chair, studying me thoughtfully, as if he's still making up his mind about what I'm saying.

Looking at my grandfather is like looking at an older version of myself—at my own black hair turned white, but just as unruly despite the intervening decades. The same patrician nose, strong brows, light brown skin. When I was young, I was fascinated by his face—even then, he looked different from most people. Smoothing out his wrinkles or tucking in the skin around his chin is a procedure that would take an hour or two at most, but unlike most residents of Alciel, he's never let the medtechs do their thing. His experience is written on his face, every line telling a story, and I like that.

Talamar, on the other hand, has taken advantage of everything the medtechs have to offer. An illness when he was young left him with permanently damaged lungs and pain that he doesn't like to discuss. It never seems to dampen his energy, but then again, he's only been fighting the rest of the council for a couple of years. They have a long time yet to wear him down.

Right now, he's grinning openly, enjoying the commotion—but he knew what I was going to say. My mothers might have raised me, but it's my bio-donor, a man who wasn't even supposed to be identified, who really understands me. At least on this. For years I didn't know him—he was allowed to pass on birthday presents, but never his name.

When I was five, a model glider started my forbidden fascination with flight. When I was ten, a sci-fi vid about an impossible cloudship that landed Below, on the actual *surface*, sent a thrill through me that never went away—though the animated beasts the shipwrecked explorers fought gave me nightmares for weeks. By the time he was outed as my bio-donor when I was fifteen, I felt like I already knew him.

Now, Talamar nods, lifting his inhaler again, eyes creased in a smile. *Go on*, his gaze says. *You can make them see what you see.*

So I draw a breath and raise my voice to cut through the arguments around me. "Esteemed council members," I try, which catches a few of them. "Your Majesty," I continue, just as loud. "Your Highnesses."

The last of them—Damerio, a sinking skeptic—falls silent, eyeing me beadily. Just waiting for his chance to launch back into his favorite argument. I hustle on with it before he can try.

"You've all been to the air festivals here on Freysna. You've all seen the stunts and the races. And you all know that the best of the gliders is the *Skysinger*. It's faster and more nimble than any of the others, its pilot more skillful, and its design simply better. And perhaps you know that half the engineers at the academy would give up their tenures for the chance to meet that pilot and spend an hour looking over his machine.

"Well, I know that pilot. And I know why the *Skysinger* is so much better than anything else in the air. It's because his engine uses tech salvaged from the sky-engines."

Beatrin's voice is very quiet when she speaks, very dangerous. "That would be illegal," she points out. "The engines are not to be touched."

"It's not illegal, it's *practical*," I retort. "We don't know what half the parts of the engines are even for, or whether they're necessary. The pilot's been working on a new kind of engine, and with the tech from the *Skysinger*, he could build a cloudship capable of landing a pilot on the surface Below and returning him safely to Alciel. With funding, and with academy support, he could do it as quickly as this time next year."

"Impossible!" Councilor Damerio finally loses his temper

and shouts his reply, standing and puffing himself up like a yellow-tailed sparra trying to impress a mate. His puffed-up hair has always reminded me of feathers, his pouched cheeks and pursed mouth doing nothing to detract from the impression of a self-important little bird. "Your Highness, with respect, the very idea that we would endanger the engines over a perfectly natural fluctuation in altitude, that we would trust a renegade glider pilot to tinker with our engines—"

"Indeed." Finally, my grandfather speaks, and the king's voice silences Damerio instantly. "Tell me, North," he says slowly. "How did you come to know this pilot?"

I can see in his steady gaze that he already knows the answer.

Trust me, I beg silently, looking back at him. *Listen to me. I can do this.*

If this doesn't work, I'm about to give up the thing that matters most to me in the world.

But it will work. It *has* to work.

I take a deep breath.

"I know it can be done," I say. "Because I'm the pilot and the engineer of the *Skysinger*. I can build you that cloudship, and I'm volunteering to pilot it."

The room erupts into chaos, councilors coming to their feet, voices raised, hands lifted, half a dozen displays from their chronos jostling for room in the projection square atop the table.

"There have been years like this before," Damerio's shouting, gesturing wildly at his bar graph. "We are not sinking!"

Talamar stands shoulder to shoulder with Gabriala, a

councilor from one of the other small islands, their voices tangling with one another.

"The small islands are sinking faster than—"

"You cannot simply vote us down every time we—"

And I'm stuck in the middle of this, mouth half-open, watching as if I'm outside my own body. Because this is the same argument they've been having for years. These are the same words. And nothing I've said has even made a dent—even the ones who believe in altitude loss aren't talking about my cloudship, aren't talking about invention, or creation, or discovery.

They're just screaming along to the same old script.

I gave them the *Skysinger*, and I've been forgotten between one heartbeat and the next.

A hand grabs my wrist, and I whip around to see Anasta, eyes huge, mouth trembling. My heartmother's always been the one to find some way to applaud everything I've tried, but right now she looks like she wants to pass out. When she silently draws me toward the door that leads to the royal quarters, I don't resist—not even when I see my bloodmother stalking furiously after us.

Nobody but my grandfather even notices us leave.

Anasta doesn't even bother making it to my mothers' room—she just stops once we're out in the hall, dropping my wrist and leaning back against a window as if she needs the support. Behind her, the clear blue of the sky stretches away forever, except for a bank of clouds that loom like a mountain from a fairy tale, ready to tumble down and bury us all.

"North," Beatrin snaps from behind me, and I spin around so I can face both of them. "You *cannot* be serious. I don't even know where to start—with your deception, with the risks you've taken, with your decision to defy us in front of the entire council? I have *never* been more disappointed than I am right now."

Anasta's buried her face in her hands, and she speaks through them, still pulling herself together. "When were you doing this?" she demands, voice shaking. "When you were supposed to be studying? Was this your research? You know how precious you are, not just to us, but to Alciel." When she lowers her hands, her eyes are brimming. "If anything ever happened to you, North—when I think about you up there in the sky, nobody knowing you need to be kept safe, gliding out over all that nothingness . . ."

"I *was* safe," I protest, trying to keep the snap from my voice, knowing I'm failing. "I'm good at this—I'm the best, Anasta. All these years telling me to search for the way I can contribute to my kingdom, and now—"

"You can't contribute if you're dead!" Beatrin snaps. "It took an army of medtechs for you to be born. What do you think happens if the heir dies and the bloodline fails? You are the Prince of the Seven Isles, second in line to the throne of Alciel, and a Guardian of the Light. Your foremost duty is to continue our line. The moment this train reaches the palace, you will tell security where this glider is, and it'll be brought back to the academy. And you will never, under any circumstances, fly that thing again."

A bolt goes through me. "You can't do that," I snarl, tossing

31

restraint to the wind—it hasn't helped me, anyway. "I'm not a child, Beatrin, you can't confiscate my toys. You can't forbid me from doing things. The *Skysinger* is mine, and if you think I'm giving it up—"

"You're *my* child," she shouts, her famous calm completely gone now. "And I can forbid you, or anyone else in Alciel, from doing anything I like. Your grandfather is the king, North, and heir or not, you're his subject. You'll do exactly as you're told."

There's a beat of silence as I try to absorb this, my heart thumping and stuttering. I knew there was a chance they wouldn't listen. I knew there was a chance it would go wrong. But now that I'm here, watching my dream crumble, I don't know what to say.

Into that silence, my chrono buzzes with a soft message notification, and Anasta's gaze drops to fix on it.

"Oh," she says softly. "Oh, I see now. You didn't do this alone, did you? Your friends helped."

"Which friends?" Beatrin demands.

"The tutor's son," Anasta murmurs. *Saelis.* "And the chancellor's daughter." *Miri.*

"Leave them out of this," I say, just as soft. "Anasta, don't."

"I'm sorry," she says simply. "But it has to stop. This infatuation with them has gone too far, North. One day your grandfather will be scattered to the clouds, and your mother will be queen—and when she follows him in her turn, you'll be king. A king cannot be a part of a three. That's where this is heading, isn't it? That's why they were willing to help you do something so incredibly stupid—that's why you started doing it to begin with. You think they love you—and you're showing off for them."

"That's not what we're talking about right now," I tell her, trying to ignore the burning in my cheeks, because I am *not* discussing my love life with my mothers, and especially not today. "And when it is something I'm deciding, I'll be doing it myself. Without consulting ancient traditions and conservative crap."

Beatrin opens her mouth, and then bites off her words when Anasta shakes her head. My heartmother always gets the job of delivering the news I don't want to hear.

"This isn't about us," she says, "or what we believe. The monarch makes a pair, because to add a third person would be to add hopeless complexity to the archipelago's politics, North. Just look at what's happened with Talamar."

"What about him? He was elected to the council by his island."

"Yes," she agrees. "But only after the journos outed him as your bio-donor. He was chosen for that role specifically because he was of no importance politically, and had no influence to wield for or against the throne. Now he has a seat on the council, because his island hopes his connection to you will bring them favor. And worse, perhaps it will."

"I can keep my personal relationships separate from politics," I snap, trying to ignore the fact that I'm in the middle of a political argument with my own mothers right now.

"You can't control gossip," Beatrin says, her tone harsh. "The preservation of the royal bloodline is our most important task, North. And what Anasta's too sweet to say is that if you make a three that includes the tutor's son, then there'll always be doubt about who fathered your heir, no matter what proof you provide."

"Why does that matter for us, when it doesn't matter for anyone else in the archipelago?" I demand. "If the owner of one of the big tech companies makes a three, nobody asks who fathered his heir. The children are raised, and they inherit."

"The royal family is not a tech company," Beatrin snaps. "The rules are different for us, because *we* are different."

I want to fight her, but I don't know how. On top of everything that just happened in the council room, the blows are piling up, threatening to bring me to my knees.

"This has gone so far beyond the edge, I don't even know where to start," she continues. "To suggest that you, of all people, could go Below—nobody has ever returned from there, North, because that way lies death. You'll turn in your glider, and you won't see those two friends of yours again, is that clear?"

The air goes out of me, and I'm left staring at her. "You're joking," I say weakly. Of all the things I thought I was risking, Miri and Saelis were never on the list. They're my best friends. Until today, I'd hoped they might be more. And even if that's impossible, I never want to lose them.

"I'm deadly serious," she says quietly. "Now we're going to go back to that table and try to salvage something from this fiasco. Clear?"

"Clear," I murmur, my thoughts fritzing like there's a bad connection in my head. "I, um—just give me a moment. I'll use the restroom."

"North," she begins, but Anasta lays a gentle hand on her arm again.

"We'll see you in there in just a minute, North," my heart-mother says.

I nod, and watch as the two of them disappear back through the door, the noise of the argument beyond it welling up, then shutting off as it slides closed.

I'm left staring at the emblem painted onto it—my family's crest. It's a stylized sky-island, borne aloft by a pair of wings. The underside of the island is smooth, the top a jagged line to represent the buildings.

In this moment, that island looks impossibly small.

I take Anasta's place, leaning against the sun-warmed dura-glass of the window, hands shaking as I try to understand what's just happened. In a quarter hour, I've lost my glider, my best friends, and my freedom.

Then I feel the faint dragging sensation that comes with the train dropping from high velocity to regular speed, which means we're approaching Port Camo. Last stop before the palace.

Before I can think about it, I'm hustling down the hallway, past windows that now look out onto the sporting district on one side, and a mural on the opposite wall. It features a parade of fantastical birds and animals, supposedly from the time before. We no longer have names for most of them—and quite a few look so stupid that I'm certain the artist made them up entirely.

I press my thumb against the SmartLock beside the door to the royal quarters. My skin tingles as the microneedles connect, and then the sensation passes. The lock is coded to just three people's DNA—my mothers' and mine—and even our attendants don't have a way inside. Beatrin says she'd rather make her own bed than give up her privacy. Today, that'll buy me time.

My fingers fumble as I unbutton my soy-silk shirt, then use it to scrub away the gold dots painted along my cheekbones. I dump it in a gold-trimmed puddle on the ground and strip down to my bamboo undershirt as I drop to my knees beside our luggage where it's piled in the corner, ready to be off-loaded.

Everything I own has gold thread woven through it, so it's impossible to pretend I'm anyone else for even a moment in my own clothes. But I press my thumb to the lock on the suitcase I took down to Port Picard for our overnight trip, and when the case opens soundlessly, I dig madly through the jumble of stuff I shoved inside this morning. At the bottom, I find one of Saelis's plain blue shirts—I try to have something with me for moments like this—and I button it up as fast as I can.

I roll back the rug to reveal the maintenance hatch and grab hold of the ring to flip it open. The track flies by beneath the carriage as I crouch and wait, swiping my fingers across my chrono's display to dictate a message to the others. "Meet me at the hangar."

The train slows, slows and stops, and I slither down through the hatch, flattening myself on my belly, listening to the chatter of the workers above me as staff board and depart the train. I've thought about doing this before, scouted it in case I ever wanted to split, but now that I'm eyeballing it, it looks tight.

Well, as Talamar says, gotta flap if you wanna fly.

And then there's a grinding noise somewhere ahead of me, and with a hum, the train's alive once more.

I really hope I got the measurements right.

The thing just about gives me a haircut on the way out, but thirty seconds later my mothers and the council are on their way to the palace, and I'm climbing to my feet, checking the platform, then clambering up onto it to make my way out.

I duck out the station gates and into an alleyway, squeezing past a pallet of old circuitry bound for recycling, keeping my head down. I need to get underground as quickly as I can— traveling this way is how I've avoided the ident cameras for the last few years. It's why today was the first time my mothers realized I've been leaving the palace. This time they'll be on the lookout, but I'm not trying to avoid them forever.

I have a point I want to make before they drag me back home and take away everything that matters to me. It's my last throw of the dice, and I'm not going to give it up.

I have to risk the grand boulevard for a minute, and I snag a pair of sunglasses from a stall, jamming them on my face and dropping a credchip as I keep moving. The afternoon sun is a huge ruby suspended skyward at the end of the wide street, gleaming at me through gray clouds. The colors to either side of the street are just as vivid, displays dancing across the storefronts, bright lights making even brighter promises. The smell of a dumpling shop wafts past me, and the shouts of a headset vendor mingle with the sound effects of the game he's got on demo.

I duck down a second alleyway and get away from the main strip. I need to head underground from a shabbier area, where there are fewer cams—that might stop them realizing where I've gone, once they think to trace me.

The capital doesn't have the slums you see on the other islands, but the support staff have to live somewhere. Like the palace, their homes are ancient, built out of rock mined from Below before the Ascension. They're a lot more solid than the buildings that have sprung up since, made of bamboo and repurposed steel, but they all have solar panels strapped to the roofs that slowly angle throughout the day to make the most of the sun. Just now they're all pointed west, making the line of rooftops along the edge of the island seem like a serrated knife.

Ten minutes later I find a service lane running behind the strip of makeshift stalls, and thirty seconds after that, I find what I'm really looking for—a manhole. Dropping to my haunches, I pull a data cord from my pocket, plug one end into my chrono, then flip up the tiny hatch beside the manhole to find the maintenance socket for the other end of it.

A wall of figures springs up above my wrist, and I use my free hand to send them sliding around like I'm conducting music, coaxing the manhole into opening up with a soft clunk as the seal releases.

Below me are the hot, bustling depths of the sky-engines and the unmistakable greasy scent of the fog that wafts through them. To others, the engine tunnels look like the chaos of Below itself, and the thickness of the air there makes them uneasy. To me, the tunnels look like freedom.

The rhythmic thump that surrounds me as I climb down calms my thoughts and drowns out my worries as the light fades away and the air grows humid and heavy. Something about the combination of air, noise, and vibration from the engines gives this place an oddly ethereal atmosphere, and the hair on my arms begins to lift in response, as it always does. I pause to shake my wrist, and the light on my chrono kicks in, casting dancing shadows as my feet hit the ground.

I'm going to get to the *Skysinger*, and I'm going to show them once and for all what she can do. I'm going to make them see how much better her engine is than anything out there, so that they *have* to take this seriously. So that they understand this isn't some stupid daydream. This is real, and I can do it.

If we don't dream—if we don't try to go Below, try to push out the borders of our tiny archipelago and see what else is out there—then what's the point of all our tech? Are we supposed to just use it to make sleeker transports and smarter chronos—to make our lives lazier and easier?

Not me. I want to explore. There's a way to solve any problem, and if we want to figure out how to survive Below so we can search it for answers, then we need to go there.

And even if I set aside my dreams of exploration, the engines might fail at some point in the future. If the sky-cities fail, everyone dies.

There are a thousand reasons this needs to fly.

So in I go.

Every island of Alciel has engines beneath it, built into the bedrock itself, but the capital's are the largest by far—they stretch the length of the island, like a second city below the first. Once you get used to the heavy, metallic feel of the air and spend some time down here, you learn that the engines are full of neighborhoods too, each with its own personality—grinding machinery, or long walls of circuitry jostling for room, or endless close-packed intersections of dark corridors. Of course, their only residents are the engineers—and the occasional trespasser.

I pull up my long-ago stolen blueprints on my chrono and figure out where I am, then set off down a hallway lined with circuitry, thousands of small red and green lights playing across the walls on either side. Centuries ago, the code that drives them would've made sense to our engineers—now we've lost that technology. Our engineers are like doctors splinting broken bones, but if anything ever went wrong—seriously wrong—with the engines, we'd have no idea how to fix them. There are circuits with no apparent purpose, sections that seem to run on nothing more than air.

Which means we'd better hope for everyone's sake that Damerio's right, not Talamar—that the cities are not actually sinking.

Or we'd better start trying to rediscover what we've lost, if only we can stop arguing long enough.

It's fascinated me as long as I can remember, that just as my own heart beats mysteriously within me, so too do the engines deep within the city. The strangeness in the air here gives some people the shakes, and for a few, even starts messing with their minds—but it never bothered me. When I was younger,

I wanted to be an engineer. That was before I understood my path led only to council meetings and ceremony.

Today I tried to make something of those council meetings, to use the fact that I get into them at all to actually make a difference. But sometimes you need to stop talking and *do*.

Miri and Saelis are waiting in the hangar, which I found on one of my first trips down here. It was when I worked out that it used to be a launch bay that I had the idea for the *Skysinger*, and this is where she sits now, waiting to hit the skies.

The *Skysinger* is the only thing in the world that's truly mine. Everything else I own is part of my office. It was made for me because I am a prince, or was used or worn by royals before me, and will be handed on to those who come after.

But my glider—it's the one thing I can look at and think, *My name is North. I built this with my own hands, and it's mine.*

It's strong and sleek, but nothing flashy. I painted the *Skysinger* a simple black, with chrome fittings polished to perfection. So many of the other gliders are much brighter, adorned with stripes and symbols that denote their pilots' successes in races and stunt competitions. The *Skysinger* is utilitarian, low-key.

I let her flying speak for both of us.

I got part of the frame secondhand from a salvage and recyc yard, and it took me a solid year of sneaking away to put her together. Saelis did a lot of legwork for me, and Miri a little as well—neither of them has much interest in aeronautics except as a means of transport from island to island, but they never minded walking into a junkyard with a shopping list, if I told them exactly what I needed.

It's her engine that makes her special. It's unique, cobbled together out of pieces of tech that I'll freely admit I only half understand. The key, though, is that they allow me to gain altitude without relying on thermals like everyone else, which means I can outmaneuver the rest of them with one hand tied behind my back, and my glider and I can slip in underneath the city to our launch bay doors at the end of each outing, leaving everyone else wondering where we went.

"Did they ask for a demo?" Miri asks, hurrying forward, grinning. Her curls are pink today, the glitter at her cheekbones blue. "We got here as fast as we could. I tell you, it was a challenge—Saelis found this antique shop, and he's such an old man, you know what he's like when . . ." Her voice dies away when she sees my face, and she halts, uncertain.

"North?" Saelis asks from behind her, only just audible above the thrum of the engines.

"They didn't ask for a demo," I say, grim. "But they're going to get one."

"Oh." Miri's face falls. "Well, crap."

"You have no idea," I mutter. But I don't want to think about it now. I want to get into the air. The skies will be full of gliders as the sun sets, and I want to use the last of the light to show my mothers and everyone who matters just how much better and easier and faster the *Skysinger* moves. They might not be watching at first, but word will reach them quickly enough, and now that they know what they know, they'll be watching a minute after that.

"Are we in a hurry?" Saelis asks, studying my face with the gentle, thoughtful expression he always wears.

42

"Little bit."

He simply nods and turns toward the launch straps as I stride over to pull on my flight suit.

"We'll go down to the promenade and watch," Saelis says, yanking the first of the launching straps over to the winch that'll stretch them taut.

The barometer looks good, the pressure even, and I rummage for my goggles and my flight suit. I hop on first one foot and then the other as I jam each leg into it, zipping it up my front over my clothes, and then pulling on my jacket.

Meanwhile, Miri helps Saelis yank the next launching strap into place. The straps work just like my slingshot used to when I was small, before Anasta confiscated it because *treasury advisors aren't for target practice*. They creak as we secure the last one, and then we haul on the lever that starts the machinery to stretch them tight.

Once I'm ready, I slither into my seat, which is perfectly fitted to my shape. I sink down until only my head's visible above the sides.

Miri slides the duraglass windshield into place, and I'm safe behind my bubble, the sound blocked out. In front of us, Saelis is sliding up the launch bay door, giving me a clear view of the sky.

I give them the thumbs-up, and they each return it, Miri taking Saelis's place by the edge of the door, one arm wound carefully around the safety strap we tied there as she checks for obstructions, the wind making grabs for her hair and clothes.

Saelis disappears behind me, to the strap release. Miri's

holding her hand out, palm flat, angled toward the ground. It's the signal for *hold*, and he does. Then a gaudy red-and-gold glider sails past the opening of the garage, yellow streamers whipping in the wind behind it. They'll be shredded soon enough, but they'll last for at least a little of tonight's aeronautics show.

That must have been what she was waiting for, because the next moment she switches to give Saelis a thumbs-up. I feel a warning thump vibrate through the tail, and then another, as the countdown begins.

Three, two, one . . .

The glider shoots out into the gray sky, trying to push my stomach backward through my spine in a quick rush.

I tip my head back to get a look at my surroundings, but Miri was right, and I'm clear. I tilt the controls gently to the left and catch the thermal that's always there in good weather, wheeling around and offering the pair of them a wave as they check that the garage door's secure, leaving it open for my return. And then I'm climbing, climbing, until the whole of the island's spread out below me.

The streets make neat grids, lit by sparkling streetlamps that blur together as I sail overhead. The brightest lights of all are the palace, and I wheel around the edge of the exclusion zone, just another glider out for tonight's show, part of the celebration marking the beginning of council deliberations at the palace. The eastern park's below me now, a long strip of dark green, the edges nibbled in by new construction, a constant source of debate in the council.

At least a hundred other gliders are wheeling around like

newly fledged hawks playing in the wind, almost all of them brightly painted and decorated, much more interesting to look at than mine.

But I'm the one everybody's going to be watching tonight.

My heartmother used to tell me bedtime tales about the lost sky-cities, other ancient archipelagos that we once knew, but forgot in the centuries since the Ascension. Whenever I'm in the *Skysinger*, I find myself imagining that they're real, just beyond the horizon. That somewhere out there in the vast, blue ocean of the sky is another prince, in another glider, looking back across the expanse at me and wondering if Alciel was ever real.

Below isn't a myth, though. It's real, and it's within reach, if only we'll try. If only I can make them see that we have to be more than we are—we have to search, and discover, and keep making ourselves better, not just because our engines might need it, but because our *souls* do.

I skirt the eastern edge of the island, close but not too close to the edge of the main thermal, letting the updraft increase my altitude as I head for the main flight. This is what I come for— these moments when I'm one with the *Skysinger*, and in perfect control. Citizens will be watching from the boardwalk below, and I'm about to give them the show of a lifetime. Conditions are perfect. The sky is an unbroken blue dome all around me, and the lower layer of clouds between us and Below is thick and stable.

I could almost—

There's a *pop* behind me, and a quick shudder runs through the glider. It's nothing dramatic, but I know instantly that something's wrong. My gut's churning as I tilt the controls experimentally to the left . . . and nothing happens.

I yank them to the right, quicker, and again, nothing.

No steering.

Skyfall.

There are few things that can go more wrong than this, and my gaze flicks forward, my chest already tight with fear. If I'd been facing the other way, I might have hoped to gradually lose altitude, to come down with the cool of the night air and land on a distant island.

But this way, there's nothing but the palace, and then the empty sky beyond. Empty sky all the way to eternity.

And I have no way to turn the *Skysinger* around.

I lean as far as I can against my restraints, craning my neck around and pressing my cheek to the windshield, so I can just make out the curve of the glider's body that houses the steering controls—and my heart stops.

The Skysinger is on fire.

I'm hurtling toward the main flight of gliders now with no chance to warn any of them that I can't avoid them, no way to scream out to any of them for help. Any other day, and the flames whipping out the back of the *Skysinger* would signal distress—but almost every glider here is rigged to impress tonight, with holographic paint jobs or cannons shooting glittering clouds of confetti, and they'll all assume these flames are just one more show-stopping trick.

There's a bright green craft coming at me from my right. It has right-of-way, and I'm reduced to flashing my external lights at it, waving both hands madly inside the cramped space, desperately trying to show the pilot I don't have my hands on the steering controls.

"Look, *look at me!*" My voice breaks as a shout turns into a scream, and I'm thumping on the inside of the glass. "Over here, over *here!*"

It's getting closer and closer now, and I can see the shape of the pilot—who must think I'm some kind of idiot out to play a game of *who's got the stronger bladder?*—and I'm screaming and thumping at the glass, grabbing the useless controls with one hand and yanking at them, as though it'll do anything at all, and we're going to—

The green glider pulls up at the last possible moment, the undercarriage nearly scraping the top of my cockpit, and I try to duck in my seat, though I'm so perfectly cushioned by it there's no way to move.

For an instant I'm relieved, and then I glance ahead, and my heart surges up into my throat as reality reasserts itself. Because I'm still heading for the palace and the empty sky beyond it—I've just bolted straight into the exclusion zone, and I wonder for a mad moment what would happen if they shot me down, because the council might know who I am, but the guards won't—and now I'm past it, and approaching the edge of the island.

And already the glider's losing altitude as the warmth of the land mass fades, and I'm yanking at the controls, someone's voice—my voice?—begging the *Skysinger* to respond, to let me turn around before it's too late. With its engine malfunctioning, I have no way to gain altitude—no way back, if I fall.

But it's too late already.

I'm out beneath the blue of the open sky, but I'm past the edge of the clouds that have always been below me. The darkened landscape beneath stretches out with nothing between it and me.

And slowly, the nose of the glider is tilting down.

THREE

NIMH

The riverstriders tie the river barges at the marshy shoreline as the sun dips down beyond the forest-sea, working together with the kind of easy synchronicity only brothers could have. Capac wears braids to match Hiret's, tied back from his face in a thick bundle against his neck. Maita's hair is unbraided, long and coiled into a pile at the crown of his head. He is the younger of the two, and has the smiling air of someone always at ease.

Dragging a river barge high enough onto shore that a sudden flood could not tug it loose is back-breaking work, and the riverstriders' brown faces gleam with perspiration. Of the three guards who've come with me, only Elkisa has spent any time on the river, though even she fumbles with the ropes as they join in the effort. She and Capac pull at the bow, while Rheesi and Bryn haul from the stern—Maita stands alone between them, muscles straining.

Capac calls for a brief halt, then bends with a groan to scoop water over his head. Maita reaches up to haul off his shirt, sodden with sweat, and uses it to swipe at his dripping shoulders. My gaze slides toward that movement as if dragged there, and it seems to take me far too long to pull my eyes away again. Mine aren't the only eyes on him either—one of my guards, Bryn, has her heart-shaped face turned his way, one corner of her mouth curled up. Distracted, she doesn't notice Rheesi dropping the rope until the sudden pull of it topples Bryn into the water.

From my earliest memories, my guards have towered over me. Infallible and mighty, bringing with them the comfort of invulnerability no matter where I went. Now, beyond the temple and its city, with their mistakes peppering the water with ripples and Bryn's face pink as she looks anywhere *but* at Maita's shoulders . . . they seem all too human.

A little shiver runs through me, and before I can examine it—or the little ache I feel at the sight of handsome Maita laughing and offering his hand to help Bryn back to her feet—I lurch from my seat and move toward the edge of the barge. "This is silly," I call, interrupting their chatter. "It will be easier with six."

"Wait, Divine One," Elkisa calls breathlessly. "In a moment you can disembark more easily."

"A little water will not harm me," I reply lightly, reaching down to grasp the gunwale of the barge before jumping into the knee-deep water. "And I wish to help." I don't say the true reason I can't stay on the barge any longer: I'm too restless to wait uselessly while they work, as though finishing this task might make morning come more quickly, and with it, the rest of my journey.

I wade over toward Maita and reach for the rope he's been

hauling on, careful to stay several paces behind him, beyond his reach. He glances down, noting the distance between us with a nervous flick of his eyes.

Capac throws Elkisa a questioning look, and when my guard merely shrugs, he warily signals us to resume hauling the barge onto the riverbank. After a few seconds, he begins to sing, a rhythmic call-and-response work song traditional among the riverstriders.

The rope tears at my palms, which are unused to its rough fiber, but the burn is nothing compared to the exhilaration of joining my people at work. The high priest would howl to see me, and the Graycloaks would scoff and call me undignified— but in this moment, I'm no longer Nimhara, Forty-Second Vessel of the Divine; I'm just Nimh.

Dragging at this rope, my feet cooled by the water, I am more real, more seen, in this private moment than when I perform the intricate dances and rituals of the divine before hundreds of worshippers, all watching me with hungry eyes.

I lean back against the pull of the rope and let my eyes rest on the shift and change of muscle in Maita's back some distance ahead of me. In another life, I might have married a riverstrider boy like him. I would've spent my days hauling on these ropes with him, or mending fishing nets, or diving for river lettuce. This could have been my world, between sun and water and the muddy borders of the forest-sea. . . .

Maita shifts his grip, turning to face me and pull against his shoulder—and we both see that the rope has slid a little in his hands, and he's too close to me. He lets go, recoiling from me so violently that he staggers back waist-deep in the water, striking the barge with a painful thunk.

Capac calls a halt as Elkisa throws her rope down and comes splashing toward us, her gaze wide with alarm. Her agitated questions are a hazy litany, my eyes still on Maita's face, as ashen as if he'd just been pulled back from the edge of a yawning abyss.

I shake my head in response to Elkisa's concern—no, I am not hurt. No, he did not touch me.

Yes, I will wait back beneath the trees while they finish securing the barge.

My body tingles as I drop down onto a fallen tree, muscles here and there twitching from such a sudden end to the unfamiliar effort. From there, I watch as the riverstriders and temple guards resume their task—Bryn says something too low for me to hear at this distance, and Maita and the others burst into tension-relieving laughter.

What good does it do to imagine another life? I ask myself, blinking and turning away, fixating on the heavy stillness of the forest in the hope that it will still my mind. *This was never for you.*

Except that it *was*, once. I was never meant to be a goddess. My predecessor, Jezara, didn't pass her divinity to the next deity upon her death, as every other living god has done in the thousand years since the Exodus. When Jezara forfeited her divinity by committing the one unforgivable, unthinkable act for our kind—touching another—she tore my people's faith apart and left only tatters for the little girl fate called to replace her.

I was five when the high priest saw that the divinity had settled upon me, and brought me to live in the temple. By the time I was six, I understood that the long chain of gods who had guided my people for a thousand years had been irrevocably broken. While Jezara, with her unthinkable actions, had been the one to shatter that link, I would always be the one left clinging to the other half of that broken piece, trying to pull the dead weight of our wounded faith back from the edge with my bare hands.

Capac begins to sing again, and the boat slides up the shore. I wait quietly with the bindle cat upon my lap and stretch muscles tired from the weight of the rope.

Night settles over the forest-sea before anywhere else, as if gathering its strength before venturing out to envelop the rest of the land. The canopy overhead is dense enough to win out against the weakening sun, and the muted browns and grays of tree and vine and earth absorb what little light makes it through the leaves overhead. The night insects are singing by the time the others finish with the barge and begin transporting supplies to set up the camp some distance from me.

When I was younger, I was scolded often for getting involved when I ought to stay removed from my people. Though I am revered by—most of—my people, I cannot ever truly walk among them.

Matias, the Master of Archives at the temple, was the unlikely source of that particular revelation.

"They want to serve, Lady," he'd said, bespectacled eyes fixed on the text before him. He hadn't put it down despite the fact that I'd burst in, upset to have been shooed away from the solstice preparations. "They've trained for it all their lives. You can be kind to them, you can show them respect and even affection, but you cannot take from them the acts that give them purpose."

Purpose.

The word had struck me so deeply I had no answer for him. From the time I was five years old, my purpose had been made clear—and yet, until I manifest with some aspect, be it healing or harvest or anything at all, I have none.

"Are you hungry, Lady?" A familiar voice at my elbow startles the bindle cat, triggering a burble of irritation and the warning press of his back claws against my thighs as he jumps off my lap and stalks off into the dark.

I tilt my head up at Elkisa, who stands by my fallen tree and watches the cat go with a faint frown. "He means no insult," I tell her. "He is a cat—he only knows rudeness as a quality others possess."

"I wish I knew why that thing has never liked me," she mutters, a bit of her formality dropping away. She leans forward, holding out my spearstaff across her palms, having fetched it from the barge.

"He is jealous," I suggest, taking the spearstaff with a smile. "He knows you are almost as old a friend as he."

That melts Elkisa's frown, and with a twitch of her lips, she ducks her head. Her humor is short-lived, though—when she looks back up at me, her eyes are grave. "I'm sorry about what happened during the mooring."

I swallow, my throat suddenly tight. "It was my fault. I know better than to try to help."

Elkisa makes a noncommittal sound, then moves to sit beside me, just beyond arm's reach—distant, to most people. Nearly an embrace, to me. "I think maybe it's your desire to help that will save us all."

I give a quick laugh, uncomfortable with the weight of what she's said, though my heart beats a little faster. "I do not know what awaits me in Intisuyu. I only know I am meant to travel this way."

I think. But that last part, I don't say.

"Do you think we'll be long in the sun lands?" she asks. "The Feast of the Dying is tomorrow night."

"It will be faster on the way home," I say. "We will be traveling with the current." Our return will be a close-cut thing, but I know that her real questions are these: *Are you truly sure of your purpose? Will we return with something to convince the high priest we were right to defy him?*

I cannot blame her for wondering. Still, I am surprised when she speaks again. "You won't tell me what this new prophecy says? You don't trust me?"

I glance at her from the corner of my eye, aching to do just that. We grew up together, she and I—a goddess and her divine guardian. A wistful part of me misses the time when we were both just children.

Although there is little chance in a life like mine for friendship, there was a time when Elkisa and I were close that way. As an initiate, she'd been slower than the others to embrace tradition. She'd seemed blessed by preternatural agility and strength, although she once confessed to me that it was no lucky blessing at all but hard work, constant and unflinching. But her affinity with blade and bow, her quick adoption of every new combat style she encountered, meant that she was granted far more leeway in other areas than her comrades. She could be a little more outspoken before she was chastised; she could fail now and then to respect the proprieties without being dismissed outright.

She's older than I am, but one soul singled out—even for possessing a greater skill than her peers—inevitably seeks another, to banish isolation with camaraderie.

But the jealousy of her fellow initiates changed as they did, age bringing perspective and admiration to replace frustration and envy. And the best fighter in the world would still never be chosen as defender of the divine if she could not respect the formality and ritual of the role.

She pulled away, as she had to. Even if the Divine One was still as lonely as she'd ever been.

I dismiss that deep, old ache. "El, I don't even entirely trust myself." The relaxation of my speech is the only intimacy I can offer her now, and it makes her smile a little. "How can I trust anyone else?"

She sighs and leans back, bracing her palms against the half-rotted wood of the fallen tree. "There's nothing in the ruins of the sun lands anymore. Not for centuries."

"Oh, but you're wrong." I turn toward her, leaning my staff against the tree. "The story of a whole people is there. Skeletons of a great metal city, even the least of them stretching taller than the temple itself."

"You've been there?" Elkisa's eyebrows rise, her surprise tinged with a hint of jealousy.

"Not since I was very young—my first pilgrimage. Before you came to train at the temple." That seems to soothe her, and I close my eyes, recalling what I can of that whirlwind, terrifying first experience of being an entire land's only hope. "I think you will like it there. I remember thinking the forest-sea seemed to have slipped its banks and crept up into the hills, as if contesting the ancient city's control of the sun lands—covering all the stone it could reach in the green fabric of vine and sapling and moss."

A muffled noise from beside me makes me open my eyes, and I find Elkisa grinning at me.

Seeing me start to frown, she lets out a little laugh. "Forgive me, Nimh. Sometimes you turn a phrase or tell a story to rival the riverstriders' Fisher King. I was just thinking—maybe your aspect will be poetry, when you manifest."

My breath huffs, so close to a snort that I'm glad the temple's Master of Spectacle isn't here to see me violate his endless lessons in etiquette and deportment. Techeki has no time for children's tales. "It's been centuries since fate has allowed us anything so lovely as poetry. I'll leave that to the riverstriders, it's their tradition."

"Before you, the divine chose the form of the goddess of healing. Isn't that something . . . I don't know. Something hopeful?"

Long ago the gods' aspects heralded times of great literature or discovery or art, sometimes even expansion, exploration, and conquest. Now . . . now my people have no use for art, for art won't feed them, or hold back the mist, or keep them safe. Over the centuries, our divinity has declined to simpler aspects—harvest, home.

Jezara, goddess of healing, let my people think for a time that the world might heal too.

"Hope?" My gaze slides from Elkisa's face as I whisper, "We had hope last time. Look how that worked out."

Elkisa doesn't answer, and I tilt my head back to gaze into the depths of the canopy overhead. The lowest branches are painted with warmth by the firelight, each successive layer fading into the night like afterimages echoing in the dark. Somewhere in the shadows, the leaves quake with the passage of a colony of lying monkeys traveling to their nighttime berths.

Elkisa sighs and rises to her feet, and when I tip my head back down, I see that the riverstriders have finished making camp and are busying themselves at one of the fires. Bryn and Rheesi are nowhere to be seen, patrolling in the darkness beyond the firelight while Elkisa stays close to me.

I'm about to suggest she go see about something to eat when she speaks. "I know you heard the ravings of that Graycloak this morning. We all pretended not to, but I know you heard him."

My gut clenches with the memory I've been trying not to think about all day.

The Graycloak had been there at dawn as if he'd been waiting for us, though no one but my guards and the riverstriders knew of my plans to slip from the temple city unseen. Perched on top of a crate of fruit, he called out to the few people moving through the floating streets, inviting them to pause a while and listen. Voice cracking, body gangly, he could not be more than fifteen years old.

Seeing us, he spun around to follow us with eyes and voice, though I wore plain robes and no crown, and my guards had left the official black-and-gold tunics of the divine guard behind. He didn't know who I was—only that until Capac's barge cleared the market, his audience was captive.

They dress her in crimson, they paint her eyes, they let her speak the sacred rituals and touch the guardian stones. The high priest, in his desperation, calls her meager magic divine, as if that word, and not the truth of what she is, will keep us enslaved to a faith we should have abandoned a thousand years ago.

Our barge slid past him, the pace of the riverstriders quickening in response, but the Graycloak's words followed me long after he himself had vanished from sight.

What aspect is she but nothingness? What power does she have but what her priests claim for themselves? The last of the gods has gone, and all that is left is nothingness in the form of an empty girl called Nimh. . . .

His words still follow me, though he and his crate, and the market, and the city and the temple that overlooks it all have vanished down the lazy curves of the river behind us. I think they will follow me until I die.

"Nimh." Elkisa's gentle voice summons me back. That childhood name, which had cut so deeply coming from a stranger in the market streets, is a balm coming from my friend.

"It doesn't matter, El."

"It does to me," says my oldest friend, her normally easy gaze carrying an odd intensity. "And it matters to you. They claim that when J——when the blasphemer allowed herself to be touched, she destroyed the spirit of the divine altogether. That she consigned this world to darkness."

Elkisa must see something in my face when I look up, for she drops down before me, one knee bracing her against the ground. "You are not empty. You are not a puppet for High Priest Daoman to use——your very presence here, against his wishes, makes that clear enough. You are *not* what they say you are."

Her face, so close to mine, makes my chest ache. I have not been touched——not a brush of the fingertips, much less a kiss or hug——since I was five years old, but the wish is as strong as it ever was——and right now I wish I could let my friend hold me.

"But I'm not what Daoman says I am either," I whisper, my pulse thudding as I hear that fear aloud for the first time. "Where is my aspect, El? The Feast of the Dying is nearly upon us, and then it will have been ten years from the time I was called. The Graycloaks will not wait another year——what if they——"

Elkisa's hand drops to the soil between us, half an inch from the edge of my boot. The nearness of it stops my voice mid-word. Her eyes search mine.

"Daoman is not the only one who can see the divine light in you, Nimhara."

There is a strange wistfulness to her voice that I've never heard before. Her eyes are almost sad, despite the warm words.

Too moved to speak, I sit silently until that pensive look is gone again, and she rocks back on one heel.

"We will go to Intisuyu," she declares. "You will decipher this new prophecy and come home knowing your purpose, maybe even with your aspect manifested. Let them claim you are less than what they are—they will only feel more ashamed when they realize they were wrong. Tomorrow, Lady. As for tonight—will you eat?"

I swallow hard and look past her, toward the campfires. Bryn and Maita sit at one of them, not quite together, but near enough. Capac is moving off through the trees with a bowl in hand, no doubt in search of Rheesi so he can deliver the guard's dinner.

"You go," I tell her, lifting my chin, letting the mantle of divinity settle back over me. Elkisa may see me falter, but she needs to see me strong too. I owe that much to someone who would put her body between me and danger without a second thought for her own life. "I want to walk along the river a while and clear my head."

"I'll come with you." The response is instantaneous.

"Please, El. A moment to myself is all I ask. I would see someone approaching by river, and to reach the barges an intruder would have to come through here and contend with you, and four others besides. I am perfectly safe."

Elkisa's eyes narrow, but she wastes no time in debating with herself. She nods, a quick and decisive gesture. "I'll come to check on you if you're not back within half an hour."

I cannot argue, so I nod my thanks and slip away into the dark.

Elkisa seems content to believe in this "new prophecy," though bits of undiscovered text crop up all the time, buried in ancient tomes or in the scribblings of the mist-touched, and most often foretell nothing of greater importance than the shifting of a stream or the birth of twins.

I think she would feel differently if she knew what I had found was a lost stanza of *the* prophecy. The Song of the Destroyer. The only sacred text that matters.

Of all the things foreseen, the Song predates every one, going back to the time of the Exodus. Some scholars say it was written by the gods themselves before they left, as explanation or apology for the rift they tore in our world. My tutors claimed it was written by the first living god, the beginning of my line, who stayed behind to guide and protect humankind when the others took to the sky.

All life happens in cycles, even the world itself, and the life of ours was drawing to an end a thousand years ago. A young god named Lightbringer was given the task of ending the world so that it might be reborn again, new and free of suffering. But when that god, also known as the Destroyer, looked into the future and saw what lay in the gaping emptiness of the space between death and rebirth . . . he left us, and fled into the sky.

The Song of the Destroyer, as central to our faith as my own existence, tells us that one day the Lightbringer will return, with the Last Star to guide him. That amid omens of rising waters and falling stars, the Lightbringer will rejoin the living god to walk the land once more, before bringing us to rest in the instant of oblivion before the world bursts forth renewed.

Scholars and priests alike have devoted entire lifetimes to studying the Song. They ask what would have happened had the Lightbringer ended the world when he was meant to, whether we would now be in a new cycle of rebirth.

Some suggest that the last thousand years of suffering and waiting for the Lightbringer's return have been a test of our worthiness, destined from the beginning. Others have gone so far as to suggest he never existed at all, that the Lightbringer is just a Fisher King's tale, no more real than the stories of the Sentinels who guard the way between worlds, or the mist-touched wraiths that wait in the thickest, darkest mist-storms to drive the unsuspecting to the edge of insanity.

The Lightbringer cannot be real, they say—for how could a god turn his back on his destiny?

I could not help but wonder if the answer might be simple: that the boy-god born to destroy the world was afraid. I suggested this once, to one of my tutors—she came as close as anyone could come to calling her living divine a blasphemer. For what hope have men if even the gods know fear?

But I too am a god—the latest in a long, long line. And I know fear; I've met it many, many times.

Could I have destroyed the world, in his place? Would I have had the courage, the *faith*, to believe all that I was to destroy would be born again?

I wish I could say yes—but the truth is that I don't know. I cannot know—no one can, unless faced with that terrible choice themselves. Maybe the answer is that no one person, divine or not, can make that choice alone.

I was twelve years old when I fully understood the implications of the Song: that the Lightbringer would *rejoin* the living god, and together they would bring about the end of the world.

Together.

I used to imagine that he would come to *me*, that I was the one preordained to stand with him against the darkness. I could not help but long for it. To have someone by my side who understood the weight of destiny, someone who would give my life purpose and meaning. Someone who could *touch* me . . .

Perhaps that is why not even Daoman believes that my lost stanza is anything other than a girlish fantasy.

But I know what happened. It was no dream. I woke in darkness a fortnight ago, drenched in sweat, my skin tingling as if a mist-storm were all around me—and when I would have gone to the window, a vision seized me.

I saw myself in the temple archives, uncovering an ancient version of the Song of the Destroyer. But as soon as my eyes fell on the page, the letters began to glow and shift, until I was dazzled by light. When I could see again, there was a new stanza there, nestled in among the old familiar prophecy. And my heart was filled with such certainty, such *purpose*, that when the vision faded, I found myself standing in the middle of my chamber, gasping, face wet with tears.

When I could move again, I ran to the shelf in the archives where I'd found the scroll in my vision. I crouched there on the tiled floor, unrolling the dusty text that had been hidden behind a row of ancient census notes, while the bindle cat batted at night insects attracted by my lamp.

The letters would not change or glow, no matter how hard I stared at them. There was no lost stanza, no sign of anything unusual.

But the ancient scroll *was* there, exactly where it had been in my vision. Though the words were missing, how could I have known of its existence unless my vision was real? Divinely inspired, showing me the path to my purpose?

That scroll meant everything.

When I showed it to the Master of Archives, he glanced at it briefly and shrugged. "The lettering is ancient, but the page is not," Matias said. "See how the edges of it are milled here? It's a copy at best. More likely, it's a fake. Young scholars and acolytes do sometimes try to speed up their rise in the ranks by claiming to have found lost examples of prophecy."

But I knew what I had seen. The lost stanza in my vision was burned into my mind with perfect clarity.

The empty vessel, it read,
will at the end of days
seek the land kissed by the sun.
For only on that journey
before a swift gray tide
will the last star fall.
The empty one
will keep the star
as a brand against the darkness,
and only in that glow

will the Lightbringer look upon this page
and know himself. . . .

The thick humidity of the forest-sea vanishes at the river's edge, the change in the air pulling me from the memory. The bindle cat is waiting for me there, as if he knew I would seek some quiet out beyond the trees. I stoop to run a finger along the underside of his chin, then step out onto one of the smaller rafts lashed to the barge. Before I was called it would've been no different from walking on solid ground. Now, I notice how unstable it feels.

I'm becoming too pampered, I think sourly, glaring down at the bundled reeds below my boots.

The words of the prophecy's lost stanza fade in my mind's eye, replaced by the Graycloak we saw at dawn, his words still ringing in my ears.

An empty girl called Nimh . . .

I could not explain to Daoman's satisfaction why the lost stanza had seized me so completely. I was *filled up* with the idea that there could be a reason, some *purpose* to this torture of a half-life.

I was empty, without aspect, because fate had chosen me for something far greater than I had guessed, surrounded by the rising, swift gray tide of dissenters. . . .

The time of the Lightbringer's return had come—and I was the one who would discover him.

Just to think it is almost too much to bear, much less speak the idea aloud, as if the telling would somehow rob it of meaning.

Or you're afraid, my mind whispers. *Too scared of failure to let anyone know how hard you're trying . . .*

As my thoughts threaten to tangle themselves together, I draw in a deep breath of the fresh air and lift my chin. I cannot afford to indulge my worries. I can worry when I've returned.

Fireflies glint among the reeds and over the water, a dazzling arrhythmic display. As if in answer, their larval offspring nestled in the creases of the river lettuce glow in a gentler, softer dance.

Like stars lured down and held spellbound by their reflections in the water, the fireflies sing a song of light and dark.

The river is one of the only places within the forest-sea that one can see the sky unimpeded by branches and canopy. It reminds me of the view from the temple spire, though there the sky feels only half-real, like a backdrop for the rich architecture and comforts of the temple itself.

Here, with the water lapping around me and the leaves along the bank whispering to each other in the river breeze, the sky feels so close and so real I could touch it. The big, dark shape of the cloudlands blocks out a section of stars, dimly purple with the last hints of sunlight shed from below the horizon.

I'm tracing the constellations of the deities who lived and died before me when I see a spark of light—*there*, where there ought to be none. Tiny at first, so dim my mind cannot tell if it's real or imagined, the light seems suspended at the edge of the cloudlands like a firefly in a spider's web.

But then I realize the light is growing, coming closer,

gaining speed and definition as it travels in an increasingly steep arc across the sky. My heart seizes as it catches up to my eyes, and my breath stops as I stare skyward so hard my eyes begin to water.

Unbidden, for I would not dare to think the words for fear of hopes dashed, comes the thought:

The empty one will keep the star as a brand against the darkness. . . .

It is no ordinary shooting star, no thin arc of silver that streaks across the sky and vanishes into the darkness—this light lingers and grows, and just as I wonder if it's headed straight to me, it plummets, streaming fire and ash, into the forest-sea beyond the river.

Even the bindle cat has seen it. And when he chirps a question at me, it's all I need to affirm that what I've seen is real.

The Last Star. The star of prophecy.

Without thinking, without *letting* myself think, I use the sharp edge on my spearstaff to sever the lines binding this raft to the barge. I take up the oar and set off toward the opposite bank of the river.

Excitement propels me on as I hurry through the trees, though all logic is telling me to turn back and fetch my guards. Haring off into the forest-sea after a falling star would seem like utter foolishness to them, but they did not read the lost stanza—they didn't feel it seep into them like warmth into a cold-numbed body.

It *could* be a trap, though I know of no magic that could summon such a vision. *This* is my divine purpose—I know it so deeply in my being that I might more easily be convinced I could fly than that I'm wrong. Finally, I will have something to offer the people who look to me every day for relief from the constant barrage of famine and plague and mist-storms. Finally, I can promise them an end to this cycle, and the beginning of a new one, free of suffering.

I can give them hope.

Lightbringer, I pray, *I will find this star. I will bring it to the lost stanza—I'll find the one who must read it by fallen starlight. Just . . . let it all be true.*

Night insects swarm at me, prevented from reaching my nose and mouth by the muffling veils I've tied around my face. The bindle cat, trotting along at my heels, vanishes to chase some hidden creature in the forest undergrowth. He always returns, and I give him his freedom.

After all, I am chasing my own hidden thing.

As I see the trees thinning ahead, I break into a run.

Beyond the forest here lies the Mirror of Divinity, a vast salt flat that stretches leagues in all directions. The water, only a finger deep, is so poisoned by salts and minerals that nothing lives there, not a single insect to stir the surface. Even the breeze from the river is gone, not a ripple disturbing the Mirror's reflection of the heavens. The bindle cat, melting out of the forest-sea beside me, takes one step into the water and hisses angrily, licking at his wet paw and loudly cursing the salt.

I leave him at the forest's edge and step out into the water, my footsteps splashing gently against the crusted minerals beneath. All that exists, above and below, is stars.

The cosmic river flows across the sky in an arc of indigo and pearl, meeting itself in the water's surface and curving away again beneath my feet. The water ripples at each step, as tremulous as my own heart.

And there, still smoldering and smoking from the fires of its descent, is the fallen star. Shadowy and dark, it seems to draw all the light around it into itself. I would be afraid, were I not so hopeful—already I know it is no bit of celestial rock, for it has structure, intention, purpose. Arcs of shadowlike wings curve toward the sky, and a tiny pinprick of light glows deep within its dark skeleton.

I can hold myself back no longer—relief and joy are too strong, and I cannot wait one more second.

Timing my steps to the drumming of my heart, I strike out across the night sky beneath my feet and toward the fallen star.

FOUR

NORTH

The glider plunges through the clouds, the world turning solid gray, my vision gone but my ears full of screaming alarms and the horrible grinding of my engine, my own ragged breathing barely audible above it all. I yank at the controls, unable to help myself even though I know it won't make a difference.

And then I burst through the bottom of the clouds and the starlit world of Below spreads out beneath me. I see dark masses that might be forests with shadowy rivers winding through them, and a huge sheet of water that gleams up at me, flat and motionless as a mirror.

I can't help looking at it all, taking it all in as it rises up to meet me, this place I so desperately wanted to see. This place that's going to kill me.

Then the *Skysinger* shudders, snapping my head back and jarring every bone in my body, and my nostrils are filled with acrid smoke and the smell of burning plastic, and instinct takes over, driving me to fight a battle I'll surely lose.

I unsnap my harness, sliding down in my chair so I can kick at the access panel by my feet, jamming the flat of my foot against it once, twice, three times, until it begins to buckle. The glider's powered by her engines, and the circuits that power them might be a smoking ruin, but that's not the only way to steer her.

My wildly kicking feet shove aside the wreckage of the hatch cover and push through, and I flail around for the thick bunch of cords that control my wing flaps. As I press hard against them with my boots, I feel the *Skysinger* start to tilt just a little, and I throw my weight sideways to help with the course correction. I can't see what I'm doing, and I'm steering by feel, but ever so slightly, I think her nose is coming up as she loses height.

Maybe, *maybe*, enough to land.

The alarms are still screaming all around me as I struggle backward, one foot jamming in the hatch as I fight to free it, hands scrabbling against the sides of the cockpit as I try to lever myself back into my chair.

I snap my harness back into place, and the next instant we're at the water, and the world's whirling by impossibly fast, and my head's spinning from the impact, and my glider's skimming the surface and sending up huge sheets of spray, tumbling, rolling completely over once, and then slowing, dragging, until everything's still.

It's a long moment before my vision clears and I can tell which way's up and which is down.

All the alarms are silent.

And to my complete surprise, it turns out I'm alive.

The *Skysinger*'s nose is crumpled in around my legs from the impact, pinning me in place. Every bone in my body hurts, and,

and . . . *there are flames coming out of the altimeter and the tilt indicator and the whole back of my glider is scorched.*

"Skyfall," I mutter. For an instant, the sudden truth of the curse—that I just *did* fall from the sky—hits me, and semi-hysterical laughter tries to well up in my throat.

I frantically hammer at the exit hatch release button, then reach up with my other hand to push at the roof of my cockpit, trying to force it up and open. But the sides of the glider are buckled, and it's jammed in place, trapping me inside with an instrument panel that's on fire.

I force my body forward, ignoring the new bolts of pain this awakens, yanking my arms this way and that in the confined space as I wrestle my jacket off, distantly hearing my own shout as I pull the sleeve down over a gash in my right arm. Then I'm pressing the jacket over the dashboard, holding it in place to smother the flames, folding it in on itself as one spot burns through.

The cockpit fills with smoke, and I choke and cough as I slap at the release button again, the glider's buckled dome screeching a protest that puts the council back in Alciel to shame. I use my good hand to bash once more at the dome itself, this time shoving it up and away, the warm night breeze hitting my face as the smoke dissipates.

I suck in a lungful of air, tilting my head back, the stars blurring into a faint tracery of white lines through the tears in my smoke-filled eyes.

I'm on the ground.

I'm Below.

I'm . . . dead.

I should have died in the fall, but soon it won't matter. There's no way up, no way home. The *Skysinger*'s engine allowed it to gain altitude, yes, but there's not nearly enough power to launch from the surface—assuming it was even intact. Assuming it hadn't burst into flames a few minutes into my flight.

How did this happen?

The thought does laps around my head as I find the seat release and push it back, slowly and carefully easing my legs out from underneath the crushed hood so I can check that they still work. After strapping my chrono back onto my wrist, I brace my left hand against the edge of the cockpit, grit my teeth, and grab at the other side with my injured right hand. I push myself up as I wriggle my hips, and I can't muffle the noise that escapes me. White-hot pain takes my vision.

When it clears, my breath's coming quick and jagged, but I'm crouching on my seat, surveying the ruins of my glider.

There's just no way the *Skysinger* failed. I check her over constantly. Tinkering around with her is my favorite thing to do, after flying her.

I lower myself down over the side and land with a splash in ankle-deep water. I grab the remnants of my jacket and wrap them around one hand as I wade up to the front of the glider. And yes, I'm aware I'm focusing on solving a tiny problem to avoid the fact that I can't solve a much, much bigger one.

We rely on thermals and momentum to glide from island to island in the sky—we have no way to fly *up*. That was the whole point of the engine I promised the council. But I haven't built the damn thing yet, and without it, there's no way for me to get home.

There are stories about those lost beneath the islands—about those who fell, never to be heard of again. The kind of stories you tell in the dark, late at night, to scare your friends. It's only really happened once that I know of, back before I was born—a man from one of the smaller islands, who fell, and—

It takes a few bashes with my wrapped-up hand, but I manage to push the panel away to reveal the engine.

It radiates heat that forces me to look away, but I see the problem the instant I turn back, shielding my face with my hand.

Something—some*one*—has sliced through my supply lines. It's a clean cut across the lot of them. A tool did this, not the crash. This was deliberate.

This was sabotage.

I know without a shadow of a doubt that it wasn't Miri or Saelis, but there are always others down in the engines. I dodge them every time I head to the hangar. Engineers, other trespassers like me. Did one of them follow me to the hangar? If they did, why do this?

Why try to kill me?

Did they know who I was?

It doesn't matter, of course. Soon, I'm going to wish I'd died in the fall. I'll slowly starve to death, unless the poisoned air or water does the job first.

I'm going to die. Here. Alone.

I may be doomed, but my body hasn't figured that out yet,

and it keeps moving. I reach for the wrist of my wounded arm so I can take off my chrono and turn on its light, then lean back into the cockpit to dig in the storage compartment for the scarf I use on colder days. I hold the chrono's strap between my teeth so I can aim the light as I wrap the scarf around my right arm in a pretty terrible bandage, panting by the time I'm done, pain racing all the way up to my shoulder.

I swipe to turn the light off again before my night vision is completely ruined, but then I remember—my *chrono*. It's not just a handy flashlight.

My heart pushes up into my throat and swells three sizes as I reach with one trembling finger to swipe the screen. You can use a chrono to send a message all the way from one end of the archipelago to the other. Maybe it can reach Alciel from Below.

The display springs to life, projecting my options above my wrist, and for an instant my heart soars. I can let them know I'm alive! I can—

I can do nothing.

Because my chrono's offering me a fraction of my usual options.

CALCULATOR TIME/DATE BIO-FEEDS SCAN
PICS NOTES MESSAGE ARCHIVE

And that's it. Anything that requires a signal—my current messages, my news feed, even the weather and wind forecasts— is unavailable. No help is coming from above.

I drop my wrist to my side, turning to take in my

surroundings. A sweep of stars lights the sky above me. The lake around me mirrors the stars and clouds, and at its edges, darkness looms.

There are no real stories about Below, only legends. But every one of them speaks of desolation. A few speak of unnatural beasts, savage and brutal, and as if the thought of them is a summons, I hear a steady splashing away to my left.

Something's out there—and coming this way.

My chest tightens, and suddenly, despite the inevitability of it, the realization hits me: I don't want to die. Not now, and *definitely* not like this.

I wade as quietly as I can toward the back of the *Skysinger*—the front is still smoldering—and press myself in against her, hoping I can crouch in the shadows and avoid the thing's notice. I've seen birds, but never an animal except in pictures. Is that what this is? What can it do? Can it see in the dark? Can it smell me?

As it splish-splashes closer, I realize it's no taller than my knee, and covered in striped hair all over its body. A long tail trails behind it, held up in the air to keep it dry, and its eyes seem to take up most of its face, though there's still room for a long, pointed nose. I press back into the glider's side as the thing marches toward me, and with a soft trill, stops right in front of me.

The noise doesn't *sound* like it wants to kill me, but for all I know it's about to unfurl a long, poisonous tongue and zap me with it.

"Hey, little . . . uh, thing," I murmur cautiously, trying to figure out whether to lunge right or left if it suddenly becomes hostile.

It blinks at me when it finds out I can make a noise, the movement slow and deliberate, and then it sniffs at me once and burbles cheerfully, as if it's replying.

Maybe it is? I have no idea how intelligent animals are. Could it understand me?

"Don't suppose you can point me to the nearest mech shop?" I ask, huffing a laugh at my own joke, and just the tiniest, tiniest bit, hoping it'll surprise me by answering.

It trills again, eyes reflecting the faint starlight as it blinks up at me. And then in an instant it's moving, turning to scamper away across the water, sending out ripples in every direction, tail whipping behind it.

"Hey, wait!" My words are a hiss, and I'm frozen in place. Did it understand me? Is it going somewhere? Should I follow it? Or is it . . .

A sound off to my left instantly answers my question. There's a group of five shapes moving toward me across the shallow mirror of the lake, creatures at least as tall as my chest. Like the little one, they're moving on four legs, and when one turns its head I see its silhouette.

There are knives coming out of the front of its face.

My brain scrambles for the right word, one I heard from Saelis when we were small. They're . . . tusks.

I've seen one bird hunt another, and I know instantly what I'm looking at: predators. I shrink in against the glider once more, holding my breath, trying to keep so perfectly still that I don't even send out a ripple. But one of them lets out a hideous, squealing grunt, and the others answer, and when they quicken their pace it's not in the direction of the little thing that had the smarts to make a run for it. They're circling around to pin me in against the side of the *Skysinger*.

I lunge for the front of the craft, my hands closing around a strut as the creatures charge toward me. The metal cold against my hands, I brace one foot against the glider's side and yank. When the pole comes free there's a piece of canvas stuck on the end, the sparks nestled in its fold springing into fire as I brandish it.

The nearest of the animals pulls up short, just outside my range, and by the light of my brand I can see it clearly. It's like my nightmares had nightmares, and those came to life—a huge pair of dirtied yellow *tusks* sit on either side of a long, blunt, hairy nose—the coarse hair covers its whole body, the muscle visible beneath it. Its teeth are just as sharp, poking out of its mouth in a vicious overbite, and long, curved horns sweep back from its head.

It snarls and grunts again. I swing the strut at it, then around to my right in an arc, forcing its nearest neighbor to pull up short as well. In a moment, four of them have formed a semicircle around me, the broken glider at my back, and I'm reduced to instinct as I work desperately to keep them at bay. But I know I can't do it forever—the fire will burn out, they'll grow bolder, they'll realize I can't stop all of them at once.

They're grunting and squealing and slobbering, and I can't tell if they're communicating or just so frenzied at the thought of

skewering me with their face knives that they can't help screaming about it. And then there's an echoing *bang* from behind me,
as the fifth finally tells me where it is by trying to charge straight
through the *Skysinger* to get me.

I yelp. And then I see another dark shape. This one is taller,
thinner, with some kind of horn rising up above it.

No, no, no, my panicked brain chants. One more attacker
will tip the balance. I can't fight one more thing—I can't even
fight these things much longer. The strut is knocked from my
hand, and I know I'm about to feel those tusks ripping me apart.

Then light bursts into blinding brilliance all around me,
throwing long, sharp shadows against the surface of the water.

For a fraction of a second, the newcomer is outlined, and
it's a person. The horn is a staff in their hand, and it's bright as
the sun—and then I'm throwing up my arm to shield my eyes,
turning in against the *Skysinger* to protect my face.

I can't see a thing, but I can hear perfectly—every individual heartbeat as my chest tries to explode. Every grunt and
squeal and splash as the creatures and their face knives run for
their lives, setting off across the mirror lake like a flock of frightened pidges.

And then silence, save for the shallow water lapping against
the sides of the glider.

Slowly I turn, lowering my arm, blinking against the white
flashes still going off in my vision.

As the white sparks slowly fade out, I see a black shape
against the starlight before me. A silhouette. And then her features start to emerge.

It's a girl. Her mouth and nose are covered by a band of cloth, and all I can make out are a pair of dark eyes, staring at me, narrowed in suspicion.

A person—an actual human, alive and staring at me.

But there aren't any *people* Below—everyone knows that.

Maybe I'm not a dead man after all.

Or maybe this girl is the next thing that's going to try to kill me.

FIVE

NIMH

The glare from the beacon spell fades, my eyes dazzled even through my closed eyelids. The sound of the mist-bent boar splashing a noisy retreat tells me to relax, but they are hungry creatures, drawn by blood, not by light or noise. Something drew them here—something wounded.

Just before I cast the beacon, I saw a streak of fire swinging this way and that against the press of the shadowy predators. In the moment, I thought it must be a piece of the fallen object, jostled by the animals. But the truth dawns on me even before I open my eyes to see the figure half-fallen back against the crumpled, smoldering object.

Someone else has come seeking the Star.

He lurches unsteadily to his feet, sending me scrambling back, clutching my spearstaff more tightly as my heart begins to pound even harder. There's nothing else inside the odd structure that fell from the sky, or at least nothing that I can see. The man—no more than a boy, really—is unarmed, and looks like he's already had to fight his way to this spot. A thick line of blood coats the right side of his face from hairline to collar, and his arm is crudely bandaged.

"Have you taken anything from this place?" I demand, disguising my fear with an air of command.

He doesn't move—he doesn't even blink, nothing to register that he heard me, much less understood me.

I lower the tip of the spearstaff, shifting my weight so that I can level it at him. I won't let some slack-jawed boy come between me and my purpose, not now that I might actually have one.

"How many others?" I snap, hoping to jar him from his stupor. "You cannot be here alone—where is the rest of your party?"

The boy continues to gape at me. He has big black eyes and an expressive mouth, and just now he looks as surprised as if *I'd* fallen from the sky along with this . . . this thing. His eyes are wide and fixed on my face with an expression oddly like one of *hope*.

"Move away." At last, my demand gets a response—his eyes switch their focus to the tip of my spear, and, swallowing, he sidles away from the smoking ruin so I can approach it.

The structure that fell from the sky is clearly broken—even without knowing what it's meant to look like, I can see the frame is bent and twisted, the outer skin crumpled and smoldering at its front from the impact with the ground. The lost stanza of the Song of the Destroyer describes the empty vessel wielding the Star against the darkness—the Star must be somewhere inside this tangle of broken construction. Keeping most of my attention on the boy, I take a step up onto part of the structure, making it creak ominously under my weight.

When I move again, there's a loud, unpleasant cracking sound, and the boy awakens all at once.

"Stop!" he cries abruptly, swallowing hard, like it's an effort. "If you break the carbon fiber there, you'll crush the wing spar. I'm going to need . . ." His eyes scan the ruin of the thing, his shoulders dropping. "Skyfall. It's never going to fly again. It can't get me back to . . ."

He speaks with a strange accent, and I don't recognize all the words he's using. Still, after a moment, his meaning hits me. "You claim you were *inside* this thing when it fell from the sky?"

"Yes." The boy's eyeing me and the spear with equal trepidation. "This is my glider."

Is he mist-touched?

I can't see his eyes clearly enough in the darkness to observe how they focus, whether they have that strange, distant quality. Either way, it's far more likely he's lying, and thinks the object that fell might be valuable.

Or he has a more sinister purpose, and knows exactly what it is I seek. If there exists a copy of the ancient version of the Song of the Destroyer, then he could be here to prevent me retrieving the Star.

Not all who dwell in the forest-sea await the Lightbringer's coming with longing and faith.

We've been staring at each other across the length of my spearstaff for some time when the boy says cautiously, "Thanks for scaring away those—things. How did you do that?"

"I used a beacon spell," I reply absently as I scan him by the light of the stars. The Lovers have not yet risen, but despite the moonless night I can make out a few details. He doesn't move, watching me with glittering dark eyes. The blood painting the side of his face gives his profile a rather warlike appearance, accenting the sharpness of his cheekbones and his aquiline nose. His lips are pressed together tightly in pain, no doubt from the wound beneath the bloody bit of rag tied about his arm.

"You still bleed," I say finally. "The boar of the forest-sea are drawn to the smell of blood, and mist-bent boar even more so. That bandage will do little to hide the scent."

I can't help but continue to stare, as if I might intuit his duplicity or his purpose by looking at him. He meets my gaze, and while he looks nervous, he does not appear malevolent. His shock is wearing off, and now I can see that look in his eyes all the more clearly. He seems—*glad* to see me. An enemy agent wouldn't, if confronted by the divinity herself at the site of the prophesied Last Star.

Perhaps he doesn't know who I am.

Slowly, his eyes not leaving my face except to flick occasionally to the tip of my spearstaff, he shifts his weight. "I don't have any intention of hurting you—can you maybe put that weapon thing away? Or at least stop pointing it at me?"

My own eyes flick to the tip of my spearstaff, which clinks

with the dangling udjet charms of a magic user. I can feel my brow furrowing, mystery adding to mystery—who can this boy be, who doesn't recognize the staff of a magician?

"Are you armed?" I ask finally, scanning his body. His strange clothes are of one piece, formfitting. Not much room to hide anything, much less a weapon larger than a small knife.

He blinks at me. "Why would I be armed?"

I blink back at him. *Why* wouldn't *you be armed?* But I don't say it aloud. I have to find whatever object or artifact fell with this thing—a glider, he called it—but I can't conduct a search of him or the structure while holding the spear between us.

"Wait there, and do not move." My order seems to strike him oddly, but he does as I ask. I climb carefully up onto the crumpled structure again, testing the creak and bend of the thing. The boy makes a few noises of protest, but eventually I'm close enough that I can lean down and examine the interior of the "glider."

There is only a small space inside it, and nothing I could retrieve and carry back to the temple. Along the front is an array of scorched levers and soot-covered glass panels, labeled with the alphabet used in our most ancient texts, unreadable by anyone but a scholar. The words they spell are nonsense to me—*ALT.* and *COMP.* and *RADIO*—but the sight makes uneasiness prickle at me.

Suddenly, I understand why: the space inside the fallen object is the exact size and shape to hold a person. I'm looking at a *seat.*

The boy is waiting where I last saw him, his eyes following my progress. He meets my gaze when I straighten and look back at him. Perhaps even in the dark, he sees some question in my half-hidden face, because he shifts his weight and speaks.

"How . . . how are you here? Did you fall from Alciel too? Or from one of the lost sky-cities, maybe? Are there others down here with you? Do you have a camp somewhere, or some sort of shelter, or . . ." He trails off, watching me, eyes widening in wonder. "Were you *born* here?"

By *here*, he doesn't mean the Mirror of Divinity. My heart is pounding with the weight of the thing I can't quite wrap my mind around. Instead, I focus on something smaller, but no less incredible: he doesn't know who I am.

I'm not wearing ceremonial red or the golden circlet that identifies me to my people when I'm home—a tactical decision, to avoid drawing attention as we travel—but my face is known throughout the lands in paintings and statues. *He* looks at me without recognition.

If he is an enemy, revealing myself as Nimhara, Forty-Second Vessel of the Divine, would be folly. I could end him here with a flick of my spear, but I won't hurt an innocent, and there's still a chance the boy's simply mist-touched and experiencing a moment of semi-lucid awareness.

And there's also a chance . . .

An enraged squeal splits the air, reverberant across the Mirror's water. The boy jumps, whirling around to search the darkness for its source.

"The boar," I tell him. "They smell you."

He turns wild eyes back on me, his wonder vanishing in his sudden fear. "How far to your . . . wherever you came from?"

"Too far for you to walk, bleeding—they will only follow you." I hesitate one moment longer, searching for any sign that this boy is a threat.

But he simply looks weary and frightened. His face is a few shades lighter than mine, but even by starlight I can see his skin is ashen—with fear or loss of blood, I don't know.

"Come," I tell him, trying to maintain my caution despite my irrational urge to trust him. "I will tend your arm."

I put a hand to my chatelaine, dipping into one of the pouches for a pinch of fireseed. The boy watches, brow furrowed, as I cup it in my palms and whisper the invocation of light—but when I toss the handful into the air, and it casts its gentle green glow in a pool around us, he scrambles back with an oath.

I eye him quizzically. Light magic is the easiest to master, and fireseed is abundant throughout the forest-sea—and yet the boy acts as if this magic is new to him.

"I mean you no harm," I say gently. "Light magic cannot hurt you, and I need to see where you are wounded. Show me?"

The boy's eyes are still a bit wild, but he does as I ask. He grasps at something by his collar and draws downward, and his body-hugging suit splits with a metallic grating noise. Now I can see it more clearly, the bandage isn't worthy of the name. It's a dirty bit of rag tied around the wound, which is sluggishly oozing blood that pools in a congealed mess at the crook of his elbow. He tugs the rag away and eases his arms free of his suit, then ties both sleeves around his waist, baring the thin shirt he wears underneath, short-sleeved and plain.

His features are more visible now in the light of the spellfire. The eyes I'd thought were black are actually a dark brown, a pleasing contrast against the lighter shade of his skin. Though his short sleeves reveal no brawny riverstrider, there is definition to the muscle of his arms that gleams bronze in the spellfire. His black hair is of a style I've never seen: shaven close on the sides up past his ears, then left to form a mop of curls on the top. Strange, but undeniably compelling.

There is a little twinge I sometimes feel when I meet someone so obviously attractive. A fluttering glimmer of something, deep, instinctual—and then the swift banishment of that same feeling. Only the tiniest pang of loss lingers to remind me of what I can never have.

I bid him hold his arm up to the light. The gash is ragged but shallow. It will likely scar, even were I more skilled at healing magic, but I can at least stop him losing more blood. I retrieve a waxed packet of Mhyr's Sunrise from my belt and ask him to hold the rent flesh open a little. He looks more dubious by the moment, and when he hesitates, I tell him, "It will seal the wound. It will hurt, but it is better to keep ill humors from festering."

"You mean it's a disinfectant? Some kind of antibiotic medicine?" He prods at the wound with his fingertips until its ragged edges come apart, and he hisses in pain.

I move closer and eye him askance. "You use strange words." I sprinkle the Sunrise powder along the interior of the wound, careful not to spill any on the rest of his skin.

He flinches. "That's not so bad," he murmurs before looking

back up at me. "You use some pretty strange words yourself. Is this more . . . magic?" He speaks the word as though he finds it humorous.

I raise my eyebrows at him. "Yes. And that is not the part that will hurt." I replace the packet and pull out the little vial of thicksweet. Before the boy can ask me what I mean, I pry out its stopper and lean over his arm to pour a thin drizzle of the clear syrup along the wound.

"Ow, that's—hrm. That's warm. Hang on, it's feeling a bit . . ." His eyes widen. "It's getting *really* warm."

"Hush." I scoop up a handful of water and close my eyes, waiting until the tangle of energies in my mind calms a little and I can cast the water over the wound.

It bursts into golden healing fire.

The boy shouts in alarm and pain and reels backward, flapping his arm uselessly for a few seconds before dropping to his knees and thrusting it into the salty lake water at our feet.

I would grab him to hold him still if I could, but I have to resort to crying, "Calm yourself—it is only a bit of healing fire!"

The salt water does little to arrest the spell, for it is not a natural flame but a magical one. The fire is quick, however, and by the time he sits up again, it's done its work. White-faced, the boy looks down at his arm in disbelief, and then back at me.

"S-some sort of chemical reaction," he mumbles, testing the wound's edge with his fingertips. The magic has sealed it well. The spellfire in the air has begun to fade, and the water disturbed by the boy's flailing has dissipated much of what lay on its surface. "You could have warned me you were going to cauterize the thing."

His reaction could not have been feigned. The alarm coursing through me at his unknown motives has faded, and in its place is curiosity, insistent and sharp. "Who are you that you have never seen a healing spell?"

The boy looks up at me, and then away. "I . . . I told you. I crashed here." And then, for just a moment, his eyes lift toward the dark, shadowy hole in the sky that is the cloudlands by night.

The strangeness of his speech, his clothes and hair, his reaction to magic, the fact that he doesn't know who I am—and most of all, the fact that the structure I saw fall from the heavens contained a place for a human form . . .

"You are saying . . . that you fell *from the cloudlands*?" I whisper, wondering, still skeptical—but when he looks at me, I see the truth in his face.

"I need to get back there," he blurts, urgency quickening his odd voice. "Can you help me?"

But my ears are roaring with the impossibility of it, my pulse rapid. Light-headed, I can only whisper, "You come from the other side of the sky?"

The boy straightens, eyes me a moment, and then nods. "I need your help to get home. My glider is wrecked, I'm thirsty and hungry . . . Will you help me?"

The cloudlands are where the gods fled a millennium ago—the only things that have ever come to us from the sky are a few artifacts here and there, relics and spells of great power. Even I have not seen them all, for many have been locked for generations within vaults of stone.

Certainly never a human boy.

I believed I was meant to come here to find the Star, some object fallen from the heavens that would help me prepare for the coming of the Lightbringer—the one to end all prophecy, the one to wipe the world clean so that it can begin afresh. I expected a spellstone or a scroll, an enchanted sword, a spellfire lantern in whose light the Song of the Destroyer would summon the bright god to us at last.

A brand against the darkness . . .

My mind conjures the memory of seeing him trying to beat back the mist-bent creatures with a burning bit of wreckage, the flames bright against the night.

Like a brand.

Maybe . . . *maybe* . . . could the Star be a human boy? Some descendant of the gods themselves, unaware now of his divinity?

How he came to fall from the sky, I don't know. How he could be the one to help me find my destiny, I can't imagine.

Of one thing, however, I am suddenly, utterly, viscerally certain: this boy is what I was meant to find here.

"I know of no magic that can raise a man into the sky," I say weakly, scanning the boy's face, trying to find some sign—any sign—that I am looking at something connected to divine destiny. "Come with me to the temple. Our archives hold many secrets and many ancient scrolls. Perhaps they hold the knowledge you seek. Legend even says that the temple was once the home of the Sentinels, who guarded the passage to the sky."

"Thank you." His face is solemn, but there's relief in his eyes, and now he even smiles at me a little. The expression suits his features. "I'm glad you found me."

He is unscarred, no sign of callouses on his hands or of wear from the elements on his face. His skin beneath his strange outer garment is clean. He is as fresh and new as if he were just formed.

My eyes fall upon the suit he wears, its sleeves tied around his waist. On the arm of one of them, I can just make out the shape of letters, distorted by the folding of the fabric—but unmistakable.

The writing of the ancients. Just like the lettering inside the fallen glider.

"Do you have names, in the sky?" I ask, not sure what I'm expecting him to tell me.

The boy smiles a little more widely. "My name's North. What's yours?"

I stare at him, bereft of words. He looks about as divinely significant as the bindle cat. But then, not even a god is born knowing their place in fate's design. I had to learn about my purpose when I was called to divinity, as any child learns about the world.

If this boy *is* the Last Star, brand against the darkness, whose light will lead me to the Destroyer and to the end of days . . .

He doesn't *know it.*

I suddenly need to breathe free, and I reach up to tug my kerchief down from my lips so that I can gulp a breath of fresh air.

"You may call me Nimh."

SIX

NORTH

Nimh leads the way across an open plain, the stars above reflected in the water around us—a thin sheet covering the ground, less than ankle-deep. It's like walking through the sky, except that it's already soaking through my boots.

It hurts to leave the *Skysinger* behind, but I can't stay with her. She can't get me home, destroyed as she is. My only hope right now is that Nimh was telling the truth, that there might be someone in this temple of hers who can help me.

Every time I look at Nimh's agile silhouette ahead of me, try to wrap my mind around the fact that she's human and she's right here, my mind staggers back. Nobody's meant to live Below, but here she is. And she talks sense, sort of. She knows medicine, or at least chemistry—and she says there are other *people*.

We're told the surface is uninhabited. We learn this from the time we first speak. I have no idea what to make of this girl, of her showing up at my crash site, except that I'm not dead yet, and I would be if she wanted me to be. For the first time since my glider stopped responding and I dipped below the city, I have hope.

And if I'm honest, there is a tingle of excitement somewhere deep in my chest. I dreamed of the surface. I dreamed of exploration.

I never dreamed of anything like this.

She's setting a decent pace, and my aches start to assert themselves, my breath forced shallow by a pain in my ribs.

"Nimh," I say, and she turns her head without breaking stride. "Could we slow down a little? I'm sorry, I'm hurt."

She shakes her head. "My . . . friend said she would come for me after half an hour," she replies. There's just enough of a pause before *friend* that I wonder what she was going to say. Is the girl she's talking about her pair? Her superior?

"Then she'll find us," I say. "And I assume she's going to notice me sooner or later. Will it be a problem?"

"Your presence will be a challenge," she says. "But I cannot have them raising the alarm when they realize I have slipped away. That will be worse."

"All right," I say, reaching for a lighter tone. "Better get introduced before I get you into trouble, then. Everything else I've met here except you has seemed to take a deep dislike to me."

I need her help. I need to be charming. I need to avoid any hint of a threat.

Her lips move, forming for the first time the faintest of smiles. She wears it well, that smile. She can't be much older than I am, a fact I missed thanks to her spear and her magic and her fighting off a horde of terrifying creatures. The smile is only there for an instant before she's walking on again. But she's moving a little bit more slowly now for my benefit, and with a private grin to myself, I follow.

The dark shadow ahead turns out to be a tangled mass of trees—any single one of them would rival the largest trees in the palace gardens for size, and these are nothing like the straight, clean lines of our orchards and ornamental gardens at home. These are tangled and wild, linked together as if they're wrestling, their limbs forming knots above us, their roots turning the ground rough and uneven beneath our feet. As we enter the forest, the starlight is blocked out, and sticks and twigs jab me as I move past them.

Pinpricks of faint yellow glow here and there for a handful of seconds, appearing and then fading again at random. I try to track them with my gaze, but they vanish before I can get a closer look. Is this more "magic"?

I'm diverted from trying to figure out what chemical could cause the glow when swarms of insects rise around us. I clamp my mouth shut and shield my nose with one hand as Nimh draws a cloth over her face. I cautiously draw breath to ask how far we are from her camp, and a horde of insects invade my mouth, leaving me coughing and spitting in their wake. The warm, damp air is close around us, clinging to my skin.

Nimh clears her throat, and from behind her scarf, she makes an odd rippling, trilling sound with her lips that seems to blend with the night noises of the forest all around us. She pauses, brow furrowed, and I take the opportunity to lean against the nearest tree and rest.

She makes the sound a little louder this time, hands on her hips. "If you do not come now," she says quietly to the forest, in the same tone my mothers used to use to get me into bed, "I shall leave without you." And then, to me, without turning her head: "North, the ants that nest in the hirta trees will bite you."

I scramble away from my tree and she sets off again, never seeming to need to check where to put her feet among the maze of roots. She moves as if this place is her home, or like she can see in the dark. It's like she's a part of it, and a million questions bubble up inside me.

I trip and nearly fall flat on my face before reminding myself to watch my own feet, and not hers.

"Who were you talking to just now?" I ask, taking a couple of quick steps to catch up with her, ducking past a vine that wants to catch me around my neck.

"The cat," she says simply.

"What's a cat?"

"What's a—" Finally I find something that can make her break stride, and she nearly trips herself, stumbling two quick steps in a row. I reach out to catch her elbow, and she yanks away before I can touch her, spinning around to glare at me as if I'd tried to murder her. She's quick to calm her expression—or at least to remove some of the fire from the eyes visible over the edge of her scarf.

"Sorry," I offer, though I'm not entirely sure what I'm apologizing for. I guess she doesn't like being touched.

She brushes aside my apology without addressing her odd reaction and turns to resume her course. "A cat is . . . there, that is a cat."

As if on cue, a dark silhouette about the size of my torso drops from the nearby trees to land square in her path. All I can make out are a pair of glittering eyes, and a suggestion of a wide, fluffy tail that rises briefly in warning, or greeting. I'm assuming that if she wants this thing to come with us, it doesn't want to kill me.

"Oh, hello," I say, trying to mask the fact that I can't tell if this *cat* is intelligent. Is it a friend? A servant? "Are you going to introduce us?"

"How would I do that?" she asks, sounding amused.

"Well, what's its name?" I try.

"Name?" She allows herself a soft huff of breath that might be a laugh. "You do not name a cat. He is a cat; he keeps his name to himself. Have you no cats in the sky?"

"None," I say. "And we don't have any of those boar either. Is he safer than them?"

"That is a complicated question," she replies. "To me, yes. To others . . . it depends. To the temple mice, he is their own personal Lightbringer."

She says the word like it's a name, and she looks sideways at me. In that moment, I'm sure she's trying to gauge my response—perhaps it's a sacred word, and if I were from here, I couldn't help but react.

But I'm not, and I'm left creasing my brow, confused, partly because I don't know what mice are either. "Their own personal what?"

"Lightbringer," she says, more slowly. "The god who will end this cycle and begin the next. The one who will remake the world."

"Of course," I say, slapping at an insect trying to bite my neck. I haven't got a clue what she means. I've heard of the worship of gods—it was a part of my education. Something my people did, long before the time of the Ascension. We had a whole club of gods then, according to the stories. Once, I asked my heartmother why we didn't have them anymore. She said that we probably stopped believing in them once we came into the sky ourselves and discovered nobody else was there.

The girl's eyeing me strangely, and I wonder just how out of place I sound right now. Who, or what, she thinks I am.

"Do you worship the Lightbringer at the temple we're going to?" I try.

"Among others," she says. "The temple is about a day's journey from here. By tomorrow night, you will see for yourself."

I'm not sure I like that answer. It's too smooth—and reveals too little. Whoever this girl is, at least one thing about her is familiar—she'd fit right in on the council at home. She considers every word before she speaks it. She isn't telling me everything. But I don't call her on it—not yet. No matter why she's taking me with her, it's better than standing in the middle of the lake with a broken glider and hungry monsters all around me. "What will happen when we get there?" I ask.

Nimh steps over a rotting log, the cat creature leaping over it in one fluid move. "There," she says, "we will search for someone who knows how to put a man back up in the sky."

It sounds fantastical when she says it, but I can't help craning my neck back to catch a glimpse of my home. The stars are blocked from my sight by the canopy of leaves overhead.

"You mentioned Sentinels," I say. "You said they might have an idea of how to get me back up in the sky. Who are *they*?"

"A story for children," she replies. "But stories often have a seed of truth, however long lost—it is said that they were a secret society of magicians who once guarded the way between worlds. The archives are vast—if any texts about the Sentinels still exist, you will find them there."

The archives are *vast*. My brain's still just about short-circuiting at the possibility of some kind of tribe down here, clinging to life after all these centuries, and they've got *vast archives*?

"The temple, is it in a camp or a village, or something larger?" I ask.

"It sits above the city," she replies. "There is not much land here that stays dry—we are just leaving the rainy months now. The temple is on a rise overlooking the forest-sea, and many of the houses in town leave during the wet season."

A city? But that would mean *thousands* of people. My brain starts spitting sparks and threatens to catch fire. But something she's said doesn't compute. "The houses *leave*?"

"Of course." She glances sideways at me. "The temple remains, but most other places float. To find food, to trade . . .

It is a rare and treasured responsibility, to spend all your life in one place."

Understanding clicks into place. If most of the surface is flooded, then cities would need to sit on top of the water. "Our cities move too—we just move the whole of them, rather than individual parts."

"Do they glide, like your craft?"

"No, they use engines, it's a different kind of propulsion."

"Engines," she says slowly, as if tasting the word. "Propulsion." Her face is keen, curious, intelligent—but my heart sinks. She clearly doesn't know what I'm talking about. How am I going to find a way to repair the *Skysinger* if these people don't know even the basics of aeronautics?

"What is *engines*?" she asks, not seeming to notice my dismay.

"They're, uh . . . I'm not sure how to explain it," I admit. My tired mind isn't sure where to start. "They're a thing you can build that creates energy, the way wind pushing on a sail does. Only you can summon the energy whenever you want, instead of waiting for the wind to blow."

"Oh, a kind of magic," she says, as if she's saying, *Oh, gravity, got it*. "I would like to learn it—is it a magic you know, or have you only seen it done?"

"It's not magic," I say. "It's science. Science means you can explain it, that you know how each part of it works. Magic is—I mean, it's science you haven't figured out how to explain yet."

"I can explain my magic," Nimh replies. "And you just said

you could not explain your engines."

Well. Maybe I should shut up, then.

"North," she says gently, "I will do all I can to help you. I could not be sure, at first, whether you were a friend or an enemy, and I am sorry if I frightened you—but I do not believe you are an enemy. So if you will call me friend, I will keep you safe."

Her dark eyes are on mine as she speaks, with a directness and sincerity that would feel almost intimate among my own people. It must be normal among hers, but it makes me want to shift my weight, clear my throat, look away.

I have to clear my throat to find my voice.

"Thank you, Nimh." I'm beginning to think I must have gotten very, *very* lucky that she was the one to find me.

She smiles and tips her head. "We are close now, cloud-lander. Come."

We reach the edge of the trees—and, I realize a moment later, the edge of more water. This isn't the shallow, reflective stuff we saw earlier. This is more water than I've ever seen outside the city reservoirs, a thick river of it slowly drifting past the shore on which we stand.

Nimh leads me down the muddy bank to where a raft's moored, and as we climb onto it, it wobbles gently beneath our weight. This probably isn't the moment to tell her I don't know how to swim, so I keep my mouth shut as she guides us across with a paddle. I breathe more easily when we reach the other side and climb onto dry—or rather, damp—land again.

A few steps from the edge of the water, though, she slows,

and with a soft chirp, the cat creature halts by her feet. She leans on her spear, tilting her head, and I try to listen too.

"Nimh?" I venture, instinctively keeping my voice soft.

"You said you came here alone," she says, and it's not a question. It's one final opportunity for me to revise my story, suspicion back in her tone.

"Yes," I say. "I give you my word."

Her measuring glance reminds me she doesn't know the worth of a prince's word—or even that I *am* a prince. I'm not dumb enough to point out the value of my word, or of *me*, until I know what she'll do with that information, so I stay quiet.

Eventually, she explains. "My people should be on guard. And they ought to be looking for me—we should have been challenged by now."

There's something about the way she says it: *my* people. It reminds me of the way my bloodmother speaks. Like a leader.

While I'm considering that, she leans down to run her fingers along the cat's spine. As if the gesture was a signal, the thing prowls alongside her as she moves on once again.

"Stay close," she says, and through the trees ahead, I see a glimmer of light. We're reaching an open space, and the way she moves now—silent, careful, that spear thing at the ready— tells me she thinks there might be danger ahead.

"Nimh," I whisper, keeping my voice low, almost inaudible. "Do I need something to use as a weapon?" There are plenty of sharp, broken sticks around. I don't know what I'm going to do with a stick if things go bad up ahead, but I'd rather have something than nothing.

Without looking back she reaches down to one of the belts that circle her waist, draws a knife from a sheath, and offers it to me hilt-first, her fingers holding the very tip of the blade. I guess she really has decided to trust me, even if she clearly doesn't want to touch me.

Maybe she thinks I have some kind of sky-sickness.

She doesn't need to tell me to be quiet now. The sounds of the forest, a cacophony before, seem to have vanished here. I try to place my feet where she puts hers, easing them down gently as the two of us creep toward the light of several campfires ahead of us. But there are no shadows of people around them, no signs of life.

The fire lights Nimh's face as we crouch at the edge of the campsite, turning her skin golden and animating her features with every flicker and shift of the flames. I follow her gaze as she scans the camp, and now I can see little canvas tents clustered around the fires, along with cooking pots, bags, and a couple of crates. It might be basic, but it's a setup for several people—and none of them seem to be present.

I'd think they were all out searching for Nimh, but she's not acting like someone who thinks her friends are just a shout away. Tension sings through her. She picks up a stone, hefts it to make sure I know what she's about to do, then lobs it out into the middle of the campsite.

It clangs off a metal cooking pot, and nobody emerges from the shadows to see what made the noise. Slowly, gesturing for me to remain where I am, Nimh rises to her feet.

Though I'm itching to follow her, I crouch obediently in place as she creeps into the abandoned camp to investigate. One by one, she lifts the flaps of the tents. At first she's careful, spear raised in her free hand, but by the end of her search she's hurrying—she's tugged down her veil from her face, breath coming quickly, open confusion in her gaze.

Eventually, she turns toward me, and I rise from where I'm hiding and walk out to join her.

"I do not understand," she whispers. "A guard should have remained at camp, even if the others went looking for me. I cannot believe that—"

Something dark falls onto her cheek, and her hand flies up to it. When her fingers come away from her skin, their tips are a vivid red. As our eyes meet, another droplet falls between us, spattering softly against the dirt.

As one, very slowly, we tilt our heads back, lifting our gazes.

I don't know if the gasp I hear is hers or mine.

A series of bundles hang from the trees above us, slowly twisting on their ropes. I stare, not understanding, as another thick, dark droplet smacks the ground between us.

And then, as if they're coming into focus, the shapes above us suddenly resolve. And I'm looking at a nightmare.

Each bundle is a mutilated body. The firelight casts monstrous shadows on their faces and flickers in their dull, staring eyes.

A sound of horror tears itself from my throat and I scramble back, away from the things overhead—but Nimh is still standing there, staring, like a sculpture in stone. All around her, the sound of dripping blood hisses into the campfires.

Her camp, her people, have been slaughtered.

A flicker of movement behind her draws my eye, a shadow in the dark. Then movement erupts all around the edge of the clearing, and before I can react, at least half a dozen black-clad figures emerge from the trees. They walk slowly, deliberately, and silently—and they're all armed, the edges of their knives and spears glinting in the firelight.

Beside me Nimh draws a shaky breath, adjusting her grip on her own spear. "You cannot win," she calls in ringing tones. "You can still turn back." There's a tremor underneath her voice, a rawness, and the words sit there in the silence, then vanish into nothing.

The cat yowls and spits his defiance, and like the sound is a signal, the shadowy figures attack.

A man with a shaved head covered in dark stubble lunges for me, sweeping his long knife around in a quick arc, forcing me to stumble back toward the fire. He doesn't make a sound, coming after me in two quick steps, and I throw myself sideways as I dodge again.

All I can hear is my own rasping breath as I spread my arms for balance, and that's when I remember I'm holding a knife too.

His lips draw back in a snarl, teeth gleaming white in the firelight, and I take a step back.

He springs forward, grabbing a handful of my flight suit, yanking me in close. His hand clamps down on my wrist, squeezing until pain shoots up my arm. My fingers are weakening—I'm hyperaware of the hilt in my hand—*No. I can't.*

Then there's a screech by his feet, and he shouts, dropping me as the cat latches onto his leg, hissing and spitting.

I have to.

I slash at the man with my knife, and there's a quick resistance and then a sickening give as the blade sinks into his gut. He stumbles backward, and I keep hold of my knife, yanking it free. It flashes red with his blood in the firelight as he falls.

I feel like someone's squeezing my lungs, and I'm afraid that I'm going to pass out, because I just *stabbed a guy*, but an instant later I remember there are more of them, and Nimh's somewhere behind me, and she needs—

I spin around, and find Nimh standing perfectly still, holding her spear aloft. Six bodies lie still on the ground around her, unmoving.

I'm caught in place, staring at her, somewhere between awe and fear. Then she turns her head to meet my eyes, and I swallow, my mouth dry.

"Nimh, I . . ."

A flash of movement behind her draws my gaze as a lone figure charges out from the trees, hand raised, blade aimed straight at Nimh's back. I shout a wordless warning and hurl my knife at her attacker. It sails through the air to bounce harmlessly off a tree, but the warning is all Nimh needs.

She whirls around, and in a continuation of that same movement, brings her spear up and catches the figure under the chin with the blunt end of it. The hooded head snaps back and the assailant falls to the ground, where the firelight reveals the features of a girl about our age.

That's when I think to turn my head and look back at my guy, but he's not where I left him. He's disappeared back into the forest, so I guess . . . I didn't kill him? I'm caught between relief that I'm not a murderer, and fear that he's still out there.

Everything in me is screaming to run, but I can't move, and the harder I try, the more I feel like I might throw up. I've never seen a dead body. I've never hurt someone—not like this.

Swallowing my bile and my horror, I force myself to slide one foot forward and then the other, and with that shuffling step, my body begins to unlock. I'm shaking as I approach Nimh.

She still hasn't moved. Her eyes are starting to glaze over, and I'm not even sure she knows I'm here. She must be in shock.

I want to pull her away from the grisly sight around us—the bodies in the trees might be her friends, even people she loves. She doesn't seem to hear me, even when I call her name in a rasping half whisper, as loud as I dare with at least one of our attackers still out there. So I reach out, ready to take her by the shoulders and give her a shake.

But then the cat's there, abruptly tangling through my legs and, without warning, sinking his teeth into Nimh's ankle.

With a jolt, she seems to come back to herself. She blinks, looks at me, and then, so violently that for a moment I can't tell what's happening, she jerks away from my outstretched hands. She moves so quickly that she falls, this graceful creature who navigated a pitch-black rainforest with nary a misstep, landing beside the prone bodies of our attackers.

Bewildered, I take a step toward her—and she scrambles back.

"You cannot touch me!" she gasps, looking at me as though I'm the thing—not the bodies hanging from the forest canopy, not the people all around her who just tried to kill us—that terrified her beyond reason.

"I was only trying to . . ." *Comfort you*, I think. *Wake you up. Get you to tell me what we do now.*

Swallowing, I let the words spill out in a confused tangle. "You weren't moving, weren't answering, I thought maybe you were in some kind of shock . . ."

But she's scrambling to her feet now, careful to keep a distance between us. "We must go, quickly. There may be more of them."

"There's at least one. I stabbed him, but he got away." I pause, then ask the question that I don't want to hear the answer to. "Are these others . . . Are they dead?"

"No," she says quietly. "But they will sleep for a day or two. If nothing comes for them in that time, they will survive. But the one who ran from you will be bringing others even now, I am sure of it."

I thought I couldn't get any more frightened—I was wrong. I glance over my shoulder, my gaze swinging wildly across the blackness of the trees beyond the ring of firelight. "Why would they come back after—after this?"

"Because they have not finished what they came here to do." Nimh's shoving things into a couple of packs, her hands shaking. She pauses then, staring down at the supplies, going so still that for a moment I think she's returned to that same shock I tried to wake her from.

Then she stands, hefting a pack in each hand, and tosses one of them toward me. Her eyes are wide, wet with unshed tears. She's quiet for a long moment, tension in her features hinting at some internal debate.

"You may be safer if you do not come with me, cloud-lander," Nimh whispers finally. "I could tell you which way to travel, how to find the temple, what to say to the guards to allow you to use the archives and find your way home."

I look down at the pack she tossed at my feet and then back up at her, as confused as I was the first time she spoke to me, over the wreckage of the *Skysinger*. "What? I don't—"

I take a deep breath and meet her eyes the way she met mine before, hoping that feeling of connection will get her to talk to me. Even now, in the midst of all this horror, there's something about her that makes it hard to look away. She's magnetic, drawing my gaze wherever I am.

Keeping my eyes on hers, I try again. "Why would I be safer without you? How can you be sure they'll come back?"

Nimh swallows, looking very young, and very sad. "Because they were looking for me."

The words hang between us, drifting like the campfire smoke. I should ask who's after her—and why they want her. I should ask her why she's so sure they'll kill anyone who's with her. I should demand she explain everything she's holding back, every truth she isn't telling me. But of all the objections and protestations flashing through my mind, all I'm left with as she meets my eyes is one thought: *She's all alone.*

I lean down to pick up the pack and swing it over my shoulders. "I'm coming with you. Let's go."

SEVEN

NIMH

My thoughts are a storm of guilt and anger and fear, pulsing and shifting with every step I take. Jolts of pain strike me like lightning through the haze of urgency and danger. My cheek, where the blood fell on it, still burns like fire. Sometimes the whole world falls away, my whole self too, and I am just a tiny ember of hurt beneath a deluge that threatens to drown me.

I need to meditate, to find some tiny grain of stillness in my mind, or I will be next to useless if we're discovered. I cannot work magic without the concentration of my will, and right now, I have nothing in my mind but chaos, as violent and uncaring as a mist-storm.

And then I hear North crashing through the undergrowth behind me, swearing strange oaths under his breath and slapping at insects, and I am all at once myself again, my feet on the ground, my eyes clear.

To let him go, to tell him he *should* go, was almost beyond my strength—to return without him, whether he is the Last Star or not, would be to give up on everything I've hoped for, to let everyone hanging in the trees have died for nothing. But if he is as important as I believe him to be, then North's life means more than my own now.

And I am the only one who knows it. Without me, he would be safer.

Despite all that logic, all those reasons to convince him to make his own way, the one truth that pounded through my thoughts in that long, long moment as he stared at me was this: *I don't want him to go.*

We move in silence for a time, until we've traveled far enough that low voices are unlikely to betray us.

"We will be out of the forest-sea soon," I murmur to North, whose footsteps behind me are beginning to falter. He's exhausted, and my throat tightens with sympathy, for surely there are no forest-seas in the clouds, and he could not have known to prepare for this. "We will go through the ghostlands, where you will find walking easier. It is a less direct route, but there are no trees, and those who are hunting me are most at home here in the shadows. We will be safer there."

North draws a breath and then chokes, no doubt on the insects he just inhaled. "You—you know who those people were, who attacked us back there? Who killed those . . ."

I try not to think of that sight, the first shocking image of the tangle of bodies overhead, so thoroughly mutilated that I could not recognize their faces—but it does no good. I think I will see them there behind my closed eyes forever. "Members of the Cult of the Deathless. I have heard of this practice. They punish followers of the one they call the *false divinity*, suspending them in symbolic exile among the gods who abandoned us."

North doesn't answer. Either he doesn't understand what I'm saying, or he's simply breathing so hard that he can't speak. I concentrate on moving as quickly and as quietly as I can, hating that I must set such a ruthless pace for him, though he keeps up with admirable determination.

"We will be safe soon," I murmur, and I do not know whether he hears me or not. I do not know whether I was even speaking to him at all.

The stars still gleam dimly in the predawn sky when we emerge from the forest-sea. Miella and Danna hang low on the horizon, twin moons locked in their perpetual dance. The trees stop abruptly here, their growth hindered by the magic of the ancients that still lingers, though all that remains of their vast city are piles of stone and twisted metal, lying still beneath their shrouds of earth and grass.

North is some distance behind me, still struggling through the undergrowth and still choking on oaths and the insects that swarm his face. If we'd had time, I would have shown him how to wind a strip of cloth across the nose and mouth. I'd have shown him the way to find a path through the tangle of vines and roots instead of fighting them. I'd have stopped to let him rest.

When he stumbles out of the deeper shadow of the trees, my heart sinks with sympathy. His face is scratched and filthy, his thin shirt is drenched with sweat and clinging to his body, and his eyes are glazed with the effort of continuing on. Even exhausted and bedraggled, he has a presence I cannot deny. He may not know his importance, but that he *is* important, I do not doubt.

"A few more steps," I say softly. "Let us put some small distance between us and the trees, and then we will rest."

North just gives a little groan in response, but his steps—which had begun to slow after seeing me—pick up again.

We keep moving until the dim glow to the east of the plain lightens enough to throw faint shadows beneath our feet. I lead us to one of the grassy hummocks that once would have been a building tall enough to touch the clouds, and even before I can tell him it's time to stop, North drops down onto a lichen-covered stone like a bird with broken wings.

I find to my surprise that when I move to sit, my legs collapse beneath me rather more quickly than I'd expected, and I hit the stone with a faint thud. All I want to do is fold over like North, but I know we cannot stay here for long, and if we hope to keep moving, we must drink and eat.

And talk.

North did not ask, back beneath the grisly canopy of corpses, why I was the one the cultists had been looking for. But I know the question cannot be far from his mind.

My own thoughts tangle as I try to order them. I cannot believe that this ignorant boy is the answer to my people's suffering—and yet I do believe it; I *must* believe it.

If he isn't—if the falling wreckage was not the star I read about in my vision of the lost stanza of the Song, if I *wasn't* meant to make this journey and risk everything to find him . . .

Then half a dozen people are dead because of my mistakes, and my arrogance, and my desperation to prove I am worthy of my own divinity. If I'm wrong, then the closest thing I ever had to a friend is dead because of me.

Elkisa.

My eyes burn as her face flashes before me. I banish the thought before I start weeping in front of the cloudlander.

The bindle cat rubs his cheek against my knee, rumbling an aggressively reassuring purr, and then turns to settle, sentinel-like, facing the tree line of the forest-sea. I turn my own eyes toward it as well, while I force my hands to rummage in my pack for the waterskin.

I drink only until the barest edge of my thirst is quenched— if we meet with no delays, the water I brought will last us. But I cannot waste what we have. I force myself up again and approach the cloudlander, swaying on my feet. He lifts his head in time to see me put the waterskin down, just at the edge of arm's reach, and retreat.

"You must drink," I say, my voice thin and bare. "You will feel better when you do."

North blinks his eyes sluggishly, but after a moment, he does as I suggest. He takes only a few sips at first, but as if the taste on his lips reminds him of his thirst, he's soon taking great swallows, until his eagerness makes him choke and lower the skin, coughing.

I busy myself sorting through our rations. The bindle cat peers into the pack, and then, with a carefully measured little hop, he jumps into it so that he can crouch there among my supplies. I smile a little, for the bindle cat is never subtle—his purr erupts even before my fingers reach the shorter, softer fur just behind his ear.

Finally, North drags himself to his feet and comes toward me. A flash of remembered panic makes me jolt away, recalling the sight of him so close back at the campsite, ready to take me by the shoulders.

North freezes, then carefully stoops so he can lay the water-skin on the ground between us, and retreats again.

When I look up, his dark eyes are waiting for mine, unreadable in the predawn darkness.

"I wasn't going to touch you," he says finally, his voice gentle despite its hoarseness.

"I know," I murmur. "Thank you."

He runs a hand through his hair, the black curls tight with perspiration, and then scrubs at his scalp in a bracing way. "I wasn't going to hurt you, back there," he adds, his voice questing for answers. "You looked so frightened, and so faraway. I only wanted to . . ."

I know what he had been about to say, the words as clear as if he'd spoken them aloud.

I only wanted to comfort you.

For the tiniest moment, I can't help but wonder. . . . From the day I was called to my divinity, I've never known someone who didn't know exactly who and what I was. Never known anyone who's ever tried to touch me, except the occasional madman, stopped by my guards long before they ever came close.

This boy doesn't know any of that. And my people would never know if . . .

I jerk my eyes down and focus on pulling food out of the pack. "To touch me *is* to hurt me. The greatest hurt you could possibly do me."

I can't see his face, but his voice is dubious as he replies. "This has something to do with your whole magic thing, doesn't it?"

"Something," I agree, moving to set out a collection of foods on a cloth in the space between us. "Here—eat a little, whether you think you are hungry or not."

North waits until I've retreated again, chewing on a strip of dried povvy, to approach the food. He glances at me, then selects the same thing, a bit of salty dried meat.

"What is this place?" he asks, turning his gaze to sweep across the plain, more and more visible as dawn approaches.

"These are the ghostlands." I smile when he turns a look of faint alarm in my direction. "There is nothing to fear. Some believe the spirits of the ancients still walk where the streets of this city once were, but I have never seen one myself."

North's expression suggests he's not quite sure whether to take my words seriously. Experimentally, he nibbles at the strip of povvy—then, looking pleased at the taste, he tears a bit free with his teeth. "These ancients," he says, politely trying not to chew while he speaks. "What happened to them?"

I let my gaze drift across the unnatural dips and rises in the landscape. "Some were my own ancestors. Others . . ." I have to remind myself not to look tellingly at him. "In the time of the ancients, the gods lived here among us. But when food grew scarce and the mist began to gather into storms, the gods abandoned us to live in the cloudlands."

North's thick eyebrows draw together, giving his face a stern, almost regal cast. The effect is somewhat spoiled by the fact that he's still working on the mouthful of povvy. He seems a bit discomfited by how long it's taking to chew. "You're saying you think . . . you think the people who ascended, *my* people, are *gods*?"

Though it's clear he's trying to sound neutral, there's a note of incredulity in his voice that cuts me.

Whoever this boy is, it's clear he doesn't think he's divine.

Perhaps, when they left us, the gods simply forgot what divinity meant.

North's still chewing, and when I don't answer, he asks, "If you believe all the gods left, then what is the temple we're going to? Why have a temple if there are no more gods?"

"There is one divinity who remained to guide my people through the centuries," I say, keeping my eyes on my own food, trying not to marvel at the novelty of explaining my own existence. "The living divine who walks among us."

North finally manages to swallow the mouthful he'd been chewing. "Where I come from, we remember religion from long ago, but no one practices it anymore. It causes so many problems—so much violence—like your cultists. Why *are* they looking for you, anyway?"

He's being so careful, and yet I can see it in his face, hear it in his voice—he speaks of religion the way he spoke of magic. Like both are somehow no more than the product of foolish minds.

My answer—*I am the living goddess, and they want to kill me*—hangs on my lips, but the words don't come out. A tiny, shame-filled part of me knows why: though he would try to hide it, this boy would find the idea ridiculous. He would find *me* ridiculous.

And, sitting here beneath the first lilac streaks of sunrise with the only person I've met since I was a child who didn't know me by my divinity first, I find I want to stay as we are just a little bit longer.

"Finish eating," I advise him, ignoring his question and entertaining the cat with one of the laces on the pack. "We ought to keep moving."

North lifts the strip of povvy and asks curiously, "What is this, anyway? I've never had anything like it."

"Povvy," I tell him. "Dried and salted and spiced."

"What's povvy? A kind of root?"

I hide my smile—no doubt he dislikes feeling ridiculous as much as I do. "No, not a root. Povvies are little rodent-like creatures who live in the forest-sea, though the ones we eat are usually raised by farmers for their meat. They get very fat if you let th—are you all right?"

North's gone absolutely still, his eyes wide, his face a mask of horror. "This—this was an animal? This was—was *alive*?"

I lean forward, alarmed, though I cannot reach out to him.

"Yes, of course—it makes excellent food for traveling, dense protein and—"

"I'm going to be sick," North mumbles, dropping the strip of povvy and lurching to his feet. The cat leaps out of the confines of the pack and stalks over to the discarded meat, flashing North a very dirty look indeed before snatching it up and then carrying it behind a nearby stone to feast in private.

"Take deep breaths," I urge North, getting to my feet as well, although I can do nothing but offer advice from a distance. "Bend down, lean your elbows on your knees—that way, yes. Keep breathing . . ."

It takes him several long moments, but he manages not to throw up. The look he finally shoots me is accusatory. "How could you—how can you eat *flesh*?"

"How can you *not*?" I reply, as confused as he. "We eat what we must—food is scarce and meat is filling. We have always done so—your ancestors did so. Have you no meat in the clouds?"

North shakes his head vehemently. "We have no animals at all. Birds, yes, but no one . . ." He stops, swallowing hard, catching his breath. "No one would ever think of *eating* one."

He looks so distressed, so suddenly forlorn and out of place, that I find myself moving quickly toward the cloth containing our meager meal and gathering up the rest of the povvy strips so that I can stash them away in my pack, out of sight.

"Wrap up what remains there and bring it with you," I tell him. "None of that is meat; it is all vegetable and grain."

North looks as if he's doubting he'll ever eat again, but he's no fool even if he is out of his depth. He gathers up the corners of the cloth, wrapping up the last of the food, and then tucks the packet into the waistband of his suit.

I rise to my feet, signaling that we must keep moving. The plains stretch as far as the eye can see, the sun touching first the very tallest of the ruins and then flowing slowly, inexorably down into the shadows below. The sky above is streaked with the thinnest of clouds, stretching like rose-gold arrows pointing toward the thick mass of white and gray that marks the under-side of the cloudlands. Wind, unimpeded here by the dense forest-sea, sweeps down across the plains, bending the grasses before it and making the hills and hummocks seem to undulate as if with remembered life.

North is quiet as we begin to walk, his eyes round, taking in every sight as if he's never seen grass and hills before.

Perhaps he hasn't, I think, watching him out of the corner of my eye. *Are there hills in the sky?* For a moment, I nearly lose myself imagining a life surrounded by mountains of cloud and oceans of empty sky.

"What's that?" North asks abruptly, his steps ceasing be-side me.

Alarmed, my eyes go first toward the forest-sea, a now dis-tant smear of dark gray-green behind us. But then I see the direction of North's gaze and follow it across the horizon. In the distance is a cluster of pink and gold, as if one lone puff of cloud held on to dawn's colors as it came and went.

I lift my head, noting the wind flowing past me, and swal-low a flicker of alarm. "A mist-storm," I tell him. "We must move quickly."

"What's a mist-storm?" he asks, eyes still on the distant, unnatural-looking cloud. "And why would we be worried about it?"

I hide my surprise by holding tighter to my spearstaff. Every time I think I understand how little North knows of this world, he shows me I haven't begun to scratch the surface of his ignorance. "The mist is . . . I cannot think how to explain it to you. It is the residue of creation, the source of all magic. But this world is old and tired, and the mist is not harmless as it once was. The mist is all around us even now, but sometimes it gathers together, drawn to itself like motes of dust, and then it storms and rages across the land."

"So, like . . . pollution? Poisoned air?"

I tilt my head. "It is one of the things your ancestors fled from, to their world in the sky."

North eyes me sidelong. I pretend not to see and start walking again. He falls into step at my side, with the bindle cat maintaining a careful distance between us. "What would happen if it caught up to us?"

"Do all cloudlanders ask so many questions?" I can hear the irritation in my voice and try to bury it. "We must keep going, North."

He falls into step beside me again, and this time the silence is heavy until he asks, his voice even, "Why worry about it? Couldn't you just use your *magic* and whisk it away?" This time, he makes no effort to hide the sarcasm in his voice.

"For one thing," I tell him, "no magician can control the

mist. We draw power from it, but we cannot direct it. For another, the mist makes magic unpredictable—it can rob even the strongest magician of her abilities, or bestow power upon those who have never been touched with magic before. It can bring illness, or great skill, or despair, or a knowledge of things to come. To some, it brings madness itself."

A warning tickle of sensation winds its way down the back of my neck, and as North opens his mouth to reply, I lift a hand to forestall him. Above us, difficult to see at first against the smoky underside of the cloudlands, is a second swirl of pink, this one tinged with green.

A second storm, and this one is gathering fast.

My throat tightens. Hiret's story about how Quenti was injured echoes in my ears—the storm that had come from nowhere and gathered so quickly he was hit before he knew to run.

The storms are no longer behaving as they ought, as they used to. They are becoming wilder, unpredictable.

"Run," I whisper.

"What?" North blinks at me, then follows my gaze. "I don't—"

"Run! *Now!*" I gesture with my spearstaff, and the bindle cat leads the way as I break into a run. Behind me, I can hear the grass rustling as North follows. Dubious he may be about the dangers of the mist, but evidently he's not willing to take his chances alone.

I'm already exhausted, and my muscles begin to burn and my head spin in protest after only a few moments. North must be hurting even more, unused to this world as he is. But as the thought of slowing my pace pops into my head, a whirl of mist stretches down out of the clouds like a grasping arm. Spindly fingers clutch at the earth not far from where we were a few moments ago, with a series of earsplitting cracks and squeals as the stone rearranges itself, twisted into spires as if reaching back toward the clouds.

North chokes out something that must be an oath in his world, and puts on a burst of speed that brings him up beside me. "Can't keep this up," he manages over the howling of the storm as it gathers the funnel back into itself and races along behind us. "How . . ."

"There," I gasp, not bothering to gesture—the place is obvious, the only shelter visible on the plains. It's the heart of this fallen city, and there are ways inside some of the rubble-formed hills. I know because I came here often in my childhood, when it was still safe to travel.

I can't stop to look at his face, but North's silence tells me he's dubious about how well the ruins will shelter us. I wish I felt as certain as I sounded.

We reach the bottom of one of the hummocks just as the storm begins to darken the sky directly above us, purpling now with its intensity. I lead North around it and between two other hills, where an uneven gash of shadow stretches across a long, uniform rise. Pointing with my spearstaff, I shout, "Inside—quick!"

He dives into the darkness, scrambling on his knees to make

room for me to follow. Every hair on my body is standing on end, and I can taste the mist—or its power—like bitter, burned caramel on my tongue. Still, I wait a moment longer. Better to be mist-touched than to bump into North in the dark.

I drop to my knees and crawl in after him, and then the storm is upon us, howling furiously past the entrance.

I can hear North's harsh breathing, but I can see little in the sudden gloom.

The dark shadow that is the bindle cat is pressed in against North at the back of the recess, identifiable by the faint glitter of his eyes, round as the twin moons. North's quavering breath tells me he must be nearly as shaken.

"A-are you all right?" he asks, his form shifting in the dark. "Are we safe here?"

"Yes." My voice shakes, so I leave him with that one answer to both questions until I'm sure I can speak without scaring him further. My eyes, adjusting to the dark, find his outline against the stone.

"How is anyone still alive down here?" North murmurs, running an unsteady hand through his hair. "Everything about this place is trying to kill us!"

The mist-storm, the cultists, the mist-bent boar . . . Was it only hours ago that I sent those creatures scrambling? My head spins, and I draw up my knees so I can rest my forehead against them.

"You have had an unusually difficult welcome," I whisper back, as if the mist-storm might hear.

North's breath hitches as though he'd laugh if he weren't so winded. "Can you make your staff glow again? One of your . . . light spells?" He says the words rather dubiously.

A flicker of irritation makes me long to retort, *You can't scoff at magic and then turn around and ask me to use it.*

Instead, I take a breath and lay a hand on the stone wall, despite how the feel of it makes my skin crawl. "I cannot in this place. There is too much sky-steel in these stones. It protects us from the mist, but it renders me . . ."

Helpless.

"Ordinary."

North makes a skeptical little sound in his throat. "So there are rules, then? For this magic you can do?"

Though his voice is kind enough, the words he chooses are clear. "Why do you ask me questions if you believe I am lying to you?"

He hesitates. "It's not that I think you're lying. I just wonder if what you call magic is just science by another name."

"I could show you the fireseed, speak the invocation, let you see the spell fail because of the sky-steel—would that convince you?"

North's breath comes out in a long sigh. "I've offended you—I'm sorry." I can hear him moving, a rustle of fabric on stone, and then without any warning at all, a dim blue glow illuminates his face.

I jerk back in surprise, my shoulder blades hitting the wall of the tunnel. "How . . ." My head spins, and not just from the presence of so much sky-steel inhibiting my powers. "You—you can use magic?" And use it *here*, surrounded by the one thing that renders all magic inert.

North's gaze flicks up, brow furrowed—then his eyes widen in surprise. "Magic? No—*science*, like I said. Technology, see?" He lifts his arm, showing me a round, glowing panel affixed to a bracelet. "It's called a chrono—a chronometer. Everyone has them up in Alciel. In the cloudlands."

My heart thuds against my ribs. "A power strong enough to work despite the sky-steel?"

"It's not *power*," he says, "not like you mean it. It's got a battery."

"And what does the battery do?"

"It . . ." He lets out a soft huff, and sounds like he wants to laugh. "Well, it provides power to the light. It stores the power, then lets it out as needed."

"It sounds very much like an instrument of magic to me," I tell him, running my fingertips over the charms ringing the blade end of my spearstaff, each one as familiar to my touch as anything in this world.

"What are those?" he asks softly.

"These are my udjet," I say, studying them by the blue glow of North's light. "They are charms, my own instruments of magic. I do not think you would understand."

"Do they represent elements?" North guesses. "Or maybe different gods you pray to? Or are they like the things in those pouches you wear, ingredients for different spells?"

"Magic requires a tranquil mind," I say. "Harmony with your thoughts. To be that still, you must know who you are—all

129

of you. A magician's udjet . . . it's an ancient word for *soul*. They remind me of who I am."

North smiles tentatively. "I like that." He looks at the charms again, reaching out to indicate one of them. "Tell me about this one."

"From a pilgrimage I made to Intisuyu, the sun lands, when I was a little girl." It was just after I was called as the living divine, but I do not say this aloud. "I found the stone among the ruins, and Daoman, my . . . my guardian, had it polished and wrapped with silver to hang as a charm."

"And this one? I think I can guess what this one's about."

I inspect the little gold figurine of a seated cat resting on his fingertips. "He has been my companion most of my life," I say. "He is a part of who I am."

"What about this one?" He moves his hand, reaching for the little sea-glass bottle, the figure of a tall-masted ship etched on the inside. I do not say to him that it is not done, touching a magician's charms without an invitation. His interest warms me.

"I always used to dream of traveling," I murmur. "My . . . friend, and I, we would tell each other stories of the lands across the ocean and make plans to go there." I reach out to touch the little bottle as well, my fingertips a breath away from North's.

Elkisa. I'm so sorry.

"You haven't been yet?" he asks.

"Not yet," I reply weakly.

He shifts his light to inspect the next of the charms, but his attention is caught by something beside me, and he blinks, then shifts to lean in closer to the wall.

"Whoa, look at this." The movement of his hand shifts the way the glow of his bracelet lands on the stone, and tiny pin-pricks of reflected light spring up and vanish as he tilts it to and fro. Then the light catches on a long seam in the rock. "Wait—this is cement?"

I blink at him, still trying to understand what he is asking.

North glances back at me. "This place—it's man-made?"

"We are in the heart of the ruined city," I answer. "An ancient city."

"And this steel you keep talking about?"

"Almost everything the ancients built contains sky-steel. You don't know this element?" I frown when his expression remains blank—everything with him requires about four times as much explanation as I think. "Metal smithed from fallen stars? The rarest and most valuable element in all creation? It repels magic, acts as a shield. It—oh, for prophecy's sake, North!" Exasperation makes me splutter to a halt.

He turns his face away, shoulders quivering. It takes me a moment to realize: he's laughing. Too tired to take offense, I find myself huffing an answering wisp of laughter, rubbing my hands over my face.

How strange, I think, feeling how warm my cheeks are. *To be huddled for our lives beneath tons of stone and find myself laughing with a divine messenger from the clouds.*

"If only I'd thought to study 'elements of Below' at the academy." North's voice is still bright with amusement as he leans his head back against the rock.

Curiosity prickles at me. "Academy? Like a school?"

North nods. "Exactly. Do you have schools here?"

"There is a seminary in the temple for acolytes who wish to become priests." I shift around until I can lay my spearstaff down, stretching fingers that had been gripping it far too tightly. "And the riverstriders have a sort of floating school where different clans gather to share and pass on their knowledge to their children. They call it learning to walk the river."

"So you're one of these river people?"

I glance at him, then away. "My mother was."

"But not you?" North's voice is quiet, with a gentler curiosity as if, somehow, he senses my reluctance to continue down this path.

"Not me, no."

North is silent for a few breaths. "So these mist-storms—I take it everyone just builds everything out of this sky metal? Because I wouldn't want to be sitting outside unaware when one of those things shows up."

"Sky-steel is too rare now. How the ancients found so much of it, or how they scattered it throughout the stone they built with, we do not know. But we have enough to protect our villages, after a fashion. And the river protects the temple, and the riverstriders."

"We're lucky you know about this place," North grants. "I guess *I'm* lucky."

For years, this was *my* place—where I could play unsupervised, for there were no people here to touch me. Daoman considered the expeditions educational for a young deity. My guards and acolytes always had too much dignity to crawl around in these tunnels, and I never told the high priest about everything I found here, for even as a child I longed to keep a few small things for myself.

So why do I want to share them with North?

"Come," I say abruptly, before I can change my mind. "I will show you something I have never shown anyone before."

EIGHT

NORTH

Half crawling as we head deeper into the ruins, every part of me hurts in new and unique ways—gashes from my crash landing, a thousand stings from the insects of the jungle, bruises and aches every time I try to flex my wrist.

Also, I'm completely convinced there are still particles of that animal I *ate* stuck between my teeth. I shudder, trying not to think about it.

What I'd thought was a cave in the rubble of a long-collapsed building has turned out to be a passageway that twists and turns its way into the hill. "Who built this tunnel?" I venture, watching the cat's fluffy hindquarters disappear from view around a bend ahead of Nimh.

"My people," she replies, without looking back—how she doesn't trip, I have no idea. She has even less of the glow from my chrono than I do.

"But they didn't build the city that's ruined here."

"No, the city is from the time of the ancients, when the gods walked among us." She steps over a fallen section of the ceiling, then moves aside so I can do the same without coming too close to her. "The tunnels were created about two centuries after the Exodus—when the gods left."

I cling to that idea, tucking it close against my heart. My people left here once. They left ruins. There's no reason to believe they didn't leave behind some hint of how they launched the sky-islands, some ancient record. If they did, I'll find it.

"Why did you build the tunnels?" I ask now.

"My people were trying to reclaim sky-steel to use for protection, but for the most part, it is spread too thinly through the stone."

I reach out, letting my fingers trail across the cool tunnel wall beside me. It's simple poured cement, I'm sure of it. No doubt mixing it with fragments of this metal of theirs made it stronger, and somewhere down the centuries her people began to believe it had some kind of power.

Something about this place feels oddly familiar, but I'm too tired to grab hold of it. I try instructing my brain to sift through old memories, run a subprogram in the background. Maybe it will come up with what this place reminds me of.

And in the meantime, I study Nimh.

She's like a torch in the darkness, pushing away the fears and horrors of the night. I let my gaze linger on her profile as she turns to round the corner ahead of me, moving slowly as she picks her way over a pile of fallen rubble.

The faint blue glow from my chrono plays across her features, her full lips, her dark eyes, her thick lashes. Her face is nothing like Saelis's rounder, softer features, her serious gaze nothing like Miri's energetic grin, but she's magnetic in a way that's undeniable.

I can't think why I find myself comparing her to my friends. Maybe it's the heartbreak of being told that I can't ever be with them—or the realization that I may never see them again.

Maybe my heart wants some way to fill the void.

A magic-wielding girl from Below. Good choice, North.

Nimh pauses as the tunnel opens up into a bigger space beyond. She turns and our eyes lock. Her gaze is steady, and for a long moment we're perfectly still.

Just the two of us in here, the storm raging outside.

Beyond these glimmering rock walls lies death, far as the eye can see. But the girl in front of me is so full of life.

I expect her to blink or look away. It's what people do when they accidentally make eye contact. But she doesn't, and I can't.

"Why do you stare at me?" she asks quietly.

"Um." I reach for words and come up short.

She tilts her head, and maybe it's a trick of the blue light, but her cheeks seem to darken with color, just for an instant. As if she senses it, she lifts her fingertips to press them against her skin.

They touch just near the dark smear made by the drops of blood that fell from the bodies up in the trees, and in that moment I remember that her friends are dead.

Skies. I'm reaching for something that's not there. *What am I doing?* She's not looking at me the way I'm looking at her, and I shouldn't even be *thinking* about this. My own cheeks are hot as I grab for the first available subject change.

"This is, uh, the place you wanted to show me?"

She carefully steps out into the larger space, and I follow.

"Hold a moment," she says, soft. "Here, I can get far enough from the walls to reach the mist that lies dormant in this place."

"Uh, mist? Like that stuff outside?" I wish my voice didn't sound so nervous. "I thought it couldn't exist in here?"

"The mist is everywhere," Nimh answers gently, though at the edge of the chrono's light I can see her lips twitch. "A little is safe enough, and necessary for magic. There is a little trapped inside this old ruin, kept here by the cage of sky-steel around it."

"How do you know all this?"

She smiles at me. "I discovered it when I was a little girl. No one else comes here."

She reaches into that utility belt she wears, drawing out a pinch of something between finger and thumb. Bowing her head, she whispers to it softly, and then tosses it up into the air. Lifting her chin, she blows gently, and the tiny particles come to life. Glowing first like a swarm of tiny insects, they glide out into a larger, darker space, each one illuminating until it's like we're standing on the edge of a galaxy.

I've got my mouth hanging open like a palace tourist, but as I gawk at the beauty of it, slowly I begin to realize what I'm seeing.

It's a huge—well, not a room, it's too big for that. There are double-height ceilings, and a series of dark openings that lead away to other spaces—some on our level, others running off a balcony around the second level. At first I think it's a grand hall, but then I figure out what I'm actually looking at. It's much simpler than that, and so completely out of place here that it startles a laugh out of me.

She shoots me an inquiring glance, and I lift one hand to gesture at our surroundings. "It's a shopping arcade," I say, pointing at the rows of cement openings where the duraglass must have been. "Those are storefronts, right?"

"There were merchants here," she agrees with a tentative smile. "I think once it was open to the sky, or they had the art of making much larger sheets of glass than we do now."

I crane my neck back to take a look. She's right—up where the ceiling should be, another gap is bridged by huge chunks of stone.

Outside might lie the plains and the ghostlands, but in front of me is evidence that, once upon a time, this really was a city.

One built by my ancestors.

I can see the bones of something familiar in it, but now it's ancient, darker and wilder. It's otherworldly, lit up by Nimh's own personal galaxy. And when I look across at her, it strikes me all over again—she's just like this arcade. Familiar and yet utterly different.

"Come with me," she says, gentle as she interrupts my dazed train of thought. "I will show you what I found here when I was little."

The floor of the arcade is flooded with old groundwater, and I notice Nimh avoids letting it touch her feet, so I do the same. If there was ever a place where something terrifying was going to be lurking, it's here.

She picks her way around the raised walkway at the edge of the ground floor, pausing once to crouch and lay her staff across a gap in the pavement so the bindle cat can run along it to the other side, neat as any acrobat. When she talked to him outside, she spoke like he understands us, and I still don't quite know how clever he is. Either way, I'm pretty sure I haven't impressed him.

I peer into an empty store, and a memory springs up in my mind. My subconscious has found a result in that search program it was running, and it's flashing like a lit-up sign.

For an instant, I'm not Below at all, not following this mysterious girl through this ancient place.

Just for an instant, I look at that dark tunnel and I'm at home. I'm underneath the city.

"North?" Nimh asks, pausing and turning back toward me.

"It's like the engine rooms," I whisper, pressing one palm against the stone again.

"Engine," she repeats. "There's that word again."

The hairs on the back of my neck are rising, because it's all clicking into place. The tunnel that led us here reminded me of the tunnels at the very base of Alciel's engines. The walls there, between the slabs of ancient circuitry, glimmer when you run your flashlight over them. I think they're infused with what Nimh calls sky-steel, just like this place.

And the mist-tainted air out on the plains—I can almost taste it again, and now I know why it freaked me out so much. It's like a turbocharged version of the thick, stifling air in our engine rooms. I spent enough time poking around down there when I built the *Skysinger*'s engine that I'm sure I'm right. They're one and the same.

My heart's beating faster, and my gaze is darting around the ancient arcade as I study it in a new light, drinking it in like it's the muddy-tasting contents of Nimh's waterskin.

If they have sky-steel and mist here, does that mean they have materials I need to build a new engine for the *Skysinger*?

"This stuff," I say, slapping my hand against the stone. "The sky-steel. You said your people came in here to dig it out? What do you use it for, to build . . ." I search for a word that might make more sense to her than *engines*. "Do you use it to make things? Machines? To power your boats, maybe?"

Nimh shakes her head slowly. "There is very little sky-steel to be had," she replies. "The gods took almost all of it with them. What little we have, we use to power the guardian stones."

"What are they?" I practically pounce on her answer.

"The guardian stones?" She blinks at me as if she's having trouble processing the fact that I don't know. "They stand at the edges of our villages. They repel the mist, just as the last remnants of the sky-steel here are protecting us now."

"So you know how they work together? The sky-steel and the mist? If someone here understands that, they can help me power my glider. Maybe I could get home."

"We . . ." She pauses, and I can tell she's choosing her words. "Maintaining the stones is the work of our divinity," she says finally.

"The god who stayed behind?" I ask. Someone here who

remembered the old skills, who knew how to maintain the same tech that powers our engines, *would* seem like a god. "Your divinity sounds a lot like a mechanic to me, Nimh. Can you get me to them?"

"I . . ." She glances down at the cat like he might have the answer. "I am not familiar with the word *mechanic*," she says eventually.

"That's all right," I say. "All I need is an introduction."

Maybe, just maybe, what Nimh's people call magic, I might call a miracle.

NINE
NIMH

I am that divinity you seek. But I can no more put you back in the sky than I can sprout wings.

The words are there, as bright and clear in my mind as if I had spoken them aloud—but I hold them back, ill at ease. North's dark eyes are lit with hope, and I can't bring myself to extinguish it. "The Divine One lives at the temple," I say instead. "I will take you there when the storm passes."

Which I hope very much will be soon, as I am due to preside over the Feast of the Dying tonight.

North grins at me, and my ribs seem to squeeze in response, as though that smile were a tangible thing, an embrace. I shiver, and I turn away.

Though he's recognized something of his own people in the ruins of our shared ancestors, this underground marketplace wasn't what I brought North here to see. The dim light scattered around us shows the edge of one of the pools, and I gesture him forward, clearing my throat. "Come, look here."

I murmur a word of caution, for the ground here is treacherous, then crouch at the water's edge. North is careful to keep a distance between us, enough that I don't feel that little edge of panic at his closeness.

"What am I looking at?" North asks, eyes sweeping across the water's surface.

I reach out with my spearstaff, so that the more concentrated light magic at its tip illuminates the pool. "Look down into the water—do you see?"

North leans forward. It's still shallow here, only a few feet deep. Nestled in the muck at the bottom of the marsh, gazing up through the water as if seeking the sky far above, is a stone face.

The cloudlander's breath catches, and his eyes widen as they fix on the staring gaze of the stone head, its features painted blue-green with algae. Finally, he looks up, scanning our surroundings until his eyes fall on a block of stone that stands not far away. "It was a statue—that pedestal in the center of the arcade, that's where it must have stood."

I ease back, unable to fight the smile that wants to answer his. His delight at finding these pieces of our shared ancient past reminds me how I used to feel, exploring these plains and the tunnels beneath them.

He heaves a long sigh, pushing back a lock of his wavy hair and looking around again at the darkened ruins. As he contemplates the ancient city, I find his face even more compelling than the one in the water. Everything is new to him—his wonder is like that one feels in a dream.

"This is incredible," he murmurs, looking back and catching me staring. "Thank you. Do you know who it is? The statue?"

My smile fades in spite of myself. I can't put off the reason I brought him here any longer. I rise and move back toward the center of the marketplace, and the empty plinth that used to hold the statue. Years have brought back the layers of grime and dirt I once cleared away as a child, but I know where to look. Reaching into my chatelaine, I draw out the reagents for Spirit's Breath and scatter them across the stone.

"What is it?" North whispers, voice hushed as if in deference to my magic—the magic he doesn't believe in.

I can't help a sidelong smile. "Do they not value patience in the cloudlands?" Focusing my will, I stretch out my hands and guide the energies within me down my arms and into my palms. Then, hovering a breath above the surface of the stone, I let my palms spread outward.

For a moment, nothing happens—then, gradually, the bits of old, dead lichen begin to shrivel and flake away, the Spirit's Breath spell burrowing through the dirt and organic detritus down to the metal that lies beneath.

North mutters something under his breath and leans closer, as if trying to figure out the trick. A tiny part of me revels in being able to show him my empty palms, even as the last of the debris falls away.

He's watching me with narrowed eyes, but, impatient, I tilt my head to indicate the plinth again. He blinks, looking down at the metal plaque that had been hiding behind the years of grime. With his attention on it, I'm free to watch him, so intently I'm half-afraid he'll sense the weight of my gaze.

He draws a breath of surprise at the engraved lettering

there—the lettering of the ancients, unreadable now to my people, except a very small handful of scholars. I am one of them—the long years I have waited to manifest have offered all the opportunities for study that I could wish. I used to wonder if I could discover my purpose if I searched hard enough. Now I know that I waited for a reason.

These words are in the language of the gods.

"Akra Chuki," he reads without hesitation, voice slowed only by a hushed reverence for being in the presence of such an ancient piece of writing. "Honored Lord and Guardian of Peace."

My heart is pounding, my body tingling. I cannot move, for fear I'll discover I imagined it—that he can't read the ancient writing after all, that I only *want* it to be true so badly that my mind conjured the moment like the mirage of water a dying man sees in the desert.

When I say nothing, North looks up at me with a smile that fades when he sees my face. "Nimh?"

"You . . ." I have to stop, breathe, summon my voice. "You really are one of them. A cloudlander."

Divine, I think, although I do not say that aloud.

North's head tilts, a hint of confusion on his face. "Ye-es. I told you I was."

I manage another breath. "You read the ancient writing," I explain, gesturing to the plaque, which gleams as brightly now in the sun as it did the day it was engraved, thanks to the spell. "North—I know you do not understand, but to me, for my people . . . this is unheard-of. Unprecedented."

Important beyond anything that has happened in centuries.

A little of his confusion clears, and he says with a small laugh that warms his voice, "You're just as big a shock to me, you know. There's not supposed to be anybody left down here."

His laughter makes me wish I could respond. I want to preserve this ease—this feeling between us—for as long as I am able.

Because soon he will know what I know: That he was sent here. That our meeting was destiny.

That he may be divine.

It is a selfish thing, to keep the truth from him. It will hurt him more later, when we reach the temple outskirts and there's no more hiding my identity. It's selfish—and it's all I have.

"The storm may have moved on," I say finally, keeping my voice even. "We ought to continue our journey, if it is safe. There is a festival at the temple tonight—you will like it, I think."

North falls into step with me easily as we head back toward the tunnels, although there's something in his voice that isn't quite right. "You said your god lives there, right? The guy who understands the sky-steel and the mist, and how they power your shield stones?"

Perhaps that note in his voice is responding to the note in mine—perhaps he knows I'm not telling him everything. I glance at him, my smile reassuring. "The guardian stones, yes. And if the Divine One cannot help you return to the sky . . . if anyone in our history ever knew how this might be done, it will be in the records at the temple."

I must get him to the temple—I am not lying, not about the

records, and not about his safety. But I dare not tell him all that I'm thinking: that if he is divine, then he could *be* the Lightbringer returned to us.

In my vision, the lost stanza seemed to say that all I had to do was show the Lightbringer that ancient copy of the Song of the Destroyer. That, somehow, looking at the scroll would unlock his understanding of who he was.

He will look upon this page and know himself. . . .

Perhaps this boy is more than a messenger. Perhaps he *is* the message.

If he is the Lightbringer, then I am the one destined to be at his side.

I'm not fated to walk this earth alone after all.

He might not yet know it, if his destiny is to end the suffering of my people and begin the cycle anew, but I know mine—to keep him safe, and help him discover his divinity. For if his fate is to end the world, I must bring him to my temple . . . and I cannot let him leave.

TEN
NORTH

Nimh's temple sits nestled in a fork of the river. The water splits there to flow around the rocky jut of land rising up over the surrounding terrain. Like a tiered cake dominating a feast, the temple overlooks the jumble of buildings and boats spread below it.

Though I saw it all from a distance, the moment of being *in* the city itself creeps up on me. There's no one place where it begins, no wall around its border, no edge of the island like there is at home. But though it's nothing like home, this is still a city, and the best place to search for the tech and the knowledge I need. Last night when I crashed, I didn't even know there were humans alive down here. Now there's an entire city. So I keep reminding myself that things are looking up.

We made our way across the plain, where the roads of the civilization that used to be here—my ancestors and Nimh's— are still raised up a little above the rest of the land. I caught glimpses of a grid now and then.

My head still sort of wants to explode, but I think I can make sense of the story her people tell. Generations ago—so long ago that even my people have lost the records of it—we left this place, and in the time since, they've turned us into gods who fled to the sky.

We repaid them by forgetting they were down here at all.

Kind of a raw deal.

But seeing the ruined city has reminded me of one thing: this *is* the world my people came from. Once upon a time, we had the technology to lift whole cities up into the sky. Surely somewhere here, perhaps hidden away in the darkest corner of Nimh's archives, is a record of how we did it. Maybe it's written like a technical manual—it wouldn't make any sense to someone who doesn't know what engines are, but I might understand it.

If this world once knew how to raise up a city . . . then they *must* still have, somewhere, the knowledge of how to raise one lost prince.

I have to meet this god of theirs.

I can't help but glance across at Nimh while she's too focused on our path to notice. I'm like a grounded fledgling here, utterly out of my element. I suppose she'd be just as out of place in my world. I wonder . . . If I can find a way back to my city, could I bring a representative from this place? Open up communications between our two peoples? It's the kind of thing a prince should think about, after all.

Nimh and I make our way past a few boats as the water begins to deepen around us. The rivers become more defined, paths hacked through the old roads to allow the shallow craft to pass. I've never seen a full-size boat before, but we used to float petals in the palace fountains and race them, and in a strange way, I see that echoed now.

At first it's just one or two of the long, thin vessels, maneuvered through murky waters by ragged owners using long poles. Then there are flat-bottomed barges made of bundled reeds. Then the foot traffic on the beaten earth paths around us is increasing, and then we're on the outskirts of the city.

We venture into what's unmistakably a market, though so early in the morning it's still waking up. Laid out on the barges, many of which carry small buildings as well as their wares, are baskets of grubby roots, bundles of shiny green lettuce-like leaves, and small silvery things with a smell that nearly bowls me over. When I break our silence to ask Nimh what they are, she shoots me a slightly concerned sidelong look, as if she's wondering if my crash landing rattled my brains.

"Fish," she says, as she holds back a smile, not realizing that the word doesn't mean anything to me.

As I consider pressing the issue, she eases deftly to one side to avoid a pair of men who threaten to brush against her arm. The crowd isn't too thick yet, but she won't be able to avoid being jostled forever.

I'd love to know why she doesn't want to be touched, but I already approached the subject, and she sidestepped. Perhaps she just has really strong preferences. I know a man who only eats even numbers of bites at his meals, a woman who only wears blue. They manage just fine. Maybe Nimh's in that camp. Maybe she just needs more time to learn to trust someone.

That's fine. Until I can get an audience with this mechanic god of theirs, I've got all the time in the world.

I watch her profile as we make our way along the path. She's so serene now, and so sure. And then I nearly stumble over the cat as he weaves between my feet, his tail raised like a flag.

Okay, cat. I have time to win you over too.

As we make our way through the city, the whole place grows busier, denser, boats scaffolded higher in precarious arrangements that remind me of the slums on the smaller islands—held together, as my bloodmother would say, with spit and good luck. Then the ground changes underfoot, and I can see paving stones beneath the accumulated dirt. Our surroundings seem subtly more permanent. Up ahead, I can see stone buildings looming above the heads of the crowd.

If I'd ever dreamed of life here on the surface, I would have envisioned huts and dirt. A ragtag handful of people barely scraping by. But there's a vibrance to the chaos of this floating, moving city that defies anything I could have imagined. This place is so big, so *real*, that I don't know how to process it.

I'm here—and yet none of this makes any sense. How did we not know about *thousands of people*? Did we just decide so long ago that everything left Below had died, that for centuries no one ever bothered to look?

I can't explain any of it, any more than I can explain what Nimh calls her "magic." My list of questions gets longer every hour I'm down here, and I'm ready for answers.

Nimh straightens a little beside me, and when I follow her

gaze, I see what's unmistakably a security patrol—they look the same no matter where you're from, walking purposefully, keeping to their formation and letting those around them make way, forcing them right to the edge of the water. A woman balancing a stack of baskets perches with one foot on a boat to make room for them, and they don't spare her a glance as she wobbles.

I step up next to Nimh, looking for a cue as to whether the patrol's presence is a welcome development, or whether we should melt to the edges of the path as well. I've spent my fair share of time dodging my family's own security over the years, so I'm ready.

She turns swiftly to catch my gaze, her brow furrowed. "North, I will not be able to stay with you once we reach the temple. Do not be afraid, though—you will be safe, I will make certain of it."

"Wait—what? Why can't you stay? Where are you going?" I'm not prepared for the lurch of alarm that hits me at the notion of my one ally vanishing.

Nimh hesitates, smoothing a hand over her hair as she glances over her shoulder at the approaching patrol. Though she's unmistakably braced for their arrival, it isn't quite fear or nervousness quickening her movements. I'm reminded instead of the way Saelis draws himself up and goes into performance mode before he heads onstage with his quartet. She's drawing some other persona around herself, warmth fading away, replaced by a strange remoteness.

Finally she lets her breath out and fixes me with a look of mute appeal. "They will ask you many questions—tell them nothing, except that you assisted me in finding my way safely back. Tell them I have invited you to stay at the temple for a time as reward for your service."

I open my mouth, about to protest, though which part I want to protest first, I'm not sure.

The guards have nearly reached us. They don't spare a glance for me—if I wanted to run, and *not* tie myself to this girl who apparently draws assassins to her like a magnet and leaves massacres in her wake, now is my chance.

It's the guard at the front, a woman with dark brown skin and black curls slicked neatly back, who first spots Nimh by my side. I see the moment it happens. Her mouth falls open, and she breaks formation to run forward and skid to a halt in front of us with the whites of her eyes showing.

"Divine One!" She seems to be having trouble finding her words, and Nimh raises her hand, showing the guard her palm.

"All is well," she says quietly. "Be at peace."

"But Goddess, we—"

Goddess?

Nimh shakes her head just a fraction, and it's enough to silence the woman. By now, the rest of her squad has caught up, and they're shuffling back into formation behind her.

"I am pleased to have an escort back to the temple," Nimh says, as though nothing weird is happening at all. I'm busy trying not to injure my neck, swiveling my head to take in first my traveling companion, then the guards, then the onlookers, who are beginning to gather.

I can feel a pulse inside my temples, and I'm blinking too

fast, breathing too fast.

Nimh said their living god was the one who maintained their guardian stones. The living god knew how to use the same mist and sky-steel we have in Alciel's engines. She told me I could find "him" at the temple.

It's one thing to have a girl explain to me that they believe in gods down here.

It's another to find out that she—and apparently everyone else—thinks she *is* one.

"Divine One?" I repeat, in a strangled whisper. "Goddess?"

She meets it with a very un-goddess-like look that clearly says *Shut up, not now,* and I close my mouth with difficulty.

Questions and suspicions are jostling for real estate in my mind—*Why didn't you tell me?* is colliding with *Did you think I wouldn't find out?* and *What other secrets did you keep from me?*

And running through all of it is a vein of . . . hurt.

I trusted her, I let her lead me here, and it's obvious now that our trust wasn't mutual. There's no other reason she'd lie to me.

"With respect, Divine One, we should wait for a larger escort," the woman's saying.

"I think," replies Nimh gently, "that if we stand here to wait, we will keep the people from enjoying their market day. We will continue on."

Well, I want to snap, *let's not stop anyone from having a nice day. That would be terrible.*

But nobody's looking at me, and the cat underlines her words with a cranky kind of yowling sound. Despite how fearsome the guard appears, she's clearly as wary of the creature as I am, because she inclines her head and signals for her troop to form up around Nimh. Nimh gestures, and without a word, they shift their formation to include me, as well. I stare at her, willing her to meet my eyes, but she won't.

One of the guards, at an urgent order from the patrol leader, sets off running ahead of us into the city. But the rest of us don't wait, and soon we're making our way through the crowd with guards dressed in black and gold flanking us on all sides.

I can see our destination—the temple at the heart of the city, raised up on a hill. It's built from great blocks of stone, and it is, without question, the largest building I've ever seen in my life. Its layers grow smaller as they rise, lined with elaborate windows and balconies. Greenery spills out here and there to mark the presence of lush gardens on the different terraces. Intricate patterns carved into the stone wind all the way from the towering heights of the highest level down to the muddy ground below. It has an undeniably ancient quality to it, a gravity, not unlike the palace in Alciel.

We're about halfway there when a second detachment of guards, moving at double time, arrive to greet us. One walks forward and sinks to his knees to present Nimh with a bundle of red cloth draped across his outstretched hands, topped with a crown of woven gold, simple in design but exquisitely crafted. She takes both—careful not to touch the guard—and when she shakes out the fabric, I can see it's a large, loose robe that opens at the front. She slips her arms into it and settles the circlet on her brow, and it's like she's flicked a switch. Like suddenly, everyone around us is seeing something that wasn't there before.

Like a ripple traveling out from a stone tossed into the middle of a fountain, the people around us sink to their knees, bowing until their foreheads touch the ground. In half a minute, only Nimh, the guards, the cat, and I are left standing. The words travel through the crowd like a whisper, growing louder, escalating into shouts.

"The goddess has returned!"

"Bless us, Divine One!"

"The goddess returns to the city!"

All along our path, people of all walks of life, those dressed in rich silks and those in rough-spun rags, are ecstatic to see her, dropping to their knees, calling out for blessings. Nimh's serene, as if she's used to it all, and the cat stalks along beside her as if they're actually here for him.

As I watch the crowd from inside the wall of our escort, there's another color that draws my eye away from Nimh's crimson: gray.

Plain gray banners hang from some of the buildings and boats, big bolts of cloth fastened to window frames, draping down into the street. And there are people wearing gray too, standing mostly in groups of three or four.

They don't drop to their knees when everyone else does. Instead, they turn their faces from Nimh, holding up one hand like they're shading their faces from the sun, like they want to avoid seeing her.

I grew up in a palace—I know politics and intrigue as well

as I know my own name. And whatever's going on with these people in gray, it's murky and it's dangerous. The cultists who tried to kill us weren't wearing gray, which makes me wonder if there are two different groups opposing Nimh.

And I can't help wondering if these people in gray might be potential allies of mine. Nimh and I worked together to get back to the city, and I mistook that for some sort of connection. Now I have to wonder if she has any intention of helping me at all.

When we reach the temple, we're escorted into a huge reception hall, lined with yet more guards. Nimh turns to their leader, inclining her head. "I must see the high priest," she says quietly. "Please see that my honored guest is accommodated."

I have time to meet her dark eyes, to try to silently communicate how much I don't want to leave her—how badly I need her to explain what's happening, to tell me I can trust her—and then she's stepping back.

As the guards escort me away, I can't help but remember what she said to me in the forest, after finding her people slaughtered in that clearing: *You may be safer if you do not come with me, cloudlander.*

ELEVEN

NIMH

I sense something is wrong before I've even reached the temple. Even before North is bustled away, glancing back at me to meet my eyes for one tense moment, I know.

My people love me. Or, at least, they *worship* me—it's only been in the last year or two that I've thought to ask myself whether that is the same thing. But despite the devotion they feel to their faith and to their goddess, it's unusual for those in the city to have quite the same reaction as those who only see me when I travel on pilgrimage.

But as my escort and I reach the first terrace, the public gathering place where anyone may come to be near their goddess, I find it's teeming with people. One man, from one of the more distant riverstrider clans based on his black-and-yellow attire, gives an audible sob while dropping to his knees when I pass. I can't help but watch as he stares hungrily after me, tears streaming down his lined cheeks.

I knew that by now I would have been missed, but I am surprised that word of my absence has reached the city in general. I am even more surprised my unauthorized journey was not covered with some cloak of legitimacy, so my priests were not forced to admit I had struck out on my own. There is no reason my people should have feared I would not return.

And yet the cries that follow us as my escort clears a path for me to ascend to the next terrace of the temple . . . There is a pitch to them I don't recognize. They sound full of tension. They feel . . . desperate.

Once inside the temple proper, the city guard gives way to a quartet of handservants—weapons are not allowed, except to my own personal guard, within the sanctity of these walls. I recognize only two of the servants. One is a lad of thirteen named Pecho, quick and eager at his studies and obviously hoping to find his way into the priesthood. The other, a moon-faced girl my own age, joined my service around the time of last harvest. She still finds herself so overcome by her proximity to me that she can hardly bring herself to speak, and more often than not spills or drops whatever she'd been charged to bring me.

The other two must be Daoman's.

Technically, all the handservants in the temple are mine, but traditionally I ask them to serve my high priest as well, to thank him for his devotion. In truth, that structure is a formality—his servants are his own, trained by him and his people, and rarely in attendance upon me.

Unless, that is, High Priest Daoman wants something from me.

I wish that I could bypass this part altogether. I wish I could skip the disappointment and the anger of my high priest and go retrieve the scroll I found in the archives. I want so badly to bring it to North—to see if it triggers the manifestation of the Lightbringer in his heart—that my whole body aches. I could be moments away from understanding my destiny, if only I didn't have to answer to Daoman.

Quickening my steps, with the bindle cat matching them at a double-time trot, I stride toward the grand atrium. The stones are smooth and familiar, polished by centuries of feet traveling this way. Some say that this temple is so ancient it dates to a time before the Exodus, when the gods still lived among us, though there are no records that go so far back.

Still, every day that I've lived here, I've felt the weight of those centuries, the momentum of generations—I find it easy to believe those stories could be true.

I'm expecting the atrium to be empty, but when Pecho and one of Daoman's servants scramble to open the door ahead of me, I find it's full of people, their heads turning to stare at me as if connected to one long string.

Daoman is in his throne-like chair near the center of the dais, resplendent as always, speaking to a middle-aged woman in fine robes. His gaze flies up to land on me, and he rises to his feet and spreads his arms in a gesture of thanks and greeting. "Divine One!" he calls in ringing tones. "Thank the prophecies, you have returned to us. We feared the worst."

The woman he's speaking to turns, and I have only a moment to notice the strips of gray silk tied like armbands just below her shoulders. Her eyes meet mine briefly before she's turning away, melting back into the crowd.

In front of so many onlookers, I can't demand an explanation. I can't reveal any insecurity or fear, or alert the spectators if there's any chance they didn't notice what I did: that my high priest was speaking to a Graycloak.

The heads follow me as I stride up the corridor lined with flowers and braziers thickening the air with incense. The chamber is filled with saffron-robed priests, with visiting dignitaries and their retinues bearing the colors and heraldry of their regions, with the members of the Congress of Elders glittering with gold and jewels.

Daoman leans over in an elaborate bow as I approach. His eyes leave my face only for the barest second, however, before he's watching me again.

In the past, as a child, I was more than content for the high priest to run this temple and see to the needs of my people. I never knew a father, except for this man before me, and the older and lonelier I became, the more he would remind me that if I could not play with the other children, could not laugh and talk with my handservants as if they were my friends, it was because I was special.

Special. Chosen. *Divine*, he would say, a light in his dark blue eyes that sparked some light in me, brought it out from beneath the layers of sadness and isolation.

But with each year that passes, with each step I try to take beyond the walls of this temple and each word I voice in opposition to his decrees, I see a little more. I see that there is a tension between us—that there always has been. That as long as I never manifest my aspect, never rise to my full divinity and command the absolute loyalty of my priests and my people, *he* is the one who has the power.

Now, as I give him no flicker of reaction to read, I sense it all the more. For a man like Daoman, power is absolute, or it is nothing. This chamber, his greeting, the audience packed into its walls like fish in a salting barrel—it's all staged.

I give him a gracious nod as he straightens from his bow. "Of course I have returned to you," I reply, echoing his words. "Did you doubt that I would?"

Daoman's brow furrows, and the glint in his eye softens. "Then . . . you do not know?" My face must give something away, some glimmer of the sudden fear that seizes me—has something happened here too?—because the high priest is uncharacteristically quick to add, "One of your guards arrived just this morning, Divine One, and brought word of what happened. Elkisa believed she was the only survivor."

Now my face gives everything away. I have to grip my spearstaff, its end planted firmly on the stone, to keep my knees from buckling, earning me an inquisitive chirp from the cat beside me. "Elkisa—she's alive?" The words are a whisper, relief building behind some dam of disbelief, of fearing to hope.

"She is," Daoman replies. His voice is quieter now, and dimly I hear the soft lapping of hushed conversation as those at the back of the chamber try to find out what's being said. "She was looking for you at the time of the attack—she said you had gone for a walk. She searched for you, but could not find you. . . ."

To wipe away the tears in my eyes would be to betray their

presence to those behind me—so Daoman, and only he, can see them glimmering there in my lashes, turning every lamp and brazier into haloed stars. At my side, the bindle cat leans heavily against my leg, rumbling a slow, insistent purr.

The high priest takes a step down from the dais, although of course he does not approach me. "We must have you examined by a healer, Divine One."

I shake my head. "I am well. I had assistance on my travels."

Daoman's eyebrows rise. "Oh? There was another survivor among your guards? I knew you would not have been so foolish as to wander alone." His smile is thin, his eyes cool.

He knows about North already.

He knows it was no guard who escorted me back, that I did indeed leave the safety of camp alone. And he wants to force me to admit that in front of all my people, many of whom were involved in the decision not to grant me permission to leave the temple in the first place. Many of whom know I did so against the high priest's orders.

I smile back at Daoman. "Surely you do not think only my guards would be concerned for my safety?" The murmuring behind me is growing louder, as it always does in a crowd this size—one person speaking makes another feel safe to do so, and another, and on and on until soon I won't be able to hear my own thoughts.

"Come," I say, cutting off whatever the high priest would have said, and stepping past him toward the inner sanctum beyond the audience chamber. Here, in front of all these witnesses, I can get away with such peremptory behavior. In private . . . in private, the dance is far more delicate. "I will tell you what you wish to know."

Daoman has no choice but to bow low as I pass, and then, with a few muttered words to those priests nearest him, he follows me through the filmy curtains, and then the thick, gilded door.

No sooner do the doors close behind us than the high priest strides past me. "Divine One," he says, voice pitched now for the quieter conversation between two people rather than a performed one in front of a crowd. "Please sit, rest. Allow me to prepare you a drink while you tell me about your . . . adventure."

I ignore the loaded pause before that final word and make my way to one of the low divans that surround the bright, mosaic-tiled table around which I've spent so many years learning from—and arguing with—Daoman. The moment I sink down onto the deep blue cushion, the cat jumps up beside me and drapes himself over my thigh, kneading at my other leg with vigor.

I ought to refuse Daoman's tonic, ought to maintain my aura of strength and calm—I ought to keep playing the game. But I'm tired, and grief and joy are tangled in my heart because Elkisa is alive—and the others are still dead. And so I let my shoulders sag, and I lean my spearstaff against the arm of the divan, and I heave a sigh as I curl my fingers through the bindle cat's long, silky fur.

"Who were you speaking to, Daoman?" My voice is low, but the words are anything but soft. When I lift my head, his hands have stopped moving, long fingers resting on the stopper of a decanter.

"Divine One?" He glances over his shoulder, but something

about my face must tell him there's no use feigning ignorance. He sighs. "They grow bolder, the Graycloaks. She was here to ask about creating an experimental Haven, now you were . . ." The decanter stopper rattles, and he turns back to frown at it as if in chastisement for betraying the tremor in his hand.

"They wasted little time," I mutter. "How many hours since they first believed I was dead?"

He begins moving again, pulling down a finely cut crystal glass and a number of different bottles and jars. "There was little time to waste," he replies finally, his voice even and remote. "From their view. With the mist-storms increasing in violence and frequency, how could your people survive during the years it would take to locate your successor?"

I stroke the bindle cat again, and he tenses as though I've pressed too hard. "So they wish to create a city where no magic, not even divine magic, can enter—because better to live without magic than to live with the mist. I assume you told their emissary how foolish that would be."

Daoman lets out a dry breath, a distant, sour relative of laugher. "Divine One, I did not get the impression she was asking me for permission."

I frown at him. "How do they intend to locate enough sky-steel to construct such a place without the temple's reserves?"

"By destroying a guardian stone and smelting the steel from its remains."

The words are even and calm, but my heart gives a lurch as he speaks. "And leave an entire village with no protection against the mist?"

"They believe it better a privileged few should survive, in these Havens of theirs, than we all fall without the light of the divine." A bottle clinks loudly, his movements a little too hasty, a little too jerky.

I hesitate, the horror of what the Graycloaks plan to do fading a little as realization strikes me. He believed, however briefly, that I was dead.

"I know you are angry with me, Daoman," I murmur. "But I brought this matter before you and the Congress of Elders more than once. I *had* to go, with your support or without."

Daoman's hands still, and he bows his head a moment. "And how many people are dead now because of your decision? How much clearer is it to the people that we cannot control the Cult of the Deathless, because you decided you didn't need my support?"

I straighten in my seat. "How many of them would still be alive if you *had* supported me?"

Daoman dashes something from a bottle into the cup, and then slams it back down on the cabinet's surface in an uncharacteristic display of temper that makes me jump in spite of myself. The bindle cat's claws come out, just pricking against my skin, his eyes going wide as he turns his head toward the priest.

His voice is taut and thin as he says, slowly, "How many new Graycloaks were forged today, do you think? Because they believed this cult of zealots could murder their divinity, because they believed they had no other recourse than to flee faith altogether and banish magic from their lives? Your mortality is what frightens them."

And you, I think, although I do not say the words aloud.

I draw a steadying breath instead. "*You* made it sound in your reports as though the Deathless were nothing, just a handful of madmen hiding in the darkest corners of the forest-sea, where they could do little harm."

Daoman reaches for a pitcher of water with which to dilute the tonic, and then turns, goblet in hand. "Many a creature is harmless unless and until one strolls into its den."

"Why did you not *tell* me how it really was out there?" I concentrate on keeping my hands quiet in my lap, instead of balling them into fists.

Daoman approaches, placing the goblet on a silver tray so that I can take it without risking touching his fingers. The cat swipes a paw at it, but the priest moves the tray out of the way with the ease of long practice.

He inclines his head as I take the glass, as if I'm doing him some great favor by accepting the drink. "We have been dealing with the problem, Divine One. Delicately. Drawing attention to it benefits no one."

I clutch the goblet, grateful to have something with which to occupy my hands. "I should have been made aware. Had I known . . ."

Daoman's lips give a wry twist, the first sign of a thawing of his fury. "It never occurred to me that you would go on your own, Nimh." The use of my name is a rarity these days. This time, it is a signal to lay down arms and call a truce.

I take a cautious sip from the goblet. For the most part, Daoman's tinctures are quite tasty, although now and then they go down bitter and burning. I wouldn't put it past him to make this one particularly nasty, as partial punishment for my recklessness. To my surprise, it is sweet and fragrant, smelling of serra buds and batala, and other herbs I have no hope of identifying.

Daoman seats himself opposite me, his posture mirroring my own, though his hands clasp in his lap rather than around the stem of a glass.

I know what he's waiting for, and after another swallow of my drink, I draw a slow, careful breath. "I was right," I say softly, keeping my voice as low as I can. This ancient temple is a honeycomb of secret passages and hidden spaces in the walls—a spy's dream. Even I don't know all its secrets. "I was right to go, Daoman."

The high priest's eyebrows shoot up. "You—what?"

Any other day, I'd be delighted to have surprised him. But what I have to tell him is too important. "I saw the Last Star, the omen described in the Song of the Destroyer and countless other prophecies—including the lost stanza from my vision."

"Your *dream*," Daoman corrects me, his brows lowering again in a frown.

"It was no dream then, and it was no dream last night, when I saw the Last Star fall. I saw it, Daoman—the herald of the Lightbringer himself."

Daoman goes very, very still. "How can you be sure?"

I school my features—for the truth is that I can't be sure *what* I saw, or found, except that North is important, and it was my destiny to find him. "Many of our prophecies speak of the Last Star, but my lost stanza told me where to find it, and it was *right*, Daoman. I am sure of what I found. Or do you doubt the power of the divine?"

It's often struck me that Daoman would have made a better politician than a priest—I've wondered more than once just how deeply his faith runs. But he looks shaken, his long face grave. "Tell me what happened. Are you saying . . . Do you believe the end of days is approaching? That you will be the last . . ."

The last goddess? And you the last high priest?

I smile a thin, weary smile. "I will tell you what I found when I have had time to consider all that I have seen. You of all people know that prophecy is never straightforward—I must study, and meditate, and put the pieces together."

Daoman's eyes have lost a little of their focus, a habit he has when his thoughts are racing ahead beyond the conversation at hand. "A pity," he murmurs, "that no one was with you to bear witness."

My lips tighten, and I place the half-drunk goblet on the low table before me with a thunk. The bindle cat's purr stops, and he fixes the priest with a level, steady stare. "You would accuse your goddess of lying?"

Daoman blinks, gaze finding mine again. "Of course not, Divine One." He inclines his head, spreading his hands in a seated bow. "I was thinking only of the challenges to come. A witness would be useful for sharing this news with your people." A pause. "Though you may wish to wait to share it until you know what it means."

For that, I give him a little smile, though even I can tell

169

how weary it must look. "You will notice I did not exactly stride through the streets declaring that the end of days has come. As I said, I will need to study and consider all that has happened. I must consult the Song again—the copy that my vision led me to find."

Daoman's eyes are suddenly hooded, and he leans back on the divan, long fingertips steepled together. "Ah," he says, and the pause that follows that single word sparks an inexplicable tension in my heart. "Divine One . . . I had hoped this could wait until you had rested, until after the Feast of the Dying."

"You hoped *what* could wait?" My voice is sharp, and I lean forward, using the very tactics of body language I learned from him. He leans back—and I press my advantage. "What has happened?"

Daoman is quiet. "The scroll you found is gone, Divinity."

Blood roaring in my ears, I reach out to grasp the arm of my divan. "*How?* How could this happen . . . ?" My voice trails off as I focus once more upon Daoman's long features.

The empty one will keep the star as a brand against the darkness, and only in that glow will the Lightbringer look upon this page and know himself. . . .

I know the words of the stanza from my vision by heart. But its implication, that the Lightbringer would awaken and learn his purpose upon reading that ancient scroll . . .

I needed to show that scroll to North, to see if he experienced a vision like my own—an awakening to his destiny. To *know*, one way or another, who he is—and if he is to remake the world with me.

"Matias alerted me to its absence only hours ago." The high priest's gaze drops, eyes falling on the crystal goblet as if he were wishing he had some of his own calming tincture. "Nothing else appears to be missing, but the scroll you believe to contain lost pieces of the Song of the Destroyer . . . it is gone."

To his credit, his voice carries what sounds like genuine regret. For a man who stoutly denied the significance of my vision, fought against my acting upon the prophecy contained therein, and would have probably very much liked to have gotten rid of the scroll himself . . . he sounds sorry.

But then . . . Daoman can sound however he wishes. Priest or politician, never have I met a better actor. A better liar.

There is one man who would lose everything, were I to discover my divine purpose and take my place at the head of our faith.

When he looks back up, he lets me catch his gaze with no sign of guilt—but then, he would show none. His eyes are sympathetic—but then, they would be. He looks exactly as he should: worried for me and for our shared faith; relieved that I am home and safe; regretful for not trusting my divine instincts and better guarding what I believed to be the most significant text of this age.

Daoman. We both know what is coming—that the shift in power between us is inevitable. Technically we are allies, but more than that, I am the closest thing he has, or ever will have, to a daughter. It happened slowly, this growing tension, so slowly that for years I could not tell the difference between the rebellion of someone taking her first steps out of childhood, and the assertion of my power as his eventual superior.

Someday, I know, my high priest—my oldest caretaker, my father—and I will be enemies until one of us emerges the victor. *But is that day today?*

Perhaps it's Daoman's tincture, or the fact that I'm finally home again after such fear and grief, or that I cannot face the truth of the scroll's loss or know what to do next without prophetic guidance—but suddenly I feel as though I cannot keep my eyes open. Blinking hard, I lean forward, forgetting for the moment the gathering tension between my priest and me, the slow and inexorable reversal of power between us. For the moment I am his charge again, just a child, waiting to be dismissed. "Oh, Daoman, can I not go see Elkisa? If she was wounded, I might be able to help. She has been one of my closest companions, and I thought she had been . . ." My voice stops short in my tightening throat.

Daoman's lips shift, then curve into a smile. "Of course," he says gently. "You may do exactly as you wish, Divine One. She is likely still with the healers. I hope, however, that once you have seen her, you will sleep. Choosing to leave so close to the Feast of the Dying was a risky choice—I can only hope you are right. Either way, though, you must rest before the feast."

The thought of presiding over such a long, complex ritual right now makes me want to groan, but I know that rest and food will restore me. This, after all, is my purpose—until I can unravel the truth about the rest of my destiny.

I give the bindle cat a stroke down to his tail, a longtime signal that I'm about to move, and he jumps to the floor graciously. When I rise, however, the high priest clears his throat.

"Divine One, before you go . . . ?"

"Yes, Daoman?"

"The boy—the one who accompanied you through the forest-sea, and who has been given lodging here in the temple—who is he?"

I reach for my spearstaff, using that extra time to gather my thoughts. "A friend, I think. At the very least, he could have left me there alone, but chose to brave the dangers of being caught at my side by the Deathless."

The golden-robed priest regards me evenly. "I see. And how long do you intend for him to reside here?"

Did Daoman take the scroll with the lost stanza? I cannot know by looking at him. I cannot tell if he knows I came back not with some talisman or jewel—that the Last Star was not some astronomical sign but rather the fall of a human boy. Has he made that vital connection, realizing that all I brought back with me was . . . North? Can he have guessed at his identity in our prophecies, the way I did?

I am sure of what I found, I said to him a few minutes ago. I should have stayed silent. I cannot know what the words meant to him.

I sigh, letting a bit of weary irritation flicker in the sound. "I cannot think about that now. Tomorrow, Daoman—tomorrow

I will think how to reward him for his service. For now, I have other things on my mind."

Daoman inclines his head, gesturing for the rather less ornate door that leads not into the audience chamber, but back into the private parts of the temple, through my own corridors. "Rest well, child," he murmurs.

I can feel his eyes on me, a heavy weight in between my shoulder blades, until the door swings closed again. In the privacy of my own corridor—there are walkways through the temple that only I am allowed to use—I allow myself to give a little shiver.

Scooping up the bindle cat and slinging him over my shoulder, letting his reverberant purr ground me, I make my way down toward the healers' wing of the temple.

My mind wanders on the journey.

I cannot say for certain why I didn't tell Daoman about North. I don't want to believe that my high priest, the man who raised me, could have stolen the scroll, but either way he ought to know what I know about North.

A cloudlander . . . the first we've seen in centuries.

The high priest would consider him a valuable object for study, even if he proves to have nothing to do with my prophecy.

Daoman would never let North leave.

But isn't that exactly why you *brought him here? To make sure he's close at hand if you need him? Didn't you yourself think that you couldn't let him leave?*

The bindle cat gives a faint yowl of protest, his claws digging gently into my shoulder blades. I'd been squeezing him—I let my arms relax with an effort. The bindle cat jumps lightly to the marble floor and gives himself a quick little groom, eyeing me crankily. I stoop, apologizing in a low voice, and he waits only a breath or two before butting his head against my chin.

I do desperately want to see Elkisa, and I quicken my steps at the thought. But as soon as I've seen her for myself, reminded myself she's alive and she's real and she's here, I know who I must see.

Say nothing, North. Wait for me.

TWELVE
NORTH

I've been cooling my heels for about an hour in this waiting room. I've already walked a dozen circuits of it, counted the ceiling tiles, composed frustrated speeches to Nimh in my head. It's not hard, given that *there's a life-size statue of her standing right there in the corner.*

She stands between two gorgeous tapestries, wearing her circlet crown on her head and a serene expression, her hands lifted toward me as if she's offering me one of the blessings her people called out for as we walked toward the temple.

The statue is beautiful, of course, but it's also very . . . Official Portrait. This is the formal version of Nimh, The Goddess. The stonework could never capture her expressive mouth, the twist of her lips when she's thinking, the way she tilts her head when she's trying to figure something out.

Still, I feel like asking the statue if it would like to fill in a few of the gaps in my information, because the list of stuff its flesh-and-blood counterpart didn't tell me is beginning to seem pretty staggering.

This has gone so far beyond the edge, I want to tell it, feeling my jaw tighten.

I mean, *I* don't even get statues at home, and I'm a prince. Just saying.

The statue sums up my problem, though, mute as it is. Nimh kept a lot from me, and what I don't know is why. I thought we were trusting each other—after what we just went through. I thought she wanted to help me.

But *does* she want to help me? Even more important, *can* she help me? If she's the closest they've got to a mechanic and she doesn't know what an engine is, then she's not the answer I'm looking for.

Which means I need to find another way out of this mess. I've been here less than a day, and I've already nearly died three or four times. I have to find a way home, and as soon as I can.

The archives she mentioned feel like my best bet, but do I have any hope of searching a place like this for what I need? Saelis would know where to look. I'd give about anything to have him with me right now.

I try for a deeper, slower breath and look down at my chrono again, turning over my wrist and studying the display. I do it out of habit—it's still not offering anything other than its off-line functions. I can see my bio readings are all still elevated, which is no surprise. I can read the time, and not much else.

I'm about to start counting the tiles again when the door swings halfway open. The woman standing in the doorway is a solemn-faced guard clad in black and gold, her dark braids drawn back from her face, with cheekbones you could cut yourself on. She's strong too, muscles showing on her bare arms. Nimh seemed pretty quick with her spear thing, and she certainly handled those cultists in the forest, but I'm pretty sure this woman could snap me in half without breaking a sweat. Her light brown face is littered with a constellation of freckles, the only thing about her that's not perfectly ordered.

But when she smiles, she's suddenly much more human. "I'm here to take you to guest quarters," she says. "You can wash there, change your clothes."

This is my chance. I cast a farewell glance at my giant Nimh statue—*wish me luck*—and risk a smile in return. "Actually," I say, walking toward the door, turning on my princely charm despite the fact that I'm completely filthy, "I was wondering if you could show me where the archives are. Ni—the Divine. One told me they're very impressive. I'm dying to see them." *Or rather, I'll die here if I don't get to see them.*

She studies me for a moment, considering this. "You do not wish to eat first?"

My stomach tries to turn itself inside out in response. *Yes!* it yells. *Yes, feed me!*

"I can wait to eat," I reply.

She inclines her head. "This way, then. My name is Elkisa."

"North," I offer in return.

"Your accent's strange, North," she says, studying me sidelong. Waiting for me to fill in the blanks.

"You think?" I reply, all innocence, shifting the topic. "So you work for the housekeeping team?" Her uniform is the same as those of the guards I saw before—if she's anything like the security team at home, that question ought to divert her away from who I am. I'm far more interested in who *she* is.

She shoots me a sharp look. "I am one of the Divine One's personal guards," she replies, turning a corner with precision. "I volunteered to escort you."

"Then I owe you." I try to keep my tone light, as if I'm not relieved someone actually came to get me out of that place. "There were only so many laps of that room I could walk."

"I am the one who owes you a debt," she replies. There's an intensity in her face that sobers me. She clears her throat. "You escorted her home safely, when we had failed. I wanted to meet you."

She cares deeply for Nimh. That much is clear. "I'm generally less impressive in person," I reply, fishing for another smile. I could use allies right now, and something tells me she might be one, if I play this right.

She opens a tall wooden door, pushing it inward and gesturing for me to walk through ahead of her.

I make it exactly three steps before I slow to a halt, my brain shorting out. The archives are like nothing I've ever seen. Vaulted ceilings soar at least three stories up into the air, lined with intricately crisscrossed brick patterns. The shelves run almost as high, wheeled ladders positioned along them at intervals so the archive workers can climb up to access the shelves upon shelves upon *shelves* of books and scrolls. Stained glass windows dye the top levels green and blue and gold, and lower down there are lamps at the end of every aisle, puncturing the darker shadows.

I've been comparing this world to home, counting the tech they don't have, but this place would give any room in the palace a run for its money.

Vast was underselling it.

My mouth falls open, and a beat too late I snap it shut again, trying to smooth out my expression, hide my hope.

Elkisa steps around me, her footsteps echoing as she makes her way up the central walkway, and I scurry along behind her. Finding a single technical manual among all these texts could be the work of a lifetime.

She halts at a desk just a little way in, where an old man with a shock of white hair, wire-rimmed glasses, and a face the same color and wrinkled texture of a walnut sits scowling up at us.

"Matias, this is the Divine One's new guest," Elkisa says. And then to me: "I'll be outside when you're ready for that bath."

She turns for the door, leaving me alone with the old man. He adjusts his glasses and looks me up and down. What he makes of my filthy clothes, bandaged arm, and dirty face, I can't imagine.

"Well," he says eventually, just as I'm reminding myself not to shift my weight like a fidgety student. "You're the talk of the temple, lad."

"North, sir." I nod at him, uncertain about the protocol.

"You have a familiar air about you, North." Matias's eyes narrow a fraction, his expression thoughtful for a long moment before it clears. "I hear we have you to thank for bringing the Divine One home safely."

I resist the urge to correct him. "She said I might use these resources to do some research?"

"A scholar, hmm?" His white eyebrows rise as he looks me over a second time. "And such an eager one that you don't stop to rest before seeking out the library. Tell me what you're looking for, and I will do my best to assist you."

Though the words are welcome, the tone is proprietary— these are *his* books, at least in his mind. I take a steadying breath. "N—the Divine One said there were documents here on flight."

Matias is already turning toward the shelves when he pauses and glances back at me. "Can you be more specific, lad? Poetry, fiction, theology . . . ?"

"Machinery." The word slips out before I can stop it, and when Matias's face doesn't change, I add, "I'm studying ways to make machines that can fly. The ancients could do it."

"So they could," he agrees. "But we cannot. Why do you search?"

"I just think the machinery is interesting," I say. "Have you ever seen any records on how they did it? Flew, I mean?"

The Master of Archives is still for so long that I start to wonder if he's forgotten the question. Then he turns and sinks slowly back down into the chair at his desk and fixes me with a steady gaze. "Where did you say you were from, North?"

Skyfall. I should've kept my mouth shut.

"I didn't say, sir."

Matias watches me for some time, then says softly, "So our

181

Nimh did find something out there after all." His eyes are sharp and keen behind his glasses.

It's the first time I've heard anyone call her by the name she gave me, instead of "Divine One" or something like it. Maybe that gleam in the archivist's eye is a sign of fondness for her— maybe they're friends. Maybe I can trust him. Maybe . . .

Matias clears his throat, and I jump a little. "I'll see what I can find for you," he says.

"I'd be grateful," I reply, injecting every ounce of sincerity I have into my tone. "In the meantime, Nimh also thought there might be something you could find on the myth of the Sentinels?"

His brows lift. "The Sentinels?" he repeats. "Perhaps we have a book of children's tales. The riverstriders and their Fisher King have kept that tale alive, but that's the only life there is to be found in it."

I force myself to take a slow breath to hide the sinking feeling of disappointment. If this man runs a library of this size, and he says there's nothing suggesting the Sentinels left behind any hint of how they guarded the way between worlds, then either they never existed, or they're so long gone they're lost to memory.

"Perhaps there will be something on flight," he says, his tone comforting. "In the meantime, I imagine Nimh would prefer you keep a low profile. Probably best if you don't wander around looking like you came out the wrong side of a battle."

I hesitate, caught between my instinct to trust this man and Nimh's warnings to say nothing at all.

I'm so utterly out of my own skies here.

Matias sifts through the stacks of paper and scrolls on his desk. With a little grunt of satisfaction, he finally locates what he's looking for—a cup—and takes a long sip from it. Then he speaks again.

"You made quite the entrance into the city today," he observes. "The goddess returning home with her mysterious companion. I wonder, are our traditions very different to those in the cloudlands?"

"I—ah—uh—" I'm caught speechless. It's one thing for us to dance around what he's worked out. It's another to say it out loud. Thankfully, he doesn't seem to need a reply.

"What you must understand about Nimh," he continues, "is that she was called by the priesthood when she was five years old. When the divinity's human vessel dies, the priesthood packs up and spreads out like so many ants evacuating a hirta tree, crawling into every nook and cranny, up and down every river, looking for the new vessel. Usually, they find a child just shy of the transition to adulthood—Nimh is the youngest ever called to become the Divine One."

"Five years old," I echo. I remember myself at that age, my mothers bribing me to stand still at important ceremonies, my grandfather solemnly winking at me from beneath his crown. I was surrounded by family, and all I had to do was avoid spilling food all over myself. I can't imagine having to try to *lead* at that age.

"Five years old," he repeats. "So that is the first basis of her difficulties. The second is that within a few years of their calling, our divinities usually manifest their aspect—this is the area in which they can perform great magic. Their aspect sets the tone for the world during their time at the head of it. War, peace, famine, feast."

"What's Nimh's . . . aspect?" I try the word out slowly.

"Ah," he says quietly. "That, we do not know. It has not yet revealed itself, though we have waited more than ten years."

"Perhaps it's an age thing," I suggest. "Everyone else manifests theirs soon after they show up, but they're older to begin with."

"Perhaps," he agrees, in a tone that doesn't agree at all. "Or perhaps her fate will take another path. Some doubt her. You may have seen them in the city." His voice dips into derision. "They wear gray as a sort of uniform, a statement against the richness of magic and faith."

"I've seen them." My voice is grimmer than I meant it to be. "Are they connected to the ones who attacked us? Attacked her, I mean?"

Matias shakes his head. "No. They would never act so openly against her. Your attackers were cultists who follow a false deity, who seek to kill Nimh. The Graycloaks merely want to remove her from power, believing that her lack of aspect means that divinity itself has left this world. But others . . . others wonder if hers will be a magic unlike any we have seen before. If this is the calm before the storm."

"So . . . your deities are the ones who can do, uh, magic?" I try to keep the skepticism out of my voice, but it's hard to say the word *magic* with a straight face.

Matias's bushy eyebrows go up, a few scraggly hairs sticking out like antennae. "There are many who can use magic, cloudlander—magicians are not uncommon; there are usually one or two even in the smaller towns and villages. The Divine One is far more than a mere magician."

"Her aspect will show up. If it's always happened before, it'll happen now," I say, wondering how I got to a place where I'm telling someone *magic will happen*. And am I defending Nimh, despite the secrets she kept?

Matias sighs. "So we must hope. Because while Nimhara is powerful, she will be even more so when she manifests. Our people need the change her aspect will bring. They need the hope. And they need the gifts she will master. They need what she will become."

"So she could be . . . what? What was the last god like?"

"The deity before Nimh was Jezara," the old man says. "She manifested as the goddess of healing. Her light could ease any illness or wound."

I wish I knew what that really meant. Did she study medicine? Did she use her skills to prevent disease? Or do they believe she could heal with just her presence?

"And when she died, the priests found Nimh." I falter at the sight of his expression. "No?"

Matias's lips are tight. "Jezara was the only goddess whose divinity passed from her before death."

Silence. "I don't know what that means," I confess.

"It is not for me to discuss. I did not write the sacred texts," he says, in a tone that reminds me of my bloodmother saying, *I don't make the rules, North.* I've always wanted to point out to her that she could if she wanted, but now, as always in this moment, I hold my tongue.

"That's enough for now," he says abruptly. "Go; I'll see what I can find."

It's an abrupt dismissal, but his gaze is fixed over my shoulder, and when I twist in my chair there's a man speaking with Elkisa, who stands in the open doorway, arms folded, with an expression that says, *This should be good.*

I thought she had left—how much did she overhear of my conversation with the Master of Archives?

Nimh trusts her guards. Does that mean I should too?

The newcomer is a bronze-skinned man with a beaky nose, a shaved head, and a mouth made for smirking. I mistrust him the second I see him, and not just because Matias shut up the moment he arrived. Whatever he says to Elkisa makes her stiffen, glance my way, and then vanish from the doorway, her steps hurried.

"Forgive me, forgive me," the new arrival says as he turns to approach. He shows me his teeth—which isn't the same as smiling. "I do hope I'm not interrupting. I am Techeki, the Master of Spectacle." I can hear the capital letters in that title—he practically pronounces them.

"How could you be interrupting?" Matias asks, his tone a lot less polite than his words. "You're always exactly where you mean to be, Techeki."

"And you must be our visitor," the Master of Spectacle says, ignoring his reply and turning to me. "I apologize for failing to meet you earlier; I was told you would be taken straight to guest quarters. Matias, you really should have let him clean himself up before you started talking his ear off."

"Is he dirty?" Matias asks blandly, looking me over as if he hadn't noticed until now.

I know all the words to this song—I've spent my life surrounded by the political games of the palace, and every instinct I have is informing me that I'm in the middle of one of those games right now. I don't want to become a pawn in what's obviously an old argument—if that happens, one of them might squish me just to annoy the other—so I come politely to my feet.

"A bath sounds great, actually," I say. "If it wouldn't be too much trouble."

Techeki considers the request, looking across at Matias as if he's deciding whether to really get into it with him, and then turns away, stalking toward the door. "Come!" he says, without looking back. I glance at Matias, who winks and gestures for me to follow him.

Swallowing the rest of my questions, I follow the oily-mannered man from the library. Despite being a head taller than Techeki, I somehow have to hurry to keep up with him as he glides along the hallway.

The room he takes me to is small but neat—it's got no windows but plenty of lamps and rich tapestries on the walls, a pile of clothes in different fabrics and colors on a bed.

"There will only be time for you to wash your hands and face," he informs me. "The feast will begin soon, and I have much to do. We must dress you appropriately. I have provided what you will need, as well as a meal. I hope these quarters will serve."

He clearly knows the room isn't humble at all, and is awaiting something—a thank-you, or for me to stare at it all in amazement or brush it off like it's nothing. He's trying to figure me out, so I stick to a polite smile.

Venturing into the washroom, I pull my shirt off over my head, then ease the knot of my makeshift bandage down until I can slip the whole thing off my arm. I hadn't even realized I was afraid to look at it. But surprised relief washes over me—the gash I sustained in the glider crash is now just a thin burn line. I test the edges of the skin and find only a dull ache, so I toss the ruined scarf into the corner.

Whatever Nimh used to cauterize it must have also contained something that speeds the healing process—I would've maybe preferred the royal surgeon's neat stitches, but I can't complain about Nimh's results.

A lever turns out to release a steady stream of water from a spout built into the wall above the sink, and I soak the cloth beside it, using it to scrub at my exposed skin as quickly as I can. There's a vivid line of bruising across my ribs, an angry, purplish-gray stripe underlining the tattoo my mothers disapproved of. It's my family crest, and for a moment, I wish the wings to either side of the sky-island were real, were mine. I wish they could carry me away from here.

But the water is bitingly cold and doesn't leave room for daydreams. I wouldn't want to linger over the "bath" anyway—it's approaching sunset now, and I haven't slept since yesterday morning.

I try to order my thoughts as the cold water hits my skin, and by the time I walk out to where Techeki waits, I've got my game face on.

"Sit a moment," he says, indicating the table. "Refresh yourself."

It's nicer than he's been so far, and I allow him to guide me to one of the chairs. He takes his place opposite me and pours from a decanter into two goblets.

I take mine, and after a moment I realize he's watching the way I hold it. *He's judging my manners.* He wants to know who I am. And Nimh's guidance didn't extend beyond *Tell them you helped me get home.* What would she want me to say? And what's best for me?

I wish I knew whether it was safer to be a helpful nobody or a noble guest. But I have no idea, and I also have a more urgent question on my mind: he's just swirling his drink around in the goblet, but he hasn't taken a sip—is it safe to drink? Am I being completely dramatic even wondering that? I've always been taught to be wary around unknown food and drink—though a tiny part of my mind notices I forgot those rules around Nimh.

Before I can decide what to do, he notices me noticing— and with a tiny little smile that I don't like very much, he lifts his drink to take a long, deliberate sip, swallowing as he lowers it. *See?* his gaze says smugly. *Safe.*

But it says more than that—he's smug because he knows

that you don't get instincts like mine drilled into you unless you're somebody. I've told him something I didn't mean to, and I could kick myself.

This guy is a player. He'd get on well with my bloodmother.

"Thank you," I say eventually—polite, but not too gushing. I don't want to give the impression I owe him anything, if I can help it.

He takes my words as a signal to resume conversation. "We must select clothes for you for the Feast of the Dying."

He speaks as if I know what that is, and I don't correct him. I assume the feast won't involve any actual dying on my part, given Nimh could have organized that already if she wanted, and nod. "I'm honored to be attending."

"Of course," he agrees. "I am eager to ensure we follow the correct protocol for such an esteemed guest, to whom we owe such a debt of gratitude. Please, tell me about yourself."

He says it so smoothly, as if the question is nothing. As if he isn't trying to slot me into a hierarchy—figure out what value I hold for him and everyone else in the temple. *Oh, old man. You have no idea whose student you're dealing with.*

I blink slowly and take my time swallowing. "About myself?" I ask, as if I barely know my own name.

"Where are you *from?*" he says, practically clicking his tongue now. "I am asking about your people, your home."

"Oh," I say, as if I understand, then proceed to completely fail to answer the question. "I just helped her make her way safely home."

He closes his eyes for a long moment, takes a breath, tries

again. "I am aware of what you have done," he says carefully. "I am asking who you *are*. I hope you are not evading the question."

Bold move, calling me out like that, but it tells me he probably doesn't think I'm powerful. I can see him trying to decide whether I'm a player or a game piece. He's leaning toward writing me off, but he definitely hasn't made that call just yet. He's too wily.

Nimh's voice is in my head: *Tell them nothing.*

She's certainly mastered that.

There was such an intensity to her face when she first saw me in the wreckage of the *Skysinger,* and in her voice as she questioned me—I'm not convinced she brought me to this place solely for my own safety.

I *want* to put my faith in her. Out there in the wilderness, she seemed kind, and capable, and fascinating—and she seemed to be almost as fascinated by me. The little seeds of something—*friendship,* my mind supplies instantly—felt real. It felt true. Here, though, I'm adrift. I *want* to be able to trust this girl, but she's left me in the middle of a game without telling me anything about the board.

Nobody at home is looking for me—no one who falls Below ever returns. They're probably planning my memorial service right now.

If I'm ever going to make it back, I'll need to make it happen myself. So for now, I choose an answer that at least shouldn't screw with Nimh's plans.

"I'm a scholar," I say. When one of Techeki's impeccably groomed eyebrows rises, I add, "In training. I was traveling to the temple in the hopes of meeting with the Master of Archives when I came across N—the Divine One. That's why I hurried straight to the library when I arrived. I didn't think I had much of a chance of talking to him in person, so when the opportunity arose . . ." I trail off with the grin that usually gets me out of trouble with my heartmother.

Techeki doesn't look convinced. I don't know if that's because he doesn't buy my story, or because one doesn't simply ask to meet the Master of Archives. But eventually he inclines his head. "I will see to it that you are escorted to Matias in the archives tomorrow for further discussion."

The word *escorted* sounds an awful lot like I'm not allowed to leave this room without a guard. It sounds an awful lot like being a prisoner.

Nimh told me she'd keep me safe. But *safe* doesn't mean *free*. It doesn't mean *allowed to find a way home*.

For that, I can't rely on anyone but myself.

THIRTEEN

NIMH

I wish that I could pace—but even among my own servants and acolytes, I can't show such obvious signs of an unsettled heart. In such a public place as the healers' wing, I must be above such displays at all times.

It's only been a few minutes since I arrived to find that Elkisa wasn't here. Though the healers said she was relatively unharmed, I can't shake the need to see for myself. I'd been focusing so much on North and his significance, that I could not allow myself to stop and grieve for my friend. Now that I know she's alive . . .

I shift my weight, but catch myself before I can start a telltale restless step. Though I long to rush off in search of Elkisa, the best way to locate my guard is to use the temple's network of secret observers. I know who many of Techeki's informants are among my staff, and I've never tried to oust them. Better I know who to keep an eye on.

The Master of Spectacle may seem frivolous and shallow, but information is his trade—and I'm certain there are plenty of the temple staff who belong to him who even I don't know about.

Still, the healers' assistant I ordered to find Techeki gave me a startled look and a half-hearted protest before giving up and scurrying off to find his master. *Find out from Techeki where Elkisa is*, I told him. *Ask her to come to me here.*

I take a deep breath, fighting my own instincts—then, just as I am ready to search for my friend myself, footsteps echo in the corridor. I hurry forward, my heart speeding—

And I stop short.

Hiret.

The riverstrider stops at the sight of me as well, her expression blank. It took me a moment to recognize her, for her long braids are gone. Her hair is cropped close to her head now, the feathers that signified her bond with her husband absent. She looks ten years older. I know I should be the one to speak, to find some healing words to offer her—but I cannot take my eyes from her. She looks so different without her braids. So different, now that her husband is dead.

Dead because of me.

"Hiret," I manage. "I—"

"I came to ask the guard who survived if she would tell me where it happened." Hiret's voice is tightly controlled. "So I might retrieve their bodies."

The riverstriders have intricate burial rituals, each clan's traditions a little different from the others, but they all involve the river. I wonder if it would bring Hiret any comfort to know Capac and his brother died so close to the water.

Would it have comforted you?

"Your task." Hiret's voice shatters the silence, which I hadn't noticed until she spoke. "Did you accomplish what you needed to?"

I blink at her, feeling slow and stupid, pinned under her grief. "Task?"

Her expression flickers with pain, or anger. I'm not sure, just now, that there is any difference. "The reason you came to Quenti's that day in the market. The reason I sent my husband to aid you—the task you could not tell me about, but could ask my family to sacrifice themselves for."

Now that I've seen that crack in her blank expression, I cannot unsee the grief behind it. I cannot unhear how very close she is to the edge. My heart is sick and pounding.

I can only think of one thing to tell her: the truth.

"I do not know for certain, Hiret." I gulp a breath. "But I think so."

Hiret's eyes widen, her voice trembling. "You *think* so?"

"I will not lie to you," I tell her, my own eyes burning with unshed tears. "I wish I were certain. I wish I *did* know. But I swear to you, I *believe*. They died for something. I *had* to be there that night."

To find North.

Hiret's anger lingers, but she pauses, gaze raking across my face. Whatever she finds there makes her take a breath, her brow furrowing as her eyes slide past mine, focusing beyond me. "How disconcerting," she whispers. "To learn that your goddess has as much need of faith as you."

This time I don't hear the footsteps that herald a new arrival. It's not until someone clears her throat that I find Elkisa standing not far away, looking between us.

I wish that I could rush toward my friend and throw my arms around her. I wish I could take her hand, I wish I could fall down at her feet and apologize, I wish I could . . .

But our reunion cannot be that way. With the entire healing staff of the temple as witness, and the grief-stricken riverstrider at my side, I must remain the Divine One—and even if we were alone, I could not hug her, touch her, assure myself that she's real and safe.

"Divine One," Elkisa says, her voice taut. She must have heard of my return, for she doesn't look surprised—but her relief is there, all over her face. "The Master of Spectacle said you were looking for me." Her eyes shift toward Hiret, and she bows her head to the riverstrider in a gesture of grief and respect.

"Hiret," I manage, keeping my voice even. "This is Elkisa. She was with us on our journey."

Hiret presses her lips together hard and returns Elkisa's nod, and she speaks again in that low, controlled voice that tells me that something deep inside her wants to fly apart at the seams. "I would like to bring my husband and his brother home. Will you mark the place for us on a map?"

Elkisa hesitates, and I know she must see the same image I do every time she closes her eyes—the bodies swinging from the trees, twisting slowly, horrors half-hidden in the shadows. Perhaps, by now, the jungle has wrought yet more ills upon them.

Elkisa has a better mask than Hiret or I, though, and she

speaks calmly in reply. "We will bring them home for you, I give you my word. You should remember them as they were—the Divine One would not want you to see them as they died. Please, let my fellow guards and I serve you in this way."

Hiret hesitates and glances to me, and though inside I wonder why I couldn't have found words as graceful as Elkisa's, I nod slowly.

"We will send a party in the morning, Hiret."

For a moment, I think she really will fly apart—that her grief will find all the weak places in her, and she will burst out with tears, with blame and a stabbing finger. I have taken from her that which she loved most, I have tested her faith, and I have given her nothing more than *I think so* in return.

But she simply nods once more, and turns wordlessly to walk from the room, leaving me alone with the only one of my party who didn't sacrifice everything for me. Silence stretches long, and then Elkisa sinks slowly to one knee, reaffirming her loyalty with that simple gesture. My throat tightens.

I was the one who took them all there. I was the one who insisted on walking alone. I was the one who left them to face the cultists without my protection, and left Elkisa to make her own way back, believing I had died, and she had failed.

"Had they been given the choice, they would all have gladly died for you, Divine One," she says quietly, as if reading my mind. "As would I."

And finally, tears spring to my eyes. Ignoring the presence of the healers and their acolytes, I drop to my own knees, making Elkisa look up in surprise.

Slowly, saying nothing, I lift my hand in my half of the old, seldom-used gesture of warmth and friendship. Elkisa swallows, her blue eyes meeting my gaze finally, and in that moment her resolve crumbles. She lifts her hand too, holding her palm outward, a breath away from mine. It's a gesture of absolute trust and faith—for should she wish to, she could tip her fingers forward and touch me, ending my life as a divine being forever.

"They did not die for nothing," I say, my voice no more than a breath. "I was right." More than anyone, I need Elkisa to understand this.

Her eyes widen, and her own voice drops to a murmur. "I have met the boy who came back with you. . . ." She trails off, a thousand questions in her gaze.

I nod, resisting the urge to look around to see if we're being observed. Instead, I keep my words vague. "He is important, El. If I am right about him, then perhaps my purpose lies clear ahead of me. Perhaps it is greater than we dared imagine."

I see the moment she wonders if I could be speaking of the one we have waited for these many centuries.

Lightbringer.

Elkisa opens her mouth, but then freezes for a long moment until her hand begins to tremble. Rather than risk it brushing mine, she drops both to the floor and then up to cover her eyes, a salute of the deepest respect of the devout toward the divine.

"I will protect him as I would you, Divine One."

Moved by this display of her faith, I whisper a blessing, and ease back to rest on my heels.

"I will find a way to be worthy of your devotion," I say quietly. "I am sorry for what you have been through."

She looks up, and with a faint twist of a smile, she pulls us both back to normality. Once again, we are friends, rather than goddess and guard. "If you think you're going for a walk without me again, you are sorely mistaken," she says.

I am so very grateful for that smile, for even that small mercy. But the weight of all that has passed pushes down on me again, and I can do no more than nod in reply and then rise, turning to hurry from the infirmary.

The cat, who had been waiting for me at the doorway, spares not a glance for my guard as we leave her behind, and trots along at my side. He's never been very fond of Elkisa, in that endearing but inconvenient way that animals—and some people—have of displaying jealousy toward anyone their chosen person cares for.

As I make my way through the halls, navigating my way toward my quarters, unbidden, a face flashes before my eyes in the darkened corridors. A delicate, handsomely featured face with a sharp nose, warm brown eyes, and a smile far too charming for his own good.

Is North the answer? Can he be connected with the Lightbringer's coming—or could he be the Lightbringer himself?

My heart tells me with every beat that he *is*. I feel a strange, undeniable compulsion to believe that he and I were destined to meet. But does that mean I, with the weight of my divinity behind me, can see through to the truth of him? Or does it just mean that I am so weary of waiting, so desperate to find a way to help my people, that I'm seeing something that isn't there?

I've returned to the temple just in time—tonight is the Feast of the Dying, one of the most significant yearly rituals. I must begin preparing for my part in it. I have no time to see North.

But I ought to tell him. I ought to tell him everything.

Perhaps tonight, during the feast, I'll find a moment or two alone with him. And yet . . . I still hesitate.

Because right now, North is my secret, and mine alone.

Ruthlessly, I banish the little tendril of yearning to keep a secret that's mine, to discover the truth about him on my own. To discover *everything* about him on my own.

I steady myself and open the door to my quarters, a dozen attendants turning toward me and sinking as one to their knees, greeting their goddess.

There is no room, in a life like mine, for wanting.

FOURTEEN
NORTH

The celebration of the Feast of the Dying begins at sunset, a solemn ritual on a large terrace that overlooks the city. Nimh stands on a platform that raises her above the others, bathed in the dying light, her arms outstretched.

She's dressed in an exquisite robe of red silk, so fine it's just this side of sheer, the edges catching in the breeze and rippling around her like a living thing. She has golden bands around her wrists and upper arms that match the crown on her head, and golden paint around her kohl-lined eyes, across her cheekbones, and at her lips.

The light seems to caress her, intensifying around her, until she's glowing, brighter even than the glorious sunset spread out across the thick forest beyond the city.

Every face, even the sun's, seems to turn toward her.

Low drums beat out a deep bass. Chanting priests act as counterpoint to her ringing voice as she carries out the ritual. I learned as I waited quietly in my place among the crowd that the ritual is all about the approach of the solstice—they're farewelling the sun, acknowledging that the shortest days lie ahead.

In three days' time, Nimh will preside over another ritual that marks the end of mourning for the sun—the Vigil of the Rising—an all-night affair where they await the sun's rising as a symbol of hope in the coming months.

I wonder how much will happen here between now and then.

Nimh's voice dips into a rhythm that's nearly musical, her hands lifting, the sun glinting off the gold bands at her arms, and in this moment she *is* the sun, come down from the sky to shine warm upon our faces. I want to just surrender to the moment, to let the beauty of it—of *her*—sweep me away.

I want to be a part of this, to share it with everyone around me, to lose myself in the crowd. But I know I have to observe, to think. I can't afford to miss *anything* that could help me.

I make myself look at Nimh objectively. She has all the presence my mothers have tried for years to cultivate in me. She's regal, distant from all of us, but not remote. After my time with Elkisa, Matias, and Techeki, I was itching to see her again, to talk to her. But the girl I'm watching now seems impossibly far from the one I know.

Still, there are so many questions I want to ask her.

I want her to tell me why she led me here without admitting who she was. I want her to tell me what she thinks will become of me—why she didn't want me to tell anyone I'm a cloudlander. What danger lies in that. Who her allies are, and her enemies, and whether they're mine. Should I trust Matias, who seemed to care for her? Should I distrust Techeki because Matias does?

But it's a battle to look at this world from the outside when everything about the ceremony urges me to step inside instead.

The ritual ends with a sigh that seems to ripple out through the crowd, and as if on some unseen signal, the gravity of the moment is over. Servants begin to light torches against the growing dark, and I'm caught up in the river of humanity that streams into the temple for feasting and dancing.

Once the feast begins, it's harder and harder to remember there was ever any solemnity about this night at all. I'll say this for them: Nimh's people know how to party. I've thrown quite a few dusk-to-dawn blowouts in my time at the palace, and I like to think I'm pretty good at it, but I have to give credit where credit's due. Techeki has *earned* the title Master of Spectacle.

The place is a riot of color, food, and music, song and laughter echoing down at us from the ceiling tiles. I'm not quite a part of the celebration tonight. I'm dressed all in black—Techeki had no other option, given my unknown status here, but I can't pretend I don't envy the gold paint daubed on those around me. Back home, my face would be painted up with exquisite flash and glitter, my clothes shot through with gold. After all the time I've spent shedding it to make my escapes from the palace, it's ironic that I miss my golden thread. But I'm trying to keep myself a blank canvas, unknown to these people, so that Nimh and I can paint me with whatever pictures we want, and later on, whatever picture will get me home.

Also, I don't know the steps to any of their dances—literally or metaphorically.

I decline an invitation from a pretty girl who wants to draw me into the middle of the crowd, and another from a handsome boy with a head full of braids, who offers me a drink I can't identify. Shooting him a rueful grin, I slip around to the far side of a column. The architecture here is spectacular, and I tip my head back as though I'm admiring the mosaicked ceiling.

Then something bumps against my ankles, and when I look down, Nimh's cat is staring at me meaningfully.

"Where did you come from, Captain Fluffypants?" I ask, dropping to a crouch and offering him my finger to sniff. He reaches up to hook it with a paw, pulling it in closer. Then he very gently bites me—not hard enough to break the skin—and turns away, stalking off a few steps. He looks over his shoulder to see if I'm following.

I only met my first cat yesterday, but I'm already clear that it's better for everyone if I do what he wants. So I follow him around the edge of the room. Bordered by columns, the huge, circular chamber has six grand entrances, but we take none of them. Instead, he butts his head meaningfully against a service door, and when I open it for him, we both slip through.

The hallway waiting for us is empty of decoration and of people, but there's a lantern hanging on a nail, and I bring it with me to light our way. After a couple of minutes and a flight of stairs that takes me up a floor, the cat pauses at a section of the wooden paneling that looks no different to me from any other and makes a loud, talky sort of noise.

"Here?" I say, holding up my lantern to study it. I knock on the wooden panel.

Nimh's voice rings out from the other side, startling me. "Come in."

Only when the cat butts his head up against the wooden paneling do I see it give a fraction. When I push on it, a door swings open soundlessly to admit us. The room inside is carved from rock, and strings of glowing lights illuminate plants that tumble down from high-up ledges. An intricately carved wooden screen lets through pinpricks of light, and the soft murmur of voices and music—it must look out on the hall I just left.

In the center of the room is a large pool, the dark water gently rippling. Nimh's standing in it waist-deep, her eyes rimmed with black, her lips dusted gold, and . . .

. . . and she's not wearing a single thing.

"North! I thought you were a handservant." Her words are like a dim buzzing, and I barely hear them. It's only when she recovers from her own surprise and tilts her head inquiringly that I realize I'm staring, and spin around to face the way I came, cheeks burning.

A distant splashing gets past the buzzing in my ears, and then the slight sound of bare feet on stone. It's a moment before I register her voice again, and I realize she's been saying my name.

"North? There is no need to be ashamed. I am my people's goddess. No corner of my life is private. None of it has ever been."

I risk a look over my shoulder. The pool is empty now except for the ripples she left behind, illuminated by the light coming through a series of screens set up just beyond it. Behind the screens . . .

I swallow. Her silhouette is unmistakable, every detail cast against the sheer fabric. An intricately carved chest sits at one end of the screen, draped with a thick, folded stack of fabric. Her staff leans against the wall beside it.

As she dries herself, the sheer fabric shows me her silhouette. I can almost imagine the warmth of her skin, steam from the bath rising off it.

"I-I-I'm sorry to interrupt," I manage, my throat dry. "I didn't realize this was a private room."

"This is my ritual bathing chamber," Nimh replies, seeming far less flustered than I am. "After the public portion of the feast's rituals, I come here to cleanse and be cleansed by the temple waters."

The rustle of fabric behind the screen is dizzying. My body feels almost as if it belongs to someone else, and I have to fight the urge to stare. She was graceful and lithe from the moment I met her, but somehow, here, away from prying eyes, she's even more so.

For skyfall's sake, North, get your shit together!

"And you did not interrupt," Nimh goes on, making me realize that I'd been standing there in utter silence. "I was planning on sending for you when I was finished. How did you find me here?"

"The cat," I rasp. That, at least, I can respond to safely. I look around for the beast, though now he's made his mischief, there's no sign of His Furriness anywhere. Figures.

Nimh laughs, the sound quiet against the revelry beyond the carved wall overlooking the party. "I should have known he would anticipate me. My robe is there, by the steps into the pool—would you mind handing it to me?"

The pool of crimson fabric is obvious when I turn. She must not have been in the water long, because when I pick up her robe, it's still warm from her body. The cloth is fine and sheer, so delicate it's hard to believe it wasn't spun by machine. I can't help but notice the way it slides across my palms, smoother than any soy-silk I've ever felt.

A tingle across the back of my neck makes me look up—and I meet Nimh's eyes where she's peeking around the edge of the screen.

"Sorry. Here." I drape the swath of red cloth across her outstretched arm, careful not to touch her.

Her eyes linger on me a moment, lips parting as though she's about to speak—but just as the silence threatens to draw out too long, she vanishes back behind the screen again. I start talking to distract myself from the silken whisper of fabric on skin.

"The ritual was beautiful," I say, turning my back against the silhouette moving on the other side of the screen.

A thought, unbidden—*You were beautiful.*

"I'm glad I got to see it."

"It is as ancient as the temple itself," Nimh replies, voice briefly muffled as she pulls her robe back on. "I love the Feast of the Dying—I love all the rituals I perform. It is a heavy burden, to be the living divine, but performing the rituals . . . I feel connected to those who came before me. I am only the latest in a long line to bless these waters."

The silhouette straightens and begins to move, giving me just enough warning to jerk my eyes away before Nimh emerges, clothed again. She crosses behind me to the more ornate door opposite the one I arrived by and calls for a servant. I instinctively step back out of sight as she murmurs a few words to the girl. Then the door closes, and we're alone again.

Nimh turns back toward me with another of those little smiles, a curious, lopsided thing—different from the way she smiles upon her people. Though her eyelashes are still darkened with kohl and her lips are still dusted with gold, she hasn't put the jewelry back on yet, and her hair falls loose around her shoulders.

"I asked for some food to be brought—I imagine you must be hungry." Her eyebrows lift a little, turning the observation into a question.

"Did you read my mind?" I ask, looking away from a statue to study her now that she's safely clothed. I'm only mostly joking. I'm less and less sure about what Nimh actually believes she can do.

"I am tempted to say yes, to see your face." She flashes me another wry smile, then gestures at an intricately carved wooden screen along the far wall. "I can see the celebration taking place from here. I saw you weren't eating and thought perhaps you could not tell which dishes contained meat."

"You're right. I couldn't figure out what was what," I admitted. "How is it that you notice everything?"

"Magic." Her smile widens, true amusement peeking through.

I like being able to make this serious girl smile.

In spite of myself, I laugh. "Fine, don't tell me."

Nimh gives a graceful little shrug. "Years of practice. I have spent a long, long time watching." She steps toward me and sits, hesitating a moment before asking, "Would you mind assisting me with my robe? I would call another handservant, but then I would have to explain your presence here, and how you arrived via my own private passageway." She nods toward the panel that the cat led me through.

"I . . . sure. What do I . . ." But I trail off as she turns, showing me the back of her robe, which gapes open down to the waist. Crimson ties dangle in a crisscrossed pattern, waiting to be drawn up and tied off.

Nimh reaches up, gathering her hair in her hands and pulling it forward over her shoulder. As she does, it sends a waft of some kind of spicy scent in my direction. Her skin is flawless, and for a long moment I can't move. It's as if my brain simply shuts itself down.

Beeeeeeep. No activity detected. Please restart.

"You should only have to draw the strings together and then tie them," Nimh is saying from far away.

There are dimples in her lower back, just above where the fabric clings to her hips.

"North?"

I blink and glance up to find her looking over her shoulder at me. A flare of panic makes me wonder what I missed while staring at her—and then I see that her cheeks are dark and her large brown eyes are fixed on my face.

"I—forgive me, Nimh." The words come tumbling out. "It isn't every day a person is asked to help dress a goddess."

Her smile flashes at me, but I can see her head duck and the curve of her cheek shift as her smile widens farther.

Carefully, keeping a tight rein on the irrational—and unhelpful—desire to let my fingers slip a little, I pull on the ends of those laces and then knot them in a neat bow just below the nape of her neck.

I'm about the let the laces fall when my eyes focus past them, to the skin of her shoulders, where the light catches against a scattering of goose bumps rising to follow the movement of my hand. Distracted, I draw my fingertips along the ties, just lightly enough to stay on this side of untying them again.

The little shiver of her skin follows my fingers all the way down. I hear her breath catch, then release, quaking. I can feel her warmth below my fingertips.

"How is it that you can live your life without touching anyone?" I find myself asking softly. "Never being touched?"

Skies, North! What are you saying? Good work with the incredibly personal questions. Truly, I have lost it.

Her fingers are still wound around her thick wealth of hair—they shift a little as I speak, as if stroking someone else's hair, a comfort. "It is all I have ever known. All I will ever know."

Her head turns, and I see her face in three-quarter profile. In this moment, hidden from the rest of the world by the carved screen at the other end of the chamber, she looks . . . *lonely.*

"Nimh, I—"

A chime by the ornate entrance makes us both jump, and Nimh is moving before I've even registered what I've heard. She slips away from me with startling quickness, taking a moment by the door to smooth down her hair and press a hand to her cheek.

I've seen Miri do that once or twice, slipping out of an alcove to be followed a second later by Saelis. I've caused it myself once or twice, and it always made my heart skip, seeing her test how flushed her face was, and knowing I caused it. Now, I'm awash in something else, a mishmash of emotions I can barely catalog.

Except for one that stands out among the others—longing.

She believes she's a goddess and you're not allowed to touch her. Seriously, North, you've got to stop.

She may have saved my life, but she didn't exactly tell me what she was getting me into. This is trouble—I should get out while my skin, and my heart, are still intact.

I stay out of sight once more, and Nimh exchanges a brief, quiet greeting with the handservant, who has delivered a stack of woven boxes, tiered like the temple itself. She bids the servant farewell and turns, padding barefoot past me to sit on the stone between the steaming water and the carved screen that overlooks the party.

"North?" she asks when she looks up to find me still standing where she left me. "Food?"

She lifts off one of the tiers, and a mouthwateringly good smell spirals out toward me on a puff of steam.

Forget protecting my heart—those are dumplings.

Everything else can wait.

FIFTEEN

NIMH

I can't stop watching North eat. On the road, his appetite was fairly well squashed— by fear, by the pain of his injuries, by his experience with the povvy. Out at the feast, while I watched him from behind my screen, he didn't eat at all. Now, though, faced with a selection of my favorites from the temple kitchens—and a promise that nothing he's eating is meat—he's not holding back.

He catches me watching him as he's licking cheese from the fingers of one hand and trying to keep his flatbread from falling apart with the other. "What? Are my table manners not up to specifications?"

Every time I start to think he's just like any young man from this world, he goes and says something like that. He doesn't speak the way we do, though I can usually understand the idea behind what he's saying. And while I'm no longer worried he might forget himself and accidentally touch me, and he never treats me with anything but respect—he also doesn't look at me the way the people of my faith do.

His easy grin falters a little, and I realize I've been staring at him rather than answering him.

"You have lovely table manners," I tell him, which for some reason makes him laugh. I had been trying to compliment him.

North raises an eyebrow at me. "So why is my eating so amusing?"

"Not amusing," I protest. "You must understand, food is an important symbol among the people here. Food is often scarce, and so feeding a person is a gesture of . . ." I hesitate, for I'd been about to say "love." I brush past that in my mind and say instead, "To watch someone enjoying a meal so much is . . . pleasing."

North leans over to snag a spiced pastry as though he's sneaking something past me. "I'm so glad I can treat you, then."

I take advantage of his preoccupation with the pastry to try to gather my wits.

My mind has been ensnared by a particular preoccupation in the last few hours: if North is the Lightbringer, then he is divine as well.

There have never been two divine beings in the world at the same time, not since before the Exodus when the gods left us. There are no rules for it.

That the living divine cannot be touched by mortals without losing her divinity is a law that has been handed down through the centuries.

But what happens if she's touched by someone carrying *his own* divinity?

My skin still tingles at the memory of his expression when he found me in the pool. His nearness when he was handing me my robe. I must fight to keep from visibly shivering whenever my thoughts go back to it.

"Are you cold?"

I blink and find North looking at me, eyebrows drawn together in faint concern. "What?"

"You're shivering. Do you want my jacket?" He brushes the crumbs from his fingertips and curls his hands around the lapels of the borrowed jacket of black silk he wore to the feast.

Quickly, I shake my head. Techeki no doubt dressed him in fine clothes from the outer layers on down—I don't think it'd be a good idea to see him in his undershirt alone. "I was only thinking. I am quite warm enough still from the waters."

Hunger sated somewhat, North lowers his hands to the stone and leans back on them. "Tell me, what's so important about the temple waters that they play such a big role in your ritual?"

I eye him askance, trying to detect any traces of that irritating air he gets when he asks about magic or faith. All I can see is curiosity.

"Water and magic have always been closely linked." I push the boxes of food aside to make room for us both at the bathing pool's edge. "Running water can act as a shield against magic, and still water can be used as a conduit for it. That is why the temple is built here, nestled in between two branches of the river, where it runs most swiftly."

"So it works like the sky-steel?" North asks, watching me curiously. "Keeps you safe from mist-storms?"

I nod. "It's a little more complicated than that, but for the most part, yes. That is also why many of my people—the riverstriders, to be specific—have made their homes on the water and rarely leave the byways of the forest-sea and the river itself."

"So your rituals honor the water?" His voice is a little tentative, as if, for the first time, he's considering the fact that his attitude toward my beliefs might actually affect my feelings.

I find myself smiling at that, if not what he's actually said. "In a way. Water from the two rivers, from the place where they split, is diverted here." I gesture toward the pool, where troughs for the two rivers feed into the pool, keeping it brimming. "When I bathe here it symbolizes the living divine uniting her people the way the waters mix here and become one river again."

North glances at me for permission, then dips his fingers into the pool with a little smile. "Nice and warm."

"They're heated by a natural spring below the temple." I reach for my cup, and the sweet wine it contains, so I can sip at it while watching North over its rim. "These rituals are some of my favorite parts of my calling."

"Mine too," North replies fervently, his attention on the steam rising from the pool—then, seeming to hear what he's said, he stiffens and looks up apologetically. "I mean—" But the spice in the pastries must catch up with him, as he bursts into a fit of coughing.

Torn between alarm and amusement, I lean forward and hold out my cup, splaying my fingers over the rim so he can grasp its base. He nods his gratitude, the paroxysm slowing enough for him to take a drink. Once he's gotten himself under control, he takes another sip, slower this time, eyes downcast at the cup.

My amusement fades as I watch him, for his face has grown serious, a few dark curls falling forward into his eyes as he traces his fingertips around the rim of the vessel, where my own lips rested not long before.

When he looks up, his gaze is searching. "Why didn't you tell me?"

My heart gives a painful lurch, as my first thought is for the prophecy, and the role I believe he is to play—the role I don't think he would understand, not without reading the scroll, not without *feeling* destiny for himself.

Then it hits me, and I gulp a breath.

"You mean, that I am a goddess among my people?" I buy myself a little time with the question, half-distracted by the way his fingers circle the edge of the cup again and again. I open my mouth to answer him, but nothing comes.

Noticing where my attention is, he holds out the cup in return, for me to take it back. "I have a guess," he says, as my fingers close around the rim of the cup, which has been warmed by his touch.

But when I would have taken it back, he holds on to it, making me look back up at him. He's watching me, an odd look on his face—his thick eyebrows are drawn in, the brown eyes curious. His expressive mouth is curved just a little in a kind of interested fascination I've never seen before.

"I think I must be the first person you've ever met who didn't instantly know who you were," North goes on, holding me captive by my grasp on the cup—though I could let go, I don't, and the smooth brass under my fingers is electric. "I think you don't have many people who treat you like a person, rather than a goddess. It would be easy to assume you were hiding things from me for some sinister reason, but . . . I wonder if maybe you were just hiding them because it was the first time you could."

With both our arms outstretched, it's almost like we're holding hands—except, of course, the surface under my fingertips is metal. I swallow. "The way you spoke about magic—the way you dismissed it—I knew you could not understand what it means to be divine, not then. You would think me a fool."

"I didn't exactly make it easy for you to tell me," North admits with a thoughtful squint. "I'm sorry if I made you feel . . . It's clear magic is a thing in your world. I can't say I believe in it the way you do, but I don't think you're a fool. I definitely don't think you're a fool."

His voice is always warmed by amusement, but just now, it doesn't feel like he's laughing. If anything, he's more solemn than usual. When I fail to reply straightaway, he draws breath to speak, but then halts, meeting my eyes.

"The strangest thing," he murmurs, scanning my features, intent. "Sitting here with you, I almost could believe in it. In all of it. There's something about you I . . . can't explain."

My thoughts are racing, along with my pulse—I wish I had that scroll, I wish I could know he was divine, I wish I could *know*, so I could . . .

We're closer than we were a few moments ago. Whether he's drawn me nearer by the cup held between us or I pulled *him* closer, I cannot say. But as soon as I realize it, I flinch and release my grip with a gasp. That makes North recoil too, and the cup goes crashing down onto the stone.

North mutters something that must be a swear word in his land, whirling away from me to fetch one of the towels I'd used to dry myself. I haven't the heart to tell him, as he begins sopping up the spilled wine, that the material is worth a small fortune and that the wine will stain.

I haven't the heart, because my own heart is still racing.

North's muttering to himself still, and I catch only fragments—*clumsy as a fledgling*—as I stare at him while he cleans up. It isn't until he's gotten most of the wine and sees my face that he stops.

"Nimh?"

"I can explain," I manage.

His brow furrows. "Explain what?"

"You said there was something about me that you could not . . . I can explain it, North. I think . . . I *believe* . . . your coming here, to this land, was prophesied long ago. You and I did not meet by chance."

His eyebrows shoot up, though for once he doesn't seem to be dismissing me altogether. He is willing to wait, and to listen.

I manage a breath with an effort, drawing on all my training at diction and speech.

"I believe the prophecy brought us together. North, this is our destiny."

SIXTEEN

NORTH

For a moment, the sounds of the party on the other side of the screen—music, distant laughter, the hum of conversation—fade away. I'm caught staring back at Nimh, no ready reply, too riveted by her serious dark eyes and her earnest expression to think.

"Destiny," I echo, buying myself time. "Like . . . fate?"

She nods, and while I'm ready to laugh at the obvious joke, there's no hint of a smile on her face. "Prophecy plays a great role among my people. I believe I was meant to be there that night and see you as you fell."

My mind flashes to the cut lines on the *Skysinger*. My crash wasn't destiny. It was sabotage.

"I–I'm certainly glad you were there," I respond tentatively. "The thing is . . . you know I don't believe in . . . This whole magic thing in general is . . . hard to swallow."

Despite my efforts to keep my expression under control, Nimh's face shows a flicker of hurt. "And you ask why I did not tell you who I was, out there in the ghostlands. Did I not heal your arm in front of your eyes?"

"You cauterized it with some kind of chemical reaction," I reply.

"It was healing magic," she insists, leaning forward, eyes alight. Though she speaks with fervent assurance, there's a flicker in her gaze—some part of her is enjoying the argument.

"Okay," I reply. I rise up onto my knees so I can discard my jacket, then reach for the hem of my shirt and draw it up over my head, letting the fabric gather around my arms. "You want to see it? It's a *burn*—better than a bleeding gash, but still a burn, Nimh. Caused by a chemical reaction that . . ." I reach for the clean bandage that replaced my dirty one when I bathed, ready to show her the burned place—and instead, when the fabric falls away, there's only a pink line there along my bicep, shiny with new skin.

Shock robs me of my indignation. I sink back on my heels, staring down at my arm. After a few moments, I glance up to find Nimh watching me. Her eyebrows rise.

"Some kind of . . . medicine," I mutter, "an antibiotic, in the chemicals."

"It was a *healing spell*, North." She leans forward to retrieve the bandage from where I dropped it, then begins to wind it back up, fingertips lingering where they trail across the fabric. "Mhyr's Sunrise and thicksweet, when mixed with water, do still burn without magic. But they only burn—they do not heal unless a magician's will directs them."

I can't prove or disprove what she's saying, partly because I don't understand about half of it. And even if I did, I can't prove or disprove her *will*. Still, I push on. "So . . . you can do *anything* with magic? Start fires and heal people, sure, but what about . . ." My mind runs through half a dozen examples from old fairy tales, and before I can stop to think, it chooses: "What about a love spell?"

Nimh's lips quirk, a clear sign of amusement, though she's gracious enough not to laugh at me. "Magic has limitations just as any other force in this world. I could cast a spell to make myself appear more beautiful to you, or I could bind the magic to a charm that would track your movements, so I could bump into you more often. But the mind is its own realm—a magician uses her will to direct her power. She cannot use that power to affect another's mind."

She pauses to scan my features for comprehension, and she gives a quick, wry smile at what she finds. "No, North, I could not cast a spell to make you love me."

"But *destiny* could?"

Her smile falters, her certainty dropping away. I realize how my words sounded—defensive and aggressive all at once.

Accusatory.

Disbelieving.

When the truth is that I *am* drawn to her, so much so that I could almost believe it *was* magic. Miri and Saelis feel so remote compared to Nimh that my heart aches.

I let the air out of my lungs, realizing that I was tensed as if for a fight. "Nimh, I'm sorry. I'm trying to understand, I promise. Maybe we talk about destiny another time, and just . . . eat some more?"

Her gaze flickers up, though it takes a few seconds to reach my face. Belatedly, I realize my shirt's still pooled around my arms, and with a start, I pull it back on over my head. By the time I can see her again, Nimh's looking a little unsettled.

"There are things we should discuss," she murmurs. "I have no wish to keep anything a secret from you, not if . . ." She trails off, catching her lip between her teeth as she thinks. The sight is so distracting that I don't even realize I'm staring until she stops.

I look up, blinking. "Sorry?"

"Have another dumpling," she suggests, nudging the dish closer to me. It's a tacit acceptance of my truce—or my plea—and I'm not above taking it.

She turns as I reach for the tray, her attention moving to the party going on beyond and below the screen. Her profile is solemn as I pop a dumpling into my mouth. She must have spent all her life watching like this.

She's always alone, I see that now. In her rank, in the ritual I saw her perform this evening . . .

The staff—the weapon—leaning against the wall by the screen never seems to leave her side, a constant reminder of her duty. She even has her own corridors to walk without company—except for the bindle cat, who still hasn't reappeared.

But Nimh doesn't seem to mind me in these secret spaces of hers, and in that realization, I suddenly catch a momentary glimpse of something else.

Nimh's not being a goddess right now. She's being a person. A person who got me dumplings. I was right before, when I thought maybe she didn't tell me what she was because she never gets a chance to be anything else.

The strange thing is, if there's anyone who can understand even a fraction of what that's like, then surely it's me.

And, as the part of my brain dedicated to fairness (heavily influenced by Saelis over the years) points out, *you haven't told her who you are either. You haven't said anything about being a prince.*

I scoot a little closer so I can look out through the carved screen as well. We're one floor up, situated behind the musicians—it's a good view.

"Tell me about the people out there," I say, changing the subject. It feels like the safest thing to do. "I see some really amazing outfits."

She's quiet, considering this, then she leans in to put her eye to one of the carved holes.

"That is the high priest," she says, "over there by the far wall, wearing the gold-trimmed robe."

"*Your* high priest," I say, trying out how it feels to say it aloud.

"Yes," she says quietly. "His name is Daoman. He leads the priests who live here in the temple. He is . . . a formidable man. He raised me, for the most part."

Which explains why you're *so formidable.* I bite down on the words and focus on the dumpling in my hand while she searches out other characters of note.

She points out Techeki talking to a guildmaster, a couple of the council members who lead the city, dignitaries from foreign governments.

It all feels oddly familiar—the cast of characters might be different from those who occupy my grandfather's palace, but their roles and the patterns they make are the same.

"You know them all," I say, when we pause for more dumplings.

She inclines her head. "I have many years of observing the rhythms of temple life. Watch now, that woman in the robes of the Congress of Elders will move around to the far side of that table, because she does not wish to dance with the leader of one of the riverstrider clans, the woman wearing blue and green. The clan is pressing the congress for a change to a trading law, and the elder does not wish to discuss it."

And as we look down, that's exactly what happens—one woman gracefully avoids the other by seeming to move around a table to investigate the snacks on the far side of it without ever looking the riverstrider's way. I whistle, impressed. "Magic," I tease, grinning.

"Too much spare time," she returns, with her own smile. "*You* did not dance tonight. I saw several people ask you."

"I love dancing," I admit. "But we do it differently, and I figured it was better to remain mysterious than to step on everyone's feet and make myself an ordinary idiot."

That draws a laugh from her, soft and musical. "You could never be ordinary."

I swallow the lump that forms in my throat at the obvious compliment. The cat, who has returned without our notice, chirps his disapproval of her laughter, and like misbehaving children we press our eyes to the peepholes once more.

"Is Matias here?" I ask.

Her breath seems to catch in her throat, and I have a feeling that if she were less restrained, she might have snorted. "He does not care for festivities" is all she says.

I wonder whether she's told him he can give me the information I asked for. But I don't press the issue, not tonight. Tonight is . . . something else. Tonight, or at least just now, the two of us are apart from the others. Joined in a way that feels different from being in the forest-sea and the ghostlands together, as though there's something between us that can only show its face when no one else is looking.

"When I saw Matias today, he told me about how you came to be the goddess," I say, thinking back to his words. "It must have been so hard, at five, to leave everything behind."

"It was necessary," she says simply. "They cannot see me as a person. They must see me as a symbol, and symbols must stay apart. They cannot be . . . longed for. Wanted."

"Are you sure?" I murmur, as the music swells on the other side of the wall, and laughter drifts up. "It seems to me that ritual is designed to foster exactly that."

She doesn't answer my question, though she meets my eyes in the dim light. "I remember when the priests came for me," she whispers, barely audible above the revelry. "My mother tried to hide me, because she did not want to give me up. She cried when they took me away. I have always treasured that memory. It was the last time anyone wanted *me*. Nimh. Not Nimhara, the Divine One."

My throat tightens at the thought of it, of all those years of loneliness since. At what her duty requires her to be.

"I'm sorry," I say softly. "For her hurt, and for yours. But what makes you so certain it was the last time?"

Her lips part, though I'm not sure even she knows what she's going to say next. We're both still and quiet, ignoring the party around us, our gazes still locked. I feel an ache in my heart—a yearning for something I can't quite name.

A few breathless moments pass, her face clearly torn. "North . . . ," she whispers finally, "there is something I should— something I would *like* to tell you—"

A deafening roar on the other side of the wall interrupts her, as if the sky has fallen and the world's ending.

We spin toward the spy holes to see the far wall of the great room collapse in a spray of stone, knocking several people down and reducing the feast to a rubble-strewn pile.

The hole in the temple wall is filled with smoke and dust, but through it I can make out the barest silhouette. Someone is standing there. Before I can gather my wits to ask Nimh what's going on, a voice from behind the rubble rises over the groans of the wounded and the frightened babble of the guests.

"Where is your goddess?" The voice is female, low and smooth, and utterly commanding. Now I can make out several other shapes flanking her, bearing weapons. "Come to me, Nimhara—you may either damn every soul in this room to death, or surrender yourself to the Deathless, and the true vessel of the Divine. I have come to take my rightful place and cast you forever into the dust."

SEVENTEEN

NIMH

A voice rings out demanding my surrender.

It is then that I see the woman standing amid the clouds of dust.

For a moment, I want to laugh—for how could anyone think they could stroll up to the temple, blow a hole in its side, and start making demands of one of the most heavily guarded people in the world? There are only half a dozen others standing among the rubble, flanking the woman in front as if participating in some strange ritual.

But then reality descends upon me in a swift, dizzying swoop and seizes me in its talons.

The Cult of the Deathless has breached my temple. My home.

The woman standing in the rubble wears a robe much like my own, but of deep indigo, little flecks of stone and centuries-old mortar speckling its skirt like stars. Gleaming relics from the ancients adorn her fingers and hang around her neck, more than I have ever seen in one place. She holds a staff like mine, although it has no blade at the end, only ceremonial charms. Her black hair is long, but twisted up and tied so that it forms a circlet along the top of her head from ear to ear—a crown, not of gold, but of darkness. At first glance, it seems she is wearing a blindfold—but then I realize it is a stripe of black painted across her face, emphasizing the brightness of her eyes in the darkness. Even at this distance, I can see them flash as they scan the room.

She must have known from the instant she could see through the dust that I was not there, and yet she makes a show of searching for me. A few of those nearest her draw back as her eyes pass over them. Her lips, a red so dark they nearly match the paint across her eyes, curve a little.

"Why have you all ceased your celebration?" she asks, her voice still pitched to carry across the chamber. "I have no wish to stop such a moving display of faith. Please, continue."

No one moves, her words hanging in the air like the dust from the collapsed wall.

"I said *continue*." When her order fails again, those eyes flash toward the musicians' dais just below my bathing chamber. "Play!" she snaps, and behind her, one of the other intruders draws a blade from his belt with a sound that lingers in the silence.

Haltingly, fumbling and out of sync with each other, the drummer and piper begin to play again, the lively tune a harsh contrast with the shock and horror of the room's occupants.

The woman lifts one hand and makes an expansive gesture, like a ruler welcoming honored guests to her throne room. "Do not be afraid," she declares. "You should rejoice—for you are the first beyond my own people to look upon the face of the one who will be your *true* goddess."

Beside me, North makes a small sound. I wrench my gaze from the screen long enough to spare him a glance. His face is grave and tense, his hands clenched tightly together. When he raises his eyebrows and glances toward the door of my chamber, I shake my head—whatever he might be proposing, I cannot move.

"I am Inshara," the woman continues, "true vessel of the divine. I am a child of two worlds, born to commune with the Lightbringer himself. The day approaches when he will infuse me with his spirit, and I will become the greatest of all divinities. I will be the Wrathmaker, the Destroyer, the Eater of Worlds. Bring your false goddess to me, for she and I must speak."

A murmur of fearful confusion slips around the chamber as my people react to her words. Some shuffle backward, some duck their heads, but not one of them show her any defiance.

My own breath catches, and I bite my tongue against the reply I want to fling at her, my anger and disbelief demanding to make themselves heard.

Everything she says is false—none of the prophecies speak of a vessel to be *infused* by the Lightbringer. Where is her Last Star? Where are any of the signs?

A flicker of movement catches my eye, and I shift, pressing my cheek to the carved wooden screen until I can see it properly. *Elkisa.*

She is moving slowly, carefully, sidling away from her post and closer to the cultists' leader. I can read the icy calm of determination as she moves between and around the guests at the party.

She is the sole survivor of the massacre at our camp. She means to kill this intruder. She means to take revenge.

"No," I whisper, and after a moment, North sees her too—his breath catches and his knuckles show white.

Inshara smiles, unaware of Elkisa's approach, and steps gracefully down the pile of rubble as though descending a grand staircase. Her guards remain where they are, covering their exit back through the hole in the wall.

A flicker of hope kindles in my chest. If Inshara keeps moving into the room, *maybe* Elkisa can reach her, stop her, before her guards can . . .

"One of you must know where she is," Inshara says, her tone almost pleasant now—indulgent, like that of a parent speaking to a child she knows has been naughty. "You could not be so foolish as to misplace a goddess."

From my vantage point above and behind the musicians' platform, I can see the piper's shaking fingers and the sweat darkening the drummer's hair. I can see heads swiveling side to side in the crowd, looking for me, or perhaps for Daoman—anyone who might take charge of the situation.

Then, like povvies scattering before a predator, the crowd parts and I see the rich saffron of my high priest's robe.

"Leave this sacred place," he commands, his voice effortlessly pitched to carry just as hers does. His face is calm, but I know he wears a mask—I know that beneath the facade, he is raging.

Inshara's flashing eyes turn toward him—and a few degrees farther away from Elkisa. My guard is nearly within striking distance. The false goddess smiles at Daoman. "High priest," she greets him, with a gracious inclination of her head. "Well met. If you bring your goddess before me, I shall let you remain among my priesthood." She adds with a touch of amusement, "Not in your current position, you understand, but you will be permitted to light incense and join in the prayers of my acolytes."

From where I stand, I can see them facing each other. Daoman's profile is motionless and stern; Inshara's smiling and certain.

"Go," Daoman says again, "and *you* will be permitted to live long enough to leave this city."

"I can't do that," Inshara replies, simulating dismay. "Not without proving to you and all those here that you have put your faith in a tragic mistake."

Movement. Elkisa is only a few paces away from where Inshara stands facing Daoman. I see her draw her blade slowly, making no sound.

Gods of my ancestors, please . . .

For the first time I can remember, I am seized with such a powerful desire to reach out and take someone's hand that I am forced to ball my own hands into fists. I squeeze them so tightly that I can feel my fingernails digging into my palms.

I glance at North and realize that now my hands look exactly like his.

Daoman's voice is ringing. "Nimhara is no mistake, Insha."

He leaves off the divine honorific—the sound of that truncated name makes the leader of the Deathless stiffen. "Even without an aspect, she holds great power."

Inshara collects herself, treating the high priest to a slow, lazy smile. "Perhaps. But you have never seen *true* power, Daoman."

With a scream of rage and effort, Elkisa launches her attack, blade raised. Inshara whirls, incanting a spell I don't know, and then moves as if throwing something invisible at my guard. Elkisa's headlong rush halts so abruptly it's like she hit solid stone—stunned, she lets the blade fall from her fingers. It clatters, metallic and harmless, to the floor.

Cries of shock and horror ripple outward through the crowd, and my own hands lose their strength as surely as Elkisa's did. I can feel North shifting his attention back toward me, confused.

"You said that you couldn't use magic to control someone," he whispers.

I swallow hard, watching Elkisa's face, the fear in her eyes like a knife in my heart. "This cultist is controlling her body, not her mind—it takes a vast amount of power."

A *divine* amount of power—but I do not say this to North.

I could not have done it.

The realization rings over and over and over in my head, surging up like a rising tide and bringing with it every doubt that ever lingered in the shadowy places of my heart.

She is more powerful than I.

As if she performs such feats every day, Inshara smiles a

little, hand still outstretched to hold Elkisa in place. "I suppose," she says lightly, "in Nimhara's absence, I shall have to give this little demonstration instead."

My guard's eyes are wide as she hangs motionless, only the balls of her feet still touching the floor, the rest of her frozen. Her fear is writ so plainly on her face that I can read it from here.

Slowly, Inshara's fingers begin to move. They curve, tip downward subtly, shifting with insidious grace.

And Elkisa's arm moves, matching that slow gesture. She gives a cry of alarm, her body shaking as she tries to fight the invisible force compelling her to move—but she makes not an ounce of headway, for her arm continues to move as Inshara's does.

The cultists' leader tips her hand down farther, farther, farther—and when Elkisa is bent nearly double, her arm outstretched to the floor, Inshara slowly closes her hand into a fist.

Elkisa's fingers wrap around the hilt of her fallen blade.

I throw myself back from the spy hole, clamping my hands over my mouth to stifle the cry that bubbles against my lips.

North does not reach for me, but he is closer than I would let anyone come under normal circumstances. "What is *happening*?" he whispers, eyes glittering in the darkened chamber.

I shake my head helplessly, too frightened to answer, too frightened to look back through the screen and watch as Inshara forces my closest, my *only* friend, to turn her own blade upon herself.

North looks over his shoulder at the spy holes, resting one palm against the wall beside my head, and then looks back at me. "Nimh—can you fight her, stop her?"

I shake my head again. "Sh-she is too strong." The voice that comes out is thin and wobbly and alien. It isn't the voice of Nimhara—it is the voice of Nimh, a little girl with no power. "She's stronger than me."

The words keep tumbling from my lips as though they're the only ones I can say. North makes a frustrated noise in his throat, looking down and flexing his fingers to stop himself touching me, shaking me out of my terror.

"Enough!" Daoman's voice, strong as ever, cuts across the rising sounds of horror and wonder down in the chamber. "You must know there is no power in this world that would compel me or anyone in this room to expose the Divine One to your threats. Every word you speak is a lie."

Daoman's tone is dismissive and furious all at once. I have no idea from where he is finding this strength—if I were at his side, witnessing up close the magic she's using on Elkisa, I would have crumpled to the ground in terror. "There is nothing you could say to convince me to take your word over Nimh's."

My heart tightens, but this time with something other than fear. Not "hers," not "the Divine One's," not even "Nimhara's." *Nimh's.*

How could I have ever doubted his loyalty to me? His faith? His love?

Summoning my strength, I give North a shaky nod and creep back toward the spy holes. Inshara and Daoman still stand opposite each other, and Elkisa still hangs frozen in place, her blade in her quivering hand.

Inshara is smiling even more widely, as if she is enjoying herself more with every moment that passes. She takes two slow, graceful steps closer to the priest, lowering her voice—although in the captivated silence, it rings just as clearly—as she murmurs, "What about the boy, Daoman? Did she tell you who he is?"

North's breath catches as my stomach drops. I turn to find his eyes on me, a new level of urgency to his confusion. I hold a finger to my lips and put my eye against the spy hole again, even as my mind races.

The missing scroll—if Inshara's people stole it—if she has spies in the palace who heard me speak of it to Daoman—if she knows I returned with a strange boy . . .

It has taken Daoman a moment to respond, surprise momentarily penetrating his facade of calm. "The boy?" he echoes.

"I *am* the vessel of the Lightbringer, priest. I know all. More than you, it seems." She laughs again. "The boy she brought back with her to this temple. The one who does not know our ways, our customs. The one she guards as jealously as if he were something very, very precious to her." She spreads her arms and calls out, "Come, boy! Let us see you."

I bite at my lip, looking again at North. This time he doesn't look back, intent as he watches the scene play out below us. His jaw is clenched, the light from the spy hole illuminating just his eye—I watch as it narrows.

Her voice intent, Inshara calls again, "I would enjoy the chance to pit my power against yours. Come, *cloudlander.*"

A ripple of gasps spreads through the chamber, even as the bottom drops out of my stomach.

"How does she know where I'm from?" North asks tightly. "Who did you tell?"

I can only shake my head, sick and dizzy with reaction. I told no one.

Daoman's face has darkened as he watches her. "You cannot know that."

Inshara's lips curl into a smile, as though she'd been waiting for this opportunity. "The spirit of the Lightbringer told me so. He also told me something else—I know who your goddess thinks he is."

"She does not think," Daoman replies, his voice ringing out, a glimpse of his anger showing. "She *knows*. The Divine One has returned from her pilgrimage with nothing less than a god for company."

North makes a strangled sound in his throat, a mix of disbelief and laughter—but he knew already, because I told him, that our gods dwell in the cloudlands. He already knew. I can barely focus on him—I'm too busy looking at Daoman.

I told him North was nobody. A boy who helped me back to the temple. But he has heard me recite the lost stanza; he knows of every other prophecy that mentions the Last Star. I should have known he would guess who I had found out in the wilds.

A moment too late, I know what Daoman is about to say.

North—stop listening. Turn away. Cover your ears.

"You are not the Lightbringer," he says, his voice rich with contempt. "You are a cultist, skulking in the shadows to hurl your knives at those who are destined to lead. Nimhara has served her people, and she has performed her ultimate duty."

No, Daoman, don't say it. . . .

I cannot look—I tear my eyes from the carved wooden screen and wish with every filament of my soul that I could touch North and pull him away. As if by keeping the truth from him, I might somehow prevent it from escaping into the world.

"Nimhara has found the Lightbringer on her pilgrimage," Daoman proclaims, his voice ringing out above the rising roar of the crowd.

North watches on, unblinking, pupil dilated in the light that shines through the crack in the wall. There's no hint of laughter in his face as my high priest proclaims the truth.

"She has found the Lightbringer, and his destiny *will* be fulfilled."

What reaction comes from below, I do not know. I can only sit, a dim buzzing in my ears, my eyes on North's face. I see his eyelashes dip once, twice. Then the narrow beam of light against his eye softens and spreads across his face as he leans back. His head turns toward me—and I cannot hide from him, not in this moment.

He reads the truth there in a heartbeat, confirmation, a wordless confession. My divinity wasn't the only thing I hid from him.

I also hid his.

EIGHTEEN

NORTH

My hands are fists. For a long moment, that's the only detail I can focus on, my brain shying away from everything I've just seen, everything I've just heard.

But as always, my gaze is dragged back to Nimh, and her expression answers the terrible question that's stirring in my gut.

She told me the gods left her people to flee to the clouds.

She didn't tell me that she thought I was a very specific god. That I had some part to play in the insanity of this place—that the murderers who came for her would come for me too.

She didn't bring me here to help me find a way home. She brought me here because she thinks I'm someone worth killing to possess.

Wrathmaker.

Eater of Worlds.

Destroyer.

Lightbringer.

I'm not any of those things. I'm no part of this. I want to run as far and as fast as I can, but I'm frozen in place.

The hectic clash of my thoughts is interrupted when Inshara speaks again on the other side of the wall.

"There is an easy way to settle this," she says into perfect stillness—the musicians have trailed off and the crowd draws back. "Bring me your false goddess, and the boy as well."

The high priest draws his robes around him, straightens his back. Nimh was right—he's a formidable man. He has his voice under control when he replies, "The Divine One is not here. And if she were, not a one of us would hand her over to *you*."

Inshara clicks her tongue at him like he's a naughty child. "I think she *is* here."

Daoman's thunderous expression darkens. "You are a dark magician and a blasphemer—your kind is not welcome here! Go now, and do not return."

Inshara lifts one hand, fingers twitching in a quick gesture, and I hear Nimh gasp beside me, a small, frightened sound.

And where she stands between Inshara and Daoman, Elkisa slowly lifts her knife, hand trembling, to press it to her own throat. The whites of her eyes showing, she tilts her head back, trying to avoid the blade. Beside me, Nimh's whimpering now, small involuntary noises escaping with each breath. I fight the urge to reach out for her, despite everything she's done to bring us to this place.

"If you insist," the false goddess says casually, "I will kill you one by one until she reveals herself, or one of you directs me to her. The choice is yours."

Nimh's eyes are closed now, and by the piecemeal light that makes it through the wooden cutouts, I can see the tears

239

streaming down her cheeks, leaving behind gray lines as they track the kohl from her eyes over her skin.

I've been trained for moments like this, and I'm sure she has been too. I hated every second of it as I sat listening to my teachers. I vowed that whatever they said, I'd give myself up in an instant for my grandfather, my mothers, for my friends.

But now I find myself here, I know the answer. I know what she has to do—what she *can't* do. And I ache for her, despite the lies she's told me.

"Nimh," I whisper, the words almost a breath. "You can't go out there. No matter what she does."

So easy to say when you're the teacher, not the student.

She nods, her jaw clenched, her face like death, her breath coming quick and shallow. She's holding on to her self-control with everything she has, and I'm not sure how much longer it will be enough.

Daoman turns his head, speaking over his shoulder to the huddle of priests behind him. He's utterly calm, but there's a note of finality in his voice, like he's making the final move in a game, and he knows it's the winning one. "Bring me the Shield of the Accord."

Nimh goes utterly still beside me, and for a long moment, it's like the whole room is holding its breath.

Then there's a rustle among the priests, like wind rippling through the branches of a tree, and they part to reveal two of their number hauling the top off what I thought was a huge ceremonial table, but turns out to be some sort of giant container.

But then they hesitate, and it's one of their assistants—a girl who can't be much more than twelve or thirteen, wearing a simple blue robe—who's brave enough to reach inside when others step back. She pulls out a heavy bundle about the size of her torso, wrapped in thick, stiff cloth that glints in the lamplight as though something metallic is woven through it.

"Nimh?" I murmur, unable to tear my eyes from it. Even Inshara is standing perfectly still.

"It is a relic made of sky-steel," she breathes, almost inaudible. "Only to be used in an hour of great need. It will extinguish the magic of all who gaze upon it."

"What?" I don't know why I'm so horrified at the idea. Magic doesn't *exist*.

The girl has staggered up to Daoman, and he must be stronger than he looks, because he takes the bundle from her with one hand, and with the other he draws off the cover in one quick movement, dropping it to the floor. He's left holding what looks like a bundle of metallic sticks, and he sends them clattering to the ground in a great pile, directing them toward Inshara with a jerk of his hand.

I expect them to start rolling in every direction, but instead, they animate immediately. It's like watching a broken robot reassemble itself in a vidshow, except the sticks are surrounding Inshara. They snap together and rise up, building one atop the other at a furious pace until she's within a tightly woven lattice that rises high above her head. A cage.

Everyone else is outside it—Elkisa, Daoman, the priests—and only hints of movement can be seen within.

Daoman speaks calmly. "Now perhaps we can talk, Insha. As you can see, your threats will avail you nothing."

Inshara shifts within her enclosure. Her hands lift again, and Elkisa jerks in place—her body taut, her back arching.

"No," the guard gasps, looking straight at the woman holding her captive. "No."

"No," Nimh echoes beside me, eyes huge and horrified. "It's not possible. . . ."

But we're watching the impossible unfold right in front of us. Daoman's mouth opens as if to protest, but no sound comes out.

And then the shield dissolves, the pieces of it losing their grip and dropping to the ground with a deafening clatter, the temple's most powerful weapon falling apart like a toy kicked by a toddler.

Inshara stands among the debris and shoots the shaking Elkisa an almost maternal look, a *please be reasonable* sort of glance, as if Daoman's attempt to rob her of her magic was nothing more than a mild inconvenience. Then she lifts her hands once more.

Elkisa can't resist. Her white-knuckled hand wrapped around the hilt of the knife, she abruptly straightens her arm, flinging it out to drive the blade straight through the deep yellow silk of Daoman's robes. It sinks all the way in, smooth and soundless, and his whole body stiffens.

He looks down at where the knife protrudes from his chest.

His eyes meet Elkisa's, and I can't imagine what he sees there.

And then he collapses at her feet, crimson pouring out

across his robes, so sudden, so *much*, that I know without any doubt that her strike found his heart.

Cries of horror and fear rise around the hall, but as Daoman's robes flutter and settle around him, the loudest cry is from beside me.

"No!" Nimh screams, throwing herself at the wooden wall that hides her bathing chamber, grabbing at the carvings as though she wants to tear them apart, climb through them. At her feet, the cat rises onto his hind legs to sink his claws into the wood, yowling his distress.

"Nimh," I whisper, helpless. "Nimh, no!"

But it's too late.

Out in the hall, Inshara is staring directly at us, as if she can see right through the wall. "High Priest," she says to Daoman's body. "What do you have to say for yourself now? Liar."

She leans down to pull the knife from his chest with a soft sound of effort, and wipes it clean on his robes. Then she points the tip of the blade in our direction.

"Our quarry's within the walls," she says, turning her head a little to address her guards. "After them. Quickly!"

Horror sweeps through me. She knows about Nimh's hidden corridors.

Nimh tears her gaze away from the woman standing over her high priest's body, both hands covering her mouth as she looks across at me, as though she needs to hold in all the sounds she wants to make.

"Run," she whispers.

NINETEEN
NIMH

In the darkened corridors, my mind is free to conjure images with blinding clarity. A time when I was small, chasing and being chased by Elkisa all throughout these corridors. Daoman, stern-faced and with hair still a youthful brown, chastising me for "running away" to one of the bolt holes in these walls and hiding there all night.

Daoman lying on the floor, still and . . .

Daoman.

North's breath is quick and harsh behind me. Some distant part of me is glad we have to run—glad I don't have to explain.

I blamed Daoman, in my mind, for the scroll that went missing—Daoman, who died for me. *Oh, gods.* I jerk my thoughts away again, unwilling to see in my mind the crimson stain spreading out across his saffron robes, the glazed, staring eyes.

No.

But how did Inshara's people steal the scroll I need so badly? A cultist would have had to infiltrate the temple and escape again without being seen.

Or they already had someone inside.

"We have to get out of the walls," I gasp, pausing just far enough ahead of North to give him time to stop before crashing into me.

"What?" North gasps, doubling over to rest his hands on his knees. "Go out into the open?"

"She must have someone inside the temple. They would know about the passages. We have to get out before they cut us off."

North doesn't groan, doesn't pause to complain. "I'll follow you" is all he says.

I have a destination in mind. The only place in the temple *not* accessible via these hidden places: the archives.

I keep us inside the walls for as long as I can, until we reach a corridor that dead-ends at an intricately carved grille. I pause there, listening hard, cheek pressed against the ornate leaves and vines. Then, touching the stone mechanism above me, I swing the panel noiselessly open.

North and I emerge in a small reception room, the grille discreetly hidden behind a silk drape. I inch around the edge of the fabric, scanning the darkened room, and then gesture for North to follow me, our feet silent on the thick carpet.

From the doorway, I can see an intersection. On the far side of it is a jumble of activity, servants running this way and that, and even a number of the city guard as well. The clanking of their armor and weapons as they march through the corridors rings hollow and painful in my chest. They aren't allowed here, in the sanctity of my temple—no armed person is, save for the half dozen or so of my own personal guard on duty at any given time.

But all that's changed—we're under attack.

The archway that opens onto the hall I need is clear, though, and I'm about to sprint across when North hisses at me. I turn in time to see one hand half-lifted, as if his instinct was to reach out and grab me before I could go—but he remembered. There is a tiny comfort in that—that this person, at least, is safe.

"The cat," North whispers, face still tinged with shock and fear in equal proportions. "He was with us in the corridor—he's gone now."

"He will find me," I tell North with more confidence than I feel. "He always does. Now, quickly," I whisper—and then dart across the hall and through the archway.

It leads to a long, downward-spiraling corridor, and momentum does half the work as we run the rest of the way toward my destination. I half skid to a halt when I see that one of the tall doors to the archives stands open, for Matias would have had them both closed against the noise of the celebration raging above all night.

I sidle closer, North on my heels, and peer around.

All looks quiet, although I cannot see the archivist's desk without opening the other door or stepping through. The pool of light always illuminating his desk is there, and while I watch, a ghastly shadow stalks back and forth through it, monstrously huge and distorted where it's thrown back against the shelves. I'm gripping my spearstaff so tightly that my hand aches.

Then the shadow turns, and suddenly it's old and familiar—Matias.

He's standing with one of Daoman's acolytes, the younger man breathing hard, winded and doubled over where he leans against the stacks.

"Nimh," the archivist cries when he turns and sees me, more emotion and animation in his tone than I've ever heard. He wobbles around the edge of his desk. "I'd hoped you'd have the sense to come here." His keen eyes take in North as well, and if he's surprised, he gives no sign of it.

"Inshara knows about the tunnels," I gasp, still catching my breath. Then, in a rush of confusion, I remember that Matias has been here all night—that he might not know what happened, that I'll have to explain, that I'll have to tell him about Daoman—

My throat closes.

Matias shakes his head, making a slicing gesture with his hand. "I know," he says, voice softening. He tips his head at the acolyte, who's watching me with wide, tear-filled eyes. When my gaze shifts toward him, he drops to his knees and raises his shaking palms to his eyes.

"Thank you," I tell him, both touched and baffled that anyone would have thought, in the chaos, to bring the information to the archivist, of all people.

Maybe Matias isn't as wholly separate from the politics of this place as I'd thought.

Matias tips his head to the side, and, after drawing himself to his feet, the acolyte bows again and then stumbles out.

"We have to get out of here," I blurt, glancing from Matias to North, who is silent and watching, his whole body tense and ready for action. His eyes meet mine briefly, then slide away, his jaw clenching. "Both of us," I add.

Matias nods. "On that we agree. Come. All is ready."

He's left his cane leaning against his desk, urgency giving his unsteady legs strength as he leads the way toward the back of the stacks. On a trolley ordinarily used for transporting books and scrolls around the archives is a rough-spun cloth, heaped over something lumpy. The archivist whips back the cloth to reveal two packs and a belt of tools—

Not a belt of tools. *My chatelaine.* The sash full of spell reagents that I carry everywhere, but of course had not worn to the ritual or the party. I'm speechless with relief, but I look up at Matias, my question in my eyes.

"I sent Pisey for your things," the archivist says, nodding after the acolyte. "He told me what was happening."

I slip my chatelaine over my head and across my shoulder and take one of the packs. When North steps forward, one hand half-stretched toward the other pack and a look of query on his face, Matias gives him a tight little smile.

"I took a guess. Yes, that one's yours."

North slips the straps over his shoulders, movements still jerky.

"North . . ." I get no further. His head snaps up so he can look at me.

His eyes are full of hurt, the depth of emotion catching me

off guard. "Why didn't you tell me you believed I was this . . . this destroyer? Some kind of mythical character in one of your stories?"

"It is no story!" I blurt, a flicker of anger rising to match his. "It is *prophecy*—and it's coming true."

He draws himself up. "It was one thing not to tell me who you were. Why couldn't you tell me who *I* was, or who your people would think I was?"

"Because I didn't know you! Because I couldn't be sure I could trust you. Because—"

"It wasn't your decision to make!" he spits. "People are trying to kill me, Nimh!"

"I know!" My voice comes quicker and more heated than I intended, and the sound of it rings in the sudden silence. I take a breath. "I know. *That* is why no one could know. Because the moment they knew you and I might be connected, they—they'd—"

My mind fills again with the image of Daoman lying still, the pool of blood beneath him stretching long spindly fingers along the grooves between the tiles on the floor. My throat closes so abruptly that I make a strangled sound before I realize I can't finish what I'd started to say.

North doesn't answer immediately, though I hear his breathing calm, and the soft shift of fabric that tells me he's taken a step closer to me. "You're going to need to tell me," he says in a low voice. "About this Lightbringer, about your prophecy, about what your people—and *hers*—want from me."

249

"I will." I try to sound contrite, but I'm too relieved by what his words imply: for me to tell him everything, he'll have to stay with me long enough to hear it. "When we're safe."

I ignore the tiny voice in my thoughts that points out *safe* might never come. "Matias." I turn to the archivist. "When I come back, I will—"

"You can't come back," Matias interrupts, rendering me temporarily speechless with surprise. Informal though he is, he never interrupts me. No one interrupts me. "Nimh—you *can't* come back, not until this is over. You must know that."

"But—"

"He's right." North has been quiet, but now he speaks up with a quiet urgency that cuts through my protestation. "If the people out there believe what she said about being some kind of god in waiting, then this temple is hers now—or will be by the time this night is over. We'll have to get out of here first and worry about taking it back later."

Matias is nodding in agreement with North. "The entire contingent of city guards couldn't hope to remove Inshara, not if what Pisey tells me of her powers is true."

"It's *not* true," I blurt out. "It can't be."

Matias's eyebrows go up. "And yet she knew who North was? Where he was from? Who you believed him to be?" He pauses. "She made Elkisa act against her own will."

I have no answer to that.

Matias sighs and shakes his head. "You must stay away, Nimh. Not unless you can come back with . . ." His eyes flicker toward North.

With the true Lightbringer. I must find some way to awaken his power—but with the scroll gone, so is the only clue the prophecy gave me to North's destiny.

I find myself staring at my old teacher and friend, wishing I could touch him, wishing I could show my gratitude. I can't help wondering if it will be the last time I see him.

The librarian's eyes soften, as if he's reading my thoughts. "I have seen leaders rise and fall and rise again in my time, child— all that matters now is that you are alive. I will send word when it is safe for you to return. Quickly, now—there is a way out just here."

I follow him down through the stacks, North behind us. He pushes at one of the shelves, and it slides noiselessly aside. Behind it, the wall is marked with a shallow carving in the stone: a pair of circles, one inside the other, with a staring eye inside the smaller.

"I thought I knew all the tunnels and spy-walks," I mumble, staring as Matias finds a hidden catch and a panel swings free at shoulder height with a faint grinding of stone, cobwebs trailing after it like tattered lace. "What is that symbol?"

Matias gives a helpless shrug, pulling one of his shelving trolleys over to serve as a means to climb up to the passageway's opening. "Something from before the time when we began keeping records again. If you ignore the other passageways leading off this one and go straight, you will find yourself not far from the south river. Avoid the crowds."

North makes a little sound, and when I look back at him, he's got his pack off and is shrugging out of the black coat he wore to the feast. "This will help hide that red robe until we can find something else for you to wear."

I slip the coat on, trying not to notice how it is still warm from his body, and how it smells a little of him. For a moment, I'm dizzy. It is, perhaps, the closest thing to an embrace that I've felt since I was five years old.

"Go, Nimh," Matias says softly.

I whirl back around to face him. "But Inshara . . . what if she——"

"It's taken me years to rid you of that habit. No more what-ifs." His eyes are fond. I used to torture him with a constant stream of questions, most of them starting with that fatal phrase. *What if I'm not the real goddess? What if I just say I manifested, and pretend? What if I did touch someone and no one else knew? What if . . .*

When I continue to hesitate, Matias flaps one hand toward the passageway in the same gesture he always used to chase me out of the stacks at mealtimes when I was a child. "We've no time for this. I'll be fine, Nimh—this Inshara won't harm the only person who knows where everything is, not if she ever wants to consult a single prophecy or text."

I swallow back my tears and nod. The opening in the wall is short and narrow, so North goes first to make sure his broader shoulders will fit. I watch him disappear into the dark hole in the wall, muttering oaths as his shoulders scrape past the narrow opening, and then climb up onto the top of the trolley myself.

I'm struck, strangely, by an old, old memory. I had climbed onto one of these trolleys as a child, despite having been told a dozen times by Matias never to stand on them, and was trying to use it to reach one of the higher shelves. Its wheels had shifted, and I had fallen, and ended up cracking a bone in my wrist. It was the first time I'd ever had to treat myself for a significant injury, for of course the healers could not touch me. I'd had to feel my own arm for the break, in too much agony to use magic to dull the pain, and then splint it and wrap it myself.

What I would not give, now, for the pain of a broken arm, if it meant not having to bear the pain of a broken heart.

Forgive me, Daoman.

I bite my lip, close my eyes, and clamber into the hole in the wall. It's to the sound of Matias letting out a long, weary sigh that I let myself vanish into the darkness.

TWENTY
NORTH

As the panel closes behind us, we're left in the dark. "I'm stopping," I warn Nimh softly, just in case she keeps moving and accidentally comes into contact. "Can you make a light?"

She doesn't reply, but a moment later a soft green glow appears, and when I look back there's a light nestled in the palm of her hand. It illuminates her face, streaked with black and gray tear tracks where the kohl around her eyes has run, and the light casts long, thin shadows ahead of us. With her free hand Nimh reaches up for her crown, then freezes when she realizes she isn't wearing it. Her eyes widen as they snap to meet mine.

"You left it back in the bathing chamber," I murmur.

She swallows. "Inshara will find it."

I ought to tell her it doesn't matter, that if this cult leader wants to pretend she's this land's savior, it doesn't change who Nimh is. But I know the importance of symbols—I know how I would feel if I saw the gleaming, platinum crown of my ancestors on anyone's head but my grandfather's.

Nimh clears her throat as if banishing her fear and grief, pushing her shoulders back. "We should go."

254

We make our way along the dusty corridor, ignoring the passageways to the right and the left as Matias told us to. This place isn't completely disused—the uneven pavers beneath our feet are clear of dust—but cobwebs hang across the hallway every so often.

We walk in silence, Nimh moving ahead of me. She's got my jacket pulled tight around her shoulders, looking strangely ordinary despite the ethereal light. She could be any girl in Alciel, borrowing a boy's jacket on a chilly evening. The tunnel curves sharply to the right, and I catch a glimpse of her profile.

Her eyes are partly hidden by the hair that falls around her face, but her expression looks as though she wouldn't flinch if the roof fell down around her. I know this look—I saw it on my grandfather's face, and my mothers' faces, when my grandmother died. I'm pretty sure I wore it myself. It's the look of someone who has crammed every part of their emotional response to a situation down into a tiny box and nailed the lid shut so they can carry out their duty.

The other thing that I remember, though, is that if you leave that box nailed shut for too long, it can become dangerously unstable.

I had Miri and Saelis to help me vent that pressure, to hold me when I cried for her, to listen while I talked about her. But Nimh only has me, and nobody can hold her when she weeps.

She lied to me about who she thinks I am, about the destiny she thinks brought me here. Perhaps she lied about believing there might be a way for me to get home. But she *didn't* stab a guy in cold blood, so of my two choices, she's the goddess I'm sticking with.

Nimh interrupts my thoughts. "This must be the way out."

We've reached a T-intersection, a solid door straight ahead of us, a much larger, much wider hallway running away to our left and right. The ceiling is high, and it leaves me feeling uncomfortably exposed. The older part of the tunnels must have reached a section that's more regularly used, because the walls are lined with lamps, their light dimmed, perhaps to save fuel during the night. Would I be able to see a threat before it was on us?

Nimh extinguishes her own light and grabs at the door's handle. She yanks it, then stops short. She tries to turn it again, and again, then kicks it, wincing at the impact. "Gods," she mutters. "Not now, not *now*."

"Locked?" I ask quietly, and she nods, a quick, tight movement.

She drops to a crouch, pulling a small leather kit from her belt of tools and pouches. When she unrolls it, I recognize with a jolt of surprise: lock-picking tools. It was a hobby of Saelis's for a little while, adopted to help me get down into one of the oldest sections of the engines beneath the city. Most things worth protecting are behind electronic locks at home, only accessible after a microneedle samples the user's blood—but nobody ever bothered to install DNA locks in the old, dusty engine room corridors. I wonder where Nimh wanted to go, that the doors were locked even to a goddess.

I keep watch, leaning my back against the wall, my skin

prickling. We're hopelessly unprotected here. And what's happening several levels above us? What has Inshara made of her rival's disappearance? How many others has she killed?

A sound somewhere in the dark of the tunnel yanks me out of my thoughts. I drop to a crouch, and as I move, I catch a glint—a flash of eerie greenish gold in the gloom.

Then with a skittering of claws against stone, the cat is scurrying toward us, his ears laid back, the closest I've seen him come to undignified haste.

I let out a slow breath of relief as he brushes past me to press in against Nimh's legs, but the sound he makes isn't a purr—it's another growl.

The realization clicks into place as I lift my gaze again. There was something about that scurry that I can't quite put my finger on, but I know what it meant. He was running away from something. Something out there in the dark.

I could have sworn there were more lights before—that the lamps stretched farther away along the hall than they do now.

A trickle of ice runs down my spine. There *were* more lights. I'm sure of it.

"Nimh," I whisper urgently, swinging back to look to the left once more. As I watch, the farthest lamp goes out, plunging another section of the corridor into darkness.

And then another, and the dark creeps closer still. I look back over my shoulder and catch a lamp behind me extinguishing itself.

One by one they're going out, the dark—and whatever it hides—closing in.

Nimh mutters something I don't catch, though I know from her tone it's a curse, and stashes her tools back in her belt, rising to stand beside me.

"Should we go back to the archives?" I whisper, my heart thumping.

She shakes her head a fraction. "There is no other way out of the temple that will not be observed," she murmurs. "It must be this door, it is our only way to the city. And if we tried to double back, they would catch us before we reached Matias."

Then a voice rings out from the black, unfamiliar and harsh. "How did you scurry down into your burrows so fast, little povvies? You scamper much more quickly than we thought."

Cultists.

My breath's coming quick and shallow now, and I'm running a desperate mental inventory, trying to think what I could use for a weapon. I can't believe I didn't ask Matias for one. But then, I've never needed a weapon in my life. Not until I fell out of my world and into this one.

Nimh's voice is very quiet. "North, stay close to the door."

"What?"

"*Don't move.*" Her tone is intent, her face blank, her hands reaching into the pockets attached to her belt.

So I press myself in against the cool stone wall by the door. *This is a nightmare*, I tell myself. *I'm going to wake up in my own bed at home. Then I'm going to be a model son for the rest of my life.*

Nimh raises both her hands, palms up, in a strange, ceremonial kind of movement like the ones I saw during the ritual earlier today. Greenish-blue light blazes from both of them—bright as day, nothing like the gentle glow I saw before——illuminating the hallway, revealing the black-clad figures sneaking up on us from both directions. I can only see Nimh by squinting, and like them, I'm frozen in place.

"Come no farther," she says, her voice ringing with absolute authority, as a deep rumble sounds within the walls.

"Come with us," calls one of the cultists. "She might let you live."

The rumble grows to a volume no one can ignore. The floor shakes beneath us, sending shocks through my body. Dust rains down from the ceiling. A shudder goes through the walls and the dust forms swirls and patterns on the floor. The paving stones below it upend themselves, buckling and breaking apart.

The cultists cry out in surprise. With a deafening crash, a slab of stone falls from the ceiling to my right, smashing into the ground between Nimh and our pursuers. It shatters on impact. An instant later another crashes down on our left, sending up swirling clouds of dust.

Nimh is utterly wild, an invisible wind rising from the ground to toss her robes and hair about. She's terrifying but composed. She looks like a predator——the cat a small, fierce hunter beside her——and everyone else in the hallway is prey.

I throw my arms over my head, shielding myself from flying debris as boulders begin to fall, piling up between us and the cultists on both sides. Nimh's whispering now, the hiss of it somehow cutting through the noise around us. She raises her hands as if *commanding* the ceiling to fall.

The air is heavy, roaring in my ears as if an impossible

storm is brewing. The ceiling shudders, then splits with a great crack. Nimh lifts her hands higher, above her head, then throws them down toward the floor. With a *boom* like a strike of lightning, the whole ceiling comes crashing down.

It forms a wall—sealing us off from the cultists on both sides—making us safe.

She sags back against the stone behind her. The blue strobe fades. The only light is the one dim lamp nearest us.

I'm still pinned against the wall—disbelieving, awestruck, and terrified. "H-how did . . . ?"

Without moving, Nimh speaks quietly, her voice aching with exhaustion. "We should go. Before they remember there is a door into this section from the outside."

I finally manage to move, stepping across a pile of rubble. "It's still locked," I point out, feeling a little like someone telling a master artist that one of the trees in her painting could use a couple more leaves.

Nimh doesn't open her eyes, though she turns her head as if she wants to answer me.

"I'll do it," I tell her, reaching for her staff and hefting it in my hands. I hesitate for a long moment over using something so clearly ceremonial for this job. But Nimh used it to help her hike through the forest-sea, and time's a factor. So I angle the butt of the staff toward the lock and bash at it, my mind racing.

What just happened?

Was it a virtual image? A hologram?

No, the stone piled up on either side of us is very real.

Something mechanical? Some kind of ancient defense system she triggered?

But how could—why *would*—the mechanism be located right where we needed it?

A distant part of my mind, observing my own scramble for logic, points out that none of these mysteries explain the intruder's control over Nimh's guard back at the party. How was *that* possible? How is any of this real?

With a final blow, the lock gives way.

The door swings open and the cat stalks forward, looking completely composed, despite the roof having fallen down around our heads. I stumble after the cat and Nimh follows. The exit leads to a dark side street that runs along the edge of the temple.

I hand back Nimh's staff. A part of me is grateful to have her on my side—to have her power and her protection.

But another part of me—a part I can't deny—is becoming afraid of her.

TWENTY-ONE

NIMH

The night is warm and quiet, and the streets and alleyways of the upper city are deserted. Most of my people are up at the temple. Are they captive—fearful for their futures? Are they revelers—celebrating my defeat?

Or are they prisoners—dying as they cry out for their goddess to save them?

I shudder, hunching my shoulders.

"Are you cold?" North's voice is soft, coming from just behind my left shoulder.

"No." I shake my head, fighting off another shiver. If it were one of my people with me, I would have used the excuse gladly. But I find I don't want to lie to North anymore, even if it means showing human weakness. "I'm frightened."

A sigh from North, and then, as he visibly pulls himself together: "Me too." He looks around and tilts his head at the mouth of a narrow alley. "In there. We can hear if anyone's following, and lose them if they are."

We pause just beyond the lip of shadow at the alley's entrance and stand for a time in silence. A faint breeze up above the streets stirs one of the pennants flying from a window. The Lovers have risen, but the silver rose of the moonlight leaches color in the darkness, and I cannot tell if the pennant is one of our multicolored flags of celebration or one of dull gray. In the distance I hear a shout—and then nothing.

The stillness chafes at me, my whole body twitching with the need to run, but I know North is right. Stealth is our best hope.

What kind of life has he led in his land in the clouds, that he is so accomplished at sneaking around and avoiding pursuers? How has it never occurred to me to wonder?

I raise my eyebrows in query at North, who nods. The streets are clear, and we keep moving.

We retrace the steps I took the morning I went to see Quenti, and my spine tingles with the strange sense of having done this before. Then, my need was not quite so dire. But then, I wasn't responsible for the deaths of two members of his family.

Steps lead down to the river's edge, where we move from stone streets onto the woven mats of the floating market walkways, abandoned in favor of the feast.

"What's wrong with one of these?" North's voice is some distance behind, and I halt so I can look back at him. He's gesturing to one of the fishing boats tied up near the edge of the river.

"We need to use a riverstrider's barge." I tilt my head, gesturing for him to keep moving. "They are swifter and safer than any other—you and I would tire of rowing that boat long before we got far enough away."

North abandons the boat he'd been examining and hurries to catch up with me again. "They've got sails or something?"

"Or something," I echo, feeling a tattered ribbon of amusement flicker once and then fade. "Let us hope a few of them chose not to attend the feast."

I can feel North's eyes on me, sidelong. After a few more steps, he speaks, his voice a soft rumble in the darkness. "Nimh . . . you're doing the only thing you can do. I may be new to this world, but even I can see how much your people need you."

His words ought to be comforting, and a part of me aches that he's even trying, given all that I kept secret from him. But the wounds are still fresh, and his touch—gentle though it is—burns.

"You cannot imagine what it feels like to be in my place," I snap, my words sharp as knives. "You believe in nothing."

North takes his time answering, time that lets me catch my breath. "That's not true. And while I've never been through anything like this, I can imagine better than most. How heavy it is, this responsibility."

A tiny undercurrent of curiosity tugs at me. "Why? Why can *you* imagine better than most?"

North tilts his head back, gazing toward the underside of the cloudlands, little more than a dark silhouette against the stars. "My grandfather . . . is the king of Alciel."

I stop so abruptly that I have to prevent myself from stumbling. "King?" I echo stupidly. "There have been no kings or queens here for many centuries." Then, my mind catching up, I continue slowly, "Kings pass on their power to their children, do they not?"

"My bloodmother is a princess, and heir to the throne." North has stopped too, and now he looks back at me, expression faintly rueful. "So I'm, you know, royalty."

"A . . . prince, isn't that the word?" I can't help the smile that tugs at my lips. "Like in an ancient poem?"

"I don't know this world's stories, but . . . yes, I'm a prince." North's face mirrors my own—his smile appears when mine does, and a few moments later, fades.

"You did not tell me this when we met," I point out.

"In Alciel, there are people who would use my family connections against the crown. I couldn't be sure you weren't one of them."

"Ah," I say, a hint of triumph warming my voice. "So you are telling me that you did not know me yet, and did not trust me, and so kept important information secret until you could be sure it was safe?"

North gives a quick, appreciative huff of laughter. "A fair point, Divine One. Though *my* secrets aren't going to get us—"

Killed.

It is true. It is my fault Daoman is dead.

And those who accompanied me on my pilgrimage.

The chill returns. I turn away, scanning the boats until I find what I'm looking for: the warm glow of lantern light in one of the barges.

My heart sinks when I identify whose it is. "Of course," I murmur, staring at the barge. It's the only light in the entire row of boats.

North glances between me and the barges and then back again. "What is it?"

I force my lungs to draw in a deep breath. "The barge belongs to a man named Quenti, one of the leaders of this clan. It was my mother's clan."

"The clan you would've been part of?"

I nod. "That is why I came to him for help when no one in the temple or the Congress of Elders supported me. That is why his niece Hiret sent her husband and his brother to escort me on the journey that led me to you."

North is quick to understand. "The people at the camp," he whispers.

I nod again, this time because I dare not speak for fear of weeping.

North straightens, moving forward so that he can turn, putting himself between me and the lighted window. "Let's just take one of these boats, Nimh—you're a *goddess*, and you're fleeing for your life."

I shake my head. "We must ask. A riverstrider's barge will not work without its keystone." I give him a little smile, though, for what he's trying to do. "We would be better off rowing ourselves in a fishing boat."

I steel myself, wishing I could summon something more gracious than dread. "Wait here."

North gives a stubborn shake of his head. "I'm going with you."

I open my mouth to protest, but when I catch sight of his face and the look of resolve there, I feel more relieved than annoyed by his refusal to do as I ask.

A knock at the door of the houseboat gets no response. I push the door open cautiously. I call a soft greeting, unable to risk anything louder. I exchange glances with North, and he puts a finger to his lips, creeping carefully toward the narrow, ladder-like staircase leading up to the second floor. There, faint light shines in the hall.

I let him go first, for in these cramped quarters, it'd be impossible to avoid being touched by an attacker, or even just a surprised apprentice or riverstrider coming out of a room. I pause at the top of the ladder as North vanishes around the corner. He's gone only a few seconds, but by the time he stumbles back out, my heart is pounding.

His face has gone ashen, his expression one of mixed fear and revulsion, and he whispers, "There's someone here, but . . . he's, um . . . There's something wrong with his face. . . ."

My chest gives a little squeeze and a lurch. "Quenti," I murmur, and gesture for North to move so I can go into the little room.

He lies where I saw him last, the colorful quilts covering his form contrasting with the pallor of his skin. My breath stops all over again when I see him. I can't tell if he is better for my attempts at healing, although I think maybe his breathing is

267

a little easier, and there are fewer lines of pain creasing his wounded flesh.

Then, to my surprise, the puffy eyelids squeeze once, then open.

"Quenti?" I whisper, lurching forward a few steps until I can lean my staff at the foot of the bed and kneel beside him.

His gaze is vague, and takes some time wandering before focusing with difficulty on my face. "Nimh?" His lips start to curve, but the movement tugs at a wounded place, and he stops with a catch of his breath. Instead, he lifts a hand, disentangling it clumsily from the quilt. "Come here, girl."

His outstretched hand blurs in my vision. "I cannot," I whisper. "Quenti, I am the living divine now—don't you remember?"

"Foolishness," Quenti mutters, still trying to reach for my hand. "Jezara is young and strong still. . . . Why won't you greet me, child?"

My breath catches in a sob, but suddenly North is there, kneeling beside me and offering his hand to the old man instead. When I look at him, blinking to clear my eyes, I see no trace of the sickened recoil I saw in the hallway. When Quenti's gnarled fingers close around his, he doesn't shrink away.

My heart gives an almost painful thud, and I must have made some noise, for North looks back at me, brows lifted. Seeing some sign of my emotion, he gives me the tiniest of sad smiles, and tilts his head slightly. *Go on.*

I swallow the knot in my throat, folding away the tangle

of gratitude and grief. *Fall apart later.* "Quenti—we need a keystone to one of the barges."

"Mmm," murmurs the old man. "My ankles are swollen today. Hiret should be here somewhere. . . . She's grieving still, poor girl. Misses her mother. . . ."

His mist-touched mind believes he is years in the past, but he still knows Hiret is drowning in grief.

I shake my head, curling my fingers into the edge of the quilt. "She is not here, Quenti, and we cannot wait for her to return. Do you know where I can find a keystone?"

Quenti closes his eyes, and for a long moment I'm convinced he's slipped back into unconsciousness. Then, with a hoarse bark of amusement, he says, "Take Orrun's barge. Idiot boy keeps his keystone just inside the door. Teach him a lesson, asking for someone to steal it."

I whisper a thank-you, wishing I could stay and talk to him until he sleeps again—or that I could be North, and give him my hand, the only bit of comfort he asked for. Instead, I reach for my spearstaff and climb to my feet.

North is gently withdrawing his hand to follow suit when Quenti's eyes suddenly fly open again, fixing on North's face as he tightens his grip.

"I know you," the old man mumbles, a sudden alertness in those vague eyes.

North glances at me, his own eyes a bit wild. "Um—no, sir, I'm not from—"

"Yes . . ." Quenti's voice is stiff and dusty, like an old

forgotten manuscript. "I've seen you before. You're from a place so far away I used to think it was just one of the Fisher King's stories . . . but it was the Fisher King who took you in. I said it was a pity his tales of Sentinels weren't true."

"The Fisher King?" North repeats the title, his brows drawing together. "Who, um . . ." He remembers too late that he should know the answer to the question, and cuts himself off, but Quenti does not question his ignorance.

"The Fisher King," he repeats. "His stories are his fish. Quick, glistening things that are always moving." The old man is animated now, energy restored as he speaks. "They jump up, and if you're quick you can catch them, and pin them in place for a while. The Fisher King is the keeper of our traditions, lad. The teller of our stories, our songs, our ballads. He knows the laws that go beyond those of the temple, that belong only to the riverstriders. He is where we go for wisdom. And my, but you have questions for the Fisher King, don't you? You, from your faraway place."

"It is the mist," I whisper to North, whose eyes go even wider at that last statement, uncannily true. "Or else the pain— he cannot know what he is saying."

Quenti's brows draw in, and his dusty voice grows heavier. "You spend too much time around our goddess, boy. She is not for you to love. . . ."

North finally succeeds in freeing his hand, and he retreats back toward the door. "I'm sorry. I won't, uh, do that anymore."

But Quenti's alarm is already subsiding, as though whatever invented memory he was reliving went dark the moment he let go of North's hand. He mumbles something, then closes his eyes, breath slowing again.

North turns that wide-eyed look on me, and I tilt my head in a silent gesture toward the door.

The breeze, though still warm, is like a dash of cold water as we stumble out of Quenti's barge and into the night.

North takes a few more steps, as if all too eager to put some distance between himself and the wounded old man in the bed. "Nimh, what the . . . What *was* that?" he blurts.

I have to wait a moment before I answer, letting the cooler air restore some of my equilibrium. "He is mist-touched," I say finally, as I turn toward the row of riverstrider barges, looking for Orrun's boat.

"The mist did *that* to him?" North gestures at his own face, his gaze creeping back toward the single lighted window above us.

"It can damage the mind and the body. Make people see things, bestow power or take it away. Sometimes it even grants the gift of prophecy."

"Prophecy," North echoes, voice equal parts confusion and skepticism.

Orrun's boat is not far from Quenti's. It's one of the newer barges, smaller than the others, though that suits our purposes fine. I move down the little woven reed pathway and step up onto the edge of the boat.

North follows me, though his mind is still up in Quenti's room. "So you're saying he somehow knew who I was and that you'd brought me here? And he's trying to warn me not to . . ."

He halts, and when I glance over at him, his eyes meet mine and then dart away.

"That was not prophecy," I tell him. "He did not even know I was the goddess—he thought I was still a little girl."

"Still. Unnerving," North mumbles, following me as I move toward the steps up to the captain's perch.

Orrun is no "idiot boy," as Quenti said—he is a man well into his thirties. But if Quenti's mind was stuck in a time ten years past, Orrun would have been younger too.

Please, I pray, reaching for the latch on the door, *let him be as foolish now as he was then.*

I step back, inspecting the inside of the door—and there, hanging from a hook, is a little chain holding the amber keystone. I let my breath out, fetching it down with trembling fingers, and step up to the controls.

North is watching curiously, no doubt wondering what *technology* will explain away how a riverstrider's barge responds to its keystone—but I pause before starting up the barge.

"Thank you," I whisper, unable just yet to lift my gaze.

"For what?"

"For Quenti. For taking his hand when I could not."

When I finally do look up, North is outlined by the moonlight that streams onto the deck of the barge. My eyes meet his, and he smiles a little, though his face is sad.

"Whether your prophecy is right about me or not," he says, with just enough of a wry twist to his voice, "we're in this together now."

I used to dream of being the one the Lightbringer came

to. Having a partner, being understood, sharing the weight of divinity with another. Despite the grief threatening to paralyze me, I can still feel the pull of that dream.

"Hey." North's eyebrows rise as he ducks his head a little, catching my gaze. "No time for zoning out. Let's put some distance between us and the temple, hmm? And maybe then you can tell me a story or two, because if your people think I'm this *destroyer*, I should probably know what that's all about."

I fit the keystone into its hollow and start priming the boat's magic—the motions are all still familiar, for all that I've not been riverfolk since childhood.

North's voice is still ringing in my ears, telling me we're a team.

I used to dream of not being alone.

And now, here is someone to stand beside me.

TWENTY-TWO

NORTH

"There is a story among my people," Nimh says, her eyes on the dark river ahead of us, hands resting on the boat's wheel. "It is said that a thousand years ago, when the gods still walked among us, the world was ready to come to an end—that existence had grown weary, and it was time for life to begin anew."

Another time, I might have asked her to skip ahead and get to the part where I'm some prophesied savior of her people. But we still have distance to put between us and her pursuers, and nothing but time.

And, if I'm being honest, I like the way she tells stories.

"To that end," she goes on, "a new god was born. He was called Lightbringer, and he was to remake the world. But he was young and untested, and when the time came, he was afraid to do what must be done.

"When the other gods decided to abandon humanity and take to the sky, he fled with them instead of fulfilling his destiny. One god stayed behind—the first living divine—and she gave us words of prophecy. They eventually became the Song of the Destroyer—the Lightbringer's story."

"This is the prophecy about me?" I interject.

She nods. "It tells us a new Lightbringer will come, and finish what the first one could not. Restore balance to this world, remake it into one where its people can thrive."

I sigh. "And you believe this prophecy is coming true now."

She echoes my sigh, unaware of how closely the sound matches—I hide my smile in the dark. "I have faith, yes." She's standing there like a statue, the cat motionless at her side, guiding the riverstrider's boat down the slow, lazy river.

The only real noise is the lapping of the engine's blades as they slice through the water at the stern—because that's what's driving this thing. An engine. It's soundless, and Nimh says it's running on magic—because what doesn't in this place—but *something* is turning the blades on the propeller. It could be a circuit that the insertion of the keystone completes. Or a reaction between the keystone and one of the materials the boat is made of.

Or the power could be magnetic—the harnessing of some kind of attraction or repulsion.

Funny thing is, after the initial rush of excitement that I might have found a power source that can help lift my own ship, I stopped really thinking about it. Glider repairs don't feel like my top priority. Ensuring Nimh's safety does.

I don't know when that happened.

"I know your people believe mine are gods—," I begin.

"Descended from gods," Nimh corrects me, voice lightening a little. "I have revised my opinion about your people's actual divinity since meeting you."

It's a dig, but I feel a rather foolish smile spread over my features. "Oh, very nice. To be fair, we didn't know we were meant to be anyone's gods."

I catch a glitter in her eyes as they shift momentarily away from the river to catch mine. "Did your people never simply look *down*?"

I lean back, this time watching the river myself. "I've wondered that once or twice since discovering you existed," I admit. "But the clouds below Alciel are pretty thick. No one's gotten a good look through them in centuries. And I suppose . . ."

"You suppose?" Nimh asks curiously.

"I suppose my people stopped wondering what else might be out there."

She's quiet for a little while, and then says very softly, "I think that would be a very hopeless sort of life."

A part of me wants to object to that, because my people are happy, for the most part, and fed and secure. But I know security isn't exactly the same as hope, and the more time I spend here, the more I wonder what we gave up when we forgot about gods and magic and the power of prophecy.

I clear my throat, hoping to change the subject. "So what is it, exactly, that I'm meant to *do*? Shouldn't I be prepared in some way?"

Nimh is quiet for a moment before she answers, her voice thin. "I promise I will be honest with you, North. I will tell you what you wish to know, I just . . ." She falters, and I fold my arms over my chest to stop myself reaching out to offer to steady her. "It is a long story, and it is full of things for which you have little patience. Magic and destiny and divine callings."

My chest constricts and I force a slow breath. It's been a long night, but for Nimh far more so than for me. "Why don't we talk about it tomorrow?" I suggest. She nods, features flickering with gratitude.

The world slips by us in the moonlight, the trees getting thicker the farther we go from the city. Great mossy blocks of stone are strewn in among the brush, as though the jungle is taking back what was once the edge of the cultivation. The ruins have been visible on the banks for some time now, and I think the temple and its surroundings used to be much bigger—that they've contracted over the centuries to huddle where they do now at the place where the rivers meet.

I'm still afraid.

Afraid of the murderers we left behind us at the temple, afraid of the animals that are out there prowling the banks, afraid of what we might have to do next—but I also see a beauty here that escaped me when I landed.

Was it really just twenty-four hours ago? Neither Nimh nor I have slept since then, and *that*, I definitely feel. When I look over at her, I see her statue-like silhouette wobble. She's like a part of the landscape, half-hidden in shadow like the trees along the bank. I rise to my feet to make my way toward her end of the deck.

"Nimh," I say softly as I approach her—and even so, she startles. "I think we should stop the boat for a little."

277

"No," she says automatically, without taking her eyes off the moonlit ripples ahead of us.

"Nobody knows how we left the city, and we've come a long way," I point out. "We need to rest, even if it's just for a few hours."

Now she glances over her shoulder, as if she might see pursuers rounding the bend. The cat makes a soft chirping noise.

"See?" I try. "Even our fearless leader is tired."

That draws just the faintest smile from her, and she concedes, turning the wheel to ease us in closer to the shore. "We need to find a place to tie up," she says.

I'm a clumsy deckhand, but I do my best, and she shows me how to sling ropes around the trees and then let them out a little, so we're firmly secured, but far enough from the bank that nothing with big teeth can make the jump to us.

Watching Nimh work gives me a little glimpse into what she might have been like, had she not been singled out by the high priest as a child. She'd have been a riverstrider like her mother, working on the water like this all her life. It's a nice thought—and a sad one.

"I saw clothes down below," she says, as the river draws us out into its current, and we come up short, the ropes taut between us and the trees. "I will borrow some from Orrun's wife. Hers will be more practical than mine."

The cat and I stay up on deck as she heads down the companionway, and when I take a seat on a crate full of cargo a minute later, he hops up next to me. "Well, Fuzz," I murmur to him. "We're what she's got now. I hope you know what you're doing, because I don't."

He headbutts me, which I decide to consider a positive development in our relationship. Then he headbutts me again, ramming against my forearm.

"He is suggesting that you pet him." Nimh's voice comes from behind me as the cat goes in for a third attempt. This time I lift my hand, and he walks along underneath it, encouraging me to stroke the length of his back, then he spins around for the return journey. It feels pretty good against my hand, and I'm about to tell him so when Nimh moves around into sight.

She wears a pair of loose trousers that could almost be a skirt, and though the moonlight wants to bleed her of all color, I can tell they're a deep russet. A dark blue shirt crosses over at the front and wraps around her torso to tie at the back, and her hair falls loose around her shoulders.

Of all the versions of Nimh I've seen so far, I know instantly that this is the one I like the most.

This is Nimh the girl. Nimh as she might have been, if she'd never become Nimhara the goddess. I sensed it for a moment when we stood behind the carved screen, watching the party unfold so close to us, but still separate.

I'm different from the other people she knows. I don't mind if she's scared, or sad. I want her to be human. I want her to feel. And if I can manage it, I want her to hope.

"Do you think Elkisa is alive?" she asks quietly, and my heart cracks a little.

"Inshara had no reason to kill her," I say quickly. "In fact, if I were her, I'd absolutely leave her alive, as a symbol of how powerful my magic was."

Nimh considers this, nodding slowly. "You sound like a prince," she says, but I only half hear her. I'm too busy trying to block out what I just said—speaking as if Inshara's magic were real, as if everything that happened didn't have some sort of logical explanation. . . .

I change the subject. "Who are the people wearing gray? I saw them when we came into the city, and I think I saw a couple of them at the party as well."

"Opponents of the temple," she says, walking across to the edge of the deck to rest her hands on the railing and gaze out at the river. "The Graycloaks. They believe the age of the divine has ended. They see the mist-storms growing stronger and more dangerous, so they wish to create Haven cities, places no mist could penetrate, but no magic either."

"Would that be so bad?" I ask, thinking of home.

She shakes her head, lifting one hand to run it through her loose hair. "We would lose so much," she says. "Everything we have built and learned over the last thousand years and more. We use magic to power everything from our boats to our lamps. But what is much worse is that the Havens could only ever be home to a few people. They would dismantle the guardian stones that protect our villages in order to build their Havens, leaving the rest of my people alone against the mist with barely any protection. They would be left to die."

"That's . . ." I'm momentarily speechless. "Barbaric. How could anyone agree to such a thing?"

"They believe that unless they act soon it will be too late to save anyone at all," she replies quietly. "They think that a storm unlike any we have seen before is coming. And when it does, our civilization will cease to exist. We will be extinct. But I am my people's goddess. I must give myself completely to the task of saving all of them."

Her voice threatens to break on those last words.

Skies, I am doing the world's worst job of comforting her. I've brought her straight back to the memory of the one she couldn't save tonight.

"I'm sorry about Daoman," I say quietly.

"We were family," she replies, soft and simple. "We were often at odds—as my power rose, his had to decline. It might even have come to a confrontation eventually. But neither of us had anyone else. He helped raise me. He cared for me."

"Skyfall, Nimh," I murmur. "I didn't know."

She shakes her head, as if chasing away the sympathy. "I spoke the rites for him as we made our way down the river," she says quietly. "Now I will do as he taught me, and focus on what is best for my people."

"What's best for your people right now begins with rest," I say.

She raises her gaze, eyes hollow. "How can I sleep?" she whispers. "Every time I close my eyes, I see him. Or Elkisa. Or the temple's devotees, cowering in fear."

I keep my eyes on hers, willing her to see that she's not alone. "I'll bring some of the blankets up on deck. We'll talk about something else. Until you feel like you can sleep."

There are blankets and cushions down below, but it's too stuffy to want to sleep there. I bring up as many as my arms will carry and begin laying them out on the deck. Once I've made us a little nest, I ease down with a groan to pat the spot beside me.

She hesitates for a moment, and the cat immediately takes advantage of the pause to claim her spot for himself. It breaks the tension, and with a soft laugh she scoops him up, cradling him in her arms as she eases back to rest her head against a cushion. "Tell me about your family, North," she says.

That I can do. That, I can distract her with.

"My family's very small," I begin. "There's just me, my bloodmother, my heartmother, and my grandfather. My blood-mother, Beatrin, is definitely the strict parent. She's a power player, the real politician in the family. My heartmother, Anasta, is softer. Because of that, people tend to underestimate her, and I think that's the way she prefers it."

"What about your grandfather?" she asks.

"He's the kind of king I wish I could be one day," I say. "He's wise, and his people love him. *I* love him. When he's scattered to the clouds, I think Beatrin will be a different sort of leader. And after her . . ." And there I trail off, because right now the question of whether I'll ever lead my people is looking pretty grim.

I scramble for something else to say before we can dwell on that possibility. "I think you'd like my bloodmother, Beatrin. Or rather, I think she'd like you, very much. She and my heartmother both keep trying to teach me how to be a better prince, a better politician, a better leader—but you seem born to it."

"Divinely chosen," she corrects me, but her tone is wry. "They sound like a formidable team, your mothers."

"They are," I murmur, trying very hard not to think about how they must be comforting each other right now. How they must believe I'm dead.

I feel Nimh's eyes on me, and after a brief pause, she's the one to change the subject. "Did a man play a part in your making?" she asks. I suppose it's a valid question—things might be different up above, especially if we're all supposed to be gods.

"Yes, a councilor named Talamar. His part was strictly biological—I only got to know him recently. It's very strange to meet someone and realize the parts of yourself that have come from them."

"What is *biological*?" Nimh asks curiously, with absolutely no concern as to the personal nature of the question she's asking.

"Um." I wouldn't usually have a problem talking about sex, but with Nimh lying here beside me on the blanket, so close I can hear her breathing, suddenly the question makes me flush. "It's . . . I mean, he provided the . . . My mothers couldn't exactly make a baby without . . ."

"Ah," Nimh says, sparing me. And, finally, her cheeks darken a fraction, eyes skittering away to fix on a loose board on the deck instead of my face. "Biological means to lie with someone."

I could correct her, but at this moment I'm too tongue-tied to manage it. She seems less discomfited, and saves me answering by changing the subject herself.

"Are there others in the cloudlands who are important to you?" she asks.

"The next most important are my two best friends, Miri and Saelis," I reply. "Miri's highborn, with all the confidence that comes from that. She jumps into anything that grabs her interest and figures out how to handle it later. Saelis is the son of one of my tutors. He's much more grounded. And he's kind." I can feel my lips curving as I think of the two of them. "Sometimes, he's a little like an old man in a young man's body, but I like that about him. Miri adds sparks to everything. Saelis makes sure we don't catch fire."

"Hmm." Nimh casts me a sidelong look, and though her eyes look incredibly tired, she manages a hint of a teasing smile. My distraction is working, at least a little.

"In fairness," I say, "he did think the glider was a very bad idea when I built it."

That earns another ghost of a smile. "You must miss them very much."

"Very much." I hesitate only for a moment—I want to share this with her. "I can show you a picture of them. Look." I bring my chrono to life so I can navigate to my photos, our faces palely illuminated by the light of the screen.

"And you are still sure this device is not magical?" she asks—I think she might be teasing.

"Technological," I reply with a faint smile, the same way I did the first time she saw my chrono. "My people invented these about a century ago, although those were pretty primitive. Now everyone has one, and they can do all sorts of things. They track our health, give us directions, even let us talk to people who are all the way on the other end of the archipelago."

"It speaks to those who are far away?" Nimh's eyes flick up to mine. "Why have you not used this far-speech to tell your people you survived your fall?"

"I tried." I keep my eyes on the chrono for the moment, afraid to let her see just how much that still hurts. "The signal doesn't reach down here."

Nimh leans forward, studying the display, and then lurches back as I touch the button that projects it as a three-dimensional holograph. She flashes me a skeptical look. "North, this *is* magic. There are hints of such things in our most treasured relics. But even I have never seen something like this."

"It really *isn't* magic," I say helplessly. "It exists because of centuries of scientific advancements and experimentation and invention. I could take it apart and show you all the circuits inside."

She nods eagerly, eyes lighting with curiosity. "Please, I would like that."

"Well . . ." I check myself, my grin turning somewhat sheepish. "I actually can't take it apart, not without breaking it. I wouldn't know how to put it back together."

Nimh raises an eyebrow at me, and an instant before she speaks, I know what she's going to say. "You told me that magic is just science you cannot explain. But here is more of your technology that you cannot explain. How can you be so certain it contains no magic?"

I can't help it—I laugh. "Just . . . look at the picture, okay?"

It's one of my favorites, from about a year ago, taken when the three of us went on a weekend trip to one of the smaller islands in the Alciel archipelago. Saelis is in the middle, one arm around Miri, the other around me in a fake choke hold. My face is contorted with laughter, and Miri's side-eyeing the both of us, her cheeks pink.

Nimh studies it, the challenge in her expression fading away to be replaced by something softer. "You seem very fond of each other." It's almost wistful, that look in her eyes.

I pause then, because there's an easy answer to that observation, and a hard one. There's one that agrees that, yes, they are my best friends, and I care about them. And there's one that opens up a far more private part of me.

"I am very fond of them," I admit. "We wanted to make a three—Miri and Saelis and me. We . . . we all felt that."

"Such unions are not allowed in your land?"

I can feel her eyes on me, though I keep mine on the picture. "Not for a prince. It simplifies matters of heredity when it comes to my eventual heir." I swallow, then continue, "I think the two of them will end up a pair. And truly, I'm happy for them. I want the very best for both of them."

"You sound like Menaran," she says. "Watching the Lovers from afar."

"Who now?"

She turns her head to study me, and her dark eyes meet mine. "Perhaps you use other names. The Lovers are what we call the moons." She lifts one hand to point at each in turn, and we both look up. "Here is Miella, and here is her beloved, Danna. Menaran was a riverstrider, and Miella was his betrothed. He had a journey to make, so he left her in the city with his sister

286

Danna. When he returned, the two were in love, and would not be parted. So he returned to the river. Now Miella and Danna dance together in the sky for eternity. Menaran is a point of light that appears every century or so."

"A comet?" I suggest.

She shrugs, so perhaps the word is unfamiliar. "A river-strider returning from his latest journey," she replies. "To pass by them and look on once more."

We stare at the moons for a while, the sounds of lapping water at the river's edge blending with the occasional creak of the wooden boat. The air moves more quickly across the water, creating a gentle breeze that cuts through the humidity of the forest-sea. My eyes automatically seek out the dark gray mass that's the underside of Alciel—I can't help but wonder if those clouds are all I'll ever see of my home again.

Then I realize that Nimh is no longer looking up at the moons—she's watching me instead, gaze curious. "Can I ask you something, North? Something personal?"

"All right." There's not much I wouldn't answer right now, not much I wouldn't do to keep the pain in her eyes at bay.

"I was wondering . . ." She looks away, gaze on the stars above us. And on the Lovers. The clouds are creeping in, threatening to obscure them. "Did you ever kiss one of your friends?"

Whatever I was expecting, that certainly wasn't it. I blink, consider the question, try to ignore the way my cheeks are heating, and nod before I realize she's not looking at me. "Yes," I say. "Yes, I did, both of them."

It feels like something I shouldn't admit to her. I don't know why. But when she looks back at me, there's only curiosity on her face, and perhaps a hint of loneliness. "What does it feel like?" she asks.

I nearly choke. I suppose I did agree to answer a question. "Well, it . . ." I have to pause, thinking back, trying to quantify the feeling somehow. "Well, this part is probably obvious, but the feeling starts at your lips. Sort of a tingle, or . . . not a tickle, but it's related. It's very enjoyable. Then it moves, sometimes to the back of your neck and down your spine, sometimes along your arms, to your fingers. And you have your eyes closed, so you forget where you are, and what's happening around you."

I've lowered my lashes while I'm speaking, and when I look up at her, she's staring squarely at me. I can't pull my eyes from her lips, still dusted with gold from the ceremony.

"It sounds . . . lovely," she murmurs.

"It, um . . ." I drag my attention up to her eyes with considerable effort, and swallow hard. "It is. I—I wish I could show you."

Those eyes of hers widen a little, the gold-dusted lips parting, and this time I see the moment in which her gaze flickers down, fixing just a moment on my mouth. Then she drops her gaze entirely. "I . . . I apologize for my questions."

"Don't," I murmur. A little thought flickers to life in the back of my mind. "Nimh. No mortal is allowed to touch you, because you're divine. But . . ."

I don't say the words, *But if I'm a god here too . . .*

I move ever so slightly closer. I can feel the heat from her skin.

She draws a breath, eyes still downcast. *Can she have already thought of the same thing?*

But she shakes her head after a long, silent moment, and shifts away.

"We do not *know*. And after what Jezara did to my people . . ." Nimh stiffens and goes on with remote certainty. "I cannot risk it."

I can see it happening, the closing down of her face, the shuttering of her soul. The girl who wanted to know how it felt to be kissed by someone who cared for her is banished to make room again for the goddess.

I swallow hard. "What did happen with her? The goddess before you? Matias wouldn't talk about it."

Nimh is quiet, and for a long moment I think perhaps she won't answer me, won't even *tell* me she's not going to answer me. But then she looks across at me once more, half-hidden in the dark. The clouds have drawn in close now, hiding the moons and the last of the stars.

"She fell in love," she says softly. "She acted upon her desires. She chose him."

She let him touch her.

"And so she lost her divinity, and was cast out," I murmur. "What happened to him?" I ask.

"Nothing," she whispers. "Did you think her touch would have incinerated him on the spot? It is the divine who loses everything—they are the one who must choose to remain apart, for the sake of their calling."

"But that's not fair. You didn't choose this life," I reply, keeping my voice soft to match hers. "Daoman chose it for you."

"Daoman *found* me," she corrects me gently. "But the divine had already chosen me for its vessel. You did not choose to be a prince, did you? Your birth chose that life for you. And you did not choose to fall from the clouds—destiny brought you to this land."

"I thought we weren't going to discuss destiny and magic tonight." I feel a smile tug at the corner of my mouth.

Her mouth curves in answer, the movement of her lips making my heart speed. "I mean to say that none of us can choose everything that befalls us in this lifetime. It only makes the choices we *can* make all the more important. I choose to remain untouched, to honor my fate. That is my choice." Her lashes dip, then lift again. "No matter how I might be tempted otherwise."

"Then I won't ask you to choose differently." I intended the words to be light, reassuring—instead, they come out like an oath. Like a warrior in an ancient story, pledging fealty to some higher power. "I never will, Nimh."

We're close enough that I can see individual stars reflected in her eyes, and the moonlight glints off the gold dust on her lips. I can't help myself—scanning her features, it's impossible not to imagine what it would be like to touch her. To hold her. To feel her hair sliding beneath my palm, to know what she tastes like.

"North," she whispers, her eyebrows lifted with regret, "I will be my people's goddess until I die."

"I know." Slowly, making certain she has plenty of time to see me move, I stretch a hand out between us. Her eyes track the movement and then flick to meet mine, a question in her gaze as her head twitches back a fraction.

I pause, hand outstretched. I want to ask her if she trusts me, but the words stick. We've only known each other a few days, and it's no easy thing I'm asking, for her to accept that I mean her—and her divinity—no harm. But as her gaze moves across my face, she smiles a little, and tilts her head back toward me.

So I reach out, bit by bit, and let my hand hover a breath away from her cheekbone, where I long to trace my fingers. Her eyes are on mine, and after a moment they widen.

"I can feel you," she breathes.

My own skin tingling at her closeness, I move my fingertips close to the planes of her cheeks, forehead, chin. Her eyelashes dip, brow furrowing, as if she wishes to concentrate every bit of herself on this moment. I move slowly, to make certain I don't touch her skin, but the slowness seems to affect us both. As I move the pad of my thumb over her lips, they part, and she lets out a quaking breath and opens her eyes.

Earlier, when she looked at me, her gaze was full of questions—lost, lonely, yearning. Now, her brown eyes are lit like embers, and my own breath stops in my throat at the sudden heat there.

She shifts away, then lifts herself up on her elbow so that her face is close to mine, a smile playing about her mouth—and then she leans forward, trusting me, now, to hold still.

Her lips are close enough to my ear that when she speaks, her breath stirs my hair.

"And you claim you cannot work magic?"

Robbed of breath, I search for words.

Then with a deafening crash of thunder the heavens open, and torrential rain begins to fall.

With a yelp, she scrambles to her feet, and I follow. Laughing, we gather up the pillows and blankets and make for shelter belowdecks.

This is what I want for her—just this small moment to laugh and run from the rain.

Even if one moment is all we get.

TWENTY-THREE

NIMH

In my dream, I am a child again, walking the byways of the floating market with my mother. She is inspecting a piece of fruit while I gaze hungrily at the vendor across the way, who is frying dough and heating honey. I want to taste it so badly I'm trembling. I am about to ask my mother if she will buy me a sweet when the barge below us gives a great shudder, nearly knocking me over. I run to my mother, but she recoils, just out of reach no matter how hard I try.

No, Nimh, she tells me. *I cannot hold your hand.*

The floor quakes again, and then begins to crumble away all around me like shale in an earthquake, until I am on a floating island, alone. Then that too fractures and disappears, and I'm falling, falling—

I wake midair, disoriented and uncertain how long I've been falling. My body gives a loud thud when I hit the floor, my head reeling as I turn to look up at the hanging berth I fell from in confusion. The sound of breathing, a faint snore, and then a mumble, makes my gaze swing over to the other side of the room—North. He is still asleep, curled up in a ball on his side, and the bindle cat sits with perfect composure and dignity on his hip, looking down at me.

The riverstrider's boat. The rain. The moments just before . . .

Still dazed, I sit up, my pulse speeding from the fall—but as I look at North, my heartbeat settles into something steadier.

I feel my face heating, the night flooding back to me in a wild rush. It's like his hand is there again, drawing the blood to my cheeks and my lips as if his fingers were a lodestone. I find myself touching my own cheek as I watch him sleep. Looking at him is like gazing at a map to a land I only ever walked in a dream—I'm utterly lost, and utterly certain I know exactly where I am, all at once.

His thick curls have tumbled down over his brow in his sleep, and my hand itches with the unbearable urge to touch them. To touch his hair would not be to touch *him*, surely. I find my hand outstretched before I've decided one way or the other, and so I linger there, fingers hovering.

Would I know? If I touched his hair, and that was enough to drive the divinity from me, would I feel it? I don't remember when the divinity settled on me—I was so young I might have dismissed it as a passing fever or an imagined sensation. Would I *know*?

I try to imagine what it would have been like for Jezara. To give up everything she knew, everything her people needed her to be, for a moment like this one. Did she feel the divinity leave her?

Did she regret her choice?

The barge gives a sudden lurch, and I grab for the ring where North's berth is strung up before I can tumble on top of him.

The shaking ground in my dream was no dream at all—the barge is moving, and it's just struck something hard enough to make my bones ache.

I stumble upright, heart pounding though I cannot think what could be happening, and make it to the ladder up to the deck.

Early morning has dawned gray and wet, the diffuse light still enough to make me squint after the dark inside of the barge. The rain has slowed, but the river is swollen and quick, and the mooring lines . . .

Are gone.

"North!" I croak, stumbling back inside. "Wake up!"

"You wake up," he mumbles, curling into a tighter ball.

I suck in a steadying breath and lean a little closer. "North, I cannot shake you—you must wake up! The river has swept us downstream, and I need your help."

The urgency in my voice gets him moving, and all it takes is one look at my face in the dim gray light and he's scrambling free of his berth.

He's close on my heels as I emerge on deck. The barge has been caught against a mud bank, the coursing river pushing it over at an angle, which explains why I fell out of my berth. For once, we don't stop to argue or converse, but work in simple, easy harmony—I shout at North to grab the starboard bow line, and he jumps down knee-deep in mud and water without hesitation. I do the same with the line at the stern, and together we haul back against the weight of the barge.

Slowly, it begins to shift, carving deep troughs in the mud of the bank until it hits firmer ground and will move no more. I gesture with one shaking arm for North to tie off his line at the trees, and when I can manage it, I do the same.

Panting, North stumbles back over toward me and then bends forward, bracing his arms on his knees. It's a few moments before he has breath enough to speak, but when he does, his voice is amused. "Next time maybe arrange for a more pleasant wake-up call."

I'm still breathing hard myself, and I lean an arm against the tree at my side. "Wake-up call?"

"It's when—you know what? Never mind." North grins, taking any possible sting out of the words, and then straightens up again. He inspects his clothes, plucking at the wet fabric and grimacing. We're both soaked to the shoulder by our efforts, but he's still wearing the heavier black fabric of the outfit he wore to the feast.

After a hopeless attempt to squeeze the water out of the hem of the shirt, he gives up and hauls it off over his head, baring a lean, brown torso and wide shoulders, and an inked tattoo along one of his ribs. For a moment, watching him wring out his shirt in his hands, I forget about my exhaustion; I forget about the rushing river and the fact that we've been swept into unknown territory; I even forget, for a blissful handful of seconds, about what happened last night at the feast.

Then my hand slips against the wet bark of the tree, and I go sprawling in the mud with an undignified yelp.

North swears and comes sloshing over toward me, slinging his wet shirt over one shoulder. "You okay?" I blink water from my eyelashes and look up. His brow is furrowed as he inspects me, his arms crossed tightly as he stops himself from offering me a hand up. "Did you trip?"

"I—yes. Tree roots." I blink at him, careful to keep my eyes on his face. My own cheeks are heating uncomfortably, and I have to do something before they are hot enough to be visible. "There were more clothes on the barge," I blurt. "Dry ones, I mean. Men's clothes too."

North nods. "Probably more comfortable in riverstrider fashion anyway. I guess we're walking now? Where to?"

That sobers me quickly enough, for I have no way of knowing how far the river took us before we snagged on that bank. I have no idea where we are—and even if I did, what kind of place could I lead us to that would be safe?

"Go change," I tell him. "I will see if I can figure out how far we traveled."

By the time North clambers back down off the grounded barge, our two packs slung over his shoulder and his arms full of cloth, I'm at the top of a tree, gazing around at a hauntingly familiar landscape.

Below me, North looks so much like a riverstrider lad that I stop and stare. He's chosen a shirt of dark green, open at the throat and rolled up over his forearms, and a pair of pants that fit rather more snugly than they're meant to. He must not have realized that the pants are made of leather, for I feel certain he'd have the same reaction to the idea of wearing something made from an animal as he did to the idea of eating meat.

North's sloshing steps stop abruptly as he realizes I'm nowhere in sight. "Nimh?" His head swings quickly side to side, and then he bellows, "Nimh!"

"Hush! Do you want to tell the whole forest-sea where we are?" But my voice sounds more amused than annoyed. It sounds almost *fond*. I clear my throat. "Look up!"

It takes him a moment to find me, turning in a slow circle as he inspects the canopy—then he mutters something under his breath, eyes widening. "Be careful, will you?"

"Do you not have trees in the clouds?" I call back, smiling.

"Not ones you can climb."

I try to imagine that—a world where none of the trees are sturdy or tall enough to bear a person's weight—and my mind refuses to oblige me. "I would teach you how, if we had time."

"I, uh, appreciate that." North makes no attempt not to sound horrified by the idea. "See anything?"

I turn my attention back to our surroundings, sweeping my eyes across a large bend in the river until they fall on an outcropping of stone shaped like an eagle's head.

Suddenly, the memory reveals itself.

I was eight years old, going on my first real pilgrimage. My mission was to offer what assistance I could to the people living in outlying villages. The whole wide shoreline of the river's bend was lined with people dressed in their brightest garb, waving streamers and pennants, calling out for my blessing. I protested the trouble they'd gone to, but Daoman took me aside and told me not to dismiss their piety—that it was the most valuable thing they had, and to display it was a matter of pride.

Daoman.

Throat tight, I make my way carefully back down the tree. North is waiting for me when my feet hit the ground. "Well?"

"There is a village not far to the north," I tell him. "Perhaps we can hide there until I can—until it is safe. If we start walking now, we should be there just after midday."

North frowns. "Is it possible Inshara has people this far from the city?"

"Very unlikely," I reply. "This is a loyal, pious village—I came here when I was young, and they treated me very kindly. If I tell them of what has happened, I am sure they will help."

"Sounds like a plan." North nods, then sees me eyeing his clothes and grins. "What, am I wearing the clothes wrong?"

No, definitely not wearing them wrong.

I shake my head with a smile, but can't resist saying, "You *are* meant to wear a sash at your waist, if you want to look like a real riverstrider. They wear the colors of their clans."

"Hmm." North's eyes flick up to me, thoughtful, before his lips curve in a smile. "I have an idea. Here, these are for you." He carefully holds out a stack of clothes. "I wasn't sure what you'd want, so I brought a few things."

I look down at the armful of clothing, then back up at him, askance, lifting up a sleeve of trailing lace with my eyebrows raised.

North shrugs. "Maybe not practical, but I thought it was pretty."

"This is . . . ah . . . not for wearing in public." When his brow furrows, I try a different tack. "It is something a bride might wear . . . after her wedding."

His mouth opens, then closes abruptly. "Oh," he manages, looking down at the garment in question for a moment. "Maybe go with the pants, then."

I'm still laughing when he stalks off, muttering, to retrieve a makeshift sash from our packs. At first I can't tell what he's doing—and then I realize that the red fabric at the top of one of the packs is the ceremonial robe I was wearing at the feast, packed carefully away.

I scarcely have time to acknowledge that kindness before North straightens, holding the long, gold-trimmed red scarf from my robes. He ties it around his waist, adjusting it here and there, then looks up at me for approval with a somewhat rakish smile. "Do I look like a proper riverstrider now?"

For a moment, my mouth moves soundlessly, as I begin and abandon several attempts at speech. Finally, I manage to mumble, "When I said they wear their clan's colors, it isn't just . . . It's a statement of loyalty, North. A symbol of . . . devotion."

North glances down, tugging at the red sash until it sits

just so. Then he looks back up with a faint smile, unperturbed. "Yes? And?"

I wonder, watching his face, if he somehow still doesn't understand the significance of wearing *my* colors. That it is a declaration, and more meaningful than he in his different culture could recognize.

But there is a frankness to his smile that makes me stop. He seems to know exactly what he is saying to me by wearing my colors. I find myself smiling back, an unfamiliar warmth in my chest. "Perfect," I tell him.

The air grows thicker and wetter as we leave the river behind us. Here, the trees grow too close for a breeze to offer any relief from the humidity. But as we reach the path I remember, and strike out to the north, our route takes us up into the hills, the altitude bringing cooler, drier air.

To the west lie the mountains, which shelter dozens of settlements along the range's base. As the world sank into disrepair, some of my people retreated to the long, winding highway of the river, while others chose the higher ground that would not flood in the wet season. The village we seek is not far from the easternmost curve of the mountain range.

Though usually I feel at home among the dangers of the forest-sea, my spine tingles as we walk through the mountains. The sensation of being watched follows me, and I catch North glancing around more often than usual—he feels it too.

About an hour from the village our path emerges from the dense forest to meet a proper road. At the fork, we pass a migrant camp, consisting of little more than a pair of covered wagons and a handful of travelers. Rarely do such bands come as far southeast as the temple—they have most likely been cast out of their own village and are seeking refuge nearer the river.

Despite my drab attire and my unadorned face, I feel their eyes on me, their gazes as thin and sharp as their hungry faces. Even in their own village, they were likely little better off than beggars, to judge from their clothing and meager possessions. Though the adults say nothing, a child sitting on a half-rotted log holds out skinny little arms and calls a blessing in the hope of getting a bit of food or a coin from the travelers.

"We must keep walking," I whisper to North, eyes burning.

North's steps slow anyway, as though he didn't hear me.

"Please, North . . ." My voice quakes. All I want to do is whisper a blessing back to the poor creature, but the longer we stay here, the more we are in danger.

But North's jaw tightens, and he digs through his pack for the little pouch of dried povvy that Matias packed among his rations. He walks back toward the camp, halting a few steps away from the child and holding out the little pouch. The boy, arms already outstretched, grabs the packet as soon as it comes close enough. Not until he looks down at his hands, tugging at the pouch's opening and smelling the pungent spices, does he seem to understand. He lifts his face toward North's, and for a moment they are both still, watching each other.

The child murmurs something, voice very quiet, and then

dashes away into one of the wagons, to hide his find or share the bounty with his family.

North's face is cold and stony when he catches back up to me, and we begin moving again in silence.

I keep my eyes on the path in front of us. "In your land, no one goes hungry." It isn't a question.

North finally lifts his head, and the sadness on his face nearly stops me dead. I cannot imagine what it must be like to live in a place where the very idea of someone going hungry is an impossible concept—but I can imagine how devastating it would be to encounter it for the first time in the eyes of a beggar child.

My own eyes are burning by then, and I find myself saying to him, "We are helping them, North."

"How?" he asks, a strange note of bitterness in his voice.

"To unravel this prophecy is to help them—to bring into being a new world, a richer world, where no one, *no one*, has to know what it is to look at hunger for the first time."

He stays quiet for a long time, until I begin to think that perhaps he won't respond at all. It's after I've snuck my fourth or fifth look at his profile that he sighs. "Forgive me, Divine One, if I don't believe that prophecies fill empty bellies."

I was already bracing myself, I realized, for that. For the reminder that he does not believe—in prophecy, or magic, or *me*.

But then, more softly, he adds, "It's hard to take comfort in someone else's faith, Nimh. I wish I could."

"What did the child say to you back there?" I ask.

North's brow furrows a bit, and he shrugs. "Nothing that made much sense."

I try out a little smile on him. "Maybe it would to me?"

"He said that a dark magician lives to the west, along these mountains. He said that she is very powerful, and not to go there." North's eyes flick toward me.

"Oh." I frown, trying to ignore the little chill settling at the back of my neck. "I know of no dark magicians in this region, but then . . ."

"But then?" North prompts me when I fail to end the sentence.

"But then, Daoman did not tell me everything he should have." My high priest's name sits a little easier on my lips, though my heart still thuds with pain when I speak. "The Gray-cloaks, the cultists. He did not want me to know how far our world had fallen."

North shifts the pack on his shoulders. "Should we avoid the village, then?"

I shake my head. "No—the village, at least, will be safe. A guardian stone protects the people there, against dark magicians as well as mist."

"So just avoid the mountains, I guess." North's gaze drifts to the side and up, where glimpses of the western mountains flicker through gaps in the trees. There's a strange note in his voice, though, and I watch him for a time before I speak.

"What is it, North?"

"He said something else, the kid back there."

"Yes?"

North's troubled gaze swings back to fix on my face. "He said these hills are haunted, and the ghosts won't let us leave."

I try to ignore the little chill that trickles down my spine. Folk tales and stories, nothing more. But then, what drove these people from the safe refuge of their guardian stone?

TWENTY-FOUR

NORTH

The village we're headed for is set into a narrow canyon at the edge of the mountains. A dry streambed runs along its bottom. We've been walking forever, tracing the path of small tributary rivers and streams. Then we climbed what felt like a thousand stairs to reach this place. We pause at the top of the hill to look back the way we came—at the rock-hewn ledges slowly descending until they're lost in the forest-sea.

"They walked a long way," Nimh says quietly.

"*They?* You mean *we*," I tell her, resting my hands on my knees.

She shakes her head. "I mean the ones who live here. When I was young, they walked to the river to greet me as I arrived to tend their guardian stone."

We push on, steep reddish-brown cliffs rising above us on either side, their tops jagged against the pale blue sky overhead. The first homes we encounter are carved into the rock itself, or perhaps into caves that were already there.

Their open windows gaze down at us, rising two, three, and

sometimes four stories to the top of the cliffs. They're dark and unblinking, *like rows of empty eyes.*

I shake the thought off with a twitch of my shoulders. *Where did* that *come from?* A soft rustle draws my attention, and for an instant I think it must be the cat, but no. There's a scrap of fabric—perhaps an old curtain—flapping in one of the topmost windows, and somehow it's worse than nothing there at all.

Where are the people?

There are rope bridges slung back and forth between both sides of the canyon like an intricate web above us, passing between and beneath one another in an impossible maze, all rickety planks and way-too-thin bits of rope in unreliable knots.

I mean, I live in the *sky*, and the very idea of trying to cross one of those things gives me vertigo.

We walk along the empty streambed down the center of the canyon, our footsteps the only sound. The unnatural silence grates on my nerves and sets off a twitch between my shoulder blades.

When I can't take the silence any longer, I whisper, "Where is everyone?"

Nimh's reply is just as quiet. "I—I do not know."

I glance to my left as we round the bend, and startle—for a moment, I thought a person was standing there. But it's a statue, and as I look ahead, a long row of them stretches out by the side of our path. They're all about my height, with tall, conical bodies hewn from stone, heads set atop them. The bodies themselves are mostly plain—some broad-shouldered and heavyset, some smaller, more slender, but their real personalities live in their faces, which are carved with fierce, sharp features, black paint daubed around the eyes.

Nimh raises both her hands to her eyes in what's unmistakably a gesture of respect. "They are the divinities that came before me," she murmurs.

Seeing such a long row of them—seeing the history she's a part of—is sobering. I walk past them quietly, only looking at them out of the corners of my eyes.

When we reach the last of the statues, the black paint becomes crisper and cleaner, more recent. The third to last is a barrel-chested man, half a head taller than any of the others.

And then comes the second to last. It's about Nimh's height, and it's clearly a woman, its midsection swelling out to round hips, a few artful lines of black paint giving it straight black hair—except for one white stripe that runs down through the black, a single white lock.

And someone's done their best to smash it, cracks running up and down its body, gashes taken out of it from head to toe.

This must be Jezara, written out of history for daring to follow her heart.

Next to it stands the statue that must be Nimh, small and slender—they've represented her as the five-year-old she was when she was called.

When I sneak a glance at Nimh, her eyes rest on the ruined depiction of her predecessor. Her face is expressionless—but I know what she must be thinking. If not for Jezara's choice, she would be with her riverclan now.

She has suffered most because of Jezara's decision. Does she hate Jezara for what she did?

Or does she, somewhere deep in her heart, feel sympathy for her? Does some tiny part of her wonder if it was a sacrifice worth making?

I wish I knew how to ask her.

Nimh straightens, her brow furrowing as she scans the abandoned village. "They should be here," she whispers, though no one else is around.

I find myself whispering back, unable to shake the feeling of being watched, listened to. "Maybe they all went down to the river, or to forage, or . . ."

"*All* of them?" Nimh turns to look back at me. "The infants, the ill, the elderly who cannot walk?"

Before I can reply, a sound cuts through the silence. Neither of us speak, freezing where we stand. Nimh's wide eyes meet mine, and for a moment everything is still. Then the sound comes again.

A child's laugh, half-lost on the wind.

Every hair on the back of my neck stands on end, but before I can say anything to Nimh, she's whirling around, sprinting off in the direction of the laughter.

I swear and scramble after her.

"I am Nimhara," she calls, "the living divine. I need shelter and aid. Can you help . . . ?"

We round another bend, the cat running out in front, and the canyon doubles its width, broad enough now for a thin slice of sunlight to reach the bottom. Buildings in various states of repair line either side, from houses carved into the rock itself, to rickety constructions of sun-bleached wood, draped with colorful fabric for roofs. The dark holes of windows in the stone houses seem to follow us.

Nimh slows to a halt, casting about for the child—then stops with an audible gasp.

She's staring at a small island of red-and-brown sand raised up at the town's heart. A small pile of rock and rubble lies atop the island in a paler gray stone.

Nimh stumbles to it and drops to her knees, picking up a piece of broken rock with one shaking hand. There are shards of broken red glass mixed in with the rock, and something minute within the stone itself glimmers for a moment in the sunlight.

"What is it?" I ask. But as I speak, I recognize that glimmer. I remember it from the cave we used to shelter from the mist-storm, and from our engines back home. It's sky-steel ingrained within the rock.

"This was the guardian stone." Nimh's voice is trembling. Then she looks up over her shoulder, her eyes wide, but her gaze steady. "Someone has destroyed it—that is why this place was abandoned. It is no longer safe from mist-storms."

I shift my weight uneasily from foot to foot. "Then we should go. Get back to the river, keep moving. There's nothing we can do here, and you're certainly not going to find help in an empty village."

But Nimh's looking around, her wide eyes full of distress. "We cannot leave," she murmurs. "Not without finding that child—they must have gotten lost, separated from the others."

I want to tell her that the laughter we heard was her imagination—that it was the wind, or birdsong.

But I heard it too.

A flicker of movement in one of the empty windows makes us both start. I realize Nimh's taken a step closer to me, though I can't tell if she's scared, or trying to protect me, or both.

"Show yourself," Nimh calls in ringing tones. Her life as a goddess has certainly trained her voice, which emerges without a quaver.

The only answer is the faintest whisper of a laugh on the breeze.

Now that my eyes are used to it, they're finding bits of movement everywhere. A flutter of a curtain here, a shift of the shadows there.

"I am Nimhara," she calls, in that same bell-like voice, "Forty-Second Vessel of the Divine."

Nimhara, the canyon whispers back, stretching the syllables on the wind. *Nimhaaaaara . . .*

Nimh turns in a slow circle, though her eyes dart this way and that, scanning the windows.

Diviiiine . . .

The words float back again just a fraction too late to be an echo. Nimh's gaze meets mine, her eyes wide. I feel her fear like a knife's blade trailing down my back.

"Let's go," I whisper. "Nimh, let's just go. The people have abandoned this place. It can't be safe."

"They did not abandon it," Nimh murmurs, reaching out

and placing her palm against the base of the broken guardian stone. "There was a mist-storm . . . Can you not feel it?"

"You mean they're . . ." I swallow, trying to imagine an entire village struck down. "Mist-touched. Like Quenti?"

"Oh, no." She stands amid the ruins of the stone, the rising wind tossing her hair around. Her eyes meet mine. "Much, much worse."

"I don't understand," I mumble, though the worst part is that I think I *do*. "Where are they, then?"

Nimhaaaaara . . ., whisper the many dark eyes in the canyon walls.

Nimh shivers, and whispers back to me, "Everywhere."

Then her eyes flick to the side, fixing on something just behind my shoulder. My body won't move, so I watch Nimh watch the thing she's just seen behind me.

Slowly, her gaze never wavering, like that of a falconer approaching a wild bird, she slips one hand into a pouch on the belt she wears. Under her breath, she murmurs something. She visibly draws herself up, fills her lungs, and then casts her fist out, tossing a powder past me.

The air sparks and flashes, half deafening me—but not enough that I don't hear the hissing, howling sound as her spell finds its target. The cold sensation crawling across my shoulder vanishes, and suddenly I can move again—suddenly I can't *not* move.

We run, feet pounding the hard-packed earth, my lungs aching, my pulse roaring. When I risk a look over my shoulder, at first I see nothing, the landscape jumbling up in my gaze as I run. Then I focus, and see movement near the guardian stone, where I'd been standing. Something is writhing, stirring inside like ice-pale smoke, against the ground.

A head takes shape in it, arching back like something straining against a set of immovable bonds. The mouth opens, enraged, and the echo of a scream comes wailing down the canyon toward us.

I stumble on a loose stone and go sprawling in the dust. Ahead is a narrow ravine that leads up out of the village—a steep climb that normally would have me groaning. Right now, it's a glorious staircase out of this nightmare.

We're headed for it when another shriek rings out. A pair of translucent hands reaches from the shadows toward us. Nimh reels back, forcing me to fling myself to one side to avoid a collision.

We whirl around, feet pounding until we reach a precipice, skidding to a halt so abruptly that pebbles skitter ahead and down into the ravine. Nimh's gaze travels along the edge until it falls upon a rickety rope bridge beyond it, leading to the far side of the canyon. It looks like it's made of string and toothpicks.

"You're kidding me," I burst out, and she looks back, incredulous, as if I'm the one who's kidding *her*.

"North, hurry!"

The cat certainly doesn't hesitate. He runs out onto the bridge on light feet, bolting for the safety of the other side. Nimh's only a moment behind him, and the whole thing wobbles crazily, but she's almost as light on her feet as the ginger streak ahead of her, every undulation seeming to carry her farther.

The second she reaches the other side, I'm after her. But I weigh more, and I have no idea what I'm doing. I cling to the ropes on either side, the bridge bucking wildly as I stumble along it. Nimh waits for me on the far side, and one look at her face tells me there's something behind me.

I twist around to see a face made of smoke contorted into an impossible scream, its mouth too wide, black holes where its eyes should be. My foot goes over the edge of the bridge as the thing's face shifts between something vaguely human and something animal, like a vidscreen flicking back and forth between two channels.

I drag myself across the last bit of the bridge as it swings wildly, and scramble after Nimh as she finds an open doorway in one of the shacks on the far side of the ravine. We throw ourselves inside, and I slam the door closed hard enough to make the entire building shake.

Nimh and I move as one toward the only piece of heavy furniture in the one-room shack: a large wooden chest. "What are those things?" I gasp, as we each take a side and drag it across the dirt to bar the door.

Daylight shines through the gaps in the wood walls. A fine layer of sandy dust filters down from the swatch of heavy fabric overhead into my hair.

"Mist-wraiths," she answers breathlessly, stumbling back from the chest until her shoulders hit the far wall. "I have heard stories—but only stories, they were only ever stories!"

"Are they what killed the villagers?"

Her head turns toward me, her eyes big black pools in the gloom. "North, they *are* the villagers."

The beggar boy's words echo in my head as if he's standing right beside me.

There are ghosts in those hills. If you keep on, they'll never let you leave.

I open my mouth, trying to think of anything other than the terror biting at my gut. Before I can speak, something thuds against the door, making the walls shudder. I jerk from the door and the chest, stumbling backward until I'm side by side with Nimh at the far wall.

"I—I can help you!" she's calling, tears in her eyes. "Please, stop—stop this. Let me bless you—let me try to ease your pain—!" She cuts herself off with a little scream as the shack quivers, air ringing with another slam against the door.

I'm breathing in quick, shallow bursts, my head spinning. "That stuff you threw at them—how much of it do you have left?"

When Nimh doesn't answer, I turn to find her staring at me, her face tight with fear. I have only to look at her to know the answer.

None.

The walls shudder again as the door takes another beating. My hand gives a jerk, some instinct to reach out for Nimh quickly thwarted by newer, harder-learned instincts. Her eyes follow the movement, then lift to my face, her own stricken.

Then, so quickly my ears ring in the sudden silence, the battering at the door stops.

The door is silhouetted by the sun outside . . . and as I stare, something shifts against its dark surface. Trying to catch my breath, it takes me a moment to understand what I'm seeing, until the door groans and shifts as if with some great weight.

A wisp of smoke is coming *through* the door—not floating, as if on the wind, but bubbling and roiling as if surging through under great pressure.

Then another wisp, and another, and another . . .

The fingers of a hand, being pushed slowly, and with great, shuddering effort, through the wood itself. The part of my brain that knows words like *predator* and *prey*—a part that never had a workout before the *Skysinger* fell—screams at me to run. It knows what my logical mind doesn't.

Magic is real, and it's going to kill me.

The fingers become a hand, followed by a wrist, followed by an elbow . . . The very bones of the shack itself groan under the pressure. . . .

And then there's an explosion of daylight, and I hear Nimh scream, and my own voice tears out of me, certain I'll feel icy fingers around my throat at any moment.

My vision adjusts, seizing upon a single crouched figure, lit all around by a shaft of light. A moment later the figure rises and I realize it's someone in a cloak, face hooded and hidden from view. The figure stands on a pool of faded blue fabric—*the roof!* She must have come in from above, while those things battered at the door.

She? Yes, definitely a woman—something in the proportions, even with a cloak, the way she moves.

She reaches into a bag slung over one shoulder, drawing out an object the size of her fist. Then, with a grunt of effort, she heaves it at the door, where it smashes into glass shards and sends a spray of liquid across the uneven boards.

A wail of pain and fury, resonating as if coming from half a dozen different throats, like a speaker squealing with dissonant feedback, slices all around the cabin—and then silence.

For a moment no one moves—the only sound is the strange, arrhythmic syncopation of three sets of lungs heaving for breath.

Then the woman whirls to face us. The mantle wrapped around her shoulders and over her head is of deep purple, jewel-like in the sun that streams in through the unroofed shack. Her skin is fair, though lined, her eyes shadowed under her hood.

"Quick now," she says, voice brisk and certain despite the wobble in it. "Help me, girl. How is your water magic?"

Nimh is half-collapsed against the back wall—what little strength fear left her, surprise took. Blinking rapidly, she wobbles to her feet, croaking, "But—what . . . *who* . . ."

"Your water magic, girl!" The woman's voice cracks like a whip, and my own muscles twitch to attention in response, though her eyes are on Nimh and have spared me not a glance. "I only have one more jar left, and there are too many of them for us to get from here to the edge of the village—can you create vapor from water?"

Nimh stares at her, mouth hanging open, as the woman pulls out a small glass jar filled with water. The moment stretches, until a faint sound from the other side of the door makes all three of us stiffen: the long, slow rasp of fingernails on rough wood.

Then, without any warning, a massive weight slams against the door. Wood splinters alongside the squeal of boards about to come apart.

The cloaked woman hesitates, hefting the jar in her hand. If she throws it at the door, she might buy us a few more moments before the shack gives way. But the howling outside now is coming from too many voices to count.

She lifts her head, her eyes falling for the first time on me. They widen, and she gives a little flinch, as if the sight of me looking back at her is a physical blow.

Then she turns and hurls the glass jar straight at Nimh.

My heart slams into my throat, and then time seems to stretch, the jar slowing as my eyes track it toward Nimh.

But no, time isn't slowing at all; the *jar* is slowing, slowing, hovering . . .

"Take a deep breath," says the cloaked woman, her voice suddenly nothing like the one she was using earlier. Where she was barking orders, now she could be trying to lull us to sleep. "Let your mind relax. Feel the sun on your hair. The breeze on your cheeks. Close your eyes, Nimh."

She speaks with such familiarity, such easy care and warmth, that she reminds me for a moment of my mothers. Nimh must feel it too, for she does as the woman says, and closes her eyes. Neither of us ask how she knows *who* Nimh is.

For a moment, all is silent. I let my eyes go to the cloaked woman and find her watching Nimh with the strangest look on her face, one I can't quite place.

Then Nimh lifts her head, opens her eyes, and the jar explodes.

I throw my arms up to shield my face, but when nothing strikes, I risk a look.

The shards of glass are all hovering in midair, forming a glittering sphere around the place the jar had been. The water is gone—or, rather, the water is *everywhere*. A dense fog fills the air, sliding through the cracks in the building, roiling out over the tops of the walls. It spreads so much farther than it should— farther than the amount in the jar would allow—down through the valley and up the other side.

A long, wailing chorus rises throughout the canyon, echoing on and on and on . . . until it fades, a last few moans lingering before silence falls.

The cloaked woman lets out a long breath. She speaks, her voice bright with relief. "Good girl."

Nimh takes a staggering step to one side, leaning heavily on her staff. The glittering sphere, all that remains of the glass jar, drops out of the air to rain down onto the dirt floor. Nimh lifts her head with a shaky smile.

"Are they gone?" I ask, my voice coming out in a raspy croak.

The woman's head turns toward me. Her hood must have fallen back when she threw the jar, for I can see her eyes now, framed by dark hair. She looks about my bloodmother's age, with a round face and wide cheekbones. This time when she looks at me, she gives no sign of that strange recognition.

"Gone for now," she says, straightening with a grimace and rubbing at one of her legs. "We have only a little time before the sun burns away this vapor, and they can return."

"How did you know water would stop them?"

"The water is infused with fine shavings of sky-steel. Mist-wraiths are creatures made of magic. I hoped."

"You . . . *hoped*?" I echo, turning toward Nimh for support.

But she's standing utterly still, her eyes wide, face ashen. Has some new horror risen up from the fog and made itself known to her? I whirl around, but she's staring only at the woman.

It's when I look back at our rescuer, and see the flicker of answering recognition there, that I understand. Her dark hair isn't *entirely* dark—a streak of white runs through it.

Just like the defaced statue we saw on our way in.

The woman bends to put her weight against the chest barring the door. She pushes it aside with a long, loud scrape of wood on packed earth, and then straightens, not quite raising her eyes enough to meet Nimh's.

"Come," mutters Jezara, Forty-First Vessel of the Divine. "We must go. *Now.*"

TWENTY-FIVE

NIMH

The goddess who gave up her divinity leads us to the foot of the western mountains, which stretch along the long, curved edge of this land like the spine of a hunched old man.

Jezara has been a dark specter looming over me, a reminder of the kind of failure I could be if my devotion ever wavered, but never real. More like a small child's bogeyman. A hated example of wasted divinity. Had I ever thought of her as a person? If I did once, I haven't in many years. She had ceased to be flesh and blood and had transformed into something larger and smaller all at once—a warning, a cautionary tale.

But she is real.

She lives in a sprawling house built into ancient ruins where the mountains take root. I see the roof first: long rows of branches, wet with mist, stretching up the side of one of the fallen buildings strung out along the base of the mountain range. Only by following that trail of wet wood can I see where the rest of the house wanders, connecting various parts of the ruins. The ancients built this place into the side of the mountains, and so the woman's home was built upward, each addition a little higher up the nearly sheer slope. The branch-covered rooftops curl up and around the paler stone of the ancients, a spider's legs cocooning its prey.

As we get closer, I see that what I thought were wooden struts shoring up some of the house's structure are actually thick beams of metal.

Sky-steel, I realize, with a jolt of horrified fascination. The ancients' method of smelting trace amounts of sky-steel along with regular iron is a magic we lost after the gods abandoned us, but the skeletons of their spires and towers are all that's left in many places. To see relics from the last time the gods lived among us used for such ignoble purpose fits with razor-edged perfection my image of someone with so little respect for the gods, and for our faith.

I cannot help but think of the beggars we passed on the road, the child North gave his food to, the countless souls lost in the mist-ruined village.

And here she sat, surrounded by sky-steel, while those poor souls suffered.

North is just behind me, a careful step and a half back. What he thinks of this place, I cannot say. But I can feel him there, and I'm aware of his every breath.

He was nearly lost to me—to the people that love him in his world in the sky—forever.

Unbidden, his words come back to me from last night, when we fled the temple on the riverstrider's barge, and lay out on deck looking up at the Lovers.

I wish I could show you.

I thought I'd been prepared for it, for the inevitable moment when my heart and my woman's body spoke louder than the divinity in me. I've looked—of course I have looked—at boys I'd glimpse during divine services, or the acolytes who kneel before me when I pass them, at one particular craftsman from town, whose hands were strong and dexterous and gentle, and so compelling I could not stop imagining what it would feel like to slip mine into them.

But none of them, not one, has ever looked back at me. Not as North does.

I wish I could show you what it is to be kissed.

I thought I had been prepared, that the strength of my forebears and the divinity I share with them would be far stronger than any fleeting, mortal attraction.

That I should come to this crossroads now is rich with irony. Now, as I prepare to face the woman but for whose failure I would be an ordinary girl, helping my mother mend fishing nets and thinking about promising my life to an ordinary boy from one of the riverstrider clans.

But for *this woman* . . .

For who could be so selfish, so uncaring, so *heartless* that she could turn her back on the entire world, leaving every person in it to suffer so that she might experience a fleeting pleasure?

Heartless, I think. And all the while my own heart reaches out toward North with the thin, weak arms of a beggar child.

Jezara clears her throat, the first sound she's made in hours. She opens the door and then stands, waiting, for North and me.

She is older than I imagined, for when I thought of her, my

323

mind always conjured up some dark shadow-self containing all the terrible decisions I would never make. But this woman looks to be in her forties, somewhat shorter than I, and round of hip and face. She wears a robe—not red, but a deep purple—with no belt, and her hair is black save for a thin vein of silver spilling down across one side.

Our escape from the mist-ruined village is a blur of fear and astonishment—I remember North leveling his gaze at the woman, naming her, and then . . . nothing, save a roaring in my ears, until I came back to myself, running along a path toward the mouth of the canyon. Since then, Jezara has led the way without speaking but to say that we can shelter in her home.

Now she looks me up and down, an eyebrow raised. "Welcome, Divine One." My face must give away some reaction, for she laughs, a quick, dry rattle of a sound that quivers and shakes loose the heavy air. "I never expected to meet you."

The words are not exactly hostile, but there's an air about her that unsettles me.

I have noticed that fighters often have a way of standing, a display of competency and physicality that permeates their natures even when they're relaxed; Elkisa has it, a tinge of tension at all times that reminds me of her readiness.

But the best fighters, the older ones who have seen more, done more—they don't stand that way. The tension is gone. They have no need to perform readiness, for *they* know they are ready, and it doesn't matter if anyone else does.

That is how this woman stands.

I open my mouth, but it's some time before the words come out: "Thank you for helping me. How did you know to save us?"

Jezara's lips give an unpleasant twist. "When they destroyed the guardian stone, there was a mist-storm over that canyon like I've never seen before. I've been patrolling the area since, looking for survivors."

"They? Who? Who would destroy the guardian stone and leave so many helpless against the mist?" But even as I ask, I realize the answer.

I remember the woman with the gray armband speaking to Daoman the day I returned alive from the forest-sea. Her request was to dismantle a guardian stone for its sky-steel, to see if they could build one of their Havens. I look away from Jezara's pointed stare. "You knew who I was. You could have let us die."

Her keen gaze flickers over toward North. She doesn't miss the red sash he wears at his waist, my colors firmly knotted there. "Then I would have no answers to my questions," she says. "And you no answers to yours. Come inside. I will show you to the room you can use to rest."

She leads us into the entryway, leaving her weapons by the door and removing the heavier mantle she wears over her robe. Then she stoops and lifts the hem of her robe, revealing a brace strapped over one leg. The skin is swollen against the leather cords, and she loosens them with a sigh of relief. Hanging the brace next to the weapons, she reaches for an earthenware lamp and a flint-striker.

How could you abandon your people? The words bubble up in my mind like water from a deep spring under great pressure. Every question I've ever wanted to scream at her, every cut and dig and blow from a decade of trying to put this land back together after she broke it. *What sort of person chooses her own happiness over the needs of an entire world?*

How? How could you do this?

How could you do this . . . to me?

"Why do you not use spellfire?" I ask instead, watching as she lights the lamp and raises it up, revealing a corridor ahead with several doors leading off at intervals.

She glances back at me, an odd look on her face—then she blinks. "Where are your guards, Divine One? Your entourage of priests and acolytes, your barges full of amenities and ease?"

I'm seized by the ridiculous urge to lie—to tell her all is well, that the land is thriving under my tenure as the living divine. That we're fine without her.

Then the bindle cat bumps his head against my calf, and I gulp a breath.

"The temple is lost," I whisper. "A false goddess, a dark magician like none I've ever seen, has taken it and is willing to kill anyone who opposes her, starting with the high priest. I cannot return, not until I find help."

Jezara turns, the lamp lowering. "The high priest? Not Daoman?" she whispers, her eyes widening. She reads the truth in my face. Grief flickers across her features before she turns away.

Before he was my father, he was hers.

"Do they know where you are, your personal guard?"

Jezara asks brusquely. "If they are about to beat down my door, tell me now. I have reason to mistrust soldiers." The words are dismissive, and she reaches for a stick leaning next to her stored weapons. Using it to support herself as she walks, she turns to lead the way down the corridor.

She's far too young a woman to need a cane—and then the truth, the importance of what she said, hits me.

She was thrown out of the temple, out of the city, by her own protectors. Her own guards. Her own Elkisas.

And they hurt her.

The corridor turns and the tiny bits of daylight around the edges of some of the stones vanish. We're underneath the ruins now, in some substructure tunneled into the mountain.

We reach a door, and Jezara pushes it open. It takes her a while to light the braziers at the corners of the room from her little earthenware lamp, but it gives me time to absorb what I'm seeing.

I expected a dank, unpleasant hole, some meager existence carved out for herself on the edge of the survivable world. I expected rubble-strewn floors and ruins about to collapse at any moment. I expected . . . darkness.

Instead, the room that comes to life in the lamplight is wide and open, inviting and warm. A fireplace stutters to life as she rakes the coals and tosses a new log onto them. The chairs and tables are nowhere near as grand as those that furnish my rooms in the temple, but they look well made, sturdy. Small touches remind me of where she came from, things she must have taken with her—a strip of gold silk stretching across one tabletop, a tiny golden statuette of the original goddess of healing atop a shelf bolted to the wall, a set of magnifying lenses of increasing magnitude, so like those Matias uses that for a moment, I am back in his archives.

Then I realize why—between the two lamps against the far wall are a set of shelves. At least a dozen books stand there in a neat row, and on another shelf, scroll-cases stacked in a triangle. Forgetting myself, I move past my predecessor, making for the shelf. If she has a copy of the Song of the Destroyer, I could ask if North might read it—perhaps its verse will help him understand this world where my explanations will not.

From behind me, Jezara's voice drawls an amused observation. "Matias must love her. I don't think I ever ran toward a bookshelf with such fervor."

Then North's voice, a little wry. "My tutors would have preferred her too."

"You have no copy of the Song of the Destroyer?" I ask, scanning the texts with some consternation.

"Why would I?" Her voice is sharp. "What do you want with it, anyway? Surely you know it so well you could recite it in your sleep."

"I thought perhaps North could read it. He's—less familiar with our faith than most."

Jezara tilts her head. Her eyes slide toward North, who straightens and begins conspicuously inspecting the golden statuette. She goes still as she stares, as if beholding something or someone lost long ago.

"It *is* true . . . ," she whispers. "I thought, when I saw you at the village . . . but then I thought I must be imagining things. You are a *cloudlander*."

North goes rigid, gaze swinging toward me in alarm. "No! I'm . . . from a far-off country. I'm——"

Jezara reaches down to grab his wrist. She holds it aloft. "You're wearing a chronometer," she says flatly.

North's mouth falls open. "*You* know what a chrono is?"

Jezara's lips twitch to the faintest of smiles, one of her eyebrows rising. "Are you so arrogant as to think that you're the *only* cloudlander ever to have come to our world?" She turns back to me. "How did you come to be traveling together?"

This time, I don't hesitate. "I had a vision that led me to him. I reached the place in time to see his glider fall in flames from the sky."

"Saw his glider fall . . . ," Jezara murmurs, her gaze distant for a few seconds before focusing on me again, with all the pinpoint precision of a beam of light through a magnifier. "You believe he is the Last Star."

Astonishment makes me take a step back, my eyes finding North's with some confusion. How could she know? How could this solitary exile know as much about my mission as I do myself?

He looks between us, and then asks slowly, "What makes you say that?"

"'*The empty one will keep the star as a brand against the darkness*,'" Jezara says.

I clutch at the back of a chair, my knees suddenly weak. The lost stanza. She has seen it.

How many times had I repeated those words to Daoman? Insisted that my vision was real, that the lost stanza was real?

Jezara knows it.

"I suppose she believes she is the empty one because she hasn't manifested." Jezara is still addressing North, though she glances at me while she speaks.

"How—how—" My mind stutters, still trying to unravel the layers of significance beneath her words.

North clears his throat, and the sound seems to unstick me.

"*How do you know the lost stanza?*" I blurt. "I only ever saw the words in a dream. It showed me a scroll, but even if you saw that scroll while you were still the divine, you *couldn't* have seen the words—they were only there in the dream. The real scroll was blank where the lost stanza was written. How . . . how?"

"Of course the version you found didn't have the lost stanza. I stole the real scroll when I was driven out of the temple. And I covered my tracks."

North exhales slowly, his eyes round. "So it did have the stanza written on it? But you left a copy that didn't."

Jezara nods, studying my face. "Are you all right, child?"

"They thought I was mad," I whisper, the blood rushing in my ears, my skin tingling. "The priests, the Congress of Elders . . . they all thought I had gone crazy. They made me think it of myself. *You* are the reason why."

"Would you like to keep berating me?" Jezara's eyebrows lift, one corner of her mouth still curved. "Or would you like to see the lost stanza yourself?"

While I stand helplessly, my heart leaping and mind racing, Jezara locates a particular stone under the corner of an undyed wool rug. With the use of an iron poker from the fire, and North's assistance, she levers up the stone and then reaches down into the cavity. Her arm goes in up to the shoulder, suggesting part of the floor beneath the stone was dug out farther. After a long, dreadful moment in which I'm certain she'll say it's not there after all, she straightens up and withdraws a dusty scroll-case littered with cobwebs.

She trails her fingers gently across its surface, clearing away the years of detritus, then sets the scroll down on the small table with the gold silk.

With trembling fingers, I reach for it.

"Why hide it like this?" North is asking while I stare down at the case, too overwhelmed to open it. "Who are you keeping it from?"

"My daughter," Jezara replies. She adds quietly, "She's gone now."

Into the silence comes a voice—my voice. "You—you had a child?"

Jezara raises an eyebrow as she turns, the hair loose down to her waist swirling gently in time with the robe around her ankles. "How else did you think they knew to cast me out? One can hide the condition for a time, longer than you might think, but not forever. Even in loose robes, it became clear."

I keep one hand curled around the scroll, my mind spinning. "Hide the . . . that means . . ." It takes longer than it should for the pieces to come together. "You were with your—with a lover for months, long enough to show you were with child, and no one knew? You . . . you *pretended* to still be divine?"

Jezara, for a moment, looks almost comically surprised. And then she laughs again, moving around until she can drop onto one of the cushioned benches before the fire.

"Child," she says with a sigh, "not a thing changed the first time the man I loved took my hand. I lost nothing. I served as goddess exactly as I had done before, and not a single person knew the difference. I didn't stop being their god when we touched—I stopped being their god when they found out."

Horror, confusion, doubt, and anger jumble for dominance in my mind as I stare at her, the woman who'd once lived where I live, walked where I alone now walk.

She's lying.

Why would she lie?

To hurt me, for she must hate anything that reminds her of her old life. But then why let me in at all?

To toy with me? Or to give me the rope with which to hang myself? Perhaps she wants me to destroy myself the way she did. Because she wants them to see that anyone can stumble. Because she wants to prove she's not the only one without a faith strong enough to . . .

What if she isn't lying?

"Why hide this scroll from your daughter?" North asks her, seemingly oblivious to the storm buffeting my mind like a leaf in a gale.

Jezara's still watching me—she, at least, is perfectly aware of the effect her words have had. "That . . . is a complicated question, cloudlander."

"North," he says. "I apologize—I forgot to introduce myself in all the . . ." He waves a hand vaguely. "You know."

"North," Jezara repeats, and holds out her hand for him to take. "Well met."

My head and North's lift at the same time, his eyes going from her outstretched hand to meet my stricken gaze. But he's too well trained, too much the polite royal grandson—he takes her hand and bows over it in an elegant, if unfamiliar, gesture of respect.

My eyes don't move from where her hand rests in his. My own palm tingles. My heart feels like it's tearing in two. It has been so long since I've touched someone that I can't even feel it as the ghost of a touch. All I feel is—wretched. Hollow.

Jealous.

I clutch the scroll like it's my only tether to sanity.

Jezara gives North a faint smile before releasing his hand. "The answer to your question lies within that text," she says, leaning back on the bench and nodding her head in my direction. "You must have memorized the lost stanza, gone over the words again and again, haven't you, child?"

I don't answer, and to my intense and suddenly visceral horror, I can feel tears pricking my eyes. *You will not cry in front of this blasphemer. . . .*

"Nimh, come sit," North suggests, his voice a safer, stronger tether than the scroll. He crosses in front of Jezara to gesture to

333

one of the benches, placing himself between me and her for the time it takes me to move. It buys me a moment, and I glance at him as I pass, too shaken to broadcast gratitude—but he smiles as if I had, and he'd understood. He winks at me as I sit.

"I did go over it again and again," I reply finally, my voice a dry croak until I clear my throat. "I spent years searching for the reason I hadn't manifested. When I saw those words in my vision, I knew. I *knew*."

Jezara studies me, inscrutable. Is she comparing my hardships to hers? I never caused hers, though she was always the cause of mine. "Child, I—"

"My *name* is Nimhara. I am the divine vessel. The leader of our people," I snap. Then I wince, for I did not project strength, but showed my weakness.

"Nimhara," Jezara echoes. Her voice is almost gentle now. "I can see why you read those words and thought . . . but this lost stanza, this prophecy, it isn't about you."

My thoughts stumble to a halt. "It *is* about me—I saw the Last Star; I found the . . ." I barely manage not to look at North. "I know it's about me."

Jezara puts her fingers to her forehead, rubbing a spot between her eyes. "This is the trouble with prophecy," she murmurs, to no one in particular. "Everyone believes *they're* the chosen one."

North is being awfully silent now.

"The empty one," Jezara recites. "What could that be but a goddess, stripped of her divinity? This prophecy, Nimh . . . it speaks of the one who will bring forth the Lightbringer."

334

She hesitates.

Then she says quietly, "My daughter. She is the one who now sits where you once sat. I named her one of the old words for *hope*."

Hollowly, the word comes to my lips as if from a long, long distance. I whisper: "Insha. Inshara the usurper. She is your daughter."

"She is the end of all." Jezara stares straight into my eyes. "She is the Lightbringer."

TWENTY-SIX

NORTH

Nimh sinks down to sit beside me on the bench. Her hands are folded neatly in her lap, but her breath is ragged as she drags it in and slowly lets it out.

"This isn't possible," she whispers, voice tense as she watches her predecessor. I don't know what to say. Of everyone in this world, I'm the least equipped to know what is and isn't possible.

Jezara moves slowly around the cozy room, straightening a trinket here, pushing a chair into line with the table. It's as though she can't keep still while she continues her story.

"When I first had Insha, I was bitter and alone," she says. "I had been stripped of my divinity, my purpose, everything I held dear, and driven out of my home."

"Where did you go?" I find myself asking quietly.

"Where could I go?" Jezara asks. "I gave birth in a village, but less than a day later, one of the men there who had been to the temple and heard the stories realized who I must be. I was driven out almost before I could walk again."

Whatever disagreement she has with Nimh, and whatever her daughter has done, it's a difficult image to stomach—the new mother staggering down the road, alone, with her hours-old baby in her arms.

"What happened to her father?" I ask.

Jezara simply shakes her head. "He was long gone. For a time, my daughter and I lived in a floating village at the far western edge of the forest-sea, and I scraped out a living as a hedge-witch, weaving charms and healing those who came to me. And then, one day . . . I don't know how, but the people of that village discovered who I was. Who Insha was."

Nimh's face is a study in confusion, but she looks up, listening to the rest of Jezara's explanation.

"For years, I put up with their hatred and their judgment. I could take it—I was a goddess, after all, and they could not hurt me." Jezara's eyelashes dip, and she lifts a hand to pass it over her face. "But Insha was just a little girl. By the time I gathered the resources to move to these remote mountains . . . she had grown up listening to the world call her mother weak, a liar and a traitor. She never had a chance to be anything other than angry."

Nimh makes a tiny sound—when I look at her, though, she's no longer watching Jezara. Her hands are tightly knotted in her lap.

Jezara is still moving around the room, picking things up, putting them down, always in motion. I wonder if she's rehearsed this speech, or imagined giving it—and if so, who she thought she'd be talking to when she did.

"I read the prophecy over and over," she continues. "And in time, I began to truly understand. I had become the empty one, but I was not empty of purpose. My Insha—Inshara—could save the world. She could bring light. That was what I taught her."

I snort involuntarily. "When she was murdering people at the temple yesterday, it didn't seem like she'd taken that lesson to heart."

Jezara's gaze drops. "You must understand, it was not always so clear what she was. The power of her conviction was inspiring. She was determined, driven—absolutely confident she could soar to heights unmatched by any before her. And the way she spoke, the way she could wrap her words around your heart and squeeze until you could see nothing but her . . . She could *make* you love her. I knew she could change everything, win back the devotion and faith that I had lost. And then . . . there was the voice."

"Voice?" I ask.

Jezara's eyes narrow, troubled and strangely fearful. "She . . . she began to hear him. The Lightbringer himself. He would visit her in her thoughts and whisper truths to her. Things she couldn't possibly know otherwise."

"But . . ." I glance at Nimh, who's still sitting motionless, staring at something beyond Jezara, beyond the room itself. Gathering up my own wits, I try again. "I thought far-speech, as Nimh called it, wasn't a magic you had here."

Jezara lifts her hands, spreading them in a helpless gesture. "I never heard his voice myself. But what began as something I believed imaginary, a child's balm in a world that hated her . . .

it *is* true. There is a divine power speaking to her, of that I have no doubt."

"I believe it," Nimh murmurs, sounding lost. "She was so powerful. They raised the Shield of the Accord against her, and she withstood it."

Jezara nods slowly. "That," she replies, "is because sky-steel doesn't hinder her magic."

Nimh's breath catches. "That's impossible."

"No." Jezara's voice is quiet. "It's just never happened before. You asked why I don't use spellfire to light my lamps. It's because I can't. They told me my divinity fled when I touched Inshara's father. But my magic remained, until my priests found a way to take that away from me too."

I glance at Nimh, who's shaking her head. "You cannot *take* someone's ability to use magic," she replies. "It is a part of the magician, just as their blood is, their breath."

"But you can, child. If you're willing to do what's required. They put a tiny amount of finely ground sky-steel into a water-skin, so that it was infused with the stuff. And then they held me and forced it down my throat."

Jezara's voice is bitter, and Nimh has one hand clapped over her mouth now, the other pressed to her heart.

"That was how you knew to make those jars, the ones you used to fend off the mist-wraiths in the village." Nimh's voice is muffled, but Jezara nods.

"You were pregnant," I say.

"Yes. I think they believed it would rid my unborn child of

any abilities as well. But it didn't drive out her magic. It gave her a resistance to the sky-steel instead."

"An immunity," I say slowly. "Early exposure at low levels. Scientifically, it makes sense."

"Nothing about this makes sense!" Nimh bursts out. Her eyes are wild, her breath ragged.

"She was special," Jezara says simply. "Chosen. And she *believed*. It took some time before she came to call the voice in her thoughts the Lightbringer, for I don't know that he ever named himself, but when she did . . ." Jezara shakes her head. "It was years too late by the time I began to wonder if the weight of her destiny had tipped her past conviction, past reason, into . . ."

"Madness." Nimh's breath catches in a sound that isn't sure whether it wants to be a sob or a laugh. My hand twitches with the urge to reach out for her.

"I think we can safely say that's happened," I say.

"Yes," Jezara agrees. "So I hid the scroll from her, realizing she could not be the one to remake the world—if she did, it would be in her image, a reflection of the hatred our people still held for me. But if that is truly her destiny . . . then I cannot stop it. None of us can."

I look across at Nimh. Her gaze is hollow. She looks as though she's been stabbed, but hasn't figured out yet if she is dead.

Before she has a chance to reply, a bell in the corner of the room begins to ring, and Jezara whips around to look at it in consternation. "Someone's coming," she says. "That is my warning system. I would not be surprised if Insha has people watching this place. Her people are devoted to her, body and soul. She most likely knows you're here."

Nimh's brow furrows. "We will not let you face her alone and powerless."

Jezara's eyes fall on her successor, a deep but brief glimpse of sympathy there in her gaze. "You'll kill us both if she comes to find you here. That corridor leads to a tunnel that will let you out among the cliffs on the other side of the valley. I will delay them as long as I can."

There's a grim edge to her voice that causes Nimh's eyes to widen a fraction. "You think she would harm her own mother?"

Jezara doesn't reply in words, but Nimh's answer is there in the sadness etching lines in the former goddess's face, the way her head bows as if under a great weight.

I stow the scroll in my bag, carefully nestling the ancient document among my food and supplies. I'm not sure what use the thing will be—even if it turns out I *can* read it, even if it turns out I am this Lightbringer, Inshara doesn't strike me as someone who would listen calmly while we explained her mistake.

Nimh looks at Jezara for a long time, and the other woman gazes back at her. I wonder what they see in each other—Jezara in the girl who took her place, and Nimh in the woman who went before. They're the only two people in this world who know what life as the living divine is like. The only two who have ever been alive at the same time to know it together.

Tension hangs between them, sharp like a taut wire.

Finally, Nimh breaks the stalemate and blurts, "How could

you do it?" She swallows a sob. "Abandon your people, abandon *us*, for a man?"

Jezara's eyes harden, the muscles in her jaw going tight. "I wondered how long it would take you to start blaming me."

"No!" Nimh snaps, her eyes burning like I've never seen—I'm not sure I ever understood just how much her people must have hated this woman until now. "You don't get to act like the victim. You didn't choose to be divine, but you certainly chose *not* to be."

"You're just a child," Jezara snaps back, an angry flush rising in her cheeks. "You know nothing about what I've suffered."

"They *needed* you, and you left them so *you* could be happy." Nimh pauses while she struggles to get her breathing under control. "Look how *happy* you've become."

I flinch and glance at the older woman, who takes a step back as if reeling from a physical assault. Then her widened eyes narrow, her expression cold and sharp.

"Nimh," I cut in, before Jezara can speak. "Nimh, we have to *go*."

Nimh backs a few steps toward the escape corridor, though she doesn't take her eyes from her predecessor. As if her flung accusations and questions have used up all her anger, she just looks exhausted now, eyes brimming.

"You did this to me," she murmurs—though whether Jezara hears, I don't know. Nimh shakes herself and ducks down into the darkness.

I turn to follow, leaving behind the cozy home that promised rest, but Jezara takes me by the arm. "They won't kill her," she says in a low voice. "Not right away. Inshara will want to publicly dethrone her. But they can kill you, and they will. You make her human, cloudlander, and so you make her vulnerable. Protect yourself—love will not shield you from their weapons."

I've got my mouth open to protest—but Nimh's already vanished down the corridor, and Jezara pushes me after her.

We make our way down a hallway shored up by more sky-steel beams. They remind me of the ribs of the concert hall back home, completely out of place amid the ancient stonework of Below. The hall ends in an old, half-rotten door. On the other side, we emerge into a long, dark tunnel.

Nimh casts her light spell with shaking hands. I fall into step behind her, and without speaking, we hurry through the winding turns of Jezara's escape tunnel, the cat trotting ahead of us.

The sun is nearly setting when we stagger through the brush concealing the entrance to the tunnel. It lets out exactly where Jezara said it would—the cliff that rises ahead of us overlooks the valley, and behind us I can see the mountains on its other side where, somewhere, Jezara is holding the cultists at bay.

At least I hope she is.

Nimh hasn't spoken since those low, tortured words she threw at Jezara before she fled. *You did this to me,* she said— and it's true. If Jezara hadn't given up her divinity for her lover, Nimh would be an ordinary girl, a riverstrider with her clan. Able to live her life as she pleased. *With* whomever she pleased.

I move up beside her, keeping my voice low. "Are you . . . ?" It would sound idiotic to say *all right,* so I trail off.

Her reply is soft. "They only threw her out when she was so far-gone with child that they could not help but see it. All those months, she was carrying out the duties of the goddess, and nobody knew. Her powers were not diminished."

I consider my response as we match strides, carefully not dwelling on what my words mean about my own beliefs. "How do we know she's telling the truth? She's the only one who ever lost her divinity, right? So how do we know what that looks like?"

"If she still carried some hint of the divine, and passed it on to her child . . ."

I frown. "Is that even possible? I thought that this divinity finds someone random, not someone connected by blood."

Nimh raises her eyes in a helpless gesture. "The living divine cannot be touched. None of them have ever borne a child. None of this has happened before, not in this cycle of the world. It took the priests years to find me after Jezara was banished. What if that was because, somehow, her divinity was passed to her daughter, and I am just a . . ." Her voice gives out. The word she hasn't said rings through my mind.

Mistake.

Her face is so stricken that I can't help but try to fix it, even though I have no idea what I believe.

"Nimh, stop it." The sharpness of my tone earns me a startled look—but startled is better than devastated. "You *are* their goddess. You prove it every day."

"Except I haven't manifested," Nimh whispers. "Every

other deity in our history did so a year or two after their calling. It has been ten years for me. What if the priests couldn't find the spark of the divine because it lived in Jezara's child, and they settled for an ordinary, if powerful, magician instead?"

"Nimh . . ." I struggle to find words. "*You* are the one meant to lead your people. Inshara is insane, you saw her back at the temple. She's a murderer. Whatever the laws of your magic and your divinity may be, you're the one your people need. All she'll do is destroy them."

Nimh's eyes are fixed on the path now. "Inshara is more powerful than I."

"No," I counter. "She knows how to do things you don't. That's not the same thing."

She turns to me, her eyes suddenly lit with such intensity that I take a step back. "The scroll," she blurts. "You must read it—find out your role in this."

I set my pack down and slowly pull out the scroll, my mind racing for some way to stall her. In this moment, I can read her heart in her eyes. Everything she believes is pinned on me being able to read this scroll of hers—to read it and experience some sort of awakening to my destiny.

"We really should keep moving," I murmur, holding the scroll in both hands, glancing back at the bushes growing around the mouth of the tunnel, still visible in the distance. "If they get past Jezara and find that tunnel . . ."

"Then we had better be sure they face two gods when they find us," Nimh retorts. "Please, North."

345

It's that plea that stops me. The window into the desperate girl under the goddess. I let out my breath and, with shaking hands, unroll the crumbling parchment.

Back home, something this ancient would be preserved beneath duraglass and under special lighting, and only scholars with gloves and face masks would be allowed near it. I'm strangely aware of my sweaty palms and my quick breath as I keep my touch as gentle as I can.

The text of their ancient verse spills down across the page. It does include Nimh's extra verse, the one she dreamed about and believes is referring to me.

The empty one
will keep the star
as a brand against the darkness,
and only in that glow
will the Lightbringer look upon this page
and know himself. . . .

But no matter how many times I read the words, nothing changes. The scroll doesn't light up, no sense of purpose settles in my chest, no new stanzas or instructions appear. I realize I'm holding my breath only after the page begins to waver before my eyes—when I let it out, a wave of relief and disappointment together sweep over me.

Did I think something was going to happen?

But when I look up, that relief turns to dread. Nimh's watching me, her eyes hollow. I don't have to speak—she can tell from looking at me that nothing has changed. Her face is like that of someone bleeding to death, like the tiniest nudge will send her crumpling to the ground.

"Nimh . . ."

"It's all gone." Her voice is thin as her gaze dims, staring through me, past me. "Everything I believed in, everything I gave for it . . . my whole *life*. And I don't know if any of it was real."

My chest aches. I can't imagine being in her place. I try to think what it would be like to discover I wasn't a prince after all, but I never had to *believe* in my royalty. The proof was there every time I pressed my hand to a DNA lock or looked at my bloodmother to see my own features reflected there. And though I would have said a few weeks ago that my life as a prince demanded sacrifice all the time, having my freedom curtailed here and there for security reasons is nothing compared to the life of isolation that Nimh has endured.

"I'm still here with you," I murmur. The words are soft, but they're enough to make her focus on my face again. "I'm real. And you've taught me to believe, Nimh. In things I can't see or touch. But more than anything, I believe in *you*. And I'm real."

Her lips tremble, as if a smile is there somewhere under the layers of grief. My eyes are drawn there, and I find I can't look away.

"I was so certain you were my destiny, and I yours," she whispers.

Even spinning out of control and losing everything she ever believed in, she has the power to steal my breath away.

Her gaze drops a fraction, mouth shifting—I recognize it as a change in thought, a mannerism I hadn't realized I'd learned—but there's an invitation there, in the slight part of her lips. Her skin is darker than mine, and doesn't flush as easily, and yet I can see color in her cheeks.

If she's no longer certain she's divine . . . then she's no longer certain she can't be touched.

"We really have to keep walking," I blurt, my voice cracking in a way it hasn't for years.

"Why?" Nimh murmurs, scarcely flinching, still watching my mouth for a moment before she looks up to meet my eyes. Her gaze is a challenge—she knows exactly why I interrupted her. "What does it matter if they find me?"

I try not to let her see how unsettled I am. "Well, for starters, death. Maybe yours, definitely mine."

I meant for the words to come out lightly, but she lifts one shoulder and turns away, hunched, arms tightly crossed. I shouldn't have broken the moment. I should have acknowledged it, given something back to her. Why didn't I?

"Then let's go," she says, starting to walk.

It's quiet after that. She keeps to her thoughts, and I let her.

A few days ago, I'd have said that prophecy was a charlatan's tool, a collection of vague predictions that anyone could twist to suit the circumstances. I'd have said magic was nothing but clever tricks.

But that was before I saw Nimh conjure a wall out of thin air as we escaped the temple. It was before I saw villagers turned into spectral creatures by the mist, and saw Nimh banish them with Jezara's sky-steel water.

The only thing I'm certain of now is that the longer I stay here in this world of Nimh's, the less I am certain about anything. If Nimh's magic is real, who's to say her prophecy isn't?

Nimh may be doubting if she was ever divine—but if she touches me now, there's no undoing that choice. I couldn't bear for her to realize later that she sacrificed everything in a moment of weakness, and that I let it happen because . . . because I *wanted* it to.

We make our way along a narrow track bordered by spindly, twisting trees, gnarled and leaning in over it like they want to snatch us up. It winds its way up along one of the cliff faces, bordered on one side by sheer rock stretching upward, and on the other by a vertical drop high enough to make the most steadfast climber blanch.

The cat seems particularly alert, his tail swishing, his nose twitching at all the new scents. The roots reach out to trip us up, and sometimes the path seems not to exist at all, but when it's wide enough, I walk beside Nimh. I want to remind her she's not alone.

Nimh walks on through the lengthening shadows, her gaze fixed straight ahead. She seems unbothered by the sheer drop to one side—in fact, she's walking so close to the edge that my chest squeezes. Each step veers a little closer, until I feel the tension snap out of me, my voice tight.

"Nimh . . ." I hesitate, because the last thing I want is to sound like her caretaker—or worse, her brother—but then I see her shoulders hunch, and she comes to a halt just on the edge of the steep drop, pebbles rattling together and then falling in a long, silent descent.

She glances back at me, one eyebrow raised, challenging me to finish the admonishment I didn't voice.

"I can't exactly grab your hand if you stumble," I point out, smiling despite the worry coursing through my veins. I don't want the moment to be heavy, but there's something about the way she's holding herself that makes the hair on the back of my neck stand up.

Nimh gives a little laugh, her face shadowed before she turns back out toward the sunset, the colors lending her dark hair a fiery hue. "Which is worth more?" she murmurs aloud, though the words sound more like a question she's asking herself. "My divinity, or my life?"

All her life, people have been telling her that the divinity she carries is the most precious thing about her—that of all her other qualities, even the breath in her body, her destiny is what matters.

And, bit by bit, it's all been torn away from her. I wish I knew how to show her the worth of what she has left.

"Your life," I tell her, before the silence can stretch. "That's an easy question, and a stupid one. Come away from there—the top of the cliff is just up ahead. It's getting dark, and we must have come far enough. We'll stop and we'll have something to eat and I promise you, you'll feel better."

She says nothing, looking down at the edge of the

cliff—where I notice, with a tingle of horror that twitches between my shoulder blades, the toes of her boots are hanging off into empty space.

"Nimh!" I take a step toward her. "It's your *life*, that's more important."

Nimh glances over her shoulder at me. "So you'd catch me," she murmurs, "if I fell?"

I'm about to snap a reply when the look in her eyes stops me cold.

I thought I'd seen hopelessness in the eyes of that child who begged for food as we passed on the way to the village. I thought I'd seen pain on Quenti's face as he clung to my hand.

But there's an emptiness to Nimh's face now that makes my heart drop down so violently I feel sick.

"You told me you believed you and I were destined to meet." I take another step toward her, keeping my eyes on hers, though the unhappiness there is painful to see. "You know all this talk of prophecy and fate freaks me out, and mostly just makes me wish I'd never even *heard* of my glider. I don't know what it means that Jezara didn't lose her divinity when she was touched, and I don't know what it means that her daughter might be the Lightbringer."

Nimh's face tightens, and I hurry to keep speaking while she's still listening at all.

"I don't know anything," I tell her, spreading my hands helplessly. "Except that I'm *glad* I fell, Nimh." My eyes burn as I say the words, not least because I've never said them even to myself—not least because to say them means turning my back

351

on my family. It means surrendering hope that I'll ever see my friends again. "I'm glad," I repeat. "Because I met you."

Nimh's eyelashes dip, then lift as she focuses on my face, her own drawn and weary. The sunset behind her is glorious, but I can scarcely see it, I'm so focused on scanning every flicker and shift in her expression.

I swallow, hunting for my voice. "What do you call that, except destiny?"

Nimh's lips twist, then press together, eyes brimming. "Oh, North—I don't know what to *do*." Her shoulders quake, and then she's spilling over with tears.

I'm about to step back, to clear the way for her to come back from the edge, when I see her weight shift. She'd been holding herself stiff and straight, and now she sags with the weight of breaking emotion—and she takes one tiny, tiny step back.

Our eyes meet, horrified, in that single instant before she begins to fall.

I lunge, grabbing at her, fighting for balance for one terrifying moment as my muscles scream and my heart tries to push its way up my throat. I'm sure we're both about to go tumbling down the cliff, but as I dig in and grit my teeth, she steadies. Her wide eyes are fixed on my face, her breath coming quickly. Then her gaze drops, and mine follows, and I realize I've caught the blade of the spearstaff, and she's clinging to its handle.

With that realization comes a line of searing pain across my

352

palm, and I quickly shift my grip until I'm holding the spear's haft instead.

Even with her life on the line, I instinctively grabbed at the staff, rather than her arm or her hand. *When did I learn to think like that?*

"Are you all right?" I pant, carefully backing up, still holding the spearstaff.

"Yes," she says, shaky, holding on to it as well, following me away from the edge of the cliff. "You?"

I finally manage to peel my grip off it, breath still coming quick. "My hand," I say, with a weak huff of laughter for how small a thing that is. "It's cut."

There's a line of red across my palm where the blade of the thing dug in, oozing blood. I'm quick to squeeze my hand into a fist and tuck it away—no need for Nimh to worry, not when a pause to heal my palm leaves us so exposed.

There are still tears on Nimh's face, although the fear of nearly having fallen, and nearly taking me with her, seems to have broken through her misery for now. "I'm sorry," she whispers, running a hand over her face. "I-I've never had to believe in my faith when no one else did. I don't know how."

"I'm pretty sure that if I were you, I'd be curled in a fetal position somewhere, hoping my mothers would fix everything." The joke finally, *finally* earns me a smile, tremulous and thin though it is. "Let's make camp, and we'll have another look at that scroll. Maybe it has some hint about what to do next."

So when we reach the top of the cliff and find a small

clearing among the scraggly forest there, we stop. We're both still shaken by the near miss, and Nimh is eyeing a glimmer on the horizon that might be an approaching mist-storm, but the silence as we make camp is companionable, rather than tense.

I go through our supplies and fetch water, pulling together a meal that leaves as much as I can manage for tomorrow. Neither of us speak until we've eased down to sit by the small fire and chewed our way through what I think are some dried mushrooms and some flatbread.

"Want to take another look at the scroll?" I venture.

"I dare not hold it near the fire, and I might need the fireseed I have—since I cannot go back to the temple to replenish it." She lets out a long, slow breath. "We must wait until daylight."

I hold up my wrist, showing her my chrono and activating the built-in flashlight. "Sometimes science really *is* the answer."

Nimh blinks, and then actually lifts a hand as if she might seize my arm to draw it near. Of course, she doesn't, but her urgency is enough to prompt me to retrieve the scroll from among my things and hand it to her. We unroll it for the second time, Nimh handling it with a lot more care than I did in the moments after we stepped out of the tunnel.

We end up laying down first my jacket, and then my spare shirt, under it, then carefully weighting the corners of the paper with small rocks cleaned of even a speck of dirt.

We lean in together over the lines of neat handwriting, and Nimh points to a section low down. "This is the extra stanza," she murmurs, her eyes wide. "In the copy back at the temple, there was only a blank spot, but in my vision the words appeared. *These* words."

When I first looked over the scroll, there wasn't time to wonder at the fact that she dreamed of this before she'd ever seen it in real life. "How could you have known?"

Her head turns a little, just enough for her to look at me through her lashes, a faint smile tugging at her lips. "Magic," she says, voice low and amused. The glance makes my chest squeeze—it's a relief to see even a hint of a smile, after the day's events.

She bends back over the text and points with one careful finger, her touch hovering above the last few lines:

The empty one
will keep the star
as a brand against the darkness,
and only in that glow
will the Lightbringer look upon this page
and know himself. . . .

"This is *you*, North," she murmurs. "I am the empty one, and you are the star. My people often used *light* metaphorically in these old texts; this *glow* could mean in your company, or your lifetime."

"Or . . ." I hesitate, realizing my sudden idea might not be the most tactful one. But when Nimh looks at me with raised eyebrows, I end up lifting my wrist. "Or it literally means by my glow."

Nimh huffs a quick, appreciative breath of laughter. Even she wouldn't go so far as to think her ancient predecessors could have predicted we'd be reading this thing by chrono-light, but it's true nonetheless.

"So how would we know if I was, um, knowing myself?" *Keep a straight face, North. Probably doesn't mean here what it would sound like back home.* Miri would be in stitches.

But Nimh bites down on her lip, uncertainty bubbling to the surface. "I thought it would be clear," she admits. "I thought you might have a vision, the way I did, or experience an awakening of suppressed memory or receive some instruction."

The paper begins to curl, one of the pebbles sliding aside as the scroll tries to return to the roll it was in for such a long time, and I reach out to carefully nudge the paperweight back into place.

Nimh makes a small sound and lifts one hand, and when I follow her gaze, I realize she's staring at my palm, which is still oozing sluggishly from where it sliced along the blade of her spearstaff. "You're still bleeding!" she exclaims, brow furrowing as she lifts her eyes to mine, faintly accusatory.

I grimace, muttering, "It looks worse than it is, I promise." I give it a little shake as I pull away, and a few droplets of blood spatter against the scroll.

Before I can wince at having defaced such a valuable ancient artifact, the whole thing . . . *flickers.*

Like a vidscreen momentarily losing power, the text phases out, then back in. The ink begins to expand and unfurl across the page, flowing out from the original lettering to form new text all around the margins and between the lines, crammed onto every available part of the scroll.

It's like watching a circuit come to life, like watching one of the DNA locks around the royal quarters activate—exactly like, since a drop of blood started it—and Nimh and I watch breathlessly as the whole thing unfolds.

The new sections are a tangle of ink, layer upon layer, some faded with the centuries, others newer and crisper.

"North . . . ," Nimh whispers tremulously.

This must be it. This must be how the Lightbringer knows himself.

I'm not even sure what I want—to see nothing, and escape this madness, or to understand every word and prove to Nimh she was right.

But when I look at it closely, it's absolute gibberish. It's like one of the bugs circling the light of my chrono fell into an ink pot, and then dragged itself all over the page in its dying convulsions. I stare down at the mess of ink with no idea what to say. I want to put off the moment of saying anything. If this is the test for the Lightbringer, then Nimh has been wrong. And all this death and sacrifice has been for nothing.

"Nimh . . . ," I start, and my voice is enough to make her lift her head, brow furrowed.

She shakes her head and extends a finger, gesturing to part of the tangled mess. "Here, this part," she says. "This is written in your ancients' lettering—can you not read it? It describes an omen that will point the way, a vision of a thousand wings. And here, it describes the blood of the gods raining down upon the earth. . . ."

It takes her a moment to realize I'm not looking at the text with her anymore. When she looks up at me, her urgency tinges with confusion. "North?"

My heart's pounding in my ears. Our eyes meet.

"Nimh, *you* can read it. You *are* reading it."

She stares at me for a long, long moment. Her eyes go to the parchment, then back up to me again. Her gaze changes while I watch, her dark eyes quickening like smoldering coals—realization spreads like a wildfire.

I don't know if I believe her prophecies. I don't know if I believe in her gods or her destiny. I don't know if I believe in any of this.

But I believe in *her*.

Because if *she* can interpret what we're seeing, that can only mean one thing to her and her people.

She is the Lightbringer.

TWENTY-SEVEN

NIMH

The words squirm and crawl up at me in the pale blue light from North's bracelet. They burrow into my eyes, into my mind, a slow and inexorable torrent. I cannot pull my eyes away—each time I think I have reached the limits of what I can see there in the knotted lines and curls of ink, some new phrase or symbol grabs my eye and hauls me back into the prophecy.

North brings me food. He tries to get me to stop and eat. I feel him lingering like a distant distraction. The bindle cat makes an attempt to walk onto the surface of the object that has interested me so much, and I pull him back so quickly that he hisses in surprise and betrayal—later I feel him crouching, warm, by my leg, rumbling with an anxious purr.

The stars move overhead. Dust blows past in the canyon below. The Lovers have set, and give no light, but I have no need of them, for I have a relic of the ancients, a gift from the gods who left us. Light brought to the Lightbringer.

Dimly, I am aware of North speaking—he wants me to stop. To sleep. To rest my eyes and my mind. It has been hours, he says. He tries to leave, pulling his arm and the light away, but when I cry out a wordless objection and look up, he freezes as he sees my face. Silently, he pulls the bracelet off his wrist and sets it down by the scroll.

Just now I cannot read his expression, cannot parse the emotion written there, for I can read only these words spread out before me. What I see in his face makes no sense—for what reason would North have to look at me with fear?

I grab the bracelet, and after a time, my ears detect the sound of his footsteps moving away. I say nothing—I can't, for my mind is already wrapped once more in the depths of the page beneath my eyes.

My entire life—everything I have been, everything I *haven't* been—has been for this moment. All those years of uncertainty—all of it was for a purpose. This purpose.

My purpose.

My aspect, manifested finally after all this time.

Lightbringer.

The words are written in layers. The oldest are in the crisp, angular text of North's people, the ancients, while the newest are less than a century old. I recognize at the edges the light, meandering handwriting of Lorateon, the god before Jezara.

And I see the others there too. I see Minyara, the goddess of the night sky, who mapped the heavens and studied the movements of celestial bodies and foretold the coming of Minyara's Flame, a heavenly visitor that hung like a pale spirit in the night sky for a week a hundred years before I was born—and more than three centuries after she died. She speaks to me now in the same handwriting I know from my own studies of her charts;

360

she tells me of the Last Star, whose light would show the Light-bringer who she was—North's light. His blood, his presence, are why I am reading these words. Minyara tells me that this vision is but the beginning of my journey.

And there is Vesseon, god of exploration, who predicted the existence of an ancient waterway to the north that would, eighty years later, become vital for the passage of ships from the eastern sea to the western, sparing our sailors and merchants the violent seas ringing the southern cape of the world. He saved countless lives when explorers finally discovered that passageway, and I read his journals as though they were epic tales, devouring one after the other. And now he writes to me, as directly and intimately as if he were writing a letter to an old, dear friend. He tells me of a place remembered in his time but lost in mine—a place beyond the end of the world, a place of beginnings and endings, where I must go to fulfill my destiny.

Alteon, whose aspect was poetry, sings me a song in his hasty scrawl of loneliness and heartache, and of choices to come that will test my devotion and my faith. Emsara, whose time campaigning as the goddess of war brought us into the peace our countries know today, tells me that blood will be shed, that blood *has* been shed, but that the shedding of blood has shaped the world, and not to be afraid. Elinix, who was without gender and who manifested the aspect of love itself, whispers to me that we who are the living gods are human still, and are so for a reason—that our humanity is as vital as our divinity, even for the one who will end this world.

Especially for her.

Alone, the phrases and pieces of words make little sense—only when read together, mixing the newest additions with words left here a thousand years ago, does meaning come to me.

There are fragments of writing I do not recognize—older sections, closer to the time of the ancestors North and I share. Words that come to me from a time before even our oldest texts, from divines whose names have been lost to that desperate era when writing itself was a luxury denied those trying to survive.

My trembling fingers hover just above the page.

This is older than anything anyone alive has ever read.

And only I—so desperate for my manifestation and so late to find it that my studies ran the full gamut of our history—could have read and understood it. Finally, I understand what none of my priests and tutors could ever tell me: this is what it feels like to discover my divine aspect.

To manifest, to have purpose.

To *know* my destiny.

My mind, which had been soaking in the words like parched soil drinks in rain, is suddenly full—the words dribble in and away, my thirst slaked, my soil saturated. And still, I cannot take my eyes from the page, cannot stop reading. My eyes move faster and faster, my heart racing. The page blurs, for I cannot even pause to blink, but the words still make their way into my mind, bypassing sight entirely.

I try to pull away, but my body will not respond—North has given up trying to interrupt my studying, and I cannot hear him nearby. All I can hear is the whispering of ancient words in my thoughts, louder each moment.

They wash over me and through me, leaving searing fire in their wake, until I am certain I am dying, burning from within, about to explode into a pillar of flame—and then comes a silence so complete that I would gasp, if I could move.

Lightbringer, the scroll whispers to me. *Listen well . . . for this is how you will end the world.*

TWENTY-EIGHT

NORTH

Wisps and curls of mist are gathering in the hollows around the clearing, slowly swirling into larger sections, coming together and then breaking apart. It's hypnotic to watch.

Nimh is still motionless, a statue—I can't even tell if she's breathing. So I focus on the mist and try to fight off the worry that wants to unfurl into panic.

How long do I leave her like this? Is she even capable of coming back from wherever she's gone? What's happening to her now, and what happens next? I almost find myself missing her, though she sits just feet away.

I've been staring at the mist tendrils for hours when I slowly begin to realize that something's changing. They're moving with more purpose than they were before, writhing sections of the stuff joining together and swelling larger with a sort of restlessness that says, *Something's coming.* The stars above us are fading, not just because dawn is near, but because the air above us is thickening. It takes me far too long to understand what I'm seeing, and when I do, I scramble up from where I was sitting against a tree.

There's a storm coming. It isn't safe to be here. How much time have I wasted, thinking about Nimh instead of properly keeping watch?

"Nimh!" I hurry over to kneel in front of where she sits, still caught in a sort of ecstatic trance. She doesn't even twitch as I raise my voice. "Nimh, listen to me, I need you to wake up!" The cat adds a yowl to my pleas, stalking in a figure eight with me at the center, his fur fluffed up in every direction.

Nimh stays perfectly still, sitting cross-legged, one hand lifted to hold her spearstaff upright at her side, the other hovering over the scroll she's still reading, her lips moving soundlessly, her eyes wide.

"Nimh, please!"

I don't dare touch her, so I push at the haft of the spearstaff where it rests on the ground, until the whole thing slides backward and falls over. As the spear topples, her hand glides up until it reaches the place where the pointy end's attached. My eyes trace its movement. I see her palm slide over the dried blood I left when I cut myself.

Instantly, her head snaps back, her unseeing gaze fixed on the mist swirling above us. She spreads her arms wide and the mist begins to move. I skitter back on my hands and knees, shoving myself away from her as the mist turns a pure, pearlescent white. It lights up the clearing like it's daytime, a brilliant flash stinging my eyes.

The mist is radiant, clinging to her like an aura, curling around her arms and legs like the cat does when he's angling to be petted. It's a living thing, and a part of her. The sight makes the hair on my arms stand up on end.

For a long moment that's the only movement around us—Nimh's frozen. The cat and I crouch together, watching her, and the luminous mist weaves a path around her body. It feels like everything's suspended, like time's stopped.

Then it all comes back in a rush, and with a blinding flash she's rising up from the ground, her arms still outflung, silhouetted perfectly against the shimmering haze. The clouds pick up speed, whirling in a quickening circle around her, spiraling up above the treetops, picking up leaves and debris and flinging them everywhere, the trees shivering and shaking. Our campfire vanishes in a whirl of sparks caught in the fierce wind and torn apart.

I slap one hand down over the ancient scroll before it can be whipped up into the air. I hunker down, letting the cat push his way in underneath the arm holding the scroll as the two of us make ourselves as small and flat as possible.

A light whirls by me and I realize it's my chrono, tumbling along with the storm. I snatch it as it flies past, pulling it in beneath me. My hands press into the cat's warm side as I shove it on over my wrist—my last link with home.

An instant later everything's perfectly still, except the leaves fluttering slowly down. When I dare to lift my head, Nimh still floats in midair, holding her spearstaff, her body glowing white. And then she speaks, her voice raw, as though the words are being ripped from her.

"The Lightbringer will look upon this page

by the light of the Star

and learn the lessons of years.

Then the Star shall light the path

in the place of endings and beginnings.

The mother of light shall speak,

And the two faces of the Lightbringer shall do battle.

The Lightbringer shall rise

that the sky might fall,

and the blood of the gods rain down."

As I stare up at her, openmouthed, suddenly it's over—she falls to the ground like a puppet with its strings cut, sprawled motionless on the floor of the clearing.

I scramble toward her, but the cat is already out in front of me, and he lands flat in the middle of her back. By the time I reach the pair of them, she's stirring.

She moves just like the cat, slow and deliberate, stretching and arching her back as she pushes herself up, shaking her loose hair away from her face and turning to meet my gaze.

But this isn't Nimh. This is some wild-eyed version of the girl I've come to know, the dawn showing me a curve to her lips, a certainty in the tilt of her head that I've never seen before. She seems almost to glow, golden and shining against the rising sun behind her, with newfound purpose gleaming in her features.

If I didn't know her as well as I do, I might think she was serene. But I can glimpse the whites of her eyes, the energy bursting from inside her in the way sparks fly off a live wire, ready to connect with something and send a deadly shock straight through it.

She lifts one hand, and the mist around us whirls into action once more, seeming to contract and intensify around her, and then suddenly fly out toward the edges of the clearing, as if some invisible blast had thrown it away from us. There it stays, roiling slowly as it circles us.

Nimh tilts her hand and it picks up speed, its circuit of the clearing's edge suddenly urgent.

She tilts her hand back the other way and it slows once more.

She's controlling it.

"Nimh?" I sound like I'm afraid of her. In this moment, I am.

"This should not be possible," she breathes, watching the mist with those heated eyes. "To control the mist is to control magic itself."

I fight the desire to step back, the memories of what the mist did to Quenti and those villagers all too fresh in my mind.

Nimh condenses the mist into a little tendril that weaves about her hand. "One might collect the rain to water a garden . . . but one does not command the rain to fall."

Her eyes lift from her hand to meet my gaze. She must read something in my face, for hers softens. "You have nothing to fear," she whispers. "See?" The current of mist stretches out toward me, beckoning like a finger. When I recoil, scrambling to my feet, a flicker of hurt crosses the not-quite-serene expression on her face. "North?"

I swallow hard. "You spoke, when you were—right before

you woke up. You sounded like you were reading from a new prophecy."

Her brow furrows, the mist receding back to settle around her like a halo, catching the rising sun. "Yes . . . I remember." She blinks, urgency cutting through her daze. "It *was* a new prophecy. You are the Last Star—by your light, I knew myself . . . the Lightbringer. You were always going to be here at this moment, and I was never going to manifest until you arrived."

"A prophecy a thousand years in the making predicted *me*?" I protest.

Her weight shifts as though she wants to step toward me, but she stops herself. She can't hide the intensity in her gaze, though, and that's enough to make me want to flee. "Jezara was wrong, North. I do not know what magic Inshara has used to convince others that she is communing with the Lightbringer's spirit. But I have never been more certain in my life. *I* am the Lightbringer. And you *are* the Star—you unlocked the scroll for me to read. Don't you see?"

"And what does that mean, exactly?" Though the mist around her is quiet now, I can still see it, like a faint iridescence in the air. Somehow, its near invisibility is worse than when it was reaching toward me—now it's waiting, lurking, like a predator in the shadows. "You've been promising since the temple to tell me what the Lightbringer is meant to do. Because all the other names for that god—Destroyer, Wrathmaker, Eater of Worlds—they all sound incredibly . . . murdery."

Her eyes are clear, and though she doesn't hesitate, her voice does quiet. "The Lightbringer is the one who ends the world."

"Ends?" My throat is tight, my body cold. "That can't mean what it sounds like."

"Do those words have another meaning in your land?" she asks. "The Lightbringer brings about the end of the world. The sky will fall, the forest-sea will burn, and the slate of creation will be wiped clean. We will see an end to the cycle of suffering and poverty and disease. A return to the nothingness from whence all this was born."

A cold feeling settles in my gut at her words. "Nimh . . . you can't be serious—you want everyone and everything in this world destroyed?"

She leans forward, her gaze intent, pleading with me to understand. "Here, we are taught as children about the cycle of creation and destruction—we all learn that the end will come, and that we will be reborn in a world without suffering. But for that to happen, all this"—a sweep of her arm takes in our surroundings: the dawn, the golden light filtering through the trees, the tumble of the river below—"must die. And so must we."

And so must we. . . .

"The sky," I manage, trying not to let my dread infect my voice. "When you say the sky will fall . . ."

"The cloudlands," Nimh says, her voice softening a little. "Yes. The gods must return to us in this new cycle."

"The blood of the gods will rain down," I whisper, echoing that line of her new prophecy.

370

Her dark eyes fix on mine. "Your people and mine were never meant to exist apart. If there is anything I know with absolute certainty, it's that our two peoples were bound together long ago. Our worlds must be reborn together."

She's talking about bringing my people crashing down to Below in what could only be a firestorm of death and destruction. An impact of that magnitude would certainly destroy this land—her people and mine would be all but vaporized. The forest-sea *would* burn. The ash and debris from that fire would block out the sun for generations. It could mean the death of everything.

Suddenly, her words are real.

The Lightbringer shall rise, that the sky might fall.

And she believes everything will somehow be reborn. Maybe eventually some kind of plant will take root again, but the idea that the world itself could ever . . .

My blood unlocked the scroll just as if it were a DNA lock in the palace. That means our tech is here, all over the place, mixed in with faith and magic and ancient prophecy. The scroll could hold the key to bringing down the sky-islands. If that's true, the end of the world is no metaphorical idea—Nimh *could* do it.

"What will it be like? After?" I ask, still hoping for a loophole and stalling for time.

"No one can say with absolute certainty," she replies. "No one in this age could have witnessed anything before its beginning. But there have been many, many remakings before. Infinite worlds, an unbroken chain of life and death and rebirth.

There will be beauty again. There will be people, just as there are people now—but the world will be full of life and hope and bounty, and the people will no longer be starving or sick or huddled against the mist-storms."

I want to crawl away from her. I want to throw up. I know I'm not concealing my expression—she must see the horror and the disgust I'm feeling. She takes a deep, bracing breath. "This world was meant to end centuries ago, North—that is why these lands are so sick, their people so full of suffering. We had a Lightbringer once, and he fled to the skies with the rest of the gods, leaving us with no hope, no end to the infinite decline of our home. Until now." Her eyes are burning with a kind of dark fire, hope and certainty and pleading all at once.

"But there are ways to fix your problems," I say, hearing the desperation in my own voice. "If I am the Star, I can show you *so many* things! In Alciel, we have technology that could help feed your people. We can turn bad water to fresh, we grow large amounts of food on small stretches of land. We probably have sky-steel all over the place without realizing it—maybe enough to shield everyone here from the mist! Maybe with the changes my people could bring to this place, it would be as if the old world *had* ended and a new one had come. After all, if nobody's ever seen this cycle happen, how can we know? *That* is what I could show you. That's how I could light your way."

"You sound like the Graycloaks!" she blurts. "Trying to postpone what is already a thousand years too late. We have suffered for centuries, North—we have starved and died and pitted brother against brother in wars over clean water to drink and a safe place to live, because we had no choice. But the world still falters, and my people are still dying, and the ones who live still do so in agony. You have seen only a fraction of our suffering, and only for a few days. I have witnessed it my entire *life*. My people have lived it for generations."

There are tears in her eyes now, but she doesn't bother to wipe them away. The dawn light catches them, making them diamonds as she continues speaking. "All my life, I have wanted nothing more than to find a way to help my people, and all my life, I have had to watch, powerless, with no hope of change. *This* is our hope. *I* am our hope. If I am the one destined to bring this gift to my people, how can I not do so?"

"How can you do it at the expense of *my* people?" I demand. "They don't want to die. They don't want to be reborn. You don't get to decide this on your own, Nimh!"

"I am deciding nothing," she replies, her voice rising to match mine. "This is not some foolish belief. Have you not seen all that has happened to bring us here, to this moment? The Star fell, the empty one found it, together they brought forth the Lightbringer . . . None of it is happening the way I thought it would, but still, here we stand!"

"Coincidence," I mutter, dizzy and sick.

"Destiny," she retorts. "Where do you think these prophecies come from? Do you think they are just pretty stories, written by delusional fools? Delusional fools like me?"

I wish I could deny it—I wish I could tell her I don't think she's delusional and I don't think she's a fool. The Nimh I know is clever and caring and resourceful and brave beyond anything I've ever had to imagine.

But maybe my idea of her was never real. My voice shaking, I try one last appeal. "All those people, Nimh. Yours and mine. They would all *die*. How can that be something you want to happen?"

"*What choice do I have?*" she cries.

"*There is always a choice!*" I snap in reply.

She exhales slowly, her eyes wet with unshed tears. "I don't want anyone to die. But everything, *everything*, is part of the cycle of death and rebirth. Even the most beautiful, massive hirta tree in the forest-sea cannot live forever. When it dies, it decomposes, returning its life to the earth, and clearing a space for the sun, and a hundred new plants spring up from its grave. The old must make way for the young—it is the way of life itself." She pauses, then adds with a hint of frustrated venom, "Or has your 'technology' conquered death itself?"

"Of course not," I say quietly. "One day my grandfather will die to make way for my mother, and she will die to make way for me. But there's a difference between that natural cycle of death and rebirth, and simply killing everyone in both our worlds."

"Life is precious to me, North, more precious than you can possibly . . ." Her voice cracks, and she passes a hand over her face, regathering herself. "Why do you think we call our destroyer the Lightbringer? It is because he—because I—*am* light, for a people living in darkness. I am hope."

"But it's not just you, is it?" I ask quietly. "I'm the Last Star. And I'm supposed to play some role in this. Well, I won't do it."

I push to my feet, my muscles aching.

"North," she says, voice aching with appeal.

I shake my head and take a step back. A shiver runs through me in the early light, and . . . and *wait*.

The shiver continues down at my wrist.

It's my chrono. My chrono is *vibrating*.

I yank my wrist up with a gasp, and Nimh scrambles to her feet to try to see what I see. The same display I've been seeing since I touched down is still there:

CALCULATOR TIME/DATE BIO-FEEDS SCAN
PICS NOTES MESSAGE ARCHIVE

But beneath it, there's a new icon. One I've seen thousands of times, but never with a leap of my heart like I'm feeling now.

NEW MESSAGE

I fumble as I try to bring it up, my finger suddenly huge and unwieldy, my lungs tightening as if someone has their arms too tight around me. *Please*, I beg it silently. *Please don't be a glitch. Please, please be real.*

Even if it's just some momentary, miraculous millisecond of reception, a chance for just one message to download, it'll be a glimpse of my old life that I suddenly, desperately need. It'll be just a fraction of a second of normalcy. It'll be a link to a place I miss with all my heart and soul.

My eyes are hot with tears as I pull the thing up, the message projecting above my chrono in the luminous green letters I'm so accustomed to.

MESSAGE: RENDEZVOUS
MEET RESCUE PARTY. LOCATION INDICATED.

There's a map sketched out beneath the two lines of text, and it's easy enough to make out the main features—the canyon and river we've been following, the forest, the temple back in the city, and the road in between. Farther east, there's a flashing X that indicates my rendezvous point. All I have to do is follow the river to get there.

My head's spinning, questions elbowing each other aside in a wrestling match. How did my people get down here safely? How are they going to get back up? How do they know this place well enough to draw this map? How did they know that I'm even still *alive*?

"North?" Nimh's voice is taut with urgency—she's watching my face, and I realize I haven't spoken.

"It's a message from a rescue party," I blurt, keeping my eyes on the map instead of her face. "They're ready to meet me, to take me back."

There's pain at the thought of leaving Nimh behind. After everything we've been through, parting like this feels wrong in every way.

But *this* Nimh, wreathed in deadly mist—I don't know who she is. If I can stop her from harming Alciel, then I have no choice—maybe leaving will be enough, taking away part of her prophecy. If not, then my people will need to defend themselves, and only I can warn them.

"Back?" Her face is stricken, desperate. "No, we have work to do. We must do this together, North."

"*We* aren't doing anything," I tell her, taking a step back. "I won't help you destroy either of our worlds." *I'm sorry*, I want to say, but I'm not—I can't be. Not now.

"But . . ." She takes a step forward, lifting one hand, the mist rising and stretching toward me as if in echo. "Our destiny—"

"I don't believe in destiny!" I snap. "None of this is *real*, Nimh! Whatever messages our ancestors left you, they've been twisted, changed over the centuries. No sane person wants to kill everything in existence. It's not right. It's not *real*."

The words hang between us, her face as wounded as if I'd slapped her.

"You cannot mean that," she whispers. Mist gathers around her, flickering along with the rise and fall of her chest as she breathes. "Not after everything you've seen."

"I'll do whatever it takes to stop you from doing this. How can you think I'd do anything else?"

The silence stretches out between us as our eyes meet, and she's the one to break it.

"You say none of this is real. But if you will go, I must tell you now. You are, North. You are real. The pull I feel toward you, the way my heart wants to reach for you—those are real."

My breath stops. I twist my fingers together, fighting against the compulsion to respond—because now she's speaking the way she used to. Not as a goddess, but as the girl who made me want to tie a red sash around my waist just to wear her colors, who asked me what it felt like to be kissed.

She must see the warring desires in my face, because she steps closer, eyes searching mine. "Are you going to pretend that's madness too?" she says softly. "Will you tell me you haven't been watching me, as I've been watching you? That what you told me as we climbed this cliff, that you and I *were* destiny, was a lie? That you don't . . ." For the first time since she woke from her daze, she hesitates, biting at her lip. "That you don't feel as I do?"

She doesn't drop her eyes or look away. She's offering up her heart, along with her faith, and as the sun breaks through the spindly trees and traces across the curves of her face, across her lips, lingering in the moisture on her eyelashes . . . I want to take what she's offering.

"Of course not," I whisper, reaching out with one hand. When we met, she would have flinched away in terror of being touched—now, she waits, trusting, eyes never leaving my face as my fingers trace the curve of her cheek a breath away from her skin. I can feel the warmth of her in the cool morning air. "Of course that part's real."

She lifts her hand as well, and I bring mine even with hers, hovering so very close to it. "Then *stay* with me," she pleads. "We will send a message to your people and tell them that you are safe."

I linger in the moment, feeling the air singing between us. Yesterday, these words would have lit my heart with fire— yesterday, I would have said yes.

Yesterday, I didn't know she wanted to destroy the world.

I take a step back, withdrawing, feeling the cold against my fingertips as I let my hand fall. "I can't," I croak.

Color rises to her face, her full eyes snapping with sudden hurt and a tiny, unvoiced question. My own chest aches as if I'd wounded myself when I wounded her. I curl my hands into fists.

When her silent appeal gets no answer, her expression grows chilly, remote.

"I could make you stay," she says, eyes square on my face. A finger of mist swirls into visibility and stretches between us. It grows into a reaching arm, curling around me until I can actually feel it pressing in, an invisible band of force that threatens to gather me close to her. The coming dawn had been turning the light around us slowly golden, but as her power ripples out through the mist, everything is white, as if a snap frost had overtaken us. "I could do that now—I could *make* you stay."

I back up, my right hand wrapped over my chrono on my left wrist, putting space between us, measuring the distance to the trees.

"So this is what you are now?" I ask her. "You talk about caring for your people, about how all this death comes from a place of love, but whatever the prophecy's made you, it sure as skies isn't anything to do with love. You could *make* me stay? What's happened to you? This time yesterday, I'd have sworn on my life that you wouldn't *dream* of betraying a friend, someone who trusted you."

"I have waited all my life for this," she shoots back, the

power of the mist around her seething and roiling. "For *you*, North!"

"To force me, to break my will? To *make* me stay, when I want to go home?"

She stares down at me, and all I can hear is my own ragged breathing, in and out, in and out.

And then all of it's gone, and she's a girl again, staring at me. Her heart is in her eyes, clear and vulnerable and familiar again. Suddenly she's the same girl who offered me dumplings when I was hungry at the feast. She's the girl who wondered with me at the statue's head in the water in the ghostlands, who stared at me with longing and loss when I said I wished I could kiss her.

"Oh, gods," she murmurs, her eyes widening with shock as the mist vanishes, dissipating into the morning air as if it had never been. Her unshed tears spill down the cheek I hovered over. "Gods, North, I'm sorry. I was just so—please, my world needs you." And then her voice drops even further, until her final words are a whispered confession: "*I* need you."

I have to remind my legs how to move, because they've locked up, holding me in place. "I wish you did."

Her breath hitches as though I've dealt her a physical blow. "Everyone will be reborn. *We* will be reborn. Not as a prince and a goddess, not with the weight of destiny on our shoulders."

Skies help me. I could almost say yes, and condemn both our worlds.

It takes everything I have to turn my back.

"If you go home," Nimh says, "I'll never be able to fulfill the prophecy." Her voice is aching. My *heart* is aching. "If I let you go, I damn the world."

I resist the urge to turn.

"If I stay, I let you damn mine."

I shift my weight, telling myself to take one step. That if I can take just one step away from her, the one after that will be easier, and the one after that easier still. I wish I were better at lying to myself.

"Wait." Nimh draws a shuddering breath. "If you will not stay here, then I would see you reach your home safely. Let me give you some small protection before you go. So that you may find your way safe from harm."

My jaw aches from clenching it, and I realize I can't open it to speak. I turn back toward her and nod.

Nimh is looking around, tear-filled eyes scanning the clearing for something. She stoops to pick up a small, round stone, out of place among the more irregular, jagged rocks around it. She curls both her hands around it and draws it close to her, cradling it against her breastbone, and closes her eyes.

I can watch her like this, with her eyes closed—memorize her features and burn them into my memory so that I won't forget. I could take her picture with my chrono, but it would just be a photo of a beautiful girl and a sunrise. It wouldn't be *Nimh*; it wouldn't be magic.

When she opens her eyes, her spell complete, I'm already stretching out my hand toward her.

"It cannot protect you from a blade or a beast," she whispers.

"But it will keep you safe from the magic of any who wish to harm you." Gazing down at my hand, she places the stone in the center of my palm, careful not to let her fingers brush mine. The stone is warm from her skin, and for a moment, it almost looks different now—a faint sheen about it, perhaps, a hint of a glow.

Then I blink, and it's only the colors from the sunrise.

When I lift my head, Nimh's eyes are waiting for me. "Keep it with you," she breathes, but her words are not so much a demand as a plea, her gaze beseeching. The tears filling those eyes spill out, painting glinting tracks of reflected dawn down her cheeks.

I want to lift my hand, touch her face, catch those tears, and hold her until she stops crying. I want her to just be Nimh again, and I want never to have heard the name Lightbringer. Instead, I close my fist around the stone and nod.

This time when I walk away, she doesn't stop me—and I don't look back.

TWENTY-NINE

NIMH

The sun rises, the slow crawl of its light revealing the valley below like the drawing back of a curtain. On the cliff the morning is already here, but for a few minutes I can stand with the light warm on my hair and gaze down over a land still sleeping, steeped in shadow.

The mist gathers around me, invisible now to the eye—but there, waiting for me. It stirs to my slightest whim, something that ought to have been impossible, for even the strongest magician alive cannot control the mist, only tap it for power.

I draw a breath, noticing how different this dawn feels than the last one that I remember, when North and I sat where the forest-sea met the ruins of our ancestors, and all I could see was the darkness of uncertainty . . . and the fragile wish to abandon destiny and stay there with the strange cloudlander I hardly knew.

The morning air dries the tears on my cheeks. I never wiped them away. For once, I didn't mind showing how I felt. All my life, I've had to be something else, something more than human. But North never really believed in my divinity, so what did it matter if he saw my humanity?

I shiver, but not from the cool breeze on my face. Humanity wasn't the only thing I showed him. I can still feel the pull of the mist, the whisper of its power, the promise that, now that I had the strength to manipulate the very fabric of magic itself, I could do anything. Make anyone *else* do anything.

I could make *you stay.* . . .

North's face in the moments after I spoke, when the mist curled closer about him, is etched into my mind's eye. Shock, disappointment, anger—but most cutting of all, *fear.* I never wanted anyone to be afraid of me.

And I never thought I would be afraid of myself. That I've manifested my aspect—the destroyer, the Lightbringer—is clear. But at what cost?

North is gone. He is a vital part of the prophecy that will save my people, and I have let him go.

I've failed them all.

I set about packing up the camp, moving slowly, my mind only half-fixed on the tasks at hand. I don't know where to go. I've had no message from Matias, and by now Inshara's agents will have no doubt doubled their watch on Jezara's house.

But I pack, because I cannot stay here. Perhaps I will just begin walking, and keep walking until my feet will carry me no farther.

It's only after I've stowed everything away that I realize the bindle cat has been gone since dawn—ordinarily, he would have found his way back again by now, having hunted down some small, scurrying thing for his breakfast. A tiny sliver of thought, both hopeful and forlorn, wonders if the cat saw our party splitting and went with the one who needed him more.

Or perhaps even the bindle cat was frightened away.

I walk back toward the scroll, which is still laid out and held open by the stones North placed at its corners. It looks like gibberish now, so many layers of messages written directly on top of one another. No matter how long I look at it, none of that deeper understanding returns to me.

Perhaps, comes an unbidden thought, *because you let him go and abandoned your purpose, you are no longer the Lightbringer.*

"What else could I do?" I burst out, my voice hoarse in the crisp morning air. "I will not become that thing—you cannot make me into a weapon so deadly that I wound all that I hold dear. I am *not* Inshara! *What would you have had me do?*"

Of course, the scroll does not answer me. The lettering remains still, revealing no new insight. The final piece of the prophecy is emblazoned in my mind as if the scroll etched it inside my skull, but already the certainty it brought me is fading away.

Without North, I have no way of learning what the "place of endings and beginnings" is, so I cannot follow the prophecy's instructions.

After everything that's happened, despite the new power I control, despite all that I now know . . . I'm back where I started.

I will not fall apart. I will think again on the latest stanza.

Perhaps there are further clues. *The mother of light shall speak . . .* Surely, that must be referring to Jezara. She is more Inshara's mother than mine, but symbolically she *is* my predecessor—her life as a living divine, her choices, are what led to mine.

I have to continue. I must go back to Jezara's house and find out what she has to say about this final piece of the puzzle. If Inshara's agents are there . . . well, very little can stop me now. I will handle them.

I sling my pack over my shoulders and then retrieve the scroll. Gazing down over the valley, I can see the curve of stone on the far side where Jezara's house burrows back into the mountains. Though I don't relish the idea of confronting her again, I'm not dreading it the way I would have expected.

After all, I've chosen against my purpose now too. I let North go free. I chose him over destiny.

The thought makes me go still, heart pounding. The guiding principle of my whole life was that I would *not* be like Jezara. Yet here I am.

I start rolling the prophecy back up, about to turn away from the view and begin picking my way back down the path to the valley floor, when something grabs my eye.

A small blossom of orange light, unfurling before me . . . no, not small, very far away. On the other side of the valley, where Jezara's house is . . .

And then the sound comes, a staccato crack and a rumble of stone, echoing back to me from every cliff and rock face, fragmented like a reflection in a broken mirror.

An explosion.

My voice tears out of me in a cry, and I drop to my knees, staring. The initial bloom of the fire is overtaken by smoke and dust, a massive dark cloud rising from the place.

I asked Jezara, surprised, if she really believed her own daughter would harm her. She did not answer in words, but I should have known what I was seeing in her face.

Gods, why didn't we understand what she was telling us? Why . . .

The mother of light cannot speak at all now.

Pieces of prophecy are crumbling all around me.

I shut my eyes, my fist tightening around the scroll until the ancient parchment crackles. My thoughts spin so violently I feel sick, hurled about like a boat in a storm. The torrent of what-ifs feels like knives, cutting me more deeply each time they swirl around me.

I've failed them. I've failed all of them, because I was weak. Because I was human. Because I loved . . .

Loved?

I open my eyes, my spinning thoughts crystalizing. I may have failed destiny, I may have chosen my heart, chosen North, over the prophecy a thousand years in the making. But there is one way I am not like the goddess who came before me.

I will *not* run away.

I cannot save the world, but I can save a few. Matias and Elkisa and Techeki and my acolytes and Hiret and the river-striders and everyone who attended the Feast of the Dying . . . Inshara has them still, because I was forced to flee. My life, my purpose, was too important to risk in a confrontation. I could not fight then.

But now . . .

A trickle of mist condenses out of the air, gathering around me. It is no gentle, calm pool—it is as wild and hungry and full of fury as the most violent of storms. But it bends to me, snapping and tugging, like a pack of dogs trained to attack, chained to my will.

Now I have power—now I can defeat her.

Because now I have nothing left to lose.

The air thickens as I draw nearer the river, the humidity wrapping around me like a familiar blanket. I'll make better time traveling by water than on foot, even upriver—I must see if Orrun's boat is still there. Though it's invisible now, I can feel the ambient mist in the air all around me. I could unbeach the boat with a thought, undoing what it took North and me both to do by hand.

The sun set a few hours ago, leaving the land in darkness that will hide me from any watchful eyes. By now, Inshara's people may well have figured out that I made my escape from the temple city via the river.

I try not to think about North making his clumsy way through the wilderness in search of his people. The bindle cat must surely be with him—and though others might scoff at the idea of a single cat for protection, they don't know about his uncanny ability to see the approach of danger.

Heart aching, mind conjuring a vision of warm brown eyes and a crooked smile, I'm almost upon the river's edge before I register the bright orange glow through the trees.

I stop dead for a moment, confusion gripping me as it seems as though the river itself must be ablaze. Then I realize what is burning: the riverstrider's boat.

Breaking into a run, I burst out of the trees just as the upper deck of the boat collapses with a dull crash, sending a spray of embers skyward. I reel back, raising my arms against the heat, searching for some way to quell the flames—but the boat is lost, pieces of it hissing as they fall into the mud.

Then the hairs on the back of my neck prickle and lift, the way they do when a mist-storm is gathering. I briefly consider summoning the mist in an effort to put out the flames, but the boat is already falling apart—and that isn't the warning the mist conveyed.

I'm not alone.

I drop down into the shadow of a tree, listening. Whoever's nearby could be responsible for setting the fire. Either way, if the last few days have taught me anything, it is to assume a stranger is an enemy until they prove otherwise.

I tighten my grip on my spearstaff. My straining eyes pick out a shadow where there should be none. The dark form of a cloaked figure leans against a tree not far away. With painstaking slowness, I creep closer, keeping to the dark spaces beneath the trees until I'm only a few paces away from the silhouette.

The quickest and safest way to render them harmless is to stab out from the darkness with the point of the spear, aiming for the bulk of the body. They would be on the ground before they even knew they'd been hit.

But I'd risk the life of an innocent.

Daoman would tell me to strike. Still, when I gather myself to move, North's voice is the one I listen to.

With a grunt of effort and a lunge, I sweep my staff sideways into the legs of the shadow, knocking them to the ground and eliciting a cry of surprise. I step up to level the point of my spear at their throat.

The shifting, flickering light of the fire distorts the scene, but I can make out the shape of the person gasping for breath and gazing dazedly up at me. As I look down, my eyes adjust to the quivering light, and I begin to pick out features.

The shadow turns out to be a man—a boy, really, his features still slim and delicate, his eyes bright and large. His hair is cropped so short it must have been shaved recently, and the paleness of his skin stands out against the mud around him. Against his fair cheeks, I can see a dark trio of painted lines, an affect I recognize from the people flanking Inshara when she broke into my temple to drive me out and murder my high priest.

Fear rises like bile in my throat, choking and burning me, numbing my tongue. The barrage of questions I had prepared vanish like illusory smoke.

A cultist.

Inshara must have sent agents down the river when she realized I was no longer in the temple city.

The boy's glittering eyes glare fearlessly up into mine. I'm not wearing my ceremonial red—there's every reason to think the boy has no idea who I am.

"What are you doing here?" I demand, after a silence that stretches far too long.

He pulls a hideous grimace and then spits at me. Instinctively, I jerk back a fraction, horrified and confused all at once—never has anyone treated me thus.

"Waiting for you, False One." His voice is harsh and defiant.

I fight the need to run all the more. He does know who I am—but if anything, he seems to be recoiling from me rather than positioning himself to try to touch me. Still, my every muscle is ready to move.

"How . . . how did you know I would be here?" I keep the tip of the spear at the boy's throat.

He sneers at me and turns his face away. I see that the lines across his cheeks continue on past his hairline, barely visible through the short-cropped hair. They're not painted at all— they're *tattooed* into his flesh.

Sickened, I harden my heart like Daoman taught me. I press the point of the spear against the boy's throat, just shy of piercing the skin. "Answer me!"

The boy gives a gurgle in response to the spear's pressure, but when I lift the point of the spear to let him breathe, the gurgle turns into a laugh. He looks back up at me, his tattoos drawing my gaze in toward his sharp eyes the way the striped petals of a huntsman rose lure flies into its deadly center.

"The true Divine One sees all," he says in a low, fervent voice. "The Divine One *knows* all. You think you know what it is to be a god?" Another laugh, the edges bright and fractured with the intensity of his faith. "Compared to her, you are a flea—while she is the sun, the moon, the stars, the . . ."

I press the point of the spear in again, and the rant turns into a gurgle. "She sent her people up the river—you saw this boat." When the boy says nothing, glaring at me, I let my breath out slowly. "Why have you come to wait for me?"

"I am a messenger, but an arm of my goddess's reach—"

"What is your message?" My voice cuts across his, surprising even me—ordinarily, such ceremony is my whole life. But now I have no patience for it.

The boy blinks at me, and then smiles slowly as his eyes unfocus and his gaze drifts upward. When he speaks again, his voice is different—higher, smoother, familiar somehow. "Sister," he recites, "I bear you no ill will, for who alive can know the weight you carry but I? Let us not war against each other but come together to help the people and land we love so much."

I recognize the familiar note in his voice. He sounds almost exactly like Inshara, his boy's voice carrying her higher one without cracking or bending under the tension.

"Come back to me," the boy continues. "Come home before the Vigil of the Rising, and I promise no one will harm you. Come home, and I will not harm your cloudlander. He cares for you very much, sister. Come home, and he is yours."

I cannot speak, cannot move. The boy's eyes roll back into place and he looks up at me, all at once drained and alight. I keep the spear where it is, though in this moment I could not stop him were he to reach up and wrest it from me.

Inshara has North.

Half a dozen images flicker through my mind, each more horrible than the last. North languishing in a cell, despairing of ever seeing his home again. North being tortured for information on my whereabouts. North, broken and bleeding somewhere, delirious with the approach of death, whispering about this boat and this place and the kiss we did not share, with his dying breath.

She could have killed him, rendering me powerless to carry out my destiny, but instead she keeps him. She knows how valuable he is.

He cares for you very much. . . .

North is still here.

I can't help the trickle of relief that breathes life back into my hands, giving them strength again. I would rather see him safe with his people than held by my enemies, but . . . now I might see him one more time.

Hating myself for the flicker of happiness that thought brings, I jerk my thoughts away and focus on the boy. Inshara could have sent a whole team of agents here to kill me or capture me if she knew I would be here alone and unprotected—instead, she sent one boy, unthreatening, easily overpowered.

I shift my weight, sliding one foot closer to the boy, and he writhes, body twisting away from me as if I were surrounded by some invisible force.

Not only does she want me alive, she's clearly given her messenger instructions not to touch me.

Why?

Does she want to strip me of my divinity publicly? To put on a show for my people, rip their faith away in such a manner that it could not be denied?

I gesture with the spear. "Move—put your back to that tree there. You are going to answer my questions."

The boy's eyes slide toward the place I've indicated, and then back. "The gods are dead," he whispers, gazing at me with those glittering eyes. They hold me, so much so that I only dimly register movement at his side. "May the one god live forever. . . ."

Something flashes in the firelight, and my eyes make out the edge of a blade. Before I can so much as leap back in anticipation of an attack, the boy holds the knife to his own chin, his eyes still on mine.

"Wait!" My voice cracks with urgency and horror as I toss my spear aside. "Don't—"

Another flash of the blade, and then it clatters to the stone. The eyes widen, blood falling in an inky curtain across the neck, spraying across my robe, my arms, pattering against my skin like a warm, wet rain.

I drop to my knees, caught between the need to act and the knowledge that I can't, my whole body freezing. I sense the invisible mist in the air shifting, all coiled power and no finesse—I could use it to crush someone into dust, but not to heal the slightest scrape.

The boy's breath gurgles, the blood still coming, a gruesome rhythmic pouring of his life onto the stone. His eyes flash, swinging wildly until they find my face again, and for the first time I see not hatred, not zealous certainty, but fear. He tries to speak and coughs blood.

He thought he would die instantly. He thought it would be

like a fairy tale, going out in a blaze of glory for the cause he worshipped. Instead, he's bleeding to death in the dark on a lonely riverbank with a girl who cannot even try to staunch his wound, futile though it would be. A girl who cannot even hold his hand as he dies.

"B-b-blessings upon you," I manage, the voice coming from somewhere within me, bypassing the frozen horror seizing my mind. "May you walk lightly through the void until you live again when the world is new."

The boy's eyes stay on mine, though I cannot tell if he is glad for my prayer or if it is an insult to him.

"M-m-may forgiveness find you, and compassion keep you until . . ."

There is no more coughing and gurgling now, no more attempts to speak or move, but the boy watches me still. He watches me, still.

"Until we meet again."

I stay there while the blood stops, for even after the rhythm of its flow fades away, it seeps from the wound. I stay there, crouched by the boy, unwilling to take my eyes from his as long as he continues to watch me.

When the last of the flames die down, it is nearly dawn again. The boy is still watching me with the last vestiges of moonlight in his eyes, and I crouch there by the smoking embers, keeping my silent vigil as morning comes.

THIRTY

NORTH

I'm covered in stinging scratches, dirt clinging to my skin and sweat in my eyes, but I can see a faint light ahead—I'm nearly there. I push a branch out of the way and duck underneath before it snaps back, and then I can't stop myself breaking into a run.

A piece of my heart is tugging me backward, but I make myself focus on the things that keep me moving forward—my mothers, my grandfather, my friends, the safety of my people. My pulse is hammering impossibly fast as I see more light between the trees ahead, the forest thinning out—it must be the clearing I'm aiming for.

When I push past the edge of the trees and stumble out onto the patchy grass, I skid to a halt with a horrible, lurching sensation in my gut.

There's nobody here.

I can't have missed them—I've been on the move for two hours at most; they *must* have allowed that much time.

Then I see the fire. It's set within a ring of rocks, a lazy wisp of smoke curling upward, plenty of wood left to burn on the log within it. It's been built recently—it must be to show me that this is the place. It must mean *Don't go far, there are people nearby.*

So I lean over to brace my hands against my knees and catch my breath, and I wait. I briefly consider shouting, but I don't know what animals are out there, so instead I try to pull myself together.

Who will it be, come to rescue the prince? Neither of my mothers would be allowed somewhere so risky, I'm sure. And how do they plan on getting us all back up? Unless . . . They'll have a way up, won't they? I wouldn't put it past my bloodmother to send a bunch of guards down here on a one-way mission to protect me until she could figure out how to get me home.

A stick snaps behind me and jolts me from my thoughts, and I spin around to see a pair of men coming out of the trees at the edge of the clearing. But those aren't uniforms from Alciel.

Those are the uniforms of Nimh's temple guard.

I turn slowly, and that's when I see the others emerging. Inshara, dressed in Nimh's red robes, with Techeki—that oily traitor—walking by her side. Elkisa is on her other side, eyes down, still captive. There are four more guards gathered around the clearing, pinning me in. No wonder they wanted me by the fire, right in the middle of the open space with nowhere to run.

"Cloudlander," says Inshara pleasantly. "I see you hurried to get here. We'll have someone tend to those scrapes once we're back at the temple." She makes me sound about five years old.

Murderer. The word almost makes it past my lips before I think better of it—her people are holding weapons, and I'm not. But my anger is spiked by bitter disappointment, my throat aching with it as I force myself to swallow, as I steady myself.

Nobody from Alciel is coming. My people all still think I'm dead.

I'm not going home.

But I'm not going to let Inshara have the satisfaction of seeing my pain. I'm not going to give her anything. So somehow, from somewhere, I find a casual voice that sounds like it's coming from someone else. "I'm not sure red is your color, Insha."

She gives me just the tiniest flicker of irritation for the fact that I've chopped the goddess part off the end of her name, and then it's hidden. She smiles, glancing down at the robe and smoothing it with one hand. "I wear what duty dictates," she says with a wry smile. "Interesting to see that you do too." Her gaze is a little keener as she takes in my sash, a match for her robe.

She's wearing Nimh's crown, and she still has on the odd assortment of trinkets and necklaces she wore when she first broke into the temple. When her hand slides down the chain that hangs around her neck, my eyes involuntarily follow it. My gaze stops short when I realize what's at the end of it. A small, square face, green numbers faintly glowing.

A chrono.

"It's a holy relic," she says, following my gaze, fingers tightening around its illuminated face. "Fallen from the gods above centuries ago. But, of course, you know what it is."

I manage to keep my mouth shut, because I *do* know what it is. Better than she does, apparently.

That thing isn't centuries old. I'd be surprised if it was even *decades* old. My grandfather has the same model, claims he can't figure out the controls on the latest designs, or focus his eyes on the holographic displays. *Where did she get it?*

"I'm interested that you wear holy relics," I say, "when a few days ago I saw you murder a high priest."

Beside her Techeki very nearly winces—it's just a slight narrowing of his eyes, and then he's as smooth as ever. I can hardly believe this guy. He spent most of Nimh's life serving her, and now he's here beside her greatest enemy without even a hint of an apology.

Inshara sighs, eyes lowering. "I would have preferred not to kill anyone," she says. "But Daoman ruled the temple with an iron fist. Nimh was discovered so much younger than any divinity before her. Did you not wonder why? It was so he could control her completely, after my mother was such a disappointment to him. He was an ambitious man. He found Nimh, he raised her, and he taught her to see the world just as he wanted it seen. He used her, and she was owed justice for it, as much as anyone was."

I want to tell her to take her false sympathy for Nimh and shove it where the birds don't fly. But I have to admit her thoughts are eerily similar to my own, when I first learned about Nimh's childhood.

Inshara's eyes are grave as she watches me, and I get the sense that she can see and measure exactly the impact of her words. "I want you to help me find Nimh," she says simply.

I snort involuntarily. "Why would I even consider doing that? Didn't we just finish discussing how you wish people didn't have to die, but apparently sometimes they do?"

There's not even a ripple in her calm. "You should consider it," she replies. "Because once you've assisted me, I can send you back to the sky, Your Highness."

My heart just about stops. She has a chrono. Could she have other tech?

But even as I want to shout a *yes* at her, the rest of what she's said strikes home.

Your Highness?

I've told exactly one person in this world about my family: Nimh.

"How could you . . . ," I begin, though words fail me before I can get any further.

Inshara raises one eyebrow. "I *do* have the spirit of the true Lightbringer speaking to me, North. He tells me many things. Like, for instance, that the boy Nimhara has cast in her version of the prophecy is actually a prince in the cloudlands. That he fell to this world by accident, not because of destiny. That his mothers worry about him very much and want nothing more than to see him safely home."

I stare at her, the bottom dropping out of my stomach. "Magic," I whisper weakly, one part of my mind marveling at the way I've come to accept magic, so much so that I'm willing to use it as a defense against the idea of divine intervention. "This is just some kind of trick."

Inshara sighs, leaning forward, her expression grave.

"Believe what you must, North. I have a way to travel the sky. I only need *you* to tell me how it works."

I blink at her. "Leaving aside that I wouldn't help you even if I could, I have *no* idea what you're talking about."

Irritation flickers across her face. "The Lightbringer tells me otherwise." She reaches up to take Nimh's crown from her head, holding it up for me to see. "This is the key. Techeki already knew. The Lightbringer told me that, as well."

My eyes snap across to the Master of Spectacle, who looks as calm as ever.

"Had I but known you desired to return to your world, I would have shared the information immediately," he says, oozing sincerity. "I only regret that I do not know how the key is used, Divine One."

Something brushes my leg, and I glance down. The cat's there, his fur fluffed up so much he's twice as big as usual. My heart swells at having someone on my side, then nearly stops— does this mean Nimh's nearby? I have to do something.

When I lift my gaze, my heart does a backflip. Elkisa's lifted her head, and she's looking at the cat as well. A moment later she meets my eyes, and though the whole thing takes only a couple of seconds, it changes everything.

Inshara's control over her has slipped. Perhaps I've distracted her—because Elkisa's easing a step forward, the movement slow.

As long as Inshara doesn't know Elkisa's free, we have a chance to overpower her. So I scramble for a reply, anything to keep her attention on me.

"If the Lightbringer can tell you that your crown's the key to going up to the sky—however that's supposed to be a thing— then why can't he just tell you how to use it? He must know, right?"

She lifts a brow. "If I am to be his vessel, I must prove myself worthy," she replies. "He has told me that *you* know. That is enough. You will tell me how to use it, and we will go to the sky together."

Now it's my turn to raise a brow. "You're kidding, right? Of all the people I'd invite home to meet my mothers, you're the very last on the list."

"That's unkind," she chides me. "I know you've already met mine."

My lungs tighten. Elkisa takes another step closer. She's nearly at Inshara's back now, her face impassive.

Inshara's watching me with an interested expression, like a scientist watching an experiment play out. Her mouth curves to a smile, and then, turning her head a little, she says, "Come on, now, don't be shy."

Skyfall, she knows.

But Elkisa doesn't look afraid to be caught or furious so much as . . . uncomfortable. I watch in confusion as her gaze slides away from mine and refuses to return, and she steps forward. I'm still waiting for her to draw her knife or rush Inshara, to produce her weapon or *something*, when Inshara turns, stretching out one hand.

Elkisa hesitates, but then slides her fingers through the

other woman's, reluctantly letting Inshara draw her close. And when Inshara tips the guard's face down toward hers, when she leans up and gives her a gentle, tender kiss, Elkisa doesn't pull away. Her hand tightens around Inshara's.

This can't be happening.

This feels like it's my own heart being carved out. Like I'm the one she's betrayed. *Oh, Nimh.*

"How long?" I manage, my voice low. "How long have you been Nimh's enemy?"

Elkisa finally meets my eyes. "I'm not her enemy, North."

A quick, sharp barb of laughter escapes me. "No? Then I'm impressed at the lengths you're going to so you can lull Inshara into a false sense of security before you attack."

Inshara actually laughs, and my free hand curls into a fist. Beside me, the cat growls low in his throat.

"It's not as simple as that," Elkisa snaps.

"You've been working against her *all this time*." I'm so angry I can barely get the words out. "She trusted you, and you took her secrets to this . . ." I don't have an insult strong enough to hurl at Inshara, who's still smiling, clearly enjoying the moment.

"Elkisa let me know when Nimh ran straight to Daoman to tell him about the new stanza that had come to her in a vision," Inshara says. "That girl really should be more careful about who guards her door."

Elkisa turns her face away, jaw squaring, and I think she tries to tug her hand free of Inshara's, but the other woman holds it too tightly.

403

"Did you help the cultists that first night?" I demand. "You were the only other person to get away from the camp—did you . . ." My stomach turns, queasiness replacing my rage.

Color floods Elkisa's face, enough to show against the light brown of her skin. "Of course not. Inshara can't control everything done in her name any more than Nimh can. She doesn't want bloodshed, not if it can be avoided."

"I don't," Inshara agrees. "I sent them there because the Lightbringer told me where you would be, when you would fall. If they'd managed to take you and Nimh, things would have gone very differently. I don't want to hurt my people; I want to lead them."

"You killed the closest thing Nimh ever had to a father."

Elkisa's hands ball into fists, but not before I can see the tremor in her fingers. "It had to be done!" she blurts, heat in her voice. "Daoman never would have let Nimh surrender herself peacefully."

"So you stabbed him in the heart?"

Unbidden, an image of Elkisa the night of Inshara's takeover looms before me. Wild-eyed, shaking, desperately trying to fight as her knife struck home at Daoman's chest. Except she was going along with Inshara's plan.

The only thing Elkisa was fighting was her own conscience.

"Nimh calls you her friend," I say quietly. "And you betrayed her."

The heat drains from Elkisa's face and voice, and the look she turns on me is hollow and cold. "I've always been honest with Inshara," she says quietly, her voice steel. "I love her, and

404

she knows that. I love Nimh too. Insha accepts that what I do, I do for both of them. You know nothing about this world, or Nimh. You could never understand. This is what she *wants*, cloudlander—she is brave and strong and devoted, but she doesn't want this life. She lives it because she must, because it was forced upon her. But if none of it's true—when the Lightbringer infuses Inshara and she becomes the living divine, then Nimh can live any life she wants. She can do everything that has been denied her for so long." There's a determination about the way she speaks that catches me off guard. She believes what she's saying.

Which means there's nothing I can say that will convince her to stop.

Inshara seems to sense my moment of weakness and presses it, her voice hard now. "The way up to the sky, North."

I clench my jaw. "No," I whisper. "Even if I knew, I'd never tell you. Not even to get myself home."

Inshara lets her breath out in a long, slow whisper of air. "One way or another, I *will* find a way to reach the cloudlands. If you won't help me, then my best scholars will be only too happy to serve their goddess and be the ones to solve an ancient mystery." She pauses, glancing at Elkisa. "Have the guards secure him. We have a journey ahead."

Elkisa nods, no longer willing to meet my eyes.

"And then," Inshara continues, "El, you can head up the search for Nimh. I don't want to count on her showing up in the name of true love—not for *this* boy—and we'll need her if we're going to convince him to help."

I'm held in place by the ice suddenly running through my veins.

If there was something I could tell Inshara about how to get up to the sky, in this moment, I'd do it, and damn the consequences.

Danger's heading for Nimh in the form of her best friend, and she's not going to suspect a thing until it's far too late.

I'm moving before I can think, lunging to my left and between two guards. Behind me I hear the cat yowl, and then someone's seizing my arm, spinning me around.

It's Elkisa. Our eyes meet as she grabs the front of my shirt, yanking me in close. An instant later, pain explodes along my temple, and I catch a hazy glimpse of her shaking out her fist as I hit the ground, the world vanishing in a whirl of darkness.

THIRTY-ONE

NIMH

I swim up out of my thoughts, pulled by the realization that I'm no longer alone with the dead cultist boy. A voice is calling my name; footsteps squish toward me in the mud.

A heavy weight drops onto my shoulders, as comforting as an arm around me. I look down and see dusty purple linen. I see my hand clutch at the fabric before I've decided to do it.

"Nimh, come back to me now. . . ." The voice is low and gentle. "Come on back now—there's a good girl."

Thoughts snap back into sync with my body, jolting as though waking from a dream. I lock eyes with—*Jezara?*

Her face is tired and travel-stained. Though her gaze is as frank and self-possessed as ever, there's a flicker in it as she looks at me, a tiny window into some deeper feeling. Dust caught in her hair and on her skin glows in the moonlight and the last of the embers, giving her an aura of gold.

My breath catches, for suddenly I see the delicate, subtle echoes of divinity in her eyes.

I never knew this Jezara. My priests and my tutors and my surrogate father taught me to revile her so well that I never wondered if she and I might be similar; so well I could not imagine sharing any traits with the villain who had cast our world into such uncertainty.

But Jezara was a goddess for longer than I've been alive, and wholly loved by her people, and for the first time in my life I can imagine her as she must have been then.

She reminds me of my mother. Back when I knew her, back when I didn't know I was divine. When I ate pirrackas with the other children and sat on the floor listening to the Fisher King telling stories.

What it must have been like to love her then, instead of hating her. To grow up worshipping the goddess of healing instead of picking at old wounds. To look back into childhood and remember this shining, golden woman floating by on festival nights while we sang and danced her praise, and knew that we were safe.

What a comfort it must be to live in the protection of a god you believe in.

My eyes fill with tears, and I gasp for a breath. Abruptly, the easy remoteness of Jezara's expression cracks and falls away, and she drops to her knees at my side.

"Oh, child," she murmurs, shoulders sagging as she reaches out toward the purple mantle she draped across me. She tugs the ends together, the pressure not unlike an embrace around my shoulders. "I know, love. I know. I *remember.*"

A sob creaks free as the bands of tension around my rib cage loosen just a fraction. My mind cannot make sense of Jezara's presence here, not when the last I saw of her was the smoke rising from the ruins of her home. Nor can it make sense of her warmth, her sympathy, when the last words we exchanged were so bitter.

"They do not understand," Jezara murmurs, her voice gentle. "They cannot know what it is they asked of us. No one knows but you and I."

There's no trace of that brusque facade in her demeanor now. Perhaps, seeing me without armor, she is laying down hers.

I shudder, straightening a little, an unspoken signal that she reads immediately; her hands fall away from the mantle she wrapped around me and she sits back on her heels. A shadow now cuts through the moonlight that illuminates her face—the golden aura is gone.

"I thought you died," I croak, suddenly light-headed.

Jezara's eyebrows rise a hair, and the smile that quirks the corner of her mouth is the human Jezara again, those divine echoes receding. "Good. I'm hoping that's what my daughter's agents will think too."

She holds out a waterskin by its strap when I cough. After quite a long swallow, I manage, "You destroyed your house on purpose?"

Jezara draws in a long, slow breath, then releases it again. "I wronged you," she murmurs, gazing at the river beyond me. "You were right to be angry. I railed all my life against my divinity—but casting it off meant it fell to you."

Her voice is quiet, sincere. And though she doesn't meet my eyes, I can still see the cost of the admission in the tight set of her shoulders.

When her eyes drift back and meet mine again, her brows lift and her face falls. "Oh, Light forgive me, but I hated you, Nimhara. This perfect, dutiful girl, chosen so young. How proud Daoman must have been. How relieved my people that they could forget me now—a new goddess had come."

"I blamed you for abandoning our people, for turning against destiny for your own heart," I whisper. "But I have done the very same thing."

Jezara's eyes widen. "The cloudlander," she murmurs. "I saw the way he . . . Did you—"

"I let him go," I whisper. "He is the Last Star, and I need him to fulfill the prophecy. But when he found a way home, I . . . I *could* have made him stay. I had that power. But I let him go."

Jezara's gaze is troubled. "You wanted him to be safe. You care for him, that much is obvious."

"But he's not safe!" I retort, my voice coming out a bit more intently than I wanted. "*Inshara* has him."

Too late I remember who Inshara is to Jezara, and I regret the bitter hatred in my voice.

Seeing my face, Jezara gives a tiny shake of her head. "It's all right. I know what she's becoming. I've always known—I just didn't want to see."

"You were too busy believing *she* was the Lightbringer."

Her expression freezes, and for a moment I regret my words—until I see that her eyes are dark with . . . guilt?

"Forgive me," she murmurs, gaze falling from mine as she

passes a hand over her eyes. "I was so angry—I wanted you to feel what I'd felt, to be as lost as I was."

My stomach twists, a sickness rising up in my gut. "What are you saying?"

Jezara's lips press together. "She is not the Lightbringer. I told you the story *she* believes. I don't know what voice she hears, but it certainly isn't a god speaking to her. You must understand, she was so lonely, so unhappy as a child—we lived among such hatred. Everyone we met punished *her* for my misdeeds. When she was a child, she found that scroll, the one with the lost stanza."

"Why would she think it had anything to do with her?" I demand. "That any of it was about you?"

"Parts of it seemed true," Jezara murmurs. "The empty one. A journey. And I had my own Star. . . . I gave up my divinity for him."

"Your own—but you did not actually *see* a star fall from . . ." My words stop as my throat squeezes.

"Your North was so surprised that I knew where he was from," Jezara murmurs. "He reminded me so much of *him*, with that skeptical mind and strange newness to the world. When I first saw you together in the mist-ruined village, I thought I was seeing *him*."

"Your lover . . . was a cloudlander," I breathe, the anger knocked out of me by shock.

"He fell, and I healed him, and eventually, he gave me Insha."

"So she saw herself in the scroll, as I did." I stare at her, mind spinning. "And you did not correct her."

"It was a bedtime story!" Jezara blurts, voice begging me to understand. "I told her she was special—I told her she was *chosen.* That all this pain and loneliness . . . was because she was destined for something bigger than us, bigger than those who'd cast us out."

I feel as though I could collapse there in the mud. "You made me think I was delusional."

Jezara's eyes are wet. "I'm sorry, Nimhara. You must understand, I lost my faith the moment the only family I had threw me out into the world, pregnant and alone. I believed in nothing—what harm in giving my daughter something to believe?"

My hands curl into fists. "Why are you here, then? Why follow me?"

"Because . . ." The former goddess sighs and gets slowly to her feet, grimacing as she rubs a hand against her bad leg to work out the stiffness. "Because I know where you must go, what you must do. I understand now what Insha has become. She is my daughter, my responsibility."

"I know she's your daughter, but—"

"Listen to me." Jezara's face is calm and grave once more—but this time it doesn't have the look of armor. "They put me in my prison, those priests—I let them make me ashamed of myself, of my own daughter. I cowered there in that box of shame and guilt and regret for so many years, and I believed that they had poisoned my daughter the way they poisoned me. But I am the one who raised her. *I* poisoned her."

I stare up at her, robbed of breath.

"I'm done hiding." Jezara looks down at me, eyes troubled but resolved. "And she's my responsibility."

"She *must* be stopped," I manage, getting to my feet and finding them wobbly beneath me. "Are you sure you can . . . Jezara, I cannot imagine she'll abandon her plans peacefully."

Jezara watches me. "Please," she says quietly. "Let me try to save my daughter, Divine One."

I'm still searching for my voice when the tiniest of sensations whispers across the hairs at the back of my neck. I freeze. Though this connection with the mist is new, it's powerful—and I recognize it immediately.

We aren't alone.

I glance at Jezara, who's watching me quizzically, having seen the change in my expression. I put a finger to my lips, and she nods, her eyes widening. Carefully, I let a little of the mist loose, fighting the urge to let it all explode from my control, like a pack of dogs.

There. A person, alone, crouched in the bushes not far away. With a jolt, I realize I can *feel* her—for she is certainly a *her*. Though I cannot quite read her thoughts through the mist, her tension feels like my own; the jumble of emotion in her heart rolls off her in waves.

She's watching us.

I get slowly to my feet, gathering up more mist even as I

reach for my spearstaff. Power builds within me, begging to be set loose—only my will contains it. With an effort, I manage to take two steps toward the figure concealed in the bushes before I let the mist free.

An invisible force rushes forward and slams into the woman, who goes sprawling with a grunt of surprise and pain. I rush up before she can recover, Jezara close on my heels. I swing my spearstaff around, ready to level it at the throat of the intruder—and I gasp as I see her face in the dim predawn light.

"Elkisa!"

My guard is ashen-faced, wide-eyed, dusty from travel and lit with emotion. "Nimh—Nimh, forgive me! Please, it's me, don't—" But there she falls short, unable to explain what force knocked her to the ground.

"Gods, El, I'm sorry. How did you . . . ?"

"The smoke from the boat. You can see it for leagues if you get above the canopy. I did not *know* it was you, but I thought if it was, you might be in danger. . . ." Her eyes drift to the side, and I realize Jezara is leaning over us behind my shoulder.

"You know this woman?" she asks, her eyes narrowing as she inspects Elkisa.

I nod, head bobbing like a float on a fishing line. "She's my guard—she's my oldest friend. We were separated, and I thought . . . But she's here. She's all right. You're all right?"

Elkisa's nodding, but my attention's split by a sudden tension in the older woman at my side.

"You trust her?" Jezara speaks bluntly, voice carrying a hint

414

of that metal-edged armor again. She's drawn herself up, one hand resting on her walking stick. I can't help but remember the flash of insight I had in her house—that her own guards were the very ones who had thrown her out of her home all those years ago.

"Of course I do!" I reply, getting myself under control with an effort. Too much effort. As if sensing my emotion, the mist is all around me. Still invisible, but waiting for danger, like a ferocious animal sensing its master's agitation. I take a deep, steadying breath, and though I'm speaking to my predecessor, my eyes are on Elkisa's face. "I trust her with my life."

To my astonishment, a muffled sound from Elkisa warns me only seconds before her head drops, and her shoulders quiver in a sob.

"Oh, El—are you hurt? Come, sit up." I draw back to make room, knowing she won't move unless she's certain she won't touch me. "What is wrong?"

I see tearstains on her cheeks as she levers herself upright. She shivers. "Who is this, Nimh?" Responding to Jezara's faint frown, Elkisa assumes one of her own, until both women are watching each other uneasily.

I hesitate only for a moment. "This is . . . well, this is Jezara, El."

Elkisa's face goes slack, and she leans backward as if her surprise is so deep it borders on fear. "Nimh—you don't under-stand! That woman is Inshara's *mother*. Inshara is her daughter. You can't trust her."

For a moment, I almost feel like laughing—but her face is so intent and serious that it sobers me. "I know, El. She told us."

"You must ask her to go—we must leave this place—come, Nimh, let us—"

"She stays!" That irritation flares, and I take a deep breath, disconcerted at how readily the mist in the air around me responds to my temper. Or—perhaps—my temper responds to changes in the mist.

"We need to go," she tells me, voice firm. "The roads will be crawling with guards once *she* realizes I escaped."

Her reluctance to say Inshara's name reminds me how frightened and full of guilt she must have been these past days under the woman's control. "I'm not leaving, Elkisa. I must save North. I won't leave him with Inshara."

Elkisa's face darkens. "No. You can't face her, she's too powerful. What if I find you someplace safe to hide? I'll get North out, then come back for you. The vigil will begin soon, they'll all be distracted. I'm sure I can reach him."

A strange uneasiness settles in the pit of my stomach. "You? But what if she takes control of you again?" I ask finally, trying to figure out why I'm so unsettled.

Though Elkisa opens her mouth, Jezara is the one who speaks. "What do you mean?" she demands, her gaze going between us. When I blink at her, she elaborates. "What do you mean, 'takes control' of her?"

Elkisa shifts uneasily, and I speak so she doesn't have to describe her own ordeal. "At the feast, when Inshara breached the temple, she used Elkisa to murder Daoman. A kind of magic

416

that shouldn't be possible—it was as though Elkisa was a puppet, and Inshara the one pulling her strings."

Jezara's eyebrows shoot up. "A puppet?" She gives a short bark of laughter. "Inshara's magic is strong. And though she is charismatic, persuasive, charming—physically controlling a person through magic is something out of a story. No one can work a spell like that, girl. Not even her."

I frown at her. "I saw it with my own eyes, Jezara. She . . ." But my gaze has flicked toward Elkisa, and there's an intensity to her face that stops me short.

When she sees me looking, she takes a step back. "She's lying," Elkisa snaps. "She's on her daughter's side after all, manipulating you. We should go, *now*."

I have seen Elkisa do astonishing things. I've seen her scale a wall four times her height in a few seconds. I've seen her defeat half a dozen trainees while unarmed. I've seen her fighting for her very life—but I don't remember her ever looking quite so afraid.

That uneasiness in my stomach gives a lurch as it clicks into place. "Elkisa . . . ," I murmur, my mind shying away from the thing it doesn't want to know. "How did you know about the deadline the cultist boy gave me? How did you know we have until the end of the vigil?"

Elkisa blinks at me. "I . . ." She licks her lips. "I overheard Inshara while I was being controlled."

But her hesitation lasted a moment too long. And she knows it too. We gaze at each other across the dirt and leaf litter between us, an infinite moment that I wish would never end—because I don't want to see who she is on the other side of it.

Then Elkisa grabs for her sword, her movements a blur—but I am different now. She does not know this part of me.

The mist is faster than she is.

A wave of force knocks her back against a nearby tree so hard that the ground itself quakes. She grunts as the air goes out of her, sword dropping from a suddenly nerveless hand.

"Skies," Jezara breathes, witnessing my power.

"This isn't possible," I sob as the mist strains to press harder. Yet the guilt and fear suffusing Elkisa's features confirms the instinct deep in my stomach. "You would never—you wouldn't—"

The mist swirls around Elkisa, pushing her up the trunk of the tree until she is dangling a foot from the ground.

"Nimh . . ." Jezara's voice is low and calm but laced with urgency. "Inshara has a way of persuading people to her cause. She is ruthless, but she is also . . . magnetic. Her talent for persuasion is disproportionate to—"

"Ni—," Elkisa squeaks, the force of the mist gathering—pressing against her rib cage. "Can't—breathe—"

"All of it—everything between us? How long have you been her spy? How long have you been my enemy? Did you ever . . ." Tears burn my eyes, but I ignore them. "Did you ever care about me?"

"Nimh!" Jezara's voice cracks whiplike beside my ear. "You're not a killer. I see your power. You must control it!"

Panting with effort and fury, I gather up my will and bend it to the mist holding Elkisa fast to the tree trunk. After a moment, Elkisa gasps a long, rattling breath as the pressure against her body eases a fraction.

Shaking, I whisper, "You killed him. You killed Daoman."

Her eyes are rimmed in red and her voice is hoarse. "Yes."

A tiny little shard of my heart crumbles away, despite what I already knew.

"He loved you too, you know." I don't bother to stop the tears—I let them spill down my cheeks. "We were both children when duty called us, and he loved you too. So did I."

Elkisa's reddened face goes redder still, tension gathering in her body until it bursts out of her in a ragged scream. She struggles against her invisible bonds, heels kicking against the tree, but she cannot move much farther than that.

"Bind her, and stay and watch her when I've gone," I tell Jezara, hardening my heart. I can only let myself care about one thing now. "I will go after Inshara alone."

Elkisa gives a cry of alarm. "You mustn't!" she croaks. "Please—you can't. You'll destroy each other." There are tears on her face now too—though whether of emotion or of sheer physical terror, I cannot know.

Jezara hasn't moved to follow my instructions—instead, she's looking past me, her round face worried. "Nimh . . . I think you should wait," she says, the normally low, steady voice quaking with the effort of sounding calm. "You don't yet understand this power of yours."

With the mist holding Elkisa fast against the tree, I glance over my shoulder.

"I don't care." I'm speaking between clenched teeth, relieved to let anger take over from the deeper, more painful thing. Fury enough to distract from the gaping wound in my heart. "I'm going to go save him. I *need* to save him."

"No! Wait! You can't!" Elkisa wails. "Inshara was going to imprison him, but he fought back. . . ."

I start to interrupt her, but she shouts over me.

"North is dead!"

I stagger back a step, the mist faltering just enough so that Elkisa slides down the tree trunk to land on her feet. Then I ball my hands into fists and the mist pushes her back again. "You're lying. You're a liar—that's all you do."

"I'm not—I'm not lying, Nimh, I swear. . . ." Elkisa's muscles strain, standing out on her arm, until she manages to get a hand to her waist. She works at something tucked into her waistband, and it takes her a few moments to pull it free and drop it to the ground between us.

It's a ragged scrap of a red sash—*my* red sash. The one North tied around his waist to look like a riverstrider. To look like *my* riverstrider.

North is dead.

The words ring in the sudden silence of my mind. Everything is still, rage and pain frozen for a long, interminable instant. I'm standing in the eye of the storm, and any moment it will pass and hurl me back down into the maelstrom.

North is dead.

A scream rips its way out of my throat. The last thing I do is command the mist to slam Elkisa's head back against the tree with a sickening crack—and everything goes white.

THIRTY-TWO

NORTH

A wash of color swims across my vision, blues and greens and golds blending together in an uncomfortable swirl. Snatches of memory dance just out of reach—a fleeting impression of trees overhead, a glimpse of the temple from afar. I see them through a shifting fog, and then they're gone again. I blink and the ceiling snaps into focus.

"Ah, he's awake," drawls a voice beside me.

I turn my head, then immediately regret it as everything washes together again. Another blink, and this time it's Techeki who comes into view. A flash of anger instantly goes through me and I swallow down nausea as I prop myself up on my elbows.

"What are you doing here?" I snap. "Not busy with your new goddess?"

Techeki stares flatly at me for a moment, then looks down to one side. When I follow his gaze, I discover the cat, who returns the man's stare and meows loudly. With a sigh, the Master of Spectacle runs one hand over his shiny head and shoots me a long-suffering look.

"If I'd chosen her side, you would still be drugged, and I would have imprisoned you somewhere far less pleasant, boy. Tell me, is Nimhara safe?"

A small shock goes through me as he uses her honorific. Mistrust is quick on its heels. "I'm not telling you where she is," I reply.

"Good, I'm glad to hear you're at least that intelligent. If she returns, I will be ready to serve. In the meantime, I do what is required to keep myself in that position. I am no use to anyone in a dungeon."

"Is that why you told Inshara she was right, that she could use Nimh's crown to get to the cloudlands?" I demand. "You know what she'll do up there."

"She already knew she was right," he replies. "I don't know how she knew—you heard her; she claims the Lightbringer told her—but denying the truth would only have proven to her she couldn't trust me. So I confirmed what she already knew, and stayed in the game a little longer."

"And your next move is to come see me," I say slowly. I'm scrambling to collect myself—of all the possibilities I imagined, Techeki telling me he's my ally just wasn't one.

"My next move was to come and see you," he agrees. "Sit up, and I'll tell you why. And drink—you have been unconscious for nearly a full day."

Dazed, I let him take my hand, and I swing my legs off the couch it turns out I'm lying on. I've been here before—it's the same room I waited in when I first came to the temple. Only one thing has changed—the statue of Nimh I wanted to shout a million questions at has been smashed from the ankles up, and it lies in piles of rubble on the carpet.

"Go on," I say to Techeki, as the cat jumps up onto the newly vacated place on the couch beside me. The Master of Spectacle nods politely to the cat, and reaches down to produce a large cup of water from the ground near my feet.

"I'm here," he says quietly, "because I know more than I have told her. I've seen the crown used to send a man to the sky. I have seen a cloudlander return to Alciel."

Hearing the name of my home on his lips steals my breath, and I nearly choke on my water. "You've *what*?"

"It was years ago, when Jezara was . . . evicted from the temple," he replies quietly. "I lacked the influence then that I have now. What I could do to serve her was keep her cloud-lander from getting himself killed, as someone almost certainly would have done once Jezara's banishment was complete."

"*Her* cloudlander?" I echo, but an instant later, the memory arrives.

Jezara knew I was from Alciel when she met me. My speech, my manner must have given me away—but that could only happen if she knew what to look for.

Are you so arrogant as to think that you're the only *cloudlander ever to have come to our world?*

"When she decided to take a lover, she didn't do it by halves," Techeki says, dry. "But to the point, he used the crown to return home—I saw it myself."

"How?"

"The cloudlander used an amulet I provided to him. It came—which is to say I stole it—from the relic stores in the archives. It was rumored to have once belonged to a Sentinel."

"Sentinels aren't real," I point out. "Everybody says they're a myth. Matias offered to get me a book of bedtime stories for children when I asked about them."

"And no doubt he was right that there is no other trace," he agrees. "But the amulet *was* a way to the sky, and the Sentinels were said to guard the passage between worlds. I imagine that's how the myth came to be attached to it. The cloudlander told me he was sure the crown was the key, and so I . . . borrowed it for him. He broke the amulet against it, and in a moment, he was simply gone, leaving only the crown behind."

My heart stutters with hope. "The amulet, what was it?"

"I cannot say, but it was believed to contain the blood of an ancient king. I cannot say what made it work."

I feel a bit sick as realization overtakes me. "He broke it, you said—you don't have another one, do you?"

"I do not."

I try to ignore the sick feeling in my gut, turning his words over for any hint of a clue as to what really happened. *The blood of an ancient king.* Could he be talking about a . . . a DNA lock?

Nimh's scroll certainly unlocked itself when touched by blood. Could the crown be the same?

I repeat the words again in my head.

The blood of an ancient king.

Slowly, the barest seed of an idea starting to take root, I say, "Nimh told me once that you haven't had kings here for a long time . . . since before the Ascension—the Exodus?"

Techeki raises an eyebrow at me. "Around that time, I think. You'd have to ask the archivist for an exact answer, if anyone could find him."

"What do you mean? Is Matias all right? He helped Nimh and me escape. If Inshara found out . . ." Guilt washes through me—I should have thought to ask earlier.

Techeki shakes his head. "He hasn't been seen since the night you fled. None of my sources have yielded even the smallest scrap of information. That *may* be good news."

I have no choice but to cling to the hope that Matias has holed up somewhere to wait out Inshara's wrath. For now, he's not here, and Techeki is. I hesitate, but only briefly. Techeki's loyalties might be questionable, but I don't see anyone else on my side around here. Maybe he knows something he doesn't realize is important—I need to give him a reason to search his memory for me. By magic or technology, I *need* to find a way home.

The blood of an ancient king . . .

Lifting my chin, I say quietly, "My family has been sitting on the throne of Alciel since the time of the Exodus."

Techeki's other eyebrow joins the first. "Not just a god, but a prince among gods?" His voice is amused, however, rather than reverent. Then realization takes hold. "You think it is possible *you* are descended from the ancient king whose blood sent the last cloudlander home."

"You wouldn't *believe* how intense my family is about making sure our bloodline is unbroken. If your ancient king was my ancestor, then I most definitely share his DNA." Remembering who I'm talking to, I add, "My blood could work just like the amulet did—if we could get our hands on the crown."

Techeki nods slowly. "It's possible," he murmurs, thoughtful. "And if we remove you from the equation, then the usurper has no way up to the sky. I shudder to think what she might be capable of should she get her hands on the powers of the gods."

Inshara, with Alciel technology, would be a formidable opponent down here . . . and anyone armed with magic would be nearly unstoppable in my world. But Techeki's point makes my stuttering heart steady a little as hope takes hold, and I say the words out loud. "My blood could be my way back home."

The cat suddenly growls low in his throat, and a moment later the door opens to reveal one of the temple guards, a woman clad in black and gold.

"It is time for the Vigil of the Rising," she says, quiet and dispassionate. "Come."

The cat trots ahead of us with his tail waving like a banner, and though the temple is hushed in what must be the predawn, it's hardly empty—they're all preparing for the vigil, I suppose.

Techeki and I follow the cat past citizens and students, and one thing that stands out to me is how *normal* everything is.

Everyone moves with quiet purpose, rather than panic, and they speak to one another in low, businesslike voices. This doesn't feel like a place that's been subject to a hostile takeover. The screams and fear from the Feast of the Dying are gone. This place just feels . . . busy.

It's like nothing ever happened—like there was a seamless

change in management, and everybody's just getting on with things.

What happened after we left? How did Inshara segue from murdering Daoman in front of everyone to this quiet, calm, everyday feeling?

I feel like the whole world's been turned upside down, and I am the only one who's noticed.

I feel like I'm going mad.

Whatever Inshara's done to convince them to return to their usual lives—some combination of her deadly charisma, her displays of power, and the promise of a solution to their woes—it's working. It's simply business as usual around here.

I wish I knew what she had planned. But I have a goal now. Her crown.

If I get it, would I use it?

Could I use it and leave Nimh to face Inshara alone?

"At the Feast of the Dying, we mark the solstice," Techeki says quietly. "We farewell the sun, knowing the shortest of days are before us. But now, at dawn, we'll see the Vigil of the Rising, and remember that the darkness is behind us, and the time of the sun once again grows longer."

The guard leads us out onto a terrace, and with a jolt, I realize we're standing where Nimh stood when she performed the Feast of the Dying. Every detail of that evening is burned into my mind, from the setting sun to the spreading stain of Daoman's blood on the stone floor during the feast afterward.

Attendants light lamps around the edge of the terrace as the guard ushers us forward. The broad stone platform looks out over the city, the stonework beneath our feet an intricate pattern on too large a scale for me to pick out. Toward the center of the terrace the design turns less freestyle and more structured—the lines in the stone are so precise, I'd say they were machine-cut if Below had tech of that kind. A knot of people is gathered there, and I catch a glimpse of crimson robes—Inshara.

She's wearing the crown.

As my eyes adjust, I can see the city below us. Straight ahead, I see the river snaking away—the same river Nimh and I fled down only a few nights before. It vanishes into the gloom, the stars hidden in that direction by large, dark banks of cloud.

The river splits to pass around the city on either side, creating one big island, though so many boats and bridges cross the water that I'd never have noticed unless I came up this high.

The city below us, where I stood during the Feast of the Dying, is a sea of lanterns and flickering spellfire. I can just make out the faces of the crowd, turned up toward us.

Flanking Inshara are half a dozen temple guards, rows of priests and attendants, some of the civilian dignitaries I saw at the feast, guildmasters and council members, and I see solemn men and women dressed all in gray.

If I hadn't known Elkisa's performance the night Inshara took over the temple was all a lie, I would assume Inshara had somehow placed these people under the same spell. Though a few of them glance at me, their gazes troubled and uncertain, most pay me little attention.

How easily she's taken Nimh's people from her. How desperate they must be for a savior, that they were ready to believe in the woman who murdered the high priest in front of everyone that night.

Or, I think to myself, feeling sick, *Inshara is just that persuasive.*

So much so that she's done what Nimh could not: unite the priests and Graycloaks alike. What must she have promised them?

Inshara makes her way toward us, crimson robes catching the lamplight. When she stops in front of me, I can't help myself—my gaze drifts up to her crown. I never really looked at it when Nimh had it—I was more interested in its wearer.

But now . . . now I see it. The crown's design is intricate, but there's a message just for me hidden within the motif.

Two stylized wings spread out on either side of a small space that's perfectly clear. And the shape of that plain little area is one I know as well as my own face. It's the outline of a sky-island.

My family's crest is on the crown, calling me home to Alciel. Our mark, left behind on this world when we fled. For a wild moment, I want to snatch the crown from her and run. If my blood really is the key, I could use it to get home, to warn my family that those below want to destroy them, that their religion demands it.

I know that's what I should do.

It should be easy to choose. I'd be leaving Nimh behind, but I can't sacrifice my people, abandon my duty, for just one girl, even this girl. It shouldn't *be* a choice.

"Cloudlander, you look very thoughtful," Inshara says, and

with a blink, I realize I'm still staring at her. The golden paint on her lips shimmers in the torchlight and she has one brow raised.

"I, um." My first attempt at an answer crashes and burns, and I feel the cat weaving through my ankles, the warmth of his fur and the easy movement of his muscle somehow comforting. "I was examining the stonework there. What's the meaning behind it?"

Techeki, at my side, murmurs an explanation, willing to work with me to stall for time. "The first symbol, on the far side of the guardian stone, belongs to the nameless god. The other, on this side, to the nameless goddess. He was the first incarnation of the living divine, and she was the second. Their names are lost, but not their aspects. He was the god of endings, and saw the Exodus of the rest of his kind to the cloudlands. She was the goddess of beginnings, and saw the start of a new world in their absence."

I have to fight to keep the shock off my face. Nobody in the world but Nimh and I have heard the words of the prophecy that came to her as she manifested.

The Star shall light the path in the place of endings and beginnings.

And here I am. The Star. In the very place I'm meant to be.

No matter how hard I try to get away from it, the prophecy keeps grabbing hold of me and dragging me back in. And I'm done running from it.

Nimh's prophecy is coming true, and it's happening now.

I'm here to play my part, and I'm here to do it for Nimh.

That realization hums through me like an electrical current, as shocking as it is impossible to ignore. I can't leave her—I *won't* leave her.

I'm here for Nimh.

"She's coming, isn't she?" Inshara murmurs, turning her gaze out across the darkened city. "I can almost feel her. She's coming to save you."

I swallow hard, my eyes on the horizon, where the stars are blacked out by a distant gathering storm. It's still a small, dark shape, flashes of lightning illuminating it from within. "You'd better hope she isn't. You might find she's a bit more than you can handle now."

Inshara's gaze swivels toward me, but when I look at her, her lips are curved in a smile. "I think she'll find me prepared."

"What are you going to do?" I ask slowly, a flicker of unnamed dread running down my spine.

"Our friends in gray stand ready at their stations," she replies, taking in the city. "On my word, they will alter the river forever. I will do what she never could have, and create a permanent barrier around the whole of the city. It will be one great Haven. Six anchors of sky-steel have been placed along the river. When they are immersed, the water will connect them, and the whole city will be ringed in protection. No one inside the ring will be able to use magic."

"No one except you," I breathe, my heart dropping into the pit of my stomach.

A million questions shout inside my mind.

Where did she get the sky-steel for the anchors?

How many guardian stones were shattered?

How many villages were lost or will be lost to her need for power?

How many died, or worse?

I feel sick.

Inshara stands tall, gazing down at the rivers. "The mist-storm grows, but it can rage as mightily as it wishes. With a single word, I will keep it from us."

We're all looking at the storm as she speaks, and there's something about the way it moves that makes the hair on the back of my neck stand up, unease prickling my skin. It breaks apart and swirls back together, and at the very center of it I keep catching glimpses of a white light.

There's something about the way it moves. . . .

"I don't think that's *just* a mist-storm."

Her head snaps toward me, which is when I realize I spoke out loud. Her voice is soft, dangerous, when she speaks—these words are just for me.

"What did you say, cloudlander?"

But I don't answer—I can't. I can't look away from the great, roiling clouds bearing down on us, suddenly moving faster, eating up the distance to the city. They're the size of mountains, twisting and writhing like a great flock of birds, tumbling over themselves to reach us, breaking apart like the water of the river when it foams around the rocks.

They're not just gray—those flashes of lightning from within are cast with greens and purples. It's like a thunderstorm trying to tear itself apart.

Inshara gives a little gasp, taking a step back from the

terrace railing. But I have no time to enjoy her alarm, because I've just seen the same thing she did.

At the center of this great mountain range of mist is a cyclone, a whirling pillar the size of the temple itself. And atop it, arms outflung, shadow large enough to cover half the city below, her hair wild, her eyes glowing white . . . is Nimh.

She's a wild creature, joined with the mist-storm, a part of the thing that's lifting her aloft. I take an involuntary step back and bump into someone behind me. I distantly feel quick needles of pain as the cat climbs me like a ladder, standing across my shoulders to watch his mistress as she approaches.

A soft growl begins in the back of his throat and builds to a feral yowl that rings out across the rooftop.

She reaches the edge of the city, the river roiling beneath her. An entire flotilla of barges tears away from the water with a muted roar that takes a few seconds to reach us. Below us, screams ring out from the crowd—and then they see her too, a physical shock going through them like a wave.

A section of wall, some ancient ruin, vanishes into the mist with a grinding and tearing of stone. A platoon of guards comes running out of a tower at the end of the higher ground, only to halt in uncertain terror as they stare up at the goddess they used to protect with their lives. Some break and run. The rest are swallowed up by the mist as Nimh advances, oblivious to—or unmoved by—the destruction all around her.

Someone knocks me off-balance as they push past me, and I lift up my hands to grab at the cat and steady him, finally tearing my gaze away to look out across the terrace. Most of the priests are cowering against the far wall, several of them on their knees, their voices raised in prayers lost to the wind.

The Graycloaks have broken, elbowing the guildmasters and council members aside as they run for the stairs and whatever safety they offer. A woman hits the ground and shrieks, covering her head with both hands as a boot lands in the middle of her back.

Inshara still stands to one side of me, Techeki to the other, and her guards ring us, but they're clinging to their last nerve, gripping their spears tight, eyes rolling to the side to check they're not the only one who's holding their ground.

"The—," Inshara begins, her voice rising in something very close to panic. But she's drowned out by the noise of the storm, and she's forced to shout: "The sky-steel, now!"

Horror washes over me and I lunge toward her, not knowing what I plan to do. All I know is that if she rings the city in sky-steel, if she kills its magic, then Nimh's mist will be gone.

She'll fall.

I *have* to believe in her—I can't let her die.

I grab for Inshara's arm to spin her around, and one of her guards is between us in an instant, catching me in the stomach with the butt of his spear and sending me staggering backward to hit the ground. The cat goes flying and somehow lands on his feet, but my breath's driven out of me, and I'm gasping. Pain blanks out my thoughts as I roll over onto my hands and knees, crawling to the railing to try to haul myself up.

The wind is rising with the mist now, the air thick and oily, my clothes whipping around me and up into my face as though they want to smother me.

"Stop," I gasp, reaching out to grab at her red robes. "Inshara, stop! I-I'll tell you how to get up to the sky!"

She freezes in place, her body absolutely motionless, her robes whipping wildly in place around her. Then she spins on her heel, holding up one hand in a signal. I'm only distantly aware of the signal being passed along, of other hands raising around us. All I know is that I've bought myself a minute. I can't let myself think about what I'm about to do in it, my heart pulling me toward home, that same heart anchored here, tied to the goddess above us.

This is my only choice.

"Promise," I rasp, still fighting for breath. "Promise you won't kill her."

"I give you my word," says Inshara slowly.

Above us the cyclone carrying Nimh has nearly reached the temple. My eyes are streaming in the wind, ragged tendrils of gray and green and violet mist twisting in broken shapes around us, Nimh an incandescent white.

I have to force the words out.

"I know how to activate the crown."

Our eyes lock, me on one knee, her standing straight-backed above me, the wind grabbing with wild fingers at her hair and robes. "Well?" she demands, eyes blazing.

"It's my blood," I gasp, heartsick, trying not to think about the cost of what I'm saying. "I'm a prince in the cloudlands. My royal blood unlocks the way."

Inshara's eyes narrow, and she holds my gaze for a long, long moment, trying to determine the truth. Satisfied, she nods, and I sag in relief, turning back toward Nimh, who still approaches, ringed by destruction on all sides.

Then, from just behind me, comes Inshara's voice again: "Lower the anchors!"

"What—no!" I try once more to stagger toward Inshara, but I'm too late. Her command has been spoken, and the signal passed along, and on the shores of the great river there are fires blazing now. By their light, I see covers coming off the enormous barges I'd assumed were cargo boats.

Bodies swarm around them, struggle and heave, and I see the splashes as the anchors enter the water.

The lights nearest to them go out instantly, and I see the signal travel along the waterways. As it meets between each anchor, the net is complete, and the lights go out across the city, darkness sweeping inward, every pinpoint of light extinguished as the wave sweeps toward us.

The people below me are invisible now, but . . . Inshara is still illuminated.

Skyfall, Jezara *was* telling the truth. Her daughter, immune to the sky-steel, stares up defiantly at the mist-storm and the wild goddess riding it, watching as it begins to tear itself apart.

Surrounded by sky-steel, Nimh screams. The sound is an echo of the mist-wraiths back at the dead village. My skin crawls horribly, and for an instant I'm sure my eardrums are going to burst. Her whirling pillar shudders once, and then implodes around her, until all that remains is a writhing orb, hovering just above the stone terrace.

"*Nimh!*"

Her name's ripped out of me as I push to my feet, as I break into a run, unsure if she's even still inside the cocoon—unsure if she's even alive. "*NIMH, NO!*"

I skid to a stop beside the roiling ball of mist, helpless. The storm within it rages, though now and then a flicker of light shows me a glimpse of an arm, a leg—she's braced, frozen, locked in a struggle with the force of Inshara's sky-steel. I reach out toward her, then snatch my hand back as a shock runs through me. I'm raging at my own helplessness, but to touch her cage of mist would surely be deadly—to become like Quenti, or worse, like the mist-wraiths.

But Nimh is in there, my heart cries. The orb hovers just in front of me, barely large enough to contain her form.

Footsteps behind me make me whirl in time to see Inshara descending to this level of the terrace. Her guards hurry after her, Techeki on their heels. She stares at the condensed, raging storm for a moment. Then she turns and snatches a spear from a nearby guard. She whirls back, raising her arm.

My muscles bunch before I've time to think it through, ready to launch me in between the spear and what's left of Nimh.

Then a voice rings out like a bell, singing across the crowd. "That's enough!" For a moment, I can't tell who spoke—and

438

then a figure shoves its way through the throngs of people to emerge just in front of us. Her gaze is lifted.

Fixed upon her daughter.

"I did not raise you to be a monster," Jezara calls, panting with effort. How she made it through the destruction below, through the wide swath of rubble that marks Nimh's path into the city, I have no idea. "Stop this now."

The spear drops from Inshara's hands, clattering harmlessly to the stone. She lifts her chin. Is it in attempt to maintain her composure? "Mother. Why are you here?"

Confusion permeates those assembled on the terrace. Many of them clearly recognize their former goddess. But they had no idea Inshara was her forbidden child. Jezara moves up the bottom few steps until she's standing just below me. "I'm here," she says, "to stop you from becoming this. This isn't who you are."

"This is *exactly* who I am!" Inshara snaps back, eyes blazing. "*I* am the one the Lightbringer speaks to! I have heard him all my life—he has told me I am special, I am chosen. *I* am chosen, not her!"

Slowly, Jezara makes her limping way up the stairs until she can stand alongside me, between her daughter and the still-struggling Nimh, fighting her own battle against the mist.

"How can you stand at *her* side?" Inshara bursts out, voice agonized. "She is nothing to you—a symbol of the world that cast you out! *I* was the one who lived with you in squalor, raised on the jeers and disgust of everyone around us. *I* was the one they spat on when I passed them in the street. *I* was the one who went hungry so that we could raise enough to leave that place. She is *not your daughter*!" Inshara's voice cracks with her intensity, the last words emerging in a ragged shout as she extends a shaking finger toward me.

"Insha," Jezara says softly.

"Do you not see what I've done?" Inshara pleads, her eyes lighting, her gaze desperate. "I've made them choose me, Mother, these people and this faith. I've made them choose us both."

"They didn't choose you," Jezara replies quietly. "They're afraid of you. You mistake terror for loyalty."

"No. Don't you see?" Inshara whispers, stretching a hand back toward the priests and guards still raggedly arrayed around her. "I've made them love me."

"Insha," Jezara says, her voice soft. "I know who you are. I am begging you now—stop this. You still have *my* love. You don't need theirs."

Inshara's face flickers, something softer responding to her mother's voice. Then her expression hardens. "I have *his* love," Inshara blurts, clutching at her chest—no, at the chrono she wears strung on a necklace that hangs there. "The Lightbringer's. And when I am ready, he will manifest his power in me."

"You hear his voice from *that*?" Jezara's voice is high with surprise. "From that necklace I gave you?"

Inshara cradles it in both hands, curling over it like she's protecting something precious. "From as early as I can remember."

Realization dawns like a cold sweat, prickling all over. Unable to resist, my hand slides down my arm to touch my own chrono. If I'd known that the *chrono* was where Inshara was hearing that voice . . . But who could be speaking to her through it?

"It can't be," Jezara mutters, confusion swamping her realization. "He was banished. He never spoke to me. I gave up on him. I presumed . . ."

Her head lifts, eyes finding Techeki's. The Master of Spectacle is watching her with a grief-stricken expression.

"Forgive me, Divine One," he whispers. "I feared you would waste your life trying to follow him."

"You found a way to send him back to the sky?" Jezara's voice stretches into a wail. Her eyes bright with tears, she takes a step forward. "I thought—I thought he *chose* to abandon me. That chronometer was all I had, and it never worked. That's why I gave it to—"

Inshara's voice cuts across her mother's. "What are you talking about?" she demands.

Jezara passes a shaking hand over her eyes. "Oh, child— that voice you hear. It doesn't belong to a god, just a man. I made that necklace from a device your father gave me before we were separated. He must have found a way to get it working, but only after I gave it to you."

Inshara's hand closes around the chrono amulet. Her face has gone still, its color draining, her eyes flat and hard. "You lie," she whispers.

"Did he never ask about me?" Jezara asks, taking another step toward her daughter, half lifting a hand in entreaty. "Never ask to speak with me?"

Inshara stands stock-still, one hand curled into a white-knuckled fist around the chrono. "I . . . I wanted to keep him for myself," she whispers. "I was only a child when I told him you were dead."

Jezara's eyes widen. "You *what?* Insha—"

"This is all some trick!" Inshara blurts, her eyes filling with tears. "He is divine. A god. The Lightbringer. He told me that this world should burn. . . ."

Her mother chokes back a sob. "Oh, Insha . . . come home, my dear." She lifts her arms in an offered embrace as Inshara stares at her. "You and I have so much to talk about. I wish—"

With a scream, Inshara stoops to retrieve her spear. In one motion she drives it home with a grunt of rage and effort. Jezara's voice cuts out as she stares down at the haft of the spear protruding from her chest.

For an instant, no one moves. No one speaks. Horror holds us all captive—even Jezara's daughter, who stares at her mother's face, her eyes round.

Then a scream rises up as if from the ground itself. It's a heartbeat before I realize where the sound is coming from:

Nimh.

The figure struggling inside the dense tangle of mist gives a jerk and curls in on itself—then, in a wave of force that knocks me clean off my feet, the mist explodes.

I roll down half a flight of steps as I hit the stone, my battered head aching, my palms scraped raw. With an effort, I manage to get my dazzled eyes to focus again. I can't see what's happening up above, but beyond the terrace . . . My breath catches.

Sweeping like a wave, the spellfire lights are coming back on again. Dazed, I look past the city to the river—and then drop to my hands and knees in shock.

The water is gone, and with it, Inshara's sky-steel barrier.

Nimh has vaporized the river.

THIRTY-THREE

NIMH

Head spinning, body aching, stars bursting in front of my eyes, all I can do for long breaths is lie there, face against the stone. Then I remember what I felt through the searing pain of mist against my skin, through the gut-wrenching effort of holding myself intact.

Jezara.

Reeling, I drag myself forward until I can see her where she's slumped in someone's arms, breath rattling in her throat. Techeki—the Master of Spectacle—is there, holding her. "Jeza," he murmurs, pressing against the wound as blood flows around the spear shaft and his fingers and becomes a crimson stain spreading across the purple mantle.

I murmur at Techeki to move, reaching for Mhyr's Sunrise and my vial of thicksweet, my eyes on Jezara's wound as I try to think how to remove the spear without killing her. But the former goddess gives a shake of her head, her eyes swinging up toward mine. "No, child." Her lips quiver, a weak attempt at a smile. "I was the goddess of healing, remember? I know when a body's wounds are beyond the help of magic."

I grit my teeth, fingers tightening around the vial of thick-sweet. "I must try."

Jezara's smile fades and her eyebrows draw together. "If I don't wish to spend my last moments breathing the scent of burning flesh, feeling the grate of broken bone on bone, that is my choice."

My every instinct tells me to ignore her wishes, to keep fighting. But I look at her face again and fall silent.

Her eyes unfocus, lips working soundlessly as if in confusion. Then her body tenses as she coughs again, the sound thick and wet this time, blood staining her lips a bright, garish crimson.

"She's such a little thing," she murmurs to the air. Then her gaze floats past my face without recognition, past North's, back to Techeki's again. "You'll look after her, won't you?"

Techeki brushes a lock of her hair back, settling it gently behind her ear. "I always have, Divine One. I always will."

"Such a little thing," Jezara repeats, her voice almost dreamy. "I wonder if it's my fault, her being called so young. . . ."

Understanding dawns, and I swallow hard. This time when I glance at Techeki, his eyes meet mine for an instant before returning to the face of his old friend and goddess.

"She will do well," Techeki tells her, eyes wet with tears. "And I will look after young Nimhara, I promise you."

Jezara starts to turn her head when her eyes find me and halt there, sense and understanding draining away. "You seem familiar, child. . . . Will you hear my blessing?"

I feel a tear slip down my cheek and splash onto my hand. Swallowing hard, I nod and bow my head with my palms to my eyes. I've never made the gesture myself—I've been its recipient since my earliest memories. But it comes easily, and as I wait, Jezara begins to speak.

"Blessings upon you," she whispers, letting her eyes close again. "Light keep you safe, and light guide you on your path. May the warmth of healing go with you. . . ." Her lips move as though she would continue speaking, but no sound comes out, and her brow furrows.

Techeki reaches down and takes her hand, his eyes on the place where his palm touches hers. The crease in her forehead eases, and the tiniest of smiles touches the corners of her lips.

"May you walk lightly," I whisper, picking up where she left off. My blessing and hers are not the same—no two deities share the same. "May forgiveness and compassion keep you, until . . ."

I spoke these words not long ago, on a lonely riverbank as a boy bled to death, as helpless then as I am now. My throat constricts, and it isn't until Techeki lifts his head, his green eyeliner smudged with tears, that I find my voice, and the rest of my farewell.

"Until we meet again, Divine One."

For a moment after Jezara's last breath sighs out of her, there's no sound. My body is empty, a dark and aching hole where once there was a heart.

I lift my eyes to see Inshara standing not far away, watching us with blazing eyes, my crown upon her head. My vision dims. Blood rushes past my ears. The world begins to fall away.

"Techeki, go," I whisper.

"What?" Techeki straightens with a jerk, unwilling to leave Jezara's body. "I must—Divine One, please—"

"*Go!*" I order him, not taking my eyes from the woman wearing my crown, my red robes—that same crimson as North's sash, tossed to the ground before me when Elkisa brought me news of his death.

Inshara has taken everything from me. My crown. My best friend. The boy I gave my heart to. My father, my people, my home, my life's purpose. And finally, the only other alive in the world who could possibly understand me.

The mist is gathering around me once more, having seen to it that the sky-steel river would not harm me again. I can feel it, roiling, waiting. I can see it, flickers of violent green and purple in the corners of my vision. It tastes coppery and strange on my tongue—it tastes like blood.

It bends to my will, this mist. I am the only person in this world who can feel its caress without being twisted beyond recognition.

Inshara has no such protection.

And I will make her pay.

THIRTY-FOUR

NORTH

I fight my way up the steps, dodging the fleeing guards and priests and Graycloaks trying to get away. I nearly stumble over something soft, then halt as a hand shoots out and grabs at my arm.

"Stop!" Techeki holds fast, my momentum whirling me around and toppling me down beside him. "They'll kill you!"

Wrenching my gaze away from Jezara's body next to him—*Oh, skies, what did I stumble over?*—I turn toward the terrace.

I freeze.

Mist screams through the air, singing like the blade of a sword. Inshara's backed against the wall of the upper terrace, summoning meager flickers of magic that do little to halt the onslaught of blows coming for her.

And Nimh . . .

Nimh is fury. The very air around her bends, as if the aura of mist and rage she's wrapped around herself is so dense not even light can pass through unaffected. She's advancing upon Inshara the way she advanced upon the city. Only this time her eyes are clear—and she's terrifying.

The mist comes faster and faster, the wind ripping at my clothes and roaring like a train passing inches away. A boulder the size of my body heaves itself up, tearing its way out of the paved terrace to smash into a hundred razor-sharp fragments that join the whirling storm around her.

I start to lurch to my feet only to find Techeki still holding me back.

"Are you mad?" he shouts, forced to put his head close to mine to be heard. "You'll be killed before you've even reached them."

"She'll destroy the temple!" I scream back, shredding my throat. "She'll destroy everything she has left. I can't let her become this thing!"

"She thinks you're dead, boy," Techeki replies, voice cracking with the effort of shouting over the din. "That's why—after Daoman, Jezara, the temple . . . I heard her, cloudlander. I heard her say your name."

I spare a glance for Techeki, shock coursing through me. She hasn't seen me—she doesn't know I'm alive.

I can stop this.

A scream from the terrace jerks my attention back. Inshara's pressed up against the stone now, and the mist is gathering around Nimh so densely she's almost wearing it like a second skin. It reaches out, stretching like another set of arms, reaching for Inshara.

"Wait—Nimh! WAIT!" The wind tears my voice away.

Before I can stop it, the mist grabs Inshara and pulls her in, her scream cut short. Both she and Nimh vanish inside the deadly whirling mass. But where I'd half expected the violent torrent to halt, Nimh's goal achieved—for surely Inshara could not survive so much mist—the storm rages on.

The force of the storm rips more stones from the terrace, one flying so close to us that Techeki's forced to drop to the ground, covering his head with both hands. I manage a single glance back over my shoulder, the ruined path of destruction that Nimh left gaping like a scar across the city.

No. I will not let her do this—for their sake, for hers.

I heave a couple of breaths to ready myself, brace my feet against the top of the stairs—and then break into a sprint.

What will the mist feel like?

Will I have enough time to stop her, to reach her, before I'm dead? Before I'm twisted? Before I'm nothing more than a ghost?

My family's faces flash before my eyes. I'll never see them again.

Miri and Saelis—I'll never hear my friends' laughter.

Nimh.

The storm hits like a wall, stones battering my body, crashing against me, slicing my skin. One tears open a gash across my face—I can feel the skin peel back with sickening certainty.

Any moment now, and the mist will have me. . . .

A blinding light, a roaring in my ears . . .

And then nothing.

Confused, I open my eyes, my arms lifted to ward stone and mist alike away from my face. All around me is mist. Up close, it's as beautiful as it is frightening—it gleams as if lit from within by every color at once, glistening like iridescent feathers. It roils around me, seething, angry—and yet I feel nothing, except a flare of heat against one hip. I lift a hand and see the mist swirl around my skin, which is unmarked and untwisted.

"North?"

I whirl around. Nimh is there, just behind me, gazing at me with round, tear-filled eyes. There's no sign of Inshara.

It's just Nimh and me, wrapped together in our own world of mist. She hovers a breath away from me, her gaze roving over my features, hungry, desperate. Her hand lifts, but halts just above my face, her fingers trembling with the desire to touch me.

"You have to stop this!" I gasp, not waiting to question my luck that, somehow, I've bought a few moments before the mist takes me. "You're destroying everything that you love out there. She isn't worth it."

"There isn't anything left that I love." The tears in Nimh's eyes spill over. "You're dead."

"I'm *right here*," I insist, wishing I could reach out and grab hold of her. "I'm not some trick of the mist. Whoever told you I was dead was *lying*."

"You can't be," Nimh cries. "The mist would destroy you. You have no protection."

My hip throbs again, and with sudden realization, I dig my hand into my pocket until my fingers close around the small, round stone Nimh gave me on the cliff top. It's so hot my instincts tell me to drop it, but I hold on, gritting my teeth.

"How are you here?" Nimh's eyes drop to fix on her protection stone and then lift to meet my gaze, wondering.

451

"Magic," I whisper.

"Oh, gods," Nimh moans, her eyes focusing again on my face—focusing on the place that's burning nearly as badly as my palm. Her hand lifts, but she halts the movement before she can touch me. Her fingers hover helplessly for a moment before a drop of blood from the gash on my cheek spatters against her skin. She stares at the crimson staining her fingertips. "You're hurt."

"But alive. Nimh—we can stop her. Take your crown back, and Inshara can't go to the cloudlands. You *don't* have to become this thing."

Her eyes travel over my features as if memorizing them for the last time. "I am the destroyer," she whispers. "I am the Lightbringer."

"You can *choose* what that means!" I try to catch her wandering gaze, try to keep her eyes on mine. "You can *choose*, understand? This power is yours—you choose what to do with it."

She opens her mouth, but whatever retort she had planned dies on her lips as she looks at me, an agony of indecision. Then I see her eyes widen, and the mist raging around us goes still.

For a moment, I want to throw my arms around her, hold her tight, relief that she's chosen humanity over destruction making me giddy.

Then I see the hand curled around her ankle.

Touching her.

Inshara.

I'm paralyzed, the world crumbling around me. The mist

falls away, the terrace and the city below it utterly silent save for the rasping of our breath. Inshara is alive—though when I see her face, my breath stops, for her manic smile stretches a fraction too wide, and her eyes flicker and glint with iridescence as if they're windows to the mist-storm raging inside her soul.

She jerks at Nimh's leg, pulling her down onto the ground where she crouches. Nimh cries out in horror and pain, and the sound goes through me like a knife.

Then, slowly, Nimh begins to glow. She's like a sunrise come to life, gold suffusing her features. She's utterly beautiful, her power on full display, and the thought of that power drained from her is unbearable. Her light catches the mist in the same way the dawn catches the clouds, growing brighter and stronger every second.

It's Inshara who speaks, who breathes the word: "Yes."

In that one syllable, all her mist-touched madness is there for the world to see.

Nimh is trying to pull away, struggling against the other woman's iron grip—the grief in her face breaks my heart, for she knows what Inshara has done to her, that she's witnessing the last moments of her own divinity.

The aura of gold swells and flares around the pair of them, and Nimh cries out again as the light begins to flow from her to Inshara where the other girl holds tight to her, as if she's dragging that light from Nimh.

I can't bear to see it, but I can't look away. The knowledge beats through me like a drum: this is the end of Nimh, and all I can do is bear witness.

But I love her, and I cannot stand to see it.

She gasps for breath as her light dims and Inshara's light brightens, and I watch helplessly as Inshara strips Nimh of her divinity.

Inshara gives Nimh a ruthless shake, making her cry out in pain. "It's all mine, more than it was ever yours," Inshara snaps. "*I* am the one the prophecy chose. I *will* become the Lightbringer. You were never destined for anything—you were *never* enough for this world."

Nimh goes still, no longer struggling, as her own fears and doubts come spilling out of the woman draining her of her power. Her eyes are dull, focused somewhere beyond Inshara, beyond me, beyond the very stone itself. For a moment, all is quiet. Then, she whispers a single word into the swirl of rising mist around them: "No."

Inshara tightens her grip. "What was that?" she asks.

Nimh's gaze snaps up, meeting Inshara's with a new, blazing intensity. "I said *no*. I am my people's goddess, and you will not stand in my way."

Inshara's sharp intake of breath is audible. Nimh's gaze is unwavering, defiant. And slowly, the balance shifts. Now Inshara grows dimmer as Nimh grows brighter. She claims her divinity, pulls it back and wraps it around herself, as stunning as any royal robe I've ever seen.

"How . . . ?" Inshara demands, teeth gritted as she tries to regain the upper hand.

But Nimh doesn't answer, all her focus on the struggle

between them. She's stronger. She's fighting, and she's winning. Inshara abruptly releases Nimh, scrambling backward.

Finally, Nimh's light settles back around her, like she's slipped into a familiar garment. Inshara's breathing hard, gasping for breath and staring at the goddess whose power she failed to banish.

We're all frozen in place. I'm afraid to breathe, afraid even to blink, for fear I'll wake to find my Nimh dark and broken under the triumphant stare of her enemy.

But my burning lungs force me to breathe—and Nimh still kneels there, poised and graceful. And unbroken.

Nimh's gaze swings around and her eyes find mine, wide and flashing with sudden disbelief and wonder.

Then Inshara's eyes flick to the side, and I realize what she's looking at.

There's something there, half-hidden by the crumbled terrace stones. It glints in the spellfire, and for a moment, no one moves.

The crown. The key to my home—the key to finding a way to destroy it.

Nimh told me once that the mist didn't just bring madness and death—that sometimes, very, very rarely, it could bring *great power*.

Inshara has been deeply, deeply mist-touched.

As one, Nimh and Inshara both lunge for the crown. But Inshara is closer.

I move without thinking, trying to give Nimh a head start

by grabbing at Inshara's ankle, but she kicks, catching me in the jaw, and as my vision momentarily fills with stars, she's gone.

Out of nowhere comes the cat, an orange streak of fury launching himself at Inshara with claws extended, raking them down Inshara's body with an unearthly yowl. She screeches in reply and flings him away—he lands in a pile of rubble and doesn't move.

We've bought Nimh enough time to grab the crown, but Inshara's right behind her, and with a cry of effort, she gets a hand on the gold band as well.

Nimh's on her knees, and she braces one foot against the ground as she hauls against Inshara's grip—grappling, the two lurch to their feet. The mist around them swirls faster and faster, glowing so brightly I'm forced to shield my eyes as I look up at them.

"Give it to me," Inshara screams, wild now, clawing at Nimh in desperation.

But before Nimh can reply, a burst of light erupts from the crown itself like a soundless explosion, sending a shock wave rippling through the mist and nearly knocking me flat again.

The cut on my cheek, I realize. *She has my blood on her hand—*
No.

I struggle back onto my knees in time to see a column of light surround the two of them. An invisible force begins drawing them both upward. Dust and bits of debris rise around them, as if the laws of gravity mean nothing at all. The golden crown hangs in the air above, glowing from a set of fingerprints against it—Nimh's, painting the surface with my blood. Inshara strains to reach up for it, her fingertips just missing its surface. I find Nimh's eyes as her toes leave the ground, hair drifting away from her shoulders like she's suspended in water.

For the first time since she defended her divinity, Nimh's eyes flash with panic as she sees me. She opens her mouth to shout, her lips forming my name, but no sound comes out—I cry out her name in response, and I see her eyes widen when she hears nothing.

I scramble to my feet and sprint for the two of them, throwing one arm up toward Nimh as she reaches down. Her fingers strain toward mine, and I rise up onto my toes, willing myself to find that tiniest bit of extra reach.

Our fingers come so close to touching that they eclipse the crown's brilliance for an instant before a sunburst of white light peeks between them, then explodes against my half-blinded eyes.

And then all of it—Inshara, the column of gold light, the roiling mist, and Nimh . . . my Nimh . . . is gone.

THIRTY-FIVE

NORTH

The crown clatters to the ground, bouncing once and slowly rolling to a halt against my shoe as I stare at the place Nimh was just a moment before. Or rather, it was once a crown—now it's twisted, melted into a dull mass of gold, scorched sky-steel circuitry exposed. The afterimage of Nimh, a silhouette of her reaching for me, is burned into my eyes, still glowing.

"No!" I grab what's left of the crown and shake it, disbelieving. I touch my fingertips to my face, ignoring the stab of pain that runs down from my cheek, and smear the crown's surface with my own blood.

Nothing.

"Take me to her, do it again!"

Techeki is walking forward, his face ashen. "It is ruined," he manages to say. "Your blood will not help us now."

"Do you know what Inshara can do to my world? Nobody believes in magic there. They wouldn't have any idea how to defend themselves against a magician."

Techeki gives a shiver. "Gods know what she is now. The

mist has changed her into something else—I fear for your people and mine, cloudlander."

I give the sky-steel crown another frantic shake. "Nimh, *do something!*"

A remnant of Nimh's mist curls around me, seems almost to caress me. Just for an instant, it feels as though fingers brush my cheek. I'm haunted by the strange certainty that the touch is Nimh's—though she's never touched me before, somehow the way the mist curves against my skin is all hers.

And then the sensation is gone.

I'm still sitting on the ground, holding the melted crown. If I stand up, if I move, I acknowledge that this has really happened. That Nimh and Inshara are gone, far beyond where I can follow. I can't do that.

Then something brushes against my leg and I start. It's the cat. He's limping as he moves, clearly in pain, but his steps are deliberate as he makes his way along my body until I can carefully gather him up in my arms. There he settles without protest, which is how I know he really must be hurting.

"We'll find her," I tell him quietly. "I promise. This isn't over."

Because I know she's alive, and she's in my world. And I know that was her touch just a few moments ago.

I know what I have to do, and I won't fail her.

Techeki offers me his hand to help me up as he speaks. "We'll search," he says quietly. "We'll find another way to the cloudlands."

Someone clears her throat behind me and I jump. When I whirl around, I'm face-to-face with a woman a little older than me, her hair shorn close to her head. She's dressed like a riverstrider—she's standing with half a dozen other riverstriders gathered just behind her.

"Forgive me, cloudlander," she says, inclining her head in a gesture of respect. "My name is Hiret, and I am a friend of your goddess. I bring greetings from the Fisher King of the riverstriders. He would meet with you, if you will see him."

Irritation sears through me. "No. I can't," I blurt. "What use are stories to me right now? I don't have time for your Fisher King."

"Not even if you knew him by another name?" The voice is resonant, rich, and grave.

The riverstriders step away, revealing the figure standing in their midst—and my mouth falls open.

At the temple, he wore plain robes—so plain I can't remember what color they were, only that he was nearly indistinguishable from the texts he guarded in his archives. Now he's in a coat of dark turquoise velvet, gold braiding decorating the shoulders and running down his arms. Around his neck, he has necklace after necklace slung one atop the other, so that most of his chest is a mass of gleaming beads that clicks and shifts when he moves.

"Y-*You* are the Fisher King?" I blurt.

Matias, Master of Archives, flashes me a grim smile. "Sometimes. I am always a protector of ancient secrets, cloudlander.

Nimhara called me Master of Archives, charged me with protecting the temple's written words. The riverstriders call me Fisher King, keeper of their stories."

I tangle my fingers in the cat's fur, still uncertain why he's chosen this moment to find me—surrounded by the rubble, still reeling from having lost Nimh and my home in one terrible instant.

Matias stoops, twitching one velvet sleeve back. "You, no doubt, will call me Sentinel, guardian of the secret ways between the worlds."

With a quiet incantation, he passes his other hand across his outstretched arm—a spot of black appears, and then, like ink dropped into water, it spreads to reveal an image tattooed on his palm: the image of a staring eye ringed by two circles. The same symbol marked on the secret passageway from the temple archives that Nimh and I used to escape together the night Inshara killed the high priest and took hold of this place.

It was there the whole time—if only Nimh or I had known what that symbol meant.

Sentinel.

Matias's eyes are soft and sympathetic, but beneath that warmth I can see a glint of something harder, sterner. "We will get her back, cloudlander," he tells me. "And save your people too."

I swallow hard and turn away, my heart too full of conflicting emotions. On the horizon are the Lovers, Miella and Danna, locked in their eternal dance as they vanish into the dawn. Above them, no more than an inky spot in the still lightening sky, is the underside of Alciel.

How many times since falling did I look up and wonder if I'd ever get home? Now the question eats at me in a way it never has before, because *Nimh* is up there, and she's all alone with a woman twisted into monstrosity who wants her dead, who wants us *all* dead. I can only pray that I have enough time.

Time to stop Inshara. Time to find a way between worlds. Time to find a way back to Nimh.

Hold on, Nimh. The thought burns in me like a beacon— perhaps if I wish it hard enough, she might feel it, might know she isn't as alone as she seems. *Hold on . . . I'm coming.*

SOMEWHERE ON THE
OTHER SIDE OF THE SKY. . . .

The transit conductor sighed, glanced down at his chrono, and then released the hand brake, allowing the current flowing through the city's patchwork of rails to propel the carriage forward. The last of his passengers, a tipsy boy with glittery blue lipstick, had disembarked two stops ago. Few people ventured out during these quiet hours before dawn, but the king—long may he be remembered—had demanded safe, free transportation throughout the city for all Alciel's citizens.

As the carriage gathered speed, the conductor let his mind wander. He fretted about his son, whose quarterly evaluation marks at the Royal Academy were still growing worse, not better, despite the sizable part of his paycheck that went to a private tutor. He wondered if any of his public transit colleagues had ever seen his son sneaking back late at night like the boy with the electric blue lips—wondered if they'd seen and not known him, or worse, seen and not told the conductor about it.

A spotlight above the conductor's viewscreen illuminated a meager stretch of track ahead of the carriage, and the conductor idly watched the ties and seams in the rails go shooting past.

I ought to bring him on shift some night after one of the prince's parties—if anything will make him work harder at the academy, it will be seeing his father cleaning up after drunk rich kids.

Then the conductor remembered about the prince. And he remembered how there would be no more of his parties, not ever again.

He barely had time to feel a flare of sorrow for the loss of the queen's son, followed so swiftly by the death of her father, for there, just beyond the hedges lining the track, rose a sudden, brilliant column of golden light. Before he had time to fully register what he was seeing, it was gone—and then, flashing in the glare of the carriage light, the figure of a woman stumbled out of the hedge and directly into the path of the carriage.

The conductor shouted a warning as he grabbed frantically at the hand brake. Mouth forming a stumbling string of epithets, he leaned all his weight against the brake, making the whole carriage jerk and stutter with a scream of tortured metal.

The woman's face, no more than a terrified glimpse of large eyes, vanished beneath the bottom edge of the viewscreen as the conductor shut his eyes, waiting for a sound he'd only heard in his nightmares just before waking, covered in cold sweat, in time for the hated dead man's shift. A scream, a sickening thump, a crunch that his very bones would remember for the rest of his life . . .

The sound never came.

The conductor's heart was still thrashing in his chest as he scrambled for the latch on the door, his hands sweaty and fumbling. By the time he spilled out onto the narrow service walkway between the hedge and the tracks, he was already trying to figure out what he would say to his supervisor, to his councilor, to his queen—to the woman's family.

He found her crouching there, nothing but a pair of eyes beneath the near-blinding glare of the carriage light. For a moment, the staring eyes were so still his heart lurched and shuddered to a halt as if compelled by its own faulty braking system, and he thought, *I've killed someone.* But then she blinked, and his heart began to beat again.

"Skyfall, lady, you scared me out of my wits—are you all right? Are you hurt?"

The woman blinked again, and then, slowly, her legs shaking and her eyes still round as ball bearings, she straightened and stood. Now the light from the stalled carriage illuminated her, and the conductor stared.

She wore red, a strange, flimsy garment that hid little as she stood there, silhouetted by the sharp glare of the spotlight behind her. She was younger than he'd first thought. Swearing at himself, he kept his eyes on her face. Her hands were raised and slightly trembling, as if ready to ward off some attack, though by what power the conductor could not guess, for she did not look capable of accomplishing much by brute force. She was lovely, if rattled and terrified, and wore makeup that stretched from temple to temple, the way the royal family did in portraits generations ago, imitating the old tradition of wearing sheer gold cloth across the eyes during certain ceremonies of state. Only instead of gold, hers was black. It had an interesting effect in the darkness, making her seem at once tiny and fragile, as well as unseen and dangerous.

Like the rail current, thought the conductor dazedly. *Invisible, undetectable, right up until it kills you at a single touch.*

"I am . . . not hurt." Her voice carried a strange accent, and she spoke haltingly, as if each word came only after exquisite concentration. Something about those eyes . . . strangely colored, flickering as if lit from within.

"You can't jump out on the track like that! You'll kill yourself!" The import of the words hit the conductor only after he spoke them, and he took a halting step toward her. "You—you weren't . . . *trying* to . . . ?"

A hiss of air from the carriage made the young woman leap back with a barely muffled shriek, her body tensing into readiness.

"It's okay, it's okay!" the conductor hurried to reassure her, baffled by her sudden terror. "It's just the compressed air in the brake equalizing!"

Her gaze darted from his face to the carriage looming over them, up to the cloudless starry sky above, and back to the conductor, as if assigning each of these things an equal amount of wariness.

When she said nothing, either about the brakes or about why she'd leaped—fallen, really—onto the tracks, the conductor eased another step forward and tried another tactic. "You're not wearing a chrono or an earring. Do you have anyone you want me to call? Your friends? Your family?"

She shrank back and the conductor cursed himself. She was younger even than his revised estimate—he said *family*, and she heard *parents*. She must be no more than a teenager.

The conductor hid a smile. Terrified or no, few kids her age *wanted* their parents called after midnight. She tilted her head, noticing the smile he evidently hadn't hidden very well, and as the harsh shadows on her face moved, he realized he'd been wrong—she wasn't anything dangerous, she was just a kid, out past her curfew, her terror split equally between the prospect of being crushed to death by carriage wheels and that of being busted by her parents.

"It's all right," the conductor said, trying a gentler version of the amusement that had leaked out earlier. "We won't call them if you don't want to. There's a diner just up the street there to the left, won't cost you much money either. Get some caffeine and some food in you, and you'll feel better. They'll have a com-station you can use once you figure out who you want to call. It's right across the street from the constables' station—it's a very safe neighborhood."

The girl seemed to change then, her manner softening, her wide eyes relaxing as her brows drew in. "I *am* looking for some-one," she said, her voice somewhat more distinct now. "Perhaps you could help me."

The conductor fought the urge to look at his chrono—the girl had clearly been traumatized by the near miss, but his supervisor would have something to say about feeble excuses if the conductor didn't start on toward his next stop.

The girl drew a quivering breath and said haltingly, "Please—I lost the chrono I was wearing, and I have none of the money for the diner. I don't remember where I should go."

She must have hit her head. A little flare of panic echoed back up at that thought, as he imagined his supervisor's reaction if he learned she'd been hurt. The conductor would never work again. But then he looked at her face, her wide eyes, her trembling lips, the way she was starting to shiver in the bite of the night winds unbroken by clouds.

She was so young, after all, and still visibly afraid, the fingers of one of her hands twitching involuntarily in an odd, perpetual dance, as if weaving something out of the air. He could almost see something there, like a shadow condensed out of the night . . . like mist.

He knew then that he would help her. He *wanted* to help her. The urge was growing to do what she needed, and as he decided that he would, it was as if a kind of pressure eased.

He'd tell his supervisor . . . he'd make something up, some reason the last carriage of the night never finished its rounds, some reason he had to abandon it on the tracks. If his supervisor had a problem with it . . . drop it all, he'd just quit.

"Who are you looking for?" he asked gently.

"I have heard there was once a man who fell down into the darkness below, and returned here to the cloudlands. I wish to speak to him." She really had very little accent after all—perhaps it was nothing more than fear that had made her sound so strange before. He'd never heard the term *cloudlands* to describe Alciel before—it was lovely. Like poetry.

The conductor blinked and then gave a nervous laugh. "They're just stories. You're old enough to know that—no one could survive a fall like that, and even if they did, they wouldn't survive long in that wasteland. And they certainly wouldn't be able to magically reappear back up here."

"No," the girl murmured. "To travel by magic into the sky is impossible, of course."

For a moment, he remembered that first impression he'd had, that of something coiled and dangerous, sweet and dark and lethal.

Then the girl smiled at him, and the memory shredded itself with gleeful abandon. "Nevertheless," she said, "I wish to speak to him. The one who fell and returned."

The conductor hesitated, his mind racing, trying to think of any way he could help this girl find who she was looking for. "A thing like that, if it had really happened . . . the whole city would know about it. Unless he was close with the councilors, or maybe even the royal family, and they pulled strings to keep it quiet."

The girl considered this. "Then take me to the king."

"The . . . You mean the queen?" A cold sweat had broken out along the conductor's forehead—a sweat not unlike the one he woke to after those nightmares with the crunching sound.

"That's what I said."

The conductor stared at her for a moment, aware that she had distinctly said *king*, and equally aware how strange it was that he didn't care. He really needed to ask for that promotion from the dead man's shift so he could work a normal person's hours. His mind was starting to unravel.

"I'm really not sure I'm the right person to arrange an audience with the king—I mean queen," he said finally. The closest he'd ever been to a member of the royal family was when the prince used to try to pass incognito around the city and everyone pretended they didn't recognize him. He'd certainly never talked to him, except to play along and wish him a good evening.

The girl's face grew somber. "And yet here we are. You are all I have." Something lurked on the end of that sentence, an empty space shaped for more words.

You are all I have . . . so far.

The conductor sighed. "All right. I can bring you to the palace, at least. Perhaps one of the guards will know what to do." It was a stab in the dark, but the girl's face lit with satisfaction and approval so warm he almost felt it on his skin.

He went to the carriage door and waited, offering her his hand as she stepped inside. Her touch was cool and steady—she wasn't trembling anymore. He closed the doors behind them both and went to his chair at the controls. "I feel like a fool for not asking sooner . . . but what's your name? What do I tell the guards when we get there?"

"My name?"

She paused while the carriage eased slowly back into motion, as if the answer to that question was one she had to search for—but then the conductor realized she was only shy, and it was the strip of black makeup across her eyes that made it difficult to read her expression.

"Tell them . . . ," she said slowly, her voice thoughtful. "Tell

470

them my name is Nimhara, and that I bring news of their lost prince. Tell them I will share it with them, but only after."

"After . . . ?"

"After I have been brought before the man who returned twenty years ago from the other side of the sky. There are things to be said between him and I. He has much to answer for—and I have *much* to do here."

The carriage sped off into the night, its spotlight diminishing into a tiny pinprick of light among the other twinkling stars of Alciel's nighttime skyline.

The conductor never saw the thing half-concealed behind the bushes where he'd stopped the carriage. He never saw the body of the other girl.

ACKNOWLEDGMENTS

This book was a dream of ours for many years before it was a reality, and we're both so happy to be sharing Nimh and North (and, of course, the bindle cat) with our readers. We pinch ourselves every day, almost unable to believe our good fortune at telling stories for a living, and telling them together. But there are plenty of people to whom we're grateful as well, and we'd like to take a moment to thank them.

We must begin with you, reader. The readers, booksellers, and librarians who pick up our stories and share them with others are the reason we do what we do. It's a big world, and we all have towering piles of books we'd like to read—we're so grateful you pick up ours, and pass them on to your friends and loved ones.

Our amazing team at Adams Literary—Josh, Tracey, Cathy, and Stephen—are there with us every time we take a new leap of faith, always wise and always kind.

Our team at Harper has been wonderful every step of the way. We have no higher thanks to offer our editor, Kristen, than to dedicate this book to her. Many thanks also to Clare, Caitlin,

Alexandra, Jenna, Alison, Michael, and to the fantastic teams in sales, marketing, publicity, and managing ed. Heartfelt thanks to Artem, for one of the most beautiful book covers we've ever seen. To Anna and all our Australian team at Allen & Unwin— thank you, as ever, for being such a wonderful home.

Many, many thanks to the friends who have been there to advise, support, or bring cups of tea (or occasionally something stronger) as we've written and rewritten this book: Michelle, Steph, Marie, Leigh, Jay, Kiersten, Eliza, Peta, Alex, Sooz, Nic, Kacey, Soraya, Ryan, the Kates, Cat, the Roti Boti crew, the House of Progress, the Asheville crew, and in particular to C. S. Pacat, for a helpful and thoughtful read of the seven millionth draft. Special thanks and love from Meg to Ryn, who kept her going through flu and fatigue while she edited.

Endless thanks as well to our families—the Spooners, Kaufmans, Cousinses, and Mr. Wolf. Jack, Sebastian, and Viola kept us company for several million drafts, but it was Icarus who lent us his very self, and lives on as the bindle cat in these pages. We miss you, buddy. To Brendan, as always, an *I love you* from Amie, and to Pip, enough love and welcome from both of us to fill two worlds.